The Last Mage Guardian

Sabrina Chase

Cover art by Les Petersen

ISBN-13: 978-0-9852704-5-2

CONTENTS

Also by Sabrina Chase

Firehearted

THE SEQUOYAH TRILOGY:
The Long Way Home
Raven's Children
Queen of Chaos

ACKNOWLEDGMENTS

This book would not have been possible without help from many people —the patient fellow-writers of STEW, non-writing friends that were still willing to read manuscripts multiple times, superlative editor Deb Taber, and my mother, who will not tolerate sloppy writing even from her own daughter. Any flaws or mistakes are entirely my own and I was probably warned about them to boot. So, no excuse.
I enjoyed writing this book; I hope you enjoy reading it.

S. Chase

CHAPTER 1

"It's a bookshop. It's been there for years. Why are you staring at it?"

Dominic blinked, suddenly aware of the wind biting through the holes in his threadbare coat. Phillipe looked at him with exasperation, stomping his feet to warm them. A bitterly cold wind blew through the streets of Dinan, stirring up yesterday's snow and bringing the promise of more.

Why had he stopped? He couldn't remember. "Why don't we go in and warm up? Perhaps they have the Solstice displays."

Phillipe shook his head. "Bodin's never has them up this early. Magic like that is expensive to maintain, you know. Why are you so fascinated by them?" He made no objection to Dominic's suggestion, though, and they began to cross the street towards the bookshop.

"I don't know. When I was young my parents would take me every year." His mother would complain about how long they took, for while his father pretended they went only for Dominic's entertainment, he loved the displays as much as Dominic did. Now that his parents were both gone, it remained a bittersweet memory.

A strong hand on his coat collar jerked him back, out of the way of a large coach pulled by two steaming horses.

"I swear you should not be allowed out of doors without a minder," Phillipe complained, giving Dominic's collar a shake for emphasis before letting go.

Dominic smiled up at his lanky friend. "Where could I find a minder that would meet my exacting requirements? Strong, capable, and willing to discuss literature and philosophy at any hour of the day…rare indeed."

They crossed the icy street without further incident. Dominic opened the heavy door with inset leaves of leaded glass and sighed with pleasure. Warm air, laced with the dry scent of leather and paper, and books as far as the eye could see. Unconsciously he began to read the spines, pulling out one book after another that caught his fancy.

"You're in the Mechanical Arts section," Phillipe muttered in his ear as he went by. "Literature is over by the far wall."

"Oh. Yes." Dominic blinked and turned to leave, but his glance snagged on an intriguing title and he stopped again. *Constructing the Tannen Firth Bridge: Being a practical Treatise on the Difficulties encountered and the Means by which they were overcome.* He'd always wondered how they had built the supports in the middle of the ocean—well, in the middle of the Alban Strait, which was essentially the same thing. He turned the pages, fascinated. As he had hoped, there were illustrations.

At length, he realized what he was doing and resolutely put the book back on the shelf. How long had he been distracted? He searched for Phillipe. They both had work to do.

A man passed by, deeply engrossed in an illustrated journal. Dominic frowned. It looked like *The Family Museum,* but he didn't recognize the cover. Had they come out with another issue? He struggled with himself for a moment, and decided to just take a look.

The snow fell softly outside the diamond-paned windows, and Dominic wandered by the neat piles of journals and papers, stopping when he saw *The Family Museum.* It was an issue he had not seen before, a special Solstice edition, which would account for why it had appeared two weeks earlier than usual. Joy surged through him as he read the list of articles inside: astronomy, magical theory, etheric harmonics, and an account of an expedition to an ancient observatory recently discovered deep in the Atlantean mountains. A sinking sensation immediately followed. He didn't have the money for luxuries like this.

A deep sigh told him his friend had found him. "What now?" Phillipe wanted to know, then saw what he was looking at. "Don't you have enough of those? You don't even let me burn them when you are finished."

"I like to read them more than once. They're interesting. Bové has an account of another expedition," Dominic said.

"Oh, he's the one that traveled to the Asean desert, right?" Dominic looked at his friend in surprise. "I read some of them. You had them all over the place."

Dominic fingered the few coins in his pocket. They were all he had to provide his supper, and he was hungry. Then again, if he had something fascinating to read, he could eat the remaining end of his stale loaf dipped in tea and he wouldn't notice. He picked up a copy of the new journal and walked resolutely away before he saw anything else.

As they walked towards the counter, Phillipe stiffened beside him and muttered an oath that earned a reproving glance from an old woman with a sable stole and muff. "You knew, didn't you?"

"What?" Dominic glanced around the front of the bookshop, seeing what had made Philippe exclaim. The Solstice displays were, at that very moment, being set up. A small horde of gape-mouthed children surrounded a man setting in motion a floating model of the sun and planets. The magician considered his work for a moment, then made a gesture that added a swift, feathery comet to the display.

Three automata, made to look like pixies, already flew about the bookshelves and the customers gathered in the aisles. Unlike the usual display automata, these had moveable limbs and eyes and were made and animated with such skill they seemed alive. Bodin's always had the best displays, as befitted a bookshop renowned for its specialty in magical texts.

"Something must have caught my attention in the street," Dominic said, apologetically. "Truly, I didn't know."

Phillipe snorted. "Were you ever tested for magic?"

"Twice," Dominic said, making a face. "My father had great hopes, but I can't even light lamps."

"We should leave now," said Phillipe. "This is pleasant, but we ought to be reading the dry, dusty tomes we spent our last guilders on so we have a faint chance of passing the graduation exam."

"What's the point?" Dominic asked, watching one of the pixies as it sat briefly on a book, wings fanning gently to and fro, before it flitted off again. "If I fail, at least I will have an excuse for not finding work." He regretted saying the words as soon as they left his mouth. Phillipe looked crestfallen.

"I asked if there were any literature positions, even assistants, but…."

"No matter. I make no doubt the weather in Nantes would aggravate my gout."

"You don't *have* gout," Phillipe snapped. "We're too poor for such genteel ailments."

"If I were an assistant at Université Nantes I'd soon develop it, or something worse. I don't want to teach, anyway." Phillipe turned to look at him, curious, and Dominic cursed himself. When would he learn to keep some things to himself? Once roused, his friend's curiosity would not rest until satisfied. "I, ah, want to write. Literature, you know. Look, there's a lighting storm!"

An illusionary storm enlivened the section of the store devoted to the natural sciences. He found it amusing they had used magic for a display of something completely non-magical.

They had to wait some time for their turn at the counter. The store was thronged with customers and the clerks looked harassed beneath their professional demeanors.

With my luck, I may be joining them, thought Dominic, feeling depressed. He was barely managing to get through the university. Even if he did graduate, which was looking more and more unlikely, what employment could he find? Phillipe complained, but he had wealthy family connections that could be relied on in times of financial crisis and a position waiting for him. Dominic had no family except for some cousins in even worse straits than he, and the meager inheritance that had supplemented his scholarship had vanished long ago.

Money was not the only problem. What he really wanted was adventure—an expedition to some uncharted corner of the globe, searching for a lost city or ancient treasure. How could he do that stuck behind a counter selling books?

No, the only adventures he would have would be the ones he made up for himself, fantastic voyages that would never be. He would never find anything out of the ordinary at a bookshop in the middle of Dinan.

Then again…his imagination took up the challenge, and as they waited to be served, he began weaving a tale based on Bodin's famous specialty.

The customer at the counter finished his business, and the tall lady ahead of them took his place. She wore a shabby traveling cloak over skirts barely half as full as fashion currently dictated and a hat with the merest trifle of a bow by way of decoration. Something about the whole appeared vaguely foreign. Soft folds of veiling draped the hat, concealing her face, and she carried a faded carpetbag as if about to depart on a journey.

He idly wondered how he might fit her into his story. *A spy*, he thought happily, *looking for a secret document hidden in an old book during the Mage War.*

The clerk looked up at her, then sharply aside. "Madame wishes?"

The lady had been tightly clutching a folded paper, which she handed to him. "I can't seem to find them on the shelves," she said, and Dominic abruptly lost the thread of his tale. What a fascinating voice! It was rich, resonant, and wholly unsuited to the shabby cloak and unfashionable hat.

Taking the paper, the clerk looked at it and then at her, startled, before looking away again. "Madame, these are books of power. I regret, but you cannot have any use for such things."

Dominic saw her fingers tighten on the handles of the carpetbag. "They are for my elderly relative. He was an *ars magica* instructor and still takes interest in research, although he is no longer able to travel."

"I see. I, ah, must consult." The clerk gave her a nervous bow and vanished into the inner offices of the store. Even though the lighting was more than adequate, Dominic could see nothing of the lady's face other than her profile behind the veiling. Shadows fell where there should have been none. The lady moved restlessly, glancing at the store entrance as though she were thinking of leaving.

The clerk returned with a senior Bodin's employee in a frock coat.

"Madame, you must understand these are not books one can leave in one's drawing room. They can interfere with other magic, with potentially disastrous results, so we cannot sell them in good conscience to someone who might not have the requisite ability to guard against this."

The senior employee seemed to be addressing the slip of paper in his hand instead of the lady.

"But my great-uncle purchased many such books here, when his health permitted."

"What is his name?"

The lady hesitated. "Yves Morlais, of Peran. Please, I am in haste. He has asked me to bring these books to him, and my train leaves within the hour."

The senior employee's expression changed to a relieved smile. "I have had the pleasure of serving Magister Morlais here for many years. Of course we would be happy to assist you." He gestured sharply to the clerk waiting nervously beside him, who took the paper and left with alacrity. "I regret to hear he is unwell." He reached beneath the counter and took out a slim pamphlet. "Perhaps he would like a copy of our latest catalog? He can then write and order books for us to send, and you will not be put to the trouble."

"Thank you, that is most kind." Did she smile? She certainly sounded pleased.

The clerk returned, harried and out of breath, with several books wrapped in silver tissue.

"Madame should understand this is for the protection of the books and to prevent any interference with other magics," the senior employee said, tapping the silver tissue. "It should not be removed save by a magician. Even to look at the binding." He gave the lady an avuncular smile.

"Oh no, he has warned me very strictly about such things," the lady said. Dominic frowned. Her words were demure, but carried an undertone of amusement.

The lady paid for her purchases and left, walking with a hurried step. Dominic watched her leave, troubled and unsure why. Something was missing....

"Dominic. Dominic! Wake up! You aren't in class, you great idiot! Come on, they are waiting for you." Phillipe looked at him more closely. "I hope you aren't ill. What's the matter with you?"

"Didn't you notice the lady?" Dominic handed most of the coins in his pocket to the clerk. He hoped the loaf was not too stale, and that the mice hadn't gotten it first.

"What lady?"

"The one before us."

Phillipe glanced eagerly about. "And I missed her? What bad luck! Was she pretty?"

"I hardly know. I couldn't see her face at all." They left, and the cold was even worse after the comfortable warmth of the shop. Dominic shoved his hands into his pockets, wishing he could afford thicker gloves.

"Are you sure you didn't just imagine her?" Phillipe asked, skeptical. "I've never seen you notice a real woman, even when they want you to. Grillot's sister has tried every trick save fainting at your feet."

Dominic started, and nearly slipped on the ice underfoot. "How strange you should say that. I saw her faint just three days ago."

"And?"

"I found another lady nearby to assist her, of course. What else could I do?"

Phillipe sighed. "Assist her yourself, which is undoubtedly what she wished." They reached the entrance to their lodging and began climbing the creaky stairs with care.

"Are you sure? I only thought to spare her any embarrassment."

Phillipe shrugged, his face bland. "There is no accounting for tastes." Dominic knew Phillipe spoke from considerable experience of feminine wiles, but it still seemed incredible to him. He couldn't even remember Mademoiselle Grillot's face; all the ladies he knew seemed to strive to look identical to one another. And why would she notice him? He had no illusions about himself, especially compared to Phillipe, who was tall, handsome, and of good family. All the things he was not. Of course, he did not take as much care of his appearance as Phillipe did, either.

Dominic unlocked the door to their rooms. Nothing had changed, except that they had gotten colder.

"Hmm. Half a scuttle left," Phillipe said, glancing at their supply of coal. "And the old man on the second floor will be leaving to visit his daughter soon."

"Yes, but Madame Caisson will be baking for the holidays," Dominic replied. The secret advantage to their quarters lay in the brick chimney that took up half of one wall. With heat from the other tenant's fires, they were able to conserve their coal.

There were shadows in the corner of the room, but they matched the light. Dominic frowned. The other shadows had not....

"It's my turn to put my bed against the bricks," Phillipe announced in a cheerful voice. After a silence, Dominic felt Phillipe's hand on his shoulder. "But perhaps you should stay there for a few more days." His friend searched his face, a worried expression on his own. "When I leave Dinan, you will write to me regularly? I'll think you've been run over by a cart, otherwise."

With an effort, Dominic shrugged off his distraction. "Of course I'll write to you." He grinned. "I doubt I'll have much else to do."

Marie poured the tea from the delicate gold-traced teapot, and Ardhuin got up to get her great-uncle's cup—then remembered. She sat back down, fighting sudden tears, and tried to concentrate on the soothing warmth as she drank.

Finally, she had to say something. "I don't understand. When he wrote to me...his last letter, he mentioned nothing of being ill."

Marie dabbed at her eyes, her thin, gnarled hands shaking. "No more he was, my dear. A blessing, and a testament to his sober and regular ways that he did not suffer through long illness. Why, I doubt he truly realized how ill he was even at the end, it happened so quick. It was easy to forget, but he *was* nearly ninety-four, or would have been in April."

There was no use in Ardhuin telling herself that she should have known, should have done something to answer his summons more quickly. What could she have done? She'd left the same day she had received his letter. A strange letter....

"There hadn't been anything…troubling him, had there? Or anyone?"

"Oh no, nothing like that," Marie said, patting her hand. "He overtaxed himself, that's all. One of his special projects he was working on, and outside in the cold. You know what he is…was like. Never took note of how long he spent out there, and is it that surprising a putrid cough would be the result?" The old cook shook her head in sorrowful exasperation. "He never would listen to sense, never!" She dusted some nonexistent crumbs from the tablecloth severely and rearranged the teapot and creamer.

Ardhuin glanced up, her own pain momentarily forgotten. A special project would mean magic. And outdoors would mean—defensive magic. There would be no other reason to spend so much time outside the protective wards of his house, unless it was magic that could not be done within them.

"You mentioned that his mind seemed to wander a little," Ardhuin said.

"He was all but dead!" Marie bristled. "And I only said I could not understand him. He kept saying your name," she continued slowly, "and something that sounded like 'they seek Oron.' I don't suppose that means anything to you?"

Ardhuin shook her head, feeling suddenly cold and hoping her reaction did not show on her face. Fortunately, it appeared Marie was not expecting any answer. His mind *had* been wandering, or he had been so delirious he had not realized who was present. While his few remaining servants were completely loyal and knew he was a magician of some repute, none knew that he had another name—Oron—or that Oron was one of the most powerful mages of Aerope.

He had written vaguely of threats, and now it seemed he thought the threat was connected to his secret. "I should have come sooner," she whispered, and felt the hot tears falling down her cheeks again.

"What could you have done, child?" Marie patted her hand again. "It was his time. Indeed, I wondered at how quickly you were able to leave your school. Did the doctor send a telegram, then? But you have been in the custom of visiting here, so perhaps they made an exception for you. He did enjoy your visits, my dear."

Ardhuin felt the smile tremble on her face. "I enjoyed them too." Knowing that she could escape to Peran had helped to fend off the tedium and humiliation of school.

"That must be why he left the house to you in such a strange way," Marie said, pouring another cup of tea with an austere expression. "He wanted you to always have it. It would have been much more practical, and kind, to allow you to sell it. Men must have *some* lure to even notice a girl, sad as it is, and if beauty is lacking, money will substitute. Although I have often thought your figure is quite charming, or could be if you would dress to show it to advantage. If you could afford to dress more fashionably, it would improve your chances."

Ardhuin felt her face heat with a combination of shame and anger. "I would rather have Peran," she said in a stifled voice. "I could live here. Alone." She had never enjoyed being noticed, and she would not mind being plain if other people would stop mentioning it to her. She loathed fashion with the same intensity as her mother loved it. It was Ardhuin's determined resistance, not a lack of funds, that kept her wardrobe out of style.

Marie uttered a shocked gasp. "At your age? Your parents would never allow it." Her expression swiftly changed to one of puzzlement. "What *is* your age, now? I would have thought it time and past for you to be done with your education, and you won't meet anyone with your nose in a book." She sniffed. Marie had not approved of the encouragement her great-uncle had given to her studious interests. If she had known he had been teaching her magic, she would have been horrified.

"My mother and father wished me to remain at the seminary until their return from the Naipon Archipelago," Ardhuin sighed. "My brothers are all off on their own business and no one is at home now. It was easier to have me stay there, since Maman intends to visit friends in Bretagne after their voyage. If I went to Atlantea, I would just have to come back again."

If only there were some way she could stay in Atlantea. Her mother's 'visits to friends' would involve far too much socializing. Parties. Dancing. Ardhuin shuddered. Even the thought of it made her feel ill. Uncomfortable clothes, her mother fussing and worrying to no purpose, and then being forced to endure the discreet stares of those present. Taller than many of the men, topped with a head of flaming red hair, and clumsy in the bargain, and her mother still could not understand why she was hardly ever asked to dance. It was pure torment.

Marie made a tsking sound. "Well, I suppose it can't be helped now." She glanced at the big kitchen clock and rose stiffly from her chair. "The coach will be here any minute now. Are you ready?"

The funeral was sparsely attended, only partly due to the cold, raw weather. The doctor was present, as was the lawyer who had drawn up his will, but Ardhuin was the only member of the family. That was not considered worthy of comment. Her great-uncle had treated Ardhuin like his daughter, and everyone else was either already dead or too far away.

Besides, she was his heir. Everyone knew he had left Peran to her—that was the easy part. If she had any questions, the lawyer could answer them for her. They did not know she had also inherited his magical possessions and obligations, and there was no one she could confide in to even know if they were real.

He'd only mentioned it once. "I have an old obligation to the Mage Guardians. Since you are my heir-magical, they may call on you when I am gone." He had said little more in response to her questions, only that they were mages from every country of the Allies and sworn to the defense of Aerope. They had been instrumental in the victory of the terrible Mage War. He rarely spoke of his part in the War, so she knew it was important when he did. Ardhuin had never heard of the Mage Guardians before, but if what he had told her was true they would naturally be a secretive group.

Marie's description of her great-uncle's fevered words worried her. If someone was seeking Oron, they might be one of these Mage Guardians. She had promised him…but how would she convince them she was the heir of Oron?

Then again, perhaps he had been imagining things. Delirious, frail, had he become confused? Remembering some earlier time? She had no way of knowing. No one from this mysterious group had contacted her. It was entirely possible they had ceased to exist, if they had ever existed at all.

A cart drawn by an old, shaggy horse was waiting outside the house when they returned from the funeral.

"The cart is here already? I had not thought we were so late," Marie fretted.

"You are packed, are you not?" asked Ardhuin.

"Well, yes, but I had not finished putting the covers on the furniture, or emptying the larder, or…." Marie took her duties very seriously.

"But the arrangements—and your granddaughter is expecting you! I can finish here, and leave tomorrow." One more blessed day of freedom.

Marie shook her head resolutely. "I cannot leave you here by yourself. The driver will just have to come back, that's all."

"But I won't be alone," Ardhuin said, suddenly remembering. "Rinaud and his wife are still here, and won't be leaving for at least a week."

Marie glanced at the cart, and then at Ardhuin, wavering. "That's true. I did not remember. Oh, but I still don't like it. The cottage is outside the walls, after all."

It took a great deal of persuasion and repeated promises to ask the Rinauds to stay in the house with her and to lock all the doors before retiring, but she finally managed to convince Marie to leave.

Ardhuin spent the rest of the afternoon finishing the chores Marie had not completed. The house was wonderfully quiet. If only she could stay like this—alone and undisturbed. She could spend hours in the library and no one would complain or say too much reading would make her squint. She could practice her magic. But no, they would not let her do it.

She went down to the kitchen to finish the last of the cleaning. In the fading light of the setting sun she saw an envelope propped against the butter crock. Frowning, she picked it up, wondering at the weight of it. Only she and the servants could have gone through the wards without assistance. When had it been left?

She took out the letter. In shaky handwriting, Rinaud explained they would be leaving early, as a friend of Madame Rinaud had offered to take them in her carriage all the way to Dinan, and would they be so kind as to arrange with the carter to take their luggage? In the envelope were two faded guilder notes and a key.

Panic spurred her to sudden action. Ardhuin ran out the kitchen door into the bitter cold, following the deep footprints in the snow left by Rinaud. She could barely see the cottage in the darkness once she left the walled garden. Slipping and stumbling, her teeth chattering, she hurried down the road and with stiff hands unlocked the door. The tiny cottage was empty except for a few pieces of old furniture and a pile of carefully marked luggage.

They were, as she had feared, gone. Shivering, Ardhuin relocked the door and went back to the house. What was she going to do? Rinaud must have left the letter when they were at the funeral, or he would have spoken to them himself. Not only was it dark, she didn't have a horse and it was too cold and too far to walk to town. Nobody knew she was all alone, or would even look for her.

Nobody knew. She stumbled on something hidden in the snow, and fell into a snow-covered pile of leaves. With difficulty, she regained her feet, wishing the garden had not been so neglected. The paths were overgrown, and the snow just made it worse. Brushing snow and dead leaves from her skirt, she carefully locked the kitchen door behind her.

A daring thought; a frightening thought, that had made her lose her balance. If no one knew she was alone in the house, they wouldn't make her leave. She lit the kitchen fire and considered. What would she do for food? There was a little left, but not much. Plenty of coal and firewood in the cellars, fortunately. And what tale would she tell the carter when he returned as Marie had instructed him? Ah, a misunderstanding! He was not to come for her, but for the luggage. And hadn't Marie mentioned sending him to fetch orders from the butcher and the baker when Rinaud was ill and couldn't go himself?

She would have to talk to the carter. Perhaps even write it out and practice it, so she wouldn't get flustered. He would know she was staying at the house, and might—no, *would* tell others. This was a small town after all, and gossip a prized commodity. She had overheard some of that gossip, about her. The kindest versions described her as plain and odd, and the superstitious considered red hair unlucky or worse. Would it really seem so strange if she decided to stay here by herself? They would probably think she was just eccentric, like her great-uncle.

The seminary...she would write to the headmistress. Something vague about the difficulties caused by her great-uncle's sudden illness, and that she needed to stay a while longer. And to send any letters to her here; that would give her enough warning when her mother returned. There was always the risk that the headmistress might learn of her great-uncle's death from other sources and wonder what was keeping her. Perhaps, then, she could say there were difficulties with her inheritance?

A heady wave of delight washed over her worries and fears. There would be trouble later, unless she was very lucky. But for now...she had freedom.

Dominic made his way up the stone stairs with reluctance, dreading his destination. He knocked on the heavy wood door.

"Come in, come in!" said a testy voice, and Dominic hastened to open the door. He did not want Professor Botrel to become impatient with him. Botrel was his last hope.

"Ah. Kermarec. Now, why did I want to see you?" Botrel's shaggy white eyebrows piled like thunderclouds on his forehead.

"You mentioned you had something to give me." Dominic couldn't help glancing at the impressive piles of books and papers that were stacked everywhere, even the floor. He hoped the good professor would not have to search for whatever it was.

"Oh yes. By the way, I have seen the results of the final examinations." The white eyebrows lifted, and Botrel looked at him over the rims of his eyeglasses. "It should not be a surprise to you, or anyone else, that you do not have the necessary qualifications to be a scholar."

He had failed. No degree, no money, no prospects.

Botrel made an exasperated noise, searching through his pockets and then the drawers of his desk. "Don't stand there looking like you've been stabbed. Now where did I put it? You passed. Barely. Aha!" He pulled out a folded letter from his tobacco pouch, shaking a few flakes free. "I hope you do not object to the odor. I wanted to be sure I remembered it, you see, and I have not yet reached the point of forgetting my pipe." He gave his gentle, elfin smile.

Dominic took the letter and readjusted his ideas. He had *not* failed. Was this perhaps an offer of employment, then?

"I took the liberty of showing that imaginary expedition you wrote to Monsieur Sambin," Professor Botrel continued, waving the pipe he was filling and scattering more flakes of tobacco over his desk. "He was quite impressed. Asked me to pass on those comments to you. How did you know about camelard hair, eh?"

Dominic shifted his attention from the letter, which seemed to be a literary critique, to attempt to deal with this new inquiry. Botrel was famous for his apparent *non sequiturs* and random questions, but more observant students had noticed his chaotic discourse usually had a hidden thread connecting the whole in a subtle way. It made conversation with him fascinating but exhausting.

"A friend of mine is acquainted with the biologist who accompanied the latest expedition to the Atlantean highlands, and introduced me. He told me they had great difficulty packing the more delicate specimens until their trail guide suggested using the hair shed by their pack animals."

"Ah." Botrel puffed happily at his pipe. "Why, pray, were you desirous of an introduction to a biologist? And that one in particular? I don't recall you at any of the literary gatherings, or even expressing an interest in meeting an author."

Dominic started to sweat. This discussion was taking a disquieting turn, and nothing made sense. Why should this M. Sambin have any interest in him or his scribbled tale? Why was that name familiar?

Then he remembered. Remembered where he had read about the Atlantean expedition, and where he had seen the name Sambin before.

"You showed my imaginary expedition to the editor of *The Family Museum?*" he asked, stunned. And Sambin had been impressed!

"Oh yes. I think you may have discovered a new field, my boy. Don't listen to those crotchety academics!" Botrel swirled the cloud of smoke about his head with wild gestures. "Universities are little more than sedimentary layers, rich with fossils. Couldn't think of a new idea if their very lives depended on it—or recognize one, either. Look at all the trouble I've had! Just because I am interested in literature that isn't fifty years old! It doesn't have to age to be of value, like wine. Take *The Little Chef,* for example. Everybody can quote from it, recognize the songs, and it's still being performed today. It's a part of our *culture* and the fools refuse to see it! Bah!" He stabbed his pipe stem at Dominic, scowling. "They call it 'popular' in the same manner a doctor would say 'diseased.' It was *popular* because it spoke to all of us!"

"Pastry competitions, sir?" Dominic asked.

Botrel sat back in his chair, his eyes hooded. "Food. Good food, not the kind that just keeps you alive for a few hours. It was written during the Mage War, you see. It was a part of it. I was still living in Fougéres when the Fire Rain destroyed the city. We only got out by following a sewerman through the tunnels. We couldn't see him or each other, it was so dark. He sang the 'Cherry Tart with Almonds' song, and we followed the sound of his voice. Never did find out what happened to him...." Botrel stared into the distance for a moment, then shook himself. "But that's all over with now. The letter...oh, you have it there. Have you read it?"

Dominic skimmed the letter's contents as quickly as he could. The account was interesting, but a trifle dry for fiction, said M. Sambin. More attention paid to the personalities and less to the technical details would make the piece of greater interest to *The Family Museum*'s readers.

"He does not appear to like it," Dominic faltered, to the glowering face of Professor Botrel.

"I assure you if he did not like it he would not have taken the trouble to write to you," the professor growled. "Blockhead! He is giving you advice! Now here is my advice to you, and at least pretend to pay attention to it. Follow what makes you forget." Botrel shook his head, chuckling. "Perhaps I should phrase that in a more felicitous manner. There are things that will not let you rest, and when you follow them you forget all else. You sought out a biologist. Why? You do not, I believe, have an interest in the study of biology. Or in geology, but you paid a visit to Professor Sharmkov. My wife and his are great friends," Botrel explained, seeing Dominic's look of shock, "and they love to gossip."

"I was merely curious—" Dominic began.

Botrel nodded so vigorously his pipe fell out. "Exactly! And according to Sharmkov, you asked intelligent questions. I will venture to guess that you made use of his answers in your tale there, eh? The exploration of the caves? Fascinating, my boy. Now. You, and the examining committee, are agreed that a scholar's life is not in your future. *That*," he said, tapping the letter Dominic still held, "is your future."

"I am afraid my need of employment is more urgent than Monsieur Sambin can meet," Dominic said. "I value your advice, but I will need time to act upon it." Phillipe was leaving in less than a week, and he could not afford their lodgings on his own. If he ruthlessly cut back on any luxuries, he could eat for a month, but no more.

He stared. Botrel was making slow, dancing motions with his arms, his eyes closed and his face screwed up in an effort of thought. "This morning, eggs for breakfast, toast burnt, Pierre, my friend writes…time to leave, AH!" He leaped from his chair, startling Dominic into nearly knocking over the coat rack. Dominic regained his balance and stared at his professor. Botrel gave another subtle smile. "My wife has a way of poaching eggs with butter. Absolutely delicious, and I tend not to notice much else when they are in front of me. I don't recall the details, mind, but it seems her friend is in desperate need of a tutor. Which is something you can do and," he dropped back into his seat and beamed at Dominic, "it would give you time to write."

Going back into the house through the kitchen, Ardhuin rummaged through the larder and settled on a slice of dried-apple pie and some cheese, which she took with her in a napkin. She ate as she went back upstairs, smiling when she saw a fallen crumb gently drift away on the floor in obedience to the cleaning spell. Her great-uncle had had a curiously practical streak at times.

She opened the carved double doors of the library, first wandering to the great window that looked down on the rose garden and admiring the view. So far her plan was working quite well. She had arranged for weekly delivery of food via the carter, and with the quarterly payment from the small fund her great-uncle had set up for her she could live, not lavishly, but well enough.

She sighed happily. No one to criticize her taste in reading, or informal eating habits, or pester her to keep her hair up. It always came down anyway, so what was the point? The only thing that kept her from complete enjoyment was her great-uncle's absence.

Selecting an old, loosely bound volume from the shelves, Ardhuin sat down at the great desk. She read for some time, nibbling cheese, with her feet propped up on the desk, happily imagining her teachers' shock if they could see her in such an improper pose. Her great-uncle had never been shocked. That, and his great height, caused her to adore him at an early age. When he called her 'petite,' it was *true*. Most men had to look up at her, and it was very tiresome.

It had been nearly two months now and she still had not discovered his final project, the one Marie claimed had kept him "outside in the cold." Perhaps she should go through his notes. The wards on his workroom, fortunately, were keyed to allow her to enter or she would have had to wait until they faded—and for wards set by a mage like Oron, that could take nearly a year. Her parents would have returned by then, certainly.

Ardhuin hesitated, then swung her feet down. They could return at any time. If she were going to figure it out, it would be best not to wait. Opening the big, heavy double library doors, she conjured a ball of magefire to light her way in the dark hallway. So much easier than fussing with a lamp, and she was always afraid she would trip and drop it and set something on fire.

She stepped through the wards of the workroom, feeling the strong resistance before they parted and allowed her to enter. As always, the careless disorder made her eyes well up. She could almost imagine her great-uncle still there, giving her a thoughtful sidelong look before setting her another test of skill. Since the servants could not enter, any cleaning was done by him, and rarely—and the cleaning spell would have been a dangerous distraction. Dust covered everything.

Almost everything. The big worktable with the racks of tuned thaumaturgical devices was relatively clear, as was an ornately carved cabinet with four panel doors. That would be the best place to start looking, since he would have disturbed them most recently.

The worktable had nothing. Ardhuin opened the cabinet and found a sheet of paper with her great-uncle's spidery handwriting. *Retention of control and precision in great workings using disparate elements,* it said, with a description below. It appeared to simply be a practice magic, to develop skill, the kind of thing he had had her do so many times.

"I can do this," Ardhuin said to herself. "A central element of light, then surrounded by a stasis, which is itself surrounded by a shielding…." It was trickier than she had thought. Keeping the separate magical elements active and not touching was crucial, or the whole thing collapsed. It took her three tries, but she finally assembled the entire structure. It looked like a filigree globe, lit from within, spinning gently in the air before her.

She smiled, feeling triumphant, then remembered what she was searching for and let the magic dissipate. Just as she turned back to the cabinet, Ardhuin felt her ears pop. She looked around, startled. Now she could hear a high-pitched creak. She went to the door and reached for the latch, encountering the wards in between. They were *shuddering*.

Ardhuin snatched her hand away. Had she done something wrong? No, the amount of power she had just used was nothing compared to the strength of the wards, and none of the components were active. She darted a glance at the worktable. Sparks and runnels of light, changing in color from green to purple to red, danced over the equipment.

Power. A fearsome amount of power. It wasn't coming from her, and her great-uncle was dead, so it had to be someone else. Someone outside.

They seek Oron. "He's not here!" she whispered, sinking to the floor and clutching the heavy leg of the worktable. It would offer no protection if the wards failed, but the instinct to seek shelter could not be overcome. Why were they attacking?

After what seemed like an eternity the multicolored sparks faded and disappeared, and when she worked up the courage to test the wards they were normal. Outside the workroom there was no sign that anything had happened, until she ventured into the library. Outside the main window, shimmers of light, like an aurora, flickered in a shell around the house.

Well. Now she knew what his last "project" was. The main house wards followed the shape of the building itself, but this formed a giant dome. Since outsiders had come and gone from that area unhindered, it must be purely for protection against magical attack. Her great-uncle had anticipated this.

Ardhuin started to shake. The attack was intended to destroy Oron— or was it? Had this mysterious enemy detected the magic she had done and thought her great-uncle was still alive, or did they know about her?

Could she leave the house and live?

CHAPTER 2

The cart creaked to a stop, and Dominic roused himself from his doze. They had arrived at the promised crossroads. At least he hoped so; he had no idea where he was or how far he was from his destination, the train station in the town of Baranton.

His first attempt at tutoring had ended on a fairly cordial note, with his return transportation being provided by the family. A series of unlucky investments had put his employer in need of retrenchment. Dominic suspected his services still might not have been dispensed with had his young charges been less eager to test the knowledge they had gained—in particular, the attempt to communicate with smoke plumes of different sizes in the manner of the Yunwiyans, which had resulted in the destruction of a favorite antique carpet.

This latest position had not gone well from the beginning, and had resulted in his unceremonious ejection from the house. He was not at all sorry to go. He had only one student this time, but he was a boy of little intellect, spoiled and indulged, who enjoyed nothing more than finding some unsuspecting animal and tormenting it to death. Dominic had found it necessary to watch him constantly.

"Tha'llt have a gert road of it," the farmer driving the cart said, waving in a westerly direction. "Hold aboot and the town be retchely then."

Dominic lifted his trunk and bag out of the back of the farmer's cart, trying to decipher what he had been told. He gave up.

"Does that road go to Baranton?" he asked, pointing at the most heavily traveled road.

"It trannelt oot," the farmer said, nodding. "Nay, ha' done, spirkin," he added when Dominic attempted to hand him a few coins. "Our hap to aid." He picked up the reins and slapped them lightly on the rump of his old horse, which plodded away.

"Thank you!" called Dominic, and the farmer raised a hand in farewell without looking back.

Dominic picked up his luggage and set off. He had been fortunate to encounter the farmer. All he had to do was find the train station and go back to Dinan. He'd saved up enough that he could survive for a few months. Now he could attempt to make a living at writing, for he was more determined than ever not to continue as a tutor.

"Time to write. Hah!" Dominic shifted his trunk to the other shoulder. "Where did Botrel get that idea?" He'd hardly dared take time to sleep in his last position. With the first family, his brief attempts at his own activities had usually resulted in catastrophes like the Great Carpet Conflagration.

Nor had he enjoyed much adult conversation. To the family, he was little better than a servant; to the servants, an outsider. He had never felt so alone. Only Phillipe's occasional letters kept him in good spirits.

Dominic trudged along the road, wondering how his few precious books had turned into lead in his trunk. It was unusually hot for a summer day, even so far south as this. He tried to keep up his spirits by whistling, but the dust soon put an end to that.

How far had it been from where he'd left the farmer? Baranton should be less than five leagues, if his guess was correct, and he'd gone farther than that. He was beginning to suspect that he had taken the wrong road. This looked nothing like it would lead to a village with a train station.

He came to another crossroad and studied the weatherbeaten signpost. The arm in the direction he was heading was missing, of course, and the sign pointing to the road that went to the left was almost completely illegible. It looked like the first letter was "P," so it couldn't be Baranton—unless the elements had altered it. The name didn't look long enough to be "Baranton" either. He glanced down the side road, uncertain. It went down a gentle slope, the road shaded by huge oak trees. He could just make out a corner of a roof beyond the trees.

Dominic hesitated, then set off down the side road. He could ask for directions at the house, and perhaps rest in the shade for a while.

At first the house looked promising—a small, rambling chateau of an unusual creamy-gold stone, the high walls nearest the road showing occasional oval windows. But as he approached more closely he could see the signs of neglect; shutters broken or missing, paint peeling, tiles missing from the roof. When he reached the gates, they were chained and rusty.

"Pfui!" He stared at them, annoyed he had been brought out of his way for nothing. Then his curiosity took hold. Why was it abandoned and empty?

He decided to explore, and since his trunk was really starting to become painful, he looked about for a place he could safely hide his belongings. A small gatehouse stood by the gate, and when he tried the door it was unlocked. The interior was bare save for a large cupboard underneath the window that faced the road. He stashed his trunk and bag inside the cupboard, out of sight, and set out on his tour.

The house and grounds stood at the edge of one of the dark, brooding forests that were to be found in Morbihan, and Dominic the writer of fantastic tales nodded approvingly. On the other side of the house a long, high stone wall hid the grounds from view. He could just see a mass of white blooms over the top of the high wall, and when he came closer, discovered they were roses. He had never seen any rose so white in his life, nor smelled one with such a delicate, sweet scent.

He closed his eyes, breathing deeply, and smiled. The discomfort of the trunk, the hot dusty road—all his difficulties seemed to fade away in his mind. Such pretty roses! He wondered if he could reach one over the wall. Then his eye caught sight of the small gate. It opened with a rusty screech.

The garden was a tangle of overgrown paths and general neglect, but he could see glimpses of color in the tall grass; vivid azure blue, fiery red mixed with orange. The white rose hedge was the least of its beauties.

Dominic suddenly realized he had to write down a description of the mysterious abandoned garden or he would lose the fresh edge of his vision. He went back to the gatehouse to get his journal.

When he got there, his bag and trunk were gone.

She had found a few hints since the attack. Since she dared not leave the house or even use magic, there was not much else to do. Tantalizing hints, but no real answer to her problem. If anything, what she had learned only made it worse.

Ardhuin reluctantly turned away from the library window and picked up her great-uncle's final letter to her, the one unsent when he died. She had it nearly memorized by now. She could feel his frustration as she read it again, wanting to warn her but still uncertain what the danger was.

I am convinced that these disquieting signs are connected to my duties as Mage Guardian. We took great care to ensure we had accounted for all the mages of the Grand Armeé, even the minor ones, so I find it hard to credit this is their work. Perhaps a gifted student found some of their notes—it does not matter now. Forgive me, petite—*but I must require you, my heir, to ensure that this is not a threat to Aerope. If it is, God forbid, you must deal with these people resolutely. The world must not see such horror again.*

She put the letter down, fighting a sudden wave of despair. How could she find out anything? The magic of the attack was unlike anything she'd ever seen. The only certainties were it was mage-level magic, and that it came from a distance. She couldn't even write to ask for help from her great-uncle's associates. Most of them were dead, at least the ones he had mentioned, and why would they believe her? Perhaps he'd planned to introduce her, overcome the storm of objections that were bound to be raised, but he had not lived to do it. Her great-uncle preferred to avoid tedious arguments.

Perhaps these unseen enemies thought he might be dead or injured, and had first sent smaller spells to be certain. They would have found the wards still up and functioning, so they had sent a stronger attack. Ardhuin drew a deep breath. If they knew where the Mage Guardian Oron lived, they would be able to discover his real name—and whether he was still alive.

She shuddered. If Oron was dead but Peran was still defended, of course they would think it occupied by his heir, or someone privy to the secrets of his life. There was no point in trying to hide the fact a magician was present. She should still be cautious, though. They did not need to know her true strength. Even more important, she should prevent them from confirming they had found the correct house. There must be other mages in Bretagne.

It just didn't make any sense. The Mage War had been over for many years and had devastated Aerope. Gaul still had not recovered. Why would anyone want to start that again?

A loud metallic creak came from outside. It took her a moment to realize what it was, and then she darted to the window, being careful to stay hidden behind the drapes. *Someone had entered the garden.*

Ardhuin peeked out. A man in a dark coat stood just inside the gate, looking about the garden. That was impossible. The Lethe roses should have stopped him. Unless he was a magician and knew how to protect himself.

Fear held her motionless. She should have thought of that. If they believed they had destroyed the mage living here, they would not fear coming to his house.

The man made an impatient gesture, as if he had forgotten something, and went out the gate again. Ardhuin cast about wildly for inspiration. She needed a weapon. Using magic directly would give it all away. The letter opener? It was sharp, but she'd have to get too close to use it. The exotic swords on the wall in the entry would just make him laugh. Then she saw the fireplace tools. Yes, a frightened woman might use a poker. It was iron, too.

She grabbed the poker and ran down the stairs to the front parlor, tripping on a hidden chair leg under the shrouding muslin covers. Easing back the curtain, she looked out the front. Her heart was pounding, her mouth dry. No sign of the stranger. She checked from other vantage points, seeing nothing until she tried the front stair landing. A glimpse of a dark head moving along the side path. Back to the garden.

What on earth was he doing? If he was checking to see if anyone had survived, why hadn't he even glanced at the house?

She moved cautiously to the kitchen, crouching down so she could see out the glass panes set in the top half of the outer kitchen door. Yes, he had returned. Ardhuin frowned. She still couldn't see his face clearly, but he seemed unhappy now, almost distraught. His shoulders were slumped in despair, and his walk was slow and tired.

This did not make any kind of sense. He wandered towards the other roses, his back to the house. She eased open the door just enough to reach her shaking hand outside the wards. She could test for illusion inside them, but it would take more power and would be more likely to be noticed.

He was not an illusion. He was, however, a problem. If he noticed any of the visibly magical roses, it would confirm he had found the right place. No other mage had ever been able to merge the natural and the magical as her great-uncle had done. If he didn't leave on his own, she would have to *make* him leave. But how?

She could see him more clearly now. His lean, clean-shaven face was all planes and angles, shadowed by the sun, but mobile—she imagined she could read his emotions as they flickered over his face. His deep-set eyes glanced searchingly all over the garden, looking…lost?

The stranger stopped by the Judgement rosebush and reached out to pick one of the flame-orange blooms. Her jaw dropped, and before she could stop herself, Ardhuin charged out the door yelling "No!"

He spun around, staring at her with an expression of shock and horror. His face was as pale as if he had seen an apparition—which, she realized with a sinking feeling, she resembled more than she should. Anyone would be frightened by the sudden appearance of a giant poker-waving woman with a wild mane of red hair. She was wearing one of her favorite dresses, too—indigo swirls on a cream background in the old-fashioned high-waisted style, decidedly unusual in cut and color. Her mother would be appalled.

Ardhuin felt her face go hot with embarrassment, which made her even more angry. She took a deep breath and pointed the poker at him. He was a trespasser and she didn't care how she looked.

He held up his hands as if to ward her off.

"M-mademoiselle. I beg you pardon, I did not intend to intrude! I thought the house was empty!"

It was a reasonable assumption to make, she had to confess. That still left some questions unanswered.

"What are you doing here?" Her voice wavered a little, but the poker didn't. "I saw you leave, but you came back."

A look of anguish crossed his face. "I was on my way to Baranton, to take a train to Dinan," he said after a moment. That part seemed true enough. She could see the dust of the road on his shoes.

"This isn't the road to Baranton," Ardhuin pointed out, suspicious.

"Damnation!" The pale face flushed. She noticed with annoyance that the reaction, which would make her look like a boiler on the point of exploding, merely made him look more interesting. Divine Providence was not only unkind, but malicious as well. "My apologies, mademoiselle. I am sadly out of temper, but that does not excuse my language. I suspected I had taken the wrong road and hoped to ask at your house for directions, but when I saw the locked gate I thought no one was living here."

Perhaps she had overreacted. "Well, there is. You want to go back to the signpost and take the left turning about half a league, then take the next road. It's not far." He looked distressed and made no attempt to leave. "The last train to Dinan leaves in a few hours," Ardhuin hinted.

"Thank you, mademoiselle." He sighed. "My plans have changed, since someone has just stolen my luggage and my money. I can no longer afford train fare." He made an attempt to smile. "I don't suppose you know anyone in town in urgent need of a tutor?"

"You had your luggage with you when you came here, did you not?" Ardhuin asked, suspicious again. "When was it stolen?"

"Just a few moments ago!" He gestured towards the gate. "I set it down to rest a moment, and walked down the path to admire the roses. When I came back it was gone."

Ardhuin frowned. The roses were not doing their job, and she had a sinking suspicion what had happened to the missing luggage. "Did you perhaps leave it in the port-cochère?" she asked.

"The little room by the gate? Yes." He looked at her hopefully. "Did you see who took it?"

She bit her lip. "Wait here, please," she said, and picked up her skirts and ran back to the kitchen, heading for the large cupboard near the pantry. Dropping the poker, Ardhuin opened the door and her shoulders sagged. Yes, there they were. A battered trunk and a well-stuffed carpetbag, both old and mended. Now, how was she going to explain that? She had to get rid of him before he noticed anything else strange. Sometimes her great-uncle had been just a trifle too clever.

Ardhuin yanked the trunk off the shelf of the cupboard, dropping it when she felt its full weight. She experienced a twinge of sympathy for her unexpected visitor. Anyone would want a rest after carrying that thing around. It took her three attempts to get the carpetbag balanced on top of the trunk, and she knew her face was red again from the effort, but she didn't want him trying to help and discovering the wards in the process.

The lost tutor was delighted to see his property again, and immediately rushed to meet her. "That is much too heavy for you! Permit me—" he gave her a warm smile as he knelt to examine them. "Wonderful! Nothing is missing. How did this happen?"

"A…misunderstanding," Ardhuin mumbled. "Deliveries for the house are left in the port-cochère, and it was assumed this was another delivery." She held her breath, but he did not ask *who* had made the assumption, or how this unspecified person had moved a trunk and a carpetbag into the house without being seen. "I am so sorry. I hope this does not delay your journey," she said, trying to smile while edging around to block his view of the garden. The Sangré rose had sensed a stranger and was getting restless. "I would be most distressed if your employers were angry with you for being late."

He laughed, and to her horror she found herself smiling back at him. Was it a spell? This was the longest voluntary conversation she'd ever had with a stranger, and he wasn't scrambling to get away from her—in fact, the reverse. He was acting exactly as if she was a proper, pretty young lady he had met by chance and wanted to talk to. Very suspicious.

"You shall not be distressed. Having been recently dismissed, I need please no one but myself in my arrival. But I should not intrude upon you any longer," he said, giving a slight bow. Ardhuin suppressed a sigh of relief.

He hefted the trunk to his shoulder, wincing a little, then bent to pick up the carpetbag and froze, staring at a shadowed corner of the garden. Ardhuin felt her heart start to pound. *You see nothing. It is all in your imagination.*

"Mademoiselle…is that rose *glowing?*"

It frightened her how quickly she reacted, and the spell she chose frightened her too. He probably was just a traveler—but if her enemies found him and learned where he had been, what he had seen, they would know Oron had been there. And they would find her. They must *never* find her.

She shaped the power as quickly as she could, stalling for time by pretending to peer in the direction he was pointing. "Isn't that just a patch of sunlight?"

He stared at her, eyes wide. "It's *blue!*"

Skin. She had to touch skin for it to work, and not his hands. Close to the head. Why was this the hardest part? She was putting a *geas* on his mind, and she balked at touching him? She had to do it. He would talk about the roses, and it was too dangerous. Somebody wanted to kill her.

Ardhuin lunged at him, grasping the lapels of his coat desperately. One finger just traced the side of his neck, and she let the spell free. "Please," she gasped. What was the least constraint she could put on him? He was looking at her with great concern, but there was no sign he knew a powerful spell had been placed on him. "Don't tell anyone about the roses."

She snatched her hands away and stepped back, feeling nauseous. He stood immobile, a faint crease of worry between his eyebrows.

"I worry that people will come…steal them. Or something," she finished, looking down at her feet.

"Of course. I will say nothing of them." She did not look up, and when she heard him speak again, it was from further away. "Goodbye, mademoiselle."

Not trusting her voice, she raised her hand in farewell and forced a smile. As soon as she heard the gate creak, she looked up to make sure he had left, and then ran back to the kitchen. She stood on the smooth flagstones and sobbed, arms wrapped around herself, suppressing the sound out of habit even though no one could hear her.

Why had her great-uncle done this to her? Why had he even *taught* her the *geas* spell? It was illegal for all but a few, specially licensed mages. Most magicians didn't even know how to do it. She was in danger because of him, and she had just put herself in even more by what she had done.

At least she hadn't placed a constraint the stranger would find repellant. He had voluntarily agreed to what she had asked. The *geas* would just make sure he did not forget.

Ardhuin dried her face, feeling tired and unclean. She opened the outside door again and wandered out into the garden, giving the *ignis fatuus* rose a scowl. She hadn't even known the stupid thing had started blooming again, and of course the stranger noticed right away. If it hadn't been for that rose, she would not have had to do the *geas*.

It was done, and she would have to live with the consequences. She went to the wall and the thick overgrowth of the climbing Lethe roses. As soon as she was close enough to smell the light lemony scent, she felt her defenses rise. They were still working, at least for her. Not for the stranger, apparently, and now she would never know why.

Ardhuin woke the next morning feeling as if she had not slept at all. She burrowed into the tangled bedclothes, trying to go back to sleep, but without success. Her thoughts were too busy reliving the events of the previous day, and any number of birds were being noisily cheerful outside her window.

"I need a cat," she said, looking at the birds blearily. They ignored her and kept singing. Perhaps a lion would be more useful. It would keep down the number of unexpected visitors. No, she needed to figure out where the attacks were coming from, stop them, and go back to school before her parents found out she was missing.

She put on an old dark blue dress from her school days and went down to the kitchen for some breakfast. Food helped, but not enough, and she decided to wash her hair. She couldn't concentrate on anything right now, and it needed it. She heated the water with magic without thinking. She *had* to get some sleep, or she was going to do something really stupid.

The smell of the lavender and chamomile soap soothed her bad mood, and by the time she was carefully combing her wet hair to help it dry, her thoughts had changed to gentle melancholy. If only this were a fairy tale like *La Travaille de Fayre*, everything would work out. Her plainness would merely be the result of a spell, she would trick the evil magicians behind the attacks with a handful of dried beans and a goat, and the wine cellar would have a secret door to Elfhame behind the '33 Nantes port.

Ardhuin braided her still-damp hair and wondered what she should do next. What she really needed was advice she could trust. Perhaps her great-uncle had corresponded with another mage, unknown to her. She would just have to be convincing, or perhaps vague about her gender, in her inquiry.

She spent the rest of the morning looking for letters, feeling uncomfortable at this invasion of his privacy but too desperate to refrain. There was nothing in his workroom. She'd already searched the desk in the library—that contained nothing but ordinary business correspondence. In a cabinet in the main bedroom she found a carved lattice-wood box with the letters she had written him from school, and she felt tears prick her eyes. Had she really said anything in them worth preserving?

A bell jangled inside the house. The front door bell. Ardhuin put the box back in the cabinet and went to the bedroom window, but she couldn't see the doorway.

The bell rang again. She ran down to the drawing room. Opening one of the windows, she leaned out. Someone stood on the front step, but she couldn't see a face. She definitely needed to get that lion.

Her visitor stepped back, searching the windows of the house, and she gasped. A wave of guilt washed over her when she recognized the stranger from the previous day. Instinctively, she ducked, trying to hide, but he had seen her.

"Mademoiselle Andrews! Good morning!" He waved.

Why was he here? He seemed quite cheerful, so presumably he had not discovered the *geas* or something missing in his trunk. She lifted her head a little higher.

"How do you know my name?" she asked, fighting panic.

He pointed down the road. "I asked in the town. My name is Dominic Kermarec. May I speak with you for a moment?"

If she said no, would he leave? On the other hand, it was probably a good idea to try to find out why he had come back. What if she had made a mistake with the *geas* and bound him to this location? No, she would have noticed a mistake that big.

She nodded at him and shut the window. She took her time going downstairs and struggling to open the big iron lock and chain on the front door, hoping he would give up and leave. When she finally got the door open, though, he was still there.

Ardhuin looked at him enquiringly. Dominic Kermarec looked much as he had the day before. She noticed this time that he was only slightly shorter than she, yet he didn't seem tall. His clothing, while well cared for and clean, still showed the effects of wear. Apparently tutoring did not pay well. At least now she was more presentable, and not nearly so nervous.

"I wished to ask if that small cottage I saw at the edge of the trees might be available for rent. It appears to be empty," he added.

Ardhuin blinked. If he were working with her adversaries, surely he must know she would be suspicious of him. But if he were not, why on earth would he want to stay here?

"Monsieur Kermarec. I was under the impression you were bound for

Dinan," she said, slowly feeling her way.

He gave a rueful shrug. "I was, yes. But I had always intended to wait some months before seeking another position, and it occurred to me that I can do so much more economically in the country. I have references," he said, earnestly offering her three folded sheets of paper.

Did spies carry references? Curious, Ardhuin read through the letters. The first was a straightforward reference from a previous employer, stating that he had been dismissed for no fault and had been exemplary in the performance of his duties.

The second was from a professor at the Université Dinan. "This Professor Botrel—what is his field?" she asked casually. Dinan had an *ars magica* college, didn't it?

"Literature," Kermarec answered, and her interest faded. No hope there.

The third reference took her some time to read. The handwriting was a scrawl, the spelling haphazard, and the subject matter decidedly unusual. She held it closer, then at an angle, shaking her head. Kermarec grinned, watching her.

"I don't know why he dismissed you," she said before she could stop herself. "I've never seen someone so clearly in need of a tutor. Why does he feel it necessary to mention that you treated the kitchenmaid with courtesy? Was he that astonished?"

"The only answers that have occurred to me would impugn the character of my former employer," he answered with mock solemnity. "It was not a happy situation."

Ardhuin shook her head. "I believe you should be congratulated on your escape." Then she remembered who she was talking to, and why. She handed the letters back. She needed a good excuse, a believable one. "I don't know how much longer I will be here. The new occupants may very well wish to use the gardener's cottage for an actual gardener. Perhaps you should inquire in Baranton for lodgings."

"I could go to Baranton when they arrive," he pointed out reasonably. "It is a pleasant town, but I feel the need for greater peace and quiet."

That settled it. He couldn't say that with a straight face if he knew anything about the attacks. But if he was just an ordinary person, could she permit him to stay and risk injury? She'd done enough to him, and he deserved none of it.

"I, ah, was thinking of hiring a gardener myself," she lied.

Kermarec scratched his chin. "I'm not a gardener, but I could at least cut the grass. For a reduction in rent."

Ardhuin scowled. Now she remembered how impervious to hints he had been earlier. Fine. If he was caught in a magical crossfire, he would have no one to blame but himself. Perhaps her enemies would find him as disconcerting as she did.

"Five guilders every two weeks, with two hours of work a day," she snapped. He nodded. Before he could say anything more, she whisked back inside and shut the door.

Maybe she should turn *him* into a lion. She'd already broken the law with the *geas;* would a transformation spell be any worse? Of course, they were very tricky to get right, and with her luck the lion would just follow intruders around and ask questions instead of eating them.

She was tired, that was all. Tired and frantic with worry. If she got some sleep she would know what to do next.

One week passed with no sign of her attackers, then two. Dominic Kermarec took up residence in the gardener's cottage, and to her surprise she only saw him twice: once to give him the key and accept the first payment of rent, and once when she warned him about the dangerous roses in the garden. She had been afraid he would come and try to talk to her, so she left notes with gardening instructions pinned to his door or hanging from the gate.

She was still angry with herself for letting him stay. She just hadn't had time to think of a good lie, and once she mentioned the gardener it had all gotten complicated. Any attempt to turn him away at that point would have been suspicious, and she still wasn't completely convinced by his story. It was better to be cautious.

Since she was a late riser, Ardhuin hadn't seen him working, but she could see evidence of it. The front lawn no longer looked like a hayfield, and the garden had emerged from the tall grass and weeds that had hidden it from view. She reflected, looking at the blooming roses from the library window, that really this had worked out better than she had expected. Even if she had hired a gardener, she would not have trusted him to remain silent about the magical roses. And it was nice to walk in the garden again.

She looked more closely and her heart sank. He'd uncovered the statues at the entrance to the ley line observatory. While the grass and vines had obscured them she could pretend they weren't there, but now they gleamed white against the dark hedge. An *amori* pair in the style of the Graeco-Roman Empire, the man offering the woman a flower as a symbol of something or other. She couldn't remember what her great-uncle had told her. Their outstretched arms formed an arch over the entrance.

When she was younger she'd stared at them in fascination, knowing something secret and wonderful was hidden in their linked gaze and echoing smiles. Now that she knew what that secret was, they only reminded her of the love she would never know.

Ardhuin frowned, realizing she couldn't simply get rid of them. The eagle eye of her quasi-gardener would certainly notice if they disappeared suddenly overnight or were illusioned to look like something less objectionable. Leaving them as they were was not acceptable either. They were in full view of the library window. Since he had caused the problem, perhaps she should persuade Dominic Kermarec to solve it.

As soon as the idea occurred to her she rejected it. The statues would require more strength than he possessed to move them, and it would be difficult to argue the task was within their agreement. Even worse, she would have to talk to him. No, it was impossible.

She spent the afternoon experimenting with new spells in the workroom. When she left to look up a reference in the library she could see the statues even more plainly than before, full in the light of the sun. Ardhuin clenched her fists, realizing she had no choice. She couldn't bear the sight of them.

She couldn't go out as she was, though. Normal women did not appear in public with their hair streaming down their backs. Ardhuin trudged up to her room, wondering how long it would take this time. Her hair, in addition to its fiery color, was fine and slippery and always coming loose. She finally managed to get the whole mass up and anchored with every hairpin she owned after a prolonged struggle. Hopefully that would be good enough.

Glowering, she left the house. This was all his fault. Didn't he realize she had other, more important things to do? Then her sense of justice reminded her that she had been at pains to have him *not* realize anything. Besides, yelling and scowling at him would not further her plans. She would have to be nice.

The closer she got to the door of the gardener's cottage the more her stomach tied itself into knots. Her courage nearly failed her when she finally stood before it, and it took her a moment to force herself to raise her hand and give a soft tap.

Maybe he wasn't in. With a rush of relief she stepped back and turned to go, but then heard the door open behind her.

"Mademoiselle Andrews?" She had to turn back, since he had already seen her. Dominic Kermarec was in his shirtsleeves and looked quite surprised. There was a smudge of soot on his cheek that made the angles of his face seem even more pronounced. She froze, suddenly unable to speak, and his expression changed to one of worry. "Oh. Have you hired a gardener?"

"No!" she blurted, astonished, then winced when she realized she'd missed a perfect opportunity to solve the whole problem. She needed to practice lying. It was becoming painfully obvious her lack of skill was a handicap. "I wanted to…to ask a favor. I mean, I need…." Behind him, she saw a table scattered with books, papers, and the remains of a meal. She felt herself going bright red with embarrassment. "I have interrupted your dinner. I am very sorry."

"It would be hard for you *not* to interrupt it, since this is in fact an extremely prolonged luncheon," he said, with a wry expression. "I had no idea it was so difficult to cook a chicken. I bought it to celebrate, but I seem to have done something not quite right—I don't see how it can still be raw inside when the outside is all but burned. My hunger got the better of me and I have been eating a bite here and there as it finishes.

Next time I will ask your advice."

Ardhuin stared at him, nonplussed. She'd never cooked a chicken either, or anything else. As a child, the cook had refused to even let her in the kitchen after the first few accidents caused by her clumsiness, and no objection had been raised when she refused to take lessons in school. He was acting as if she were an ordinary young lady again.

Some of her confusion must have shown on her face. He cleared his throat and stood back from the doorway. "But you wished to ask me something, Mademoiselle Andrews. Please, come in."

He looked about the interior of the tiny cottage, then went and quickly took his jacket off the back of the only chair, picked up a book lying on the seat, and offered the chair to her. Ardhuin didn't want to sit down or even come inside, but she did so. Perhaps it was just her imagination, but he kept glancing at her with what seemed like apprehension. Now that she thought about it, perhaps she had been rather abrupt in their previous conversations.

"What are you celebrating, Monsieur Kermarec?"

He picked up a printed magazine from the table, opened up the front page, and handed it to her. "This," he said, indicating a line in the listed contents.

It said, *Under the Earth: A dramatic tale of exploration and adventure by D. Kermarec.* "You are an author," Ardhuin said softly. "I congratulate you."

"It's my very first publication," he said with obvious pride. "The editor of this magazine has even asked me to send more."

Ardhuin turned back the cover, studying the engraved illustrations, then looked at the contents again. "What is your tale about?" she asked, intrigued.

"A team of explorers that endeavor to find an entrance to the Earth's center in the deepest caverns known. You may borrow it if you like," he offered, and grinned. "I already know how it ends."

"You are very kind," Ardhuin said, feeling an unexpected spurt of happiness. She looked up. Dominic Kermarec was staring at her with an air of startled puzzlement. After a moment, he shook his head.

"I beg your pardon. You reminded me of something I had forgotten. What is it you wished to ask me?"

Ardhuin clutched the magazine, feeling nervous again. "Those two statues in the garden. Can you…move them? By yourself?" It seemed ridiculous now. While he appeared more athletic than a typical scholar, it would take a great deal of strength to shift two heavy stone statues.

He blinked. "Where do you wish them moved?"

"Anywhere I won't have to look at them," she snapped, and felt her face go red when he stared at her in astonishment.

"But—you object to them?"

She kept her gaze on the floor. "Yes. I object to them," she mumbled. "Can you do it?" She glanced up again.

He rubbed his chin, looking out the window thoughtfully. "I have an idea that might work. I will need some timbers and some rope, though."

Ardhuin stood up. She suddenly wanted desperately to get out of the cottage, out into the open air. "Look in the carriage house, on the other side of the entrance. If you don't find anything of use I will give you money to purchase what you need in town. Thank you," she said, remembering to smile.

She felt her smile start to slip when he accompanied her out the door. "It is my pleasure to assist you. If I had not been able to stay here I doubt I would have finished my story. Now I need to write another." He held up one hand to shield his eyes from the rays of the setting sun. "Do you know if there is a library in Baranton? I need to find a set of Gridel's Lectures."

"In Baranton? No." Ardhuin looked down at the magazine in her hands. She felt ashamed of her earlier suspicions. Dominic Kermarec was just an aspiring writer with too much curiosity. He had always been courteous, even when her behavior was brusque or actually rude. He was no danger to her. There was no reason she shouldn't help him—and considering what she had done to him, it might be a way of making reparations.

"I believe I might have a set," she stammered quickly. "You may borrow the volumes you need." There, she'd done it. Her heart was beating so fast she felt a little faint.

He brightened. "Thank you! Would you mind if I got them now? I can read while I wait for the chicken to be done."

Panic froze her, and she forced herself to breathe again. She hadn't intended for him to come to the house. But then, did it really matter? Nothing obvious needed hiding in the house itself. Perhaps it would be better to get it over with as quickly as possible. Then she could take a prescriptive powder and recover from the shocks of the day.

"Of—of course." She started walking down the path back to the house.

Kermarec walked beside her, relaxed and looking about as they went. "This is a beautiful place. How long have you lived here?"

"A few years," Ardhuin said carefully. He might be safe, but she didn't want to give him any potentially dangerous information.

He raised his eyebrows. "And before that?"

She could give him potentially misleading information, though. "I'm from Atlantea."

He stopped in his tracks, staring at her, then continued on, shaking his head. "You don't sound Atlantean. I mean, your name is foreign, but you have no accent at all."

Ardhuin opened the garden gate. "Oh, I went to school in Bretagne for several years," she said, and increased her pace. She had to open the wards fast enough that he would not feel anything when they went through. Of course, he waited to allow her to enter first, and she had no difficulty opening and closing them without detection.

He followed her through the house, looking with admiration at the interior. When she opened the doors to the library, she heard him gasp behind her.

"Gridel's Lectures are here," Ardhuin said, gesturing to the section of wall under the balcony.

"I begin to understand why you never leave the house," Kermarec commented, going to one knee to get a better look at the titles on the bindings. "And why you spend so much time here."

Ardhuin frowned. "How…why do you say that?"

He smiled faintly and indicated the large window that faced the garden. It was almost completely dark outside.

"I can see the light from my cottage." He started selecting volumes from the shelf. "Hmm. I don't see the volume of lectures on astronomy."

She made a noise of exasperation. "I think I know where it is. I will return in just a moment." She closed the library doors behind her and threw a delicate web of power over them, keeping the main thread with her as she hurried up the stairs. If he tried to leave the library before she returned, she'd know. Not that he would get anywhere if he did. The wards would prevent him from leaving the house until she opened them.

Up more flights of stairs, to the servant's rooms, and then the steep, narrow staircase to the cupola at the top of the house. The missing volume was still there, opened to the page of illustrations of the interaction between solar flux and terrestrial ley lines. Two pieces of smoked glass lay beside it, the ones she and her great-uncle had used to view an eclipse.

She picked up the book, which smelled slightly musty, and carefully went back down the steep stairs. How long ago had that been? How she had loved to escape from school on her vacations, and how she'd hated to go back when they ended.

The library doors were still closed, according to her spell. She paused on the landing, paging through the book of lectures and remembering how much her great-uncle had loved learning new things.

The sudden scream nearly made her drop the book. She flew down the stairs, heart pounding. Was it an attack? She'd felt nothing on the wards. The screams continued, coming from the library. Was Kermarec hurt? Ardhuin gestured the library doors to open, too impatient to care if her use of power was detected.

She didn't see him anywhere on the lower level. The screaming had stopped. She listened more carefully, walking slowly around the edge of the library. A sort of harsh, sobbing breath came from the upper level. She picked up her skirts in one hand and ran up the spiral stair.

There he was. Collapsed in a heap, unconscious, in front of the cabinets where the magic books were stored. She'd left one unlocked, evidently. It was open, and he was clutching the most dangerous book in the collection, one that had powerful defenses.

She felt cold and sick. Dominic Kermarec was a spy after all.

CHAPTER 3

Dominic scanned the shelves in growing wonder, barely noticing the sound of the library doors closing. It was a large room; books lined two walls completely. Glass-fronted cabinets framed a large window on another wall, and the remaining one featured a massive stone fireplace, deeply carved. He looked up and saw that the library had a gallery along two sides as well. He sighed in sheer bliss.

The library was like a temple to books. He'd been surprised at the richness of the interior of the house, and the signs of disuse. Most of the furniture was swathed in white covers. But here, everything was alive. The rich wood glowed in the light of the sconce lamps, and in the center space, before a large carved desk, were deep, padded leather chairs around a thick carpet of foreign design.

How many books did she have? Whoever had chosen them had eclectic taste. He started to walk slowly along the wall, fighting the urge to take a volume out and start reading. Each title was more interesting than the last—the ones he could read, at least. Many were in languages or scripts he did not recognize.

The cabinets were full of intriguing things, too. Dominic went over to examine them more closely, but saw the spiral staircase to the library gallery and hesitated, glancing at the door. The mysterious Mademoiselle Andrews still had not returned.

He put his hand on the rail and started up. What was it about her that seemed so familiar? There had been a strange sense of *something* he could not identify from the first time he had encountered her, but tonight the feeling of recognition was like a blow. Was it what she had said? He couldn't possibly have met her before—even *he* would remember a woman like her. And it wasn't just her amazing hair, either. The long lines of her face, the determined jaw and angled brows, all gave the impression of something wild. When he had opened the door to her knock, his immediate impression had been of a half-tame creature, poised to attack or flee.

The stair rail had an impressed scale pattern on its surface, and the central pole featured a seadragon winding around it, highlighted in blue-green mother-of-pearl. A very rich house indeed. Then why was it essentially abandoned?

The gallery level had an even more far-ranging selection of books. Poetry, again in any number of languages, and fairy tales. At least he thought they were fairy tales. The drab, matter-of-fact bindings did not match the titles. He could no longer resist his curiosity, and opened one to find a series of meticulous sketches of an ancient stone building.

Here the priests would meet when the lunar phase most troubled the natural etheric flow, and would mingle their blood in a single golden cup that all would drink therefrom, that none would be able to set power over the others.

Dominic put the book away, feeling disturbed. No, not a fairy tale, at least not one for children. He glanced down at the lower level, wondering if he had been forgotten. She was unpredictable, but that would be beyond anything he'd yet seen from her.

Everything about her was a mystery. As far as he could tell, she never visited anyone or received callers, and he had seen no servants in the house. Was she truly alone? That might explain her reluctance to talk to him.

Perhaps she could no longer afford servants, and kept the house out of stubborn pride. Perhaps she feared losing it. Dominic frowned, suddenly realizing she was certainly worried about something. The first time he'd actually seen her smile was when he'd given her the magazine to read.

He continued along the shelves. Idly, he noticed the carpeting had an unusual glittery, silvery design. The gallery took an unexpected turn into an alcove. The books here were in glass-fronted cabinets. Their shelves had only a few titles in languages he was accustomed to, but he didn't stop to read them. Another book had caught his eye. *I wonder what the binding is, to give it that effect,* he thought, fascinated. *Fur? Black suede?* It seemed to swallow up the light, like it was wrapped in shadow. The cabinet door was slightly ajar, and he opened it further and reached for the book.

Pain lanced up his arm, doubling him up, dropping him to the floor. Spasms contorted his body, and he cried out. He tried to let go of the book, but his hand would not respond—and the pain got worse and worse. With the last of his strength, he desperately tried to strike the book out of his hand by hitting it against the edge of the shelf. He succeeded in shifting it but could not muster the energy to try again before the world went dark.

His awareness returned in slow-moving waves. At first, all he knew was a bone-deep fatigue and profound relief that the pain had stopped. Sharp twinges announced themselves when he tried to move. There was a dull ache at the back of his head—had he hit it when he fell? He couldn't remember.

Dominic opened his eyes and drew a sharp breath. He wasn't on the upper level anymore. He was sitting in one of the leather chairs on the main floor of the library, and it appeared he would remain there for some time, since he was tied to it. Not that he would have been able to stand if he were free. How his head ached!

It hurt to move, but he twisted stiffly and looked about as much as he could. The library was still empty, but now a white opaline glass lamp glowed on the big desk.

He felt strangely calm. Yes, he appeared to be in trouble, but the odds were he would soon find answers for some of the questions that had been bothering him. That was worth a headache.

Dominic heard the library doors open behind him and the sound of quick footsteps. Mademoiselle Andrews appeared. She breathed deeply, as if she had been running, and held a glorious red-gold rose in full bloom stiffly away from her in one hand. It looked like the same kind of rose he had nearly picked in the garden.

She started when she saw him looking at her. He couldn't tell if she was surprised to see him there, or if she had not expected him to be conscious.

Mademoiselle Andrews swallowed and continued forward slowly. "You aren't a very good spy," she said, her voice shaking a little. "Or didn't they warn you?"

Dominic struggled to speak. His head ached even more, and his jaw was stiff, too.

She had the same expression he remembered from the first time he had seen her—both fierce and frightened, her troubled eyes the grey-green of a stormy sea—but now there was a trace of hurt there. She thrust the rose at him as if it were the iron poker.

Soft petals brushed his bruised face, bringing with them a cloud of tangy scent. He took a deep breath reflexively, too confused to draw back. The same rose, and now she was forcing it on him instead of driving him away. She had looked so otherworldly that day, like a goddess of the Old Beliefs come back to life. A goddess of fire. He could see it even now. Tendrils of fiery hair had escaped her coiffure and hung about her face and down her back, as if the thin veneer of modern times she hid behind was beginning to crack.

"I'm not a spy," he said. His throat was raw. He remembered screaming, now.

She blinked with surprise and stepped back. Then she frowned, but not at him. At the rose. "How can I be sure it works?" she murmured, and held it to his face again. Dominic stifled a sneeze. "Say something that isn't true," she demanded.

She seemed absolutely sane. She just didn't make any sense. "Very well. I'm a pastry che-AUGGGHH!" His arms strained against the ropes, trying to get his hands free. His throat had suddenly constricted as if he were being strangled. The invisible hand released, and he fell back, gasping for air, feeling his heartbeat pound in his ears.

Mademoiselle Andrews gave a small, satisfied sigh. "Oh, good. I was afraid you were immune." Then her gaze sharpened. "You *aren't* a spy?" She seemed disappointed. "Then what were you doing with *Umbra Aetherium Thaumatiis?*"

He stared at her in complete confusion.

"The book I found you with," she explained.

He struggled to remember. "Was that the black book? I couldn't read the title...did I open it? It just looked strange, I suppose. I wondered what the binding was made of."

Her face went slack for a moment. Had he said the wrong thing?

"It looked strange, and you wanted to see what it was made of," she repeated in a flat voice. Her shoulders sagged. "My head hurts."

"Then there are two of us," Dominic snapped before he could stop himself. She compressed her mouth and reached for him. Dominic drew back instinctively, but she simply tucked the rose into the lapel of his jacket and moved away again.

"If you don't like getting headaches—and who does?—you should not ignore well-intentioned magic intended to keep the inquisitive from finding things that will give them headaches," she said, picking up a footstool and positioning it near his chair with a thump. She gathered her skirts and sat down. "Or worse. That white rose hedge is there for a reason, you know. But you never noticed it, or the protective spells on the book that should have made you ignore it completely. It's very dangerous."

Dominic had the feeling he had violated a point of magical etiquette. "Why are there...I mean, magic books? And the white roses are magical too? What do they do?"

"It's very clever, actually. Just a slight amount of forgetfulness, and..." she broke off, and her interested expression changed to a scowl. "You are supposed to be answering *my* questions, Monsieur Kermarec. Now—why did you come here?"

"To borrow the volumes of Gridel's Lectures, of course. Aaah—and to talk to you," he said quickly, feeling his throat begin to constrict. He'd been damnably curious about her, and look where it had gotten him. Tied up and ensorcelled.

She went completely still, suspicion and doubt revealing themselves in flashes on her face. Then she glanced at the rose, and her expression became one of pure puzzlement. "I meant to this place. To Baranton," she said in a small voice.

"The position I, ah, left involuntarily was in a town to the north. Josselin. It is cheaper to travel by train, but Josselin is not yet on a rail line and Baranton is the nearest station. A farmer took me most of the way."

"And the rest…what you told me when I found you? That was true?" There was a doubtful expression in her eyes when she glanced at him.

If he said it aloud, she would believe him. Because of the rose. Dominic was at a loss as to why she thought he had an ulterior motive, but it seemed to worry her greatly. "I was lost and came to your house to ask my way. I thought the house was empty." She said nothing for a moment, sitting on the footstool with her hands clasped around her knees. Her long face looked sad and troubled. "It is empty, isn't it? Except for you."

She ignored him, her brow furrowed in thought. "Have you ever heard of Oron?"

"No." This seemed to please her, and he relaxed a little.

"What of…Yves Morlais?" Her voice was very soft. He could barely hear her.

"N–errgh." Dominic coughed and blinked. He did know something? How could the damn rose know more than he did?

That strange, strong feeling of recognition—was it connected? She was leaning forward now, her gaze intent on his face.

"I can't remember," he whispered. "You said something earlier that made me think I had met you before. In Dinan. But that's impossible. I…Mademoiselle Andrews?"

Her face had gone deathly pale. She stood up suddenly and walked towards the window, gazing out at the darkness beyond. "This impossible event. When did it take place?" He could hear the strain in her voice.

"A few weeks before the last Solstice. I was with my friend in a bookstore." Dominic hesitated, remembering more. Beginning to understand. "I overheard a lady ask for books of magic for Yves Morlais. A lady who sounded much like you. But I could never quite see her face…."

"How can you see things you aren't supposed to?" she cried, turning sharply and flinging her arms wide.

"How am I supposed to know what I shouldn't see?" Dominic asked, feeling his temper fray. "Am I really being held captive with a broken head merely for overhearing a name in a bookstore?"

"Well, no, but…no, of course not!" she protested, her face twisting with distress. "I don't understand. You go right for the magic even when…what magical training do you have?"

Not again. Phillipe had never believed him either, but now he had the rose to support him. "I have no talent whatsoever. I was examined twice." He closed his eyes and leaned his head back until the chair reminded him of his bruises and he sat up sharply.

"Your head isn't really broken, is it?" She sounded genuinely concerned.

"It hurts," Dominic said, mindful of the rose in his lapel.

She came back to the footstool. "I'm sorry," she said. "I don't want to do this, but I have to. I have to understand."

It almost sounded like she was pleading with him.

He shifted in the chair, wondering what compelled her to do this. "Who is this Yves Morlais? Is he the magician who made these roses? Why don't you ask him all these questions?"

Her face twisted. "Oh, how I wish I could." She sank her head down on her hands. "If he were here…." She dropped her hands, and for a moment Dominic caught a glimpse of wild desperation in her stormy eyes. "He's dead. He was my great-uncle, and he left his house to me."

Dominic hesitated. "Mademoiselle Andrews, if you are afraid of spies, of people stealing your great-uncle's magic, perhaps you should sell this place."

She gave him a wry, distracted smile. "I can't." She rubbed at her forehead, making a small sound of aggravation. "I have to think this through. No magical ability, but you are drawn to magic. Hmm. I wonder…." She jumped up and went to one of the curio cabinets, hunting through a narrow drawer. She came back to Dominic with three ivory balls in her hands.

"Which one looks most interesting to you?" she asked, watching his face with a look of eager anticipation.

At first glance they appeared identical. Slightly larger than billiard balls, they had the yellow patina of age and a faint pattern of cracks in addition to an overall flower and vine carving that covered the surface. What was she trying to do? He tried to ignore the throbbing in his head. If he humored her, maybe she would let him go.

"That one." He gestured as well as he could for being tied down.

"You are sure?" Her face revealed nothing.

He nodded. She slowly tipped her hands forward. Two balls fell to the carpet and rolled away. He felt one bump against his foot.

The ball he had pointed to was still floating in the air, and Mademoiselle Andrews was smiling. He felt his breath catch. She had a beautiful smile, as beautiful as it was rare, that transformed her face like a sunrise chasing shadows.

"I was right!" she said, delighted.

"But I don't have any magic. Or do I?" Dominic asked, equally confused and excited. Something had happened.

She shook her head, her earlier wary mistrust gone and replaced with interest. "No, you don't have magic. You can *see* magic. That's why redirection spells don't work on you. It's like posting a big sign with gold lettering that says 'Don't Look Here.' How fascinating!"

Dominic drew a sharp breath. Many things that had puzzled him throughout his life began to make more sense. Those damn Solstice displays, for one. Phillipe had been right after all. He *had* seen something.

Mademoiselle Andrews glanced down at the ropes holding him as if she had forgotten they were there. Her smile faded. "I suppose I should make absolutely sure," she said to herself. "Has anyone asked you questions about this place, or who lives here?"

"No."

"Do you have any interest in the books of magic in this house?"

"I want to know where they are, so I can avoid them," Dominic answered, shuddering.

She knelt and started untying the ropes. "You really should get some training in your talent, you know. Magic is so prevalent nowadays; they use it for everything."

Dominic rubbed his arms, wincing, and stared at the still-floating ivory ball. It turned gently in place. "I just guessed. How can you be so certain I have talent?"

The corners of her mouth twitched upward, and she pointed at the rose still in his lapel. "I asked which one looked most interesting. You can't lie, remember? You don't know what you see yet, but you do see it." She removed the rose, and he noted how she took care to keep it well away from her.

He stumbled and nearly fell when he tried to stand, but after a few minutes his head stopped swimming and he could walk unsteadily.

"I apologize for looking at your books without permission," Dominic said slowly. He still hadn't figured out all the mysteries. He still didn't know why she was so afraid, but he had inadvertently added to her fear and he wanted to make amends, if possible.

Mademoiselle Andrews' quick flush of color glowed and faded. "I'm sorry I didn't warn you about them. And for tying you up," she mumbled, not looking at him.

"Then let us say no more about it," he said, offering his hand. She took it, but released it instantly.

"Are you well enough to leave?" she asked, accompanying him as he slowly made his way to the door.

He nodded. He had another wave of dizziness on the stairs, but from there he was able to manage on his own. She let him out the back door to the garden, and he waved goodbye to her as she stood in the light, watching him go.

The blue glowing roses lit his way to the gate.

Dominic felt perfectly recovered the next day, with the exception of the lump on his head and a few bruises. He stood in the doorway and admired the beautiful country morning. He would never have a view like this in Dinan.

He would not have to contend with magical roses there, either. After his experiences last night he was reluctant to return immediately to his garden work. She *had* warned him about the roses, and now he had seen what one of them could do.

He rubbed his throat, taking a deep breath. "I'm a pastry chef," he announced, and smiled in relief. The effects were not permanent. How long did they last, though? He'd have to ask her. And what of the other roses?

Dominic took a thoughtful tour of the rose garden on his way to the carriage house. The blue glowing one he had first seen probably just glowed, but was there any other magic to the rose with clear emerald petals, besides the fact of its existence? One she had told him on no account to go near. It shook and rustled violently as he walked by, trailing vines lashing out and falling back again. A litter of small white bones lay around it, and once he had seen a dead bird snarled in its branches. It made him wonder what manner of man her great-uncle had been to create such things.

The carriage house had some items he could use to move the statues, but not everything he needed. Perhaps he should go to the village now, before the sun got too high. Besides his own errands, he had some items to purchase to make his statue-moving apparatus.

He glanced up at the house on his way to the road, wondering if Mademoiselle Andrews was happy there. Did her great-uncle's magic force her to stay?

Dominic stood to one side of the road to let a mail coach go by, and then followed it across a low stone bridge. He passed by the first of several clumps of chestnuts that grew outside Baranton, glad of the shade. He tried to recall anything objectionable about the statues Mademoiselle Andrews wanted him to move, but failed. Some prudish Atlanteans found the art of the late Empire shocking, but these statues were from the early Empire and quite modestly draped, considering. He'd have to ask her.

That assumed he'd ever be able to ask her anything. Dominic shook his head. Why, why had he tried to look at that damn book? She'd probably never let him in the library again.

He entered the town proper, so he had to pay attention to where he was going. It was busier than usual because this was the market day, and people had set up stalls to sell their wares in the central square. Baranton was not a large town, but the square boasted a small marble fountain and a statue of Queen Anne VI, weathered by the centuries.

He bought a loaf of bread and a fruit pie from a farm woman who wore the old-fashioned starched lace coif and who was possessed by barely contained curiosity.

"Na, yours is a face I've not seen before. You'll be visiting, then?"

"Yes, for a few months or so. Perhaps longer." Each time he came to town the people grew marginally more friendly and willing to talk. He had hopes of being able to ask questions in ten years.

"It's not the widow Retaille's you are staying at, is it?"

"No, at a cottage at the chateau, there." He gestured in the proper direction.

All amusement left the woman's face. Her neighbors in the market also grew silent and their eyes went to him.

"You've actually seen her, then? Spoken to her?" asked a grizzled old man selling chestnuts. His eyes were wide when Dominic nodded. "He don't look spellified," he added in an aside to the others.

"Now, it was the old lord that had the Gift and he'll be dead six months this Lammas," said the farm woman. "You'll have him thinking we're simple in the head."

"You don't hear no strange noises at night, or see strange lights a' flickering where there shouldn't be none?" persisted the old man, despite the woman's attempt to shush him.

"Have people seen strange things at night?" Dominic asked, intrigued. "I haven't noticed anything, but then I'm a sound sleeper." He thought of the glowing roses, and his head suddenly ached.

"What a strangeness!" said the young egg girl shyly. "I'd never heard any say she'd speak."

"She's talked to him, right enough," the old man grumped. "Else he'd not be staying there."

"She could have a letter left," the egg girl objected. "Always she be doing that, if there's aught she's needing."

The old man sniffed. "That's foreigners for you. I don't trust 'em."

Dominic kept quiet, suspecting that the definition of foreigners included anyone not born in Baranton.

"Honest." A surprisingly deep voice made itself heard, coming from a powerfully built young man with pale eyes. He was dressed as a laborer and carried a large basket on one shoulder. "Pays what she owes, afore time."

"True enough," agreed the woman. "T'wod be a good thing, more foreigners being like her."

"She is Gaulish?" the egg girl asked, looking alarmed.

"Naw," the chestnut seller said with great disdain. "She come from Atlantea. Kin to the old lord, she is, an' he left the place to her."

"And he told you himself, bein' such a good friend of yours!" the woman said scornfully. "Jehan Guern, your tales put me out of patience."

"Master Brenn, what drew up the will, might have some notion what got put in," said old Jehan with awful dignity, "and it was him that told me."

Seeing the argument continue with no sign of abating, Dominic gathered up his purchases and left. He visited the post office, finding a letter from Phillipe, and then the ironmonger's, where he spent an interesting hour discussing forging techniques with the smith before recollecting his errand and buying the pulleys he needed.

The pulleys were heavier than he'd planned for, especially with the other things he'd purchased, but he was unwilling to leave anything behind. Before he had gone far, he heard a familiar deep voice. It was the young man who had defended Mademoiselle Andrews in the market.

"Goin' back?" he said, seated on the bench of an ancient cart. "Take you. Bringing the weekly order."

"Yes, please!" Dominic said gratefully. He put his purchases in the back of the cart and climbed up beside the driver. Glancing back at the contents of the cart, Dominic saw the tall basket the man had been carrying earlier. It was now full of parcels, two loaves of bread, and a barely visible wheel of cheese. The driver clicked his tongue at the horse. After considering the matter dispassionately for a minute or so, the horse moved forward.

The big man, whose name was Michel, was silent all the way to the chateau after introducing himself. When they reached the port-cochère, Michel easily hefted the basket and placed the contents inside the cupboard. He took out a letter from his shirt pocket and was going to put it in as well.

"I'll take that to her, if you like," offered Dominic. It would save her, or someone, a trip and might help improve her opinion of him.

Michel gave him the letter, then turned his strange pale gaze to Dominic. "Want to be watchful," he said, jerking his head towards the house. "It's a powerful place. Have a care what you do."

Dominic slowly shook his head. "I don't understand."

"Land's strong there. Things don't work the same." Apparently exhausted by such a long speech, he said not another word as he climbed up on the cart and drove away, nodding farewell.

Dominic scratched his head, trying to puzzle out the meaning of what seemed to be a well-intentioned warning. Eventually he shrugged. He'd probably find out what he'd been warned about after he did it. He went to the back door after depositing the heavy gear in the carriage house, and raised his hand to knock.

He couldn't touch the door. An invisible barrier prevented it. Despite the heat of the day, he felt a chill shudder over his skin. He felt over the door, the frame, the wall of the house. The same barrier existed in a smooth, continuous form as far as he could reach.

Dominic stared at the letter he held as if it could explain what was happening. It had a foreign black-and-purple stamp, and was addressed to Miss Ardhuin Andrews at Peran, near Baranton in Morbihan. He remembered the name Peran from the encounter in the bookstore— more confirmation, if he needed it.

Ardhuin. It suited her. Hadn't that been the name of a pagan Alban queen?

He could go to the front door and ring the bell. Then he remembered one of the items Michel had delivered, a soft cheese. It would not do well sitting in the port-cochère in this heat. He should get that too.

When he got to the port-cochère and opened the cupboard, it was empty. He stared at the bare shelves and rubbed his chin, thinking. Remembering. He went to the door and looked at the ground outside. There were his footprints and Michel's. No others. No one else had entered the port-cochère.

So, he was dealing with a magician's house, was he not? Dominic took the letter and placed it inside on the top shelf and waited. Nothing happened. Something else had to occur—what?

"Oh, of course." Dominic sighed and closed the cupboard door. Michel had not commented on the disappearance of his goods, so he had never seen them disappear. When Dominic opened the door again, the letter was gone.

There was no other explanation; it had to be a spell. But who had done it? Could you leave a spell that functioned for months without assistance?

There was something else he didn't understand. The house must be warded. He'd read about wards in *The Family Museum;* it was one of the first issues he'd purchased. They were hard to do, he recalled, especially large ones. They faded over time, and the magician had to cast the spell from inside.

He'd gone inside the house last night. Now he could not. A magician had cast wards in the intervening time. Was the magician still there? Was that who Mademoiselle Andrews was afraid of?

CHAPTER 4

Dominic heaved on the rope, and the statue rocked and then slowly lifted. So far, his device worked just as he had planned. He pulled again. The heavy weight swayed and the beams creaked but held. A trickle of sweat ran down his neck, but he didn't dare do anything about it. First, get the statue down intact.

He tried not to think about how valuable the statues were. His arms shaking with exertion, he slowly lowered the marble man down to the modified two-wheeled handcart he'd made. Nothing else in the carriage house would fit through the garden gates. The statue sank into the sacking and straw, and Dominic let out a pent-up breath.

The remaining statue looked like it was reaching out to where her companion had been, trying to bring him back. Dominic felt strangely guilty.

"Don't worry, you'll be together again soon," he said, and carefully lifted the handles of the cart. It was very heavy now, and it took all his effort to get it moving.

Slowly, he passed the circular enclosure with its strange stone pedestal. It looked like an odd sundial, but instead of a central gnomon it had small crystal posts arranged about the edge.

Well, this was a triumph of one man's will against nature. Except for the pulleys, he'd made all the equipment himself, and he was quite pleased with how well his plan had worked. Perhaps he could use it for a story. Someone forced by circumstance to build everything he needed from raw materials. A series of stories, maybe. The man could be shipwrecked far from civilization, with no hope of rescue. He'd have to write M. Sambin and see if he was agreeable to the idea.

He maneuvered the cart and its cargo into the carriage house and to an empty stall. That should count as out of sight, as she had ordered. Mopping at his forehead, Dominic wearily pulled the empty cart back to the garden for the second statue.

He glanced up at the library window. Nobody was visible there now, but he'd caught glimpses of movement as he'd worked. He sat down on the tail of the handcart to rest, stirring up a cloud of dust from the straw.

On the topic of moving heavy objects, how had he gotten from the gallery to the lower level of the library that night? He was quite sure he hadn't done it himself, and while Mademoiselle Andrews was a tall, healthy young woman, it would have taken considerable strength and agility to carry a man down that narrow spiral staircase. Perhaps she had simply dumped him over the railing. No; if that were the case he would have much worse bruises and probably broken bones in the bargain.

Someone else had moved him, and then disappeared. Recalling what Michel had referred to as a weekly delivery, Dominic concluded this mysterious person must subsist on air. He doubted two people could live on so little.

The second statue gave him considerable trouble. First, it would not drop onto the cart correctly. He had to winch it back up three times. When he finally got it in the right place, he discovered it put the cart out of balance, but he was too tired to lift it up again. It took him over an hour to move it to the carriage house. Why couldn't the mysterious invisible person come out to help him? That would have been greatly appreciated.

Dominic took the handcart back one last time to remove the pieces of his lifting apparatus. Mademoiselle Andrews was in the garden when he got there, and to his utter astonishment was engaged in trimming buds from the vicious rosebush. The trailing vines were moving, but in a slow, thoughtful way that made no attempt to catch or harm her. When he came closer, though, one vine lashed out at him.

"How can you get so near to it?" Dominic asked, backing away.

"It knows me," she said simply, moving one of her full white sleeves away from the thorns with one hand. She trimmed another bud with her long fingers.

"You aren't going to let it bloom?"

She wrinkled up her face. "They smell horrible. Fortunately, it never has very many."

He watched her for a moment, thousands of questions jostling in his mind, wondering if he could ask any of them without making her leave. She hadn't looked up once since he had returned, and what he could see of her face was pale and drawn.

Perhaps questions should wait. "I'll put everything in the carriage house, in case you should have need of it again."

"Thank you." Her voice was barely audible. He picked up the handles of the handcart. "How—how long do you intend to stay?"

Dominic put the cart down again. "Through the winter, at least. I sold another story last week! Why...oh. You have hired a gardener."

At this she finally looked at him, and he saw the flash of puzzlement in her grey-green eyes. She had never intended to hire a gardener—she, with her fear of strangers and concealment of her roses always a concern? He tried to keep his sudden understanding from showing.

"Wouldn't it be better for you to be in the city? I mean, for your writing," she said, her words stumbling over one another.

He smiled. "On the contrary. Here I have peace and quiet." Then another reason for her concern made his stomach sink. "You would rather I go." She must still be angry about the incident in the library, and he could not blame her. He must have given her a considerable fright.

Her face turned a sudden, furious red, and she turned her attention back to the rosebush she was trimming. "It's dangerous for you here." Her voice was tight and upset. "There's too much magic, and I can't tell you where all of it is."

"If it is dangerous, why do you stay?" Dominic asked, skeptical.

She gave a quick, nervous smile. "I'm not drawn to it like you are, and I have…protections." She ran one finger along a thin branch of the vicious rose, and it curled around her wrist for a moment before letting go.

"You say I can see magic," he said, feeling his own face heat with embarrassment when he realized how challenging that sounded. "I mean, you showed me I can. Is there some way I can learn how to use this to avoid the dangers here?"

She was silent for a moment. "Very well," she said, so softly he barely heard her. "I think I can help you." She stepped away from the rosebush and turned towards the house. "Come back this evening."

He watched her go, then returned to his work. As he dismantled his device, Dominic turned over what she had said. Sometimes he thought she was afraid of him, and then he would recall something that made him think she was afraid *for* him. At least she did not seem to be angry.

From the garden, Ardhuin watched the golden light of the setting sun, glad now that she had decided to wear the brocade. The evenings were starting to get cool. The dress was suitable for what she was going to do, too. It was a tea gown, meaning it was both conventional enough for her to be allowed to wear it at school, and comfortable. Mostly, she liked the rich green color of the fabric.

The squeak of the gate alerted her to Dominic Kermarec's arrival. She fought down the panicked impulse to hide, to run back in the house and refuse to let him in. Truly, she was the most cowardly, pathetic creature, completely unsuited for the heavy responsibility her great-uncle had given her. She didn't even have the resolution to tell him to go away.

He knew about the books of magic now, and that was dangerous too. She refused to put yet another *geas* on him, so it was best to keep him here. A good reason, and it would have been even better if she had thought of it before deciding to let him stay.

He was looking cleaner than when she had seen him last. She could still see damp curls of black hair along his neck. He smiled in greeting, and she actually took a step backwards before she stopped herself.

"My great-uncle had a collection of magical curiosities," she blurted, before he could say anything. Her mouth was suddenly so dry she had to swallow before continuing. "I-I'll show you, and you can guess which ones."

He nodded without saying anything, and followed her into the house. Ardhuin glanced at him sideways. Was she imagining things, or did he seem apprehensive too?

She was excruciatingly conscious of her greater height, giant feet, and all her other shortcomings with him nearby. It wasn't fair she had to let him into her house, her one refuge. It wasn't fair that he seemed to have a presence larger than he actually was. She opened the double seadragon doors of the library with a jerk.

"On the desk," she said, and pointed.

Dominic glanced at her and went forward, stopping and making a careful detour when he saw an open book she had left on a chair. She felt a twinge of guilt.

"Don't worry," she said. "I locked up the dangerous ones."

"How can you be sure you found them all?" Dominic asked, not looking reassured.

If she had only locked the cabinet as she should have, the whole incident would never have happened, but she had gotten careless living by herself. And of course she could not inform him *how* she could tell which were the magic ones.

Dominic had reached the desk and was looking at the miscellany on the blotter, perplexed.

"These have magic?"

"Three of them do," Ardhuin answered. "Look at them carefully, and see if you can tell which ones."

He stared at them intently, his lips compressed and brow furrowed. Ardhuin watched, a sinking feeling in her stomach as she saw him look increasingly frustrated. He didn't really believe, she could tell.

She'd made it hard, too. The magical items all looked ordinary, and she'd mixed them in with exotic, non-magical things like the jeweled brooch and the silver puzzle ball.

"They don't look different at all," he said finally, throwing up his hands in defeat. "This isn't working."

She felt frustrated, too, trying to help him see something she could not. "Look again," she said, feeling helpless.

He took a deep breath, looking out the window at the rose garden before turning his gaze back to the desk. He started, and pointed to one of her personal items, off to the side.

"What's that?" he asked. "It looks like a giant beetle wing made of stone."

Her eyebrows rose in surprise. "That is a fossilized dragonscale. It has some residual magic. Very good!"

"An actual dragonscale?" He stared at it in delighted wonder. "Aren't they rare?"

"Yes, but one of my father's friends worked on the excavations in Atlantea and Yunwiya. You weren't looking directly at it, were you? Try just glancing at them, like you were scanning the bookshelves."

She held her breath as he screwed up his face with effort, looking without looking directly. At the end of half an hour he had found all three of the magical items, and had not guessed incorrectly once.

"They look…bright," he commented. "Or clearer. I think I am beginning to see it," he said, looking at her eagerly. "Can I try again?"

Ardhuin scooped up the decoys, putting them in a pile on a nearby chair, and went to one of the curio cabinets, studying the contents while thoughtfully chewing her lip.

"Do you know what they do?" Dominic asked. He held up the filigree inkwell.

"Mmm. If you tip it, it doesn't spill," she said. Very useful for someone with her clumsy habits. "The silver half-guilder is a real coin, but it has a spell on it to make it easy to find. You could give it to someone you wanted to follow, as long as they didn't spend it. The glass jar is for collecting insects. It has a vital stasis field to keep them alive." She should give that to her father; he would find it very useful in his work.

"You seem to know quite a bit about these things," Dominic commented.

"I spent a great deal of time here, while I was going to school. All my holidays." She could see his interest, and the questions forming behind his eyes. Quickly, she made her selection and returned with a glass flute, an egg speckled with purple, and a handful of walnuts carved with grotesque faces and added them to the items on the blotter.

It didn't stop him.

"What of your family?" he asked. "Couldn't you go home?"

She shrugged, frowning. "Atlantea is too far, and with my brothers off on their own my parents travel frequently." She gestured. "I hardly know where they are sometimes." At the present moment that was rather an advantage, since it meant she could quite easily prevent her mother from discovering she was not, in fact, still at the Metan Seminary for Young Ladies in Rennes.

Dominic examined the new assortment of objects in the unfocused way he had discovered worked best, and made his choices. They continued like this for some time, with her adding new things and removing others. And always, constantly, answering his endless questions.

She struggled to preface her answers with "my great-uncle told me" or "I read somewhere," but sometimes she forgot. She didn't think he noticed. He was too enthralled with what he was learning, and strangely, she found it enjoyable teaching him.

"I can't explain it, but these two things look similar to me," Dominic said, holding up the glass insect jar and the ivory juggling ball, which she had retrieved when he asked about it. "Obviously, not in their outward aspects," he added, grinning.

Ardhuin considered. "Well, they have similar elements. Vital stasis starts with the ordinary stasis as a basis, and the juggling ball uses that too. How extraordinary, that you can tell what *kind* of spell is present! I had no idea that was even possible. For someone with no talent you learn very quickly," she teased, then felt her face go hot at her daring.

He laughed then, and was about to say something when the clock on the mantel struck the hour. Ardhuin looked at it and gasped.

"Have we really been doing this for three hours?"

Dominic also looked a little startled at how late it was. "I beg your pardon, but it was so interesting I did not keep the time in mind."

"I think that will do for tonight. There's a book you might want to read—a sort of magic primer." She darted to the shelves, running her fingers over the spines and pulling out the familiar fat volume bound in brown calf, her longtime friend. "Oh, and I finished reading your story," she said, picking up the magazine from a side table as she returned. She gave him a shy smile. "I enjoyed it very much. I will have to find a way to subscribe, if there will be others like it."

"There will be if I have any say in the matter," Dominic said with vehemence. "I have the strongest of motivations. The only alternative occupation for me is that of tutor, and I begin to think death preferable. You don't have to subscribe unless you wish to," he added earnestly. "I would be happy to let you read what I finish. I have to make a fair copy to send for publication in any case."

Ardhuin clapped her hands together in delight. "Yes! That would be wonderful. But you should know," she said as she led the way out of the library, "you don't ever have to work as a tutor again. Your gift will permit you to obtain employment with any magician who can afford your fee."

Dominic gaped at her, looking incredulous. "What do you mean? A magician would know magic without any help at all, wouldn't they?"

She held up a finger. "Ah, but they can't *see* it. Not unless they use special tools or spells, which can change what is there—and in any case they aren't very accurate. And there are…my great-uncle told me there are many times when precision is crucial. People like you are quite rare, more rare by far than magicians. You would almost be able to name your price."

"I am very much in your debt," Dominic said warmly, taking her hand and shaking it before she could move away. "You have saved me from a terrible fate."

"I think you exaggerate," she said, amused and embarrassed at the same time. "Was it really that bad?"

He sighed. "I had not suspected how ingeniously destructive small boys can be. I certainly do not recall being so myself. For example, how did three boys, the eldest not yet ten, move a large carpet from an upstairs room to the carriage drive and set it on fire in the space of a half-hour?" Ardhuin could not help chuckling, and he assumed an air of mock dudgeon. "I assure you it is no more than the truth. And in addition—"

As they passed the door to the workroom, Dominic stopped short. He stared at it, and Ardhuin felt herself go cold.

"Don't!" she cried, just as his hand reached out to touch it.

He could see the wards. The wards on her workroom. What had she done?

Dominic swallowed, his face pale. "It's *moving*," he said, pointing. "How—?"

"No." There was nothing she could do now. She had taught him too well. "It doesn't concern you." She hid her hands in her skirts, so he would not see them shaking.

"This house has a lot of magic," he said finally.

"Yes." Her voice was so faint she could barely hear it herself. "And most of it is dangerous."

Dominic found the book on magic fascinating in many ways. The content, of course, was so distracting he had to force himself to attend to his daily tasks. It appeared to be an introductory text for beginning magicians. Strangely, it had no lettering at all on the binding. It also bore the marks of having been used by a student. Coffee stains, penciled markings, and dogeared corners brought back many memories.

Dominic continued reading it while eating his dinner, reflecting that he had not seen or heard from Ardhuin since she had given it to him. He had overstepped some boundary when he had noticed the magical door. It hadn't been the first time he'd done something like that, and it was very frustrating to not know where those boundaries were.

He glanced out his window, admiring the view lit by the full moon. The night was beautiful, scattered with stars and edged by the sharp, inky shadows of the trees. Thin clouds faintly veiled the moon.

Dominic returned to the book, absently wishing he had a more comfortable chair. Immersed in his reading, he soon forgot the hard seat, until a knock at his door startled him. In his haste to reach the door he almost knocked his chair over.

He opened the door to disappointment. Instead of Ardhuin, Michel the deliveryman stood outside, his cap crushed in his two strong, capable hands. In the darkness behind him, Dominic could see several other people, some bearing lanterns. Curiosity replaced his first emotion.

"Is there something wrong?" he asked, considerably astonished.

"It's Alain, Madame Daheron's son, gone missing. They think he was coming here, and he's not returned these four hours. We'd...." He gulped, and gripped his cap even more tightly. "We're wanting to look for him."

"I don't understand. You think he came to my house?"

One of the lantern-bearers came closer, and Dominic recognized the old war-veteran postmaster. "His mother worries for the lad, and rightly. He has a withered arm, you see. Of course he wishes to be thought well of by the other boys and will do pranks of this nature, but nothing this dangerous before. We were thinking *you* could ask her, since you have spoken to her on other occasions."

Understanding dawned. They wanted him to speak to Mademoiselle Andrews on some matter. "Please forgive me, but I do not completely comprehend. What do you wish her permission to do?"

"Go to Ankou's Bones," Michel said, swallowing hard. He pointed to the dark, shadowed hill behind the chateau. "Her lands."

Dominic reached for his jacket. "I would be happy to assist you. Perhaps one of you should go with me, though, in the event that she has questions."

There was an interlude of shifting feet and awkward silence, and then Michel stepped forward. He nodded silently at Dominic.

"I hope you will excuse my curiosity, but why are people so reluctant to talk to Mademoiselle Andrews?" Dominic asked as they walked up the path to the house. If she was in the habit of hitting people with pokers and tying them up, the matter explained itself, but he suspected he would have heard if that were the case.

Michel finally managed to speak. "The magic of the old lord."

"Yes, but he's been dead for some time." There was a question forming in his mind about exactly how long Yves Morlais had been dead, though. What had the woman in the market said?

"Happens the magic don't always die with them," Michel said simply. His eyes were darting nervously as they got closer to the chateau. He lowered his voice. "Some say she's been cursed."

That had been in Chapter Two: Misconceptions of Magic. According to the beginning magic book, curses were merely a popular myth. He wasn't going to argue about it with Michel, though, since he could see it would be like arguing with a stump.

Dominic saw the gate to the garden and decided to check the back entrance. "Stay here," he said to Michel, and ran off. He remembered Ardhuin didn't want anyone seeing her roses. The ward was visible over the back of the house, so he returned to the side path.

"Where did you go?" Michel said as soon as he saw him. His eyes were wide with terror. "You vanished!"

"I just went—" Dominic gestured, turning as he did so and seeing the bank of white roses pouring over the garden wall. They gleamed with moonlight and with magic, and he remembered what Ardhuin had said about them creating forgetfulness. "I'm sorry. I wanted to see if the back door was open."

Michel's breathing slowed, but he stayed closer to Dominic as they went around to the front entrance.

Dominic now understood why the front doorpull was on a long angled bracket away from the wall. This permitted it to hang outside the wards. He pulled it once, listening hard for the sound of the bell, then twice more.

They waited silently, for what seemed like hours. Then Dominic heard the sound of the lock being turned, and the door opened, but only a crack. He could see the ward was still there.

"What is it?" Her voice sounded tight, and a little frightened.

Dominic explained the situation as best he could. Michel stood like a stone, not even daring to come up the steps to the door.

The door had opened enough that Dominic could see her face in the shadows. There was a long silence.

"Mademoiselle Andrews?"

"I will go with them."

"What?" Dominic said, startled. Ardhuin appeared almost as frightened as Michel, but her determined jaw was prominent in a way he was beginning to recognize.

"I know Ankou's Bones well. Have them wait for me," she said, and shut the door.

Dominic turned back to Michel. "Perhaps you should go tell the others," he said, wondering what was going on. "I will wait for her here."

Michel nodded vigorously, and left. After a few minutes, Dominic heard the door open again, and he saw a hole form in the magic of the ward just large enough to permit Ardhuin to leave. It closed behind her. He noticed she did not bother to lock the door.

She had changed to a dark dress and wore a thick shawl and a familiar hat with veiling. The hat that hid her face with magical shadows, which he had first seen in Dinan. He could barely see her in the darkness.

"There is no need for you to come," he protested. "It will be dark and difficult going, not suited for ladies." It bothered him that he could not see her face.

"I want to go," she said, in a voice that had more stubborn determination than interest in it. "I know where the trails are, and I've traveled rougher ones in Atlantea."

Dominic could see the crowd of searchers before his cottage, the beams of their lamps flashing as they shifted them in their hands. There was no voiced objection when Ardhuin joined the group, but he noticed everyone kept their distance from her and never looked at her directly.

"You are coming, too?" she said when she saw Dominic walking beside her towards the hill.

"It is a pleasant night for a moonlight stroll," he answered, smiling.

"It's a full moon, too," Ardhuin said. "Drat. That will make it worse."

"I beg your pardon?"

She made a sharp gesture towards the hill and leaned closer to him. "This hill is a ley line focus. The tales the country folk tell about fairy paths have an element of truth in them, you know. To primitive magicians, it must have felt like an evil spirit lived here, interfering with their spells. Ley lines are influenced by the lunar phases, so a full moon makes them even more unpredictable."

"How does that affect us?"

There was a noticeable hesitation before she answered. "It affects the non-magical too. It makes things seem confusing. It is not surprising the child got lost."

They walked up a narrow trail through the black woods, and the winds that rushed through the branches made eerie sounds all about them. As they hiked steadily uphill, the trees began to thin out and great stone outcroppings became visible. The searchers began to call out the boy's name as they fanned out over the rocky hillside. It was strangely bright out; whole streams of light came through the trees.

"This is never going to work," Ardhuin muttered, stumbling on a rock. "Those lamps are too feeble for them to see if he's at the bottom of one of the caves." She turned her head sharply at a rustling sound in the underbrush, and pulled her shawl close to her.

"There are caves here?" asked Dominic, surprised.

"That's what they are called, but really they are just vertical shafts in the rocks. They make strange sounds when the wind is in the right direction. This whole hill is supposed to be the bones of Ankou's victims, and the sounds their spirits wailing. Just the thing to appeal to a young boy." She looked about, hesitating. Dominic wished he had some indication what she was thinking, but he couldn't see her face. "There's one now. Why don't you try that one, and I'll find another?" She darted away before he could say anything.

Dominic dutifully went to the edge of the shaft, peering down. The strange light was quite adequate for him to see it was empty of any small boys, but he shouted anyway.

Where had Ardhuin gone? He turned away to look for her, catching a flash of light from the corner of his eye. At least it looked like light, but she didn't have a lantern. Everything was confusing here. Where was the light coming from? It couldn't all be moonlight. She had mentioned ley lines interfering with magic. Perhaps they were magic too, and he could see with them.

She staggered as he came up to her, as if caught in a strong wind, but it was calm here.

"Let's go this way," she said, and her voice sounded eager. She stumbled again, and Dominic took her arm to steady her. Something hard in a pocket of her shawl bumped against him. "I beg your pardon… it's the ley lines," she said breathlessly. He could feel her hand shaking.

She led him away from the main body of searchers, down a narrow path to a depression in the side of the hill, carpeted with moss and ferns. The ground was soft and damp underfoot. They had passed several of the rock shaft openings without stopping to look at them, but here

Ardhuin headed straight for a cleft in the ground and peered in.

Dominic looked too, and gasped. "I see something! A boot, right by the patch of gravel at the bottom. Alain! Can you hear me?"

The boot shifted, and he could just hear a sobbing breath. The boy was at the bottom of a very deep shaft, one that was narrow and obstructed with rocks.

"I-I'm c-c-cold," came a small, faint voice.

"We'll have you out in two shakes," Dominic said, recognizing the sound of a very frightened boy. "Are you hurt?"

"M-my leg. D-doesn't m—move."

Dominic ran up to the top of the depression and started shouting for the other searchers. In a few minutes, they appeared from the shadows. They did not have trouble with their footing as Ardhuin had, but they seemed to have difficulty seeing obstacles that Dominic could see quite clearly.

This was a very strange place. He could see why it was the focus of legends; it seemed so alive. Even the air he breathed was richer, somehow. Full of the scent of crushed leaves and mud and bark, cool and invigorating.

They gathered at the cleft, discussing how to rescue Alain. The smallest member of the search party was still too big to fit between the rocks clogging the shaft.

"He can't climb?" Ardhuin asked Dominic in a whisper.

"I suspect his leg is broken, and he only has one good arm," he explained.

"Poor child," she murmured. Dominic blinked. The tight fear in her voice had gone, and it had returned to the usual warm richness that made him want her to say anything, just so he could listen.

The postmaster carefully lowered a length of rope down the shaft, twitching it in an effort to get it past the obstructions. For the next half-hour, they tried and failed to get the rope down to the boy, who could no longer speak from shivering.

Michel held the rope now, and the postmaster urgently discussed with the other searchers the possibility of going back to Baranton for someone who could climb down and reach Alain.

Dominic saw the flash again, and this time he was careful just to glance to the side, unobtrusively. Now he could see it *was* magic, flowing from Ardhuin's hands. He felt a chill course over his skin, and he clenched his hands with the effort to keep silent. She was doing magic. Part of him wanted to dance with delight at figuring out the puzzle that had perplexed him for so long, and part of him was stunned by the revelation. Women didn't *do* magic. They were supposed to lack the necessary mental strength, even if they had the ability.

They had apparently neglected to inform Ardhuin of this. He stood silent, watching the magic infuse the rope and guide it down. The magic looked like it was being battered about by a wind, though, and the tension in Ardhuin's posture told him something was causing her difficulty.

"He's got it!" Michel's surprised voice cut short the discussion among the others, and they crowded around the cleft again. Michel's powerful arms pulled up the rope, slowly and carefully.

It seemed an eternity before Alain emerged from the shaft, but he came in view at last; a ragamuffin boy with tears and blood visible on his dirty face.

Michel carried him carefully down the hill, wrapped in coats. When Ardhuin stumbled again, Dominic once more took her arm. There was a scent close to her…what was it? Sharp, and one he associated with smoke.

Gunpowder. He suddenly knew what she had in her shawl pocket, with a certainty that surprised him. She was carrying a gun. But why? What could possibly be so dangerous on that hill she wanted to be armed? Why would she want to go there if it *was* so dangerous? Nothing made sense, and the more he learned, the more confused he became.

The search party did not linger when they reached the path to the main road, but the old postmaster did stop long enough to shake Dominic's hand and thank him with visible emotion. He also shook Ardhuin's hand, which made her stiffen in surprise, and Dominic grinned. She stood immobile for a moment and then seemed to recollect herself.

"Thank you for your help," she said in a quiet voice, starting back to the chateau.

"Permit me to assist you further, and see you to your door," Dominic said promptly. It was still a beautiful night, although not as bright as it had been, and he was reluctant for it to end. Besides, if she was afraid enough to go armed, he should make sure she got home safely.

She didn't object, but she didn't say anything, either. He couldn't tell how she felt about it. Dominic frowned. This had to stop.

"Why do you wear that hat?"

"I prefer to…to not be seen. I mean, for people to not look at me."

It was wonderful to hear her voice. It had so much richness and depth, and her words flowed with changing speed like water in a rocky stream. He still wanted to see her face. If he could convince her to smile….

"But why? I've never seen you wear it here before. I don't like it. I can't see you." A small part of him wondered at his rude persistence. What was wrong with him? It was none of his concern what she chose to do.

A sudden wave of dizziness made him stop, shuddering. The sounds, the scents, even the feel of the ground under his feet overwhelmed him. He barely heard her say, "You *want* to see me?"

"Yes," he gasped. His vision cleared, and he took a deep breath. He saw they had reached the gate to the garden, and he opened it for her.

How rough and hard the metal was, and cool to the touch—a soothing coolness that seemed to flow slowly through his fingers and into his bones. Dominic followed Ardhuin through the gate and let go.

It was a mistake. The instant he released the gate, the magic roses all glowed like beacons to his inner sight, and the chateau blazed with the magic of the wards. He held up his hands to keep it back in vain, his head swimming, and felt himself fall. He hit the ground hard, landing on one shoulder.

The pain was a distant thing, noticed but not important. Dominic stared up at the moon, marveling at the faint opalescent colors that shimmered over its surface. Why had he never noticed that before?

"What's wrong?" He heard the fear in Ardhuin's voice and struggled to sit up. He should not worry her like this and add to her troubles. It was not courteous.

Why did his head swim so? He closed his eyes, resting his head in his hands and trying to collect himself, but a rustling sound made him snap them open again. Ardhuin was kneeling beside him. At least he thought it was Ardhuin. How could he tell?

"Where are you?" Dominic said, straining to see past the magic and shadows that surrounded her.

"I'm here, really…look. See?" She lifted shaking hands and pulled her hat off. Dominic sagged with relief and nearly collapsed on the ground again. Yes, it was she. The moonlight dimmed the fire of her hair, coming loose from its arrangement from her hurried action, but the worried face that looked at him was Ardhuin's. "What's wrong? Are you ill?"

Her hand touched his forehead only briefly, but the touch felt like lightning, like fire, a pleasure so intense it hurt. Its sudden absence was pure agony.

Dominic groaned. "No! Please…don't go away…."

"You *are* sick—what am I going to do? How am I going to fetch the doctor without leaving you?" Ardhuin looked frantically about the garden as if searching for inspiration. "If they've done this…."

She needed help. He wasn't quite sure what she needed help with or how, but he responded immediately, reaching out to find her in the soundless confusion of light and magic that surrounded them.

His hand touched a loose tendril of hair and stopped, letting it slide over his fingertips. It was sunlight made solid, a caressing, warm wind bringing a nameless scent that made his heart pound. His dizziness cleared again.

"I'm not sick," Dominic managed to whisper. Mad, perhaps, but not sick. He watched with detachment as his hands seemed to move of their own will, drowning in the rich waves of hair that slid from the top of her head as he dislodged them.

Her sea-green eyes stared at him, her face at first pale and immobile with shock, then twisted with distress. "What did they do? I don't understand! Why would they do this to you?"

She was unhappy. He tried to smooth out the unhappiness he saw there, and discovered the softness of rose petals and an echoing pulse beneath her translucent skin that made his own race. How beautiful she was!

"Help me," he whispered. "Ardhuin...." The pale flame of her face drew him closer, until he could feel her quick breath on his skin. The faint screaming voice of conscience in his mind vanished the instant his lips touched hers.

The sensation burned white-hot in his mind, driving all other considerations away except his need for her. Dimly, he was aware of her arms about him, of a feeling of lifting and motion, of flashes of brightness that were not light. He thought he heard her voice, so rich and entrancing, saying "I'm sorry, I'm sorry...forgive me...."

For a brief moment he wondered why he should forgive *her*, but the question was soon lost and forgotten. Even though he held her with all his strength, she was too far away. He had to get closer, closer still, or his heart would explode from the fire within and he would die.

CHAPTER 5

Ardhuin wandered restlessly through the house, her thoughts still confused and shaken. If she kept moving, it was easier to forget about what had happened; to stop worrying about the trouble she was in. And sometimes a sudden, vivid memory would flash into her mind and she could feel her face heat to a deep, deserved scarlet.

At first she was merely aware of a relaxed, drowsy contentment when she awoke. Then, growing more alert, she realized she was not alone, that someone's bare arm held her close, and then she suddenly remembered who held her and why.

Panic seized her completely. What had she done? Dominic would be furious when he realized. Her only impulse was to get away before he woke and saw her, and in a confused, tangled rush she scrambled out of bed, grabbed her clothes, and ran.

It really was fortunate the servants were gone, Ardhuin thought, struggling to do up her dress as she ran. She must look like a madwoman with her hair streaming down her back, and there was no time to fix it, she had to get away. Illusion, that would have to do for now.

When she reached the main stairs, she stopped. She was doing this the wrong way. She should be illusioning Dominic instead. He would realize something had happened as soon as he woke up in her room, if he hadn't already. Could she remember what the inside of his cottage looked like well enough to convince him?

She ran back, now terrified he would be awake. Carefully, she eased open the door, gathering shadow around her. Would that even work with him, or would the magic reveal more than the shadows concealed? Would illusion work, for that matter?

She carefully parted the ivory damask bedcurtains and peered inside. Dominic was still deeply asleep; the sharp angles of his face even more pronounced in shadow. He'd barely moved since she'd left; one arm was still curled around the fold of blanket where she'd been.

Ardhuin frowned. Was that normal? It would work to her advantage if he was a deep sleeper; she could move him to the cottage and he would never know. She concentrated, feeling the delicate threads tug on her senses, telling her the magic was formed and awaiting her bidding.

Dominic groaned, a half-strangled sound deep in his throat, and writhed. His face contorted with pain, and Ardhuin quickly dissipated the levitation spell. He collapsed into unconsciousness again.

That was *definitely* not normal. Ardhuin stared at him, noticing his face was flushed and damp with sweat. Working up her courage, she reached in and touched his forehead. It was burning with fever.

Her knees buckled, and she had to sit on the edge of the bed for a moment. Dominic was very sick, probably because of her. What was she going to do? How could she summon the doctor without revealing too much? There was a limit to eccentricity, especially for young women. But what if he died?

She was *quite* sure this was not a usual development of an…intimate encounter. Surely the stories would mention such a thing? He had acted so strangely, as if he had mistaken her for someone else. Someone he thought beautiful and desirable. She had gone along with his misperception, even encouraging it, snatching at the chance to know what it was like to be loved.

Magic was to blame somehow; she wasn't sure how. If it was a spell, it was one she had never heard of. It had even affected her, making her feel at one point as if she would explode or go mad with the overwhelming sensations that shuddered through her.

She fetched cold water and a cloth and bathed his forehead while she tried to decide what to do. His pulse was quick but steady, which she recalled being mentioned as a good sign. Were there any medical texts in the library?

He didn't look so flushed now. She kept up her efforts, and a few hours later it was clear his fever had broken. Ardhuin nearly wept with relief. Poor Dominic. First the defensive spell on the book, and now this. She really wasn't good for his health.

She ought to be sorry, but she wasn't. Even now. She could live out the rest of her lonely life with the memory. Just once, she could pretend she was desired. Even if she still didn't understand how it had happened. For a brief time, she had felt beautiful.

But she didn't want Dominic to pay the price for her bad behavior. Ardhuin reached out to check for any returning fever. He stirred under her hand, sighing, and she started and snatched her hand away. Dominic turned his head restlessly, groaning, then opened his eyes and looked at her. Immediately he cried out and clenched them shut again.

Ardhuin stood for a moment and struggled not to burst into tears. She felt like she'd been slapped. It was the horrible dancing class all over again. Then she realized the light from the sun had fallen full on his face through the open curtains.

"I'm sorry, I'm sorry…." She ran and closed all the blinds on that side of the room, then peeked in at the bed again. "Is that better?"

She could just see him nod, very slightly, in the gloom, and she felt absurdly happy. He wasn't dying. He might hate her, but he was alive to do it.

The drawn expression of pain on his face faded a little, replaced by confusion. He struggled to speak, and when he did, his voice was faint and raspy.

"Not my bed."

Her happiness evaporated into panic. "Don't talk! You've been very ill." Yes, that was good. Leaving would be even better. "I…I'll get you some water."

She twitched the curtains closed again, ignoring the weak sounds of protest inside, and ran out of the room. What was she going to say? How could she possibly explain? She proceeded slowly to the kitchen, trying to decide what to do.

He'd been confused. He also had been quite sick. He might not remember everything that had happened, or perhaps he could be persuaded it was the result of delirium. Ardhuin brightened for a moment, then reality set in. She would have to be very careful, and think about what she told him. If there was one thing she could count on, it was that he would ask questions.

She found a crockery pitcher and filled it from the pump at the sink. He was probably hungry, too—wasn't there some kind of special food for invalids, like calves' foot jelly? Marie would be bound to have some stored up, if it hadn't all been used in her great-uncle's last illness.

Ardhuin searched the pantry with no luck, then remembered the cold room in the cellar. Rather than bother finding a lamp, Ardhuin conjured up a ball of magefire, which reminded her she had still not determined the cause of Dominic's illness.

Her first instinct was to attribute it to an attack by her enemies, but that didn't make sense. She'd done a careful scrying on the hill to find the lost boy, and the only people on it were herself, Dominic, and the searchers, all of whom were from Baranton. In addition, why would her enemies attack Dominic instead of her, and in such a way?

It was related to magic, though. She was sure of it. She opened the door of the cold room, shivering as she stepped into the frigid air. Another spell of her great-uncle's. The shelves were almost completely empty, but on one there were three small glass jars sealed with wax and labeled "beef jelly." One had gone bad, but the other two looked fine. Ardhuin took one and stepped quickly out of the cold room.

The door to the wine cellar was just a little further down, and she hesitated. Her great-uncle had been sparing in his use of strong spirits, but she had seen him partake after a rather strenuous magical bout, explaining that brandy was of great use in countering thaumatic shock. Certainly, his hands had stopped shaking after the first glass. Maybe

Dominic would benefit from some brandy too, since he seemed to have a rather severe case of thaumatic shock. It would also help cloud his inquisitive mind.

Ardhuin made her way slowly and carefully back upstairs, now burdened with the jar of beef jelly, a spoon, a dusty bottle of brandy, the jug of water, a tumbler, and a glass for the brandy. She nearly had a disaster when she reached the door and had to unburden herself to turn the handle. She should have gotten a tray, but she didn't know where the servants had kept them.

Tiptoeing softly into the room, she first placed the jug on the bedside table, and returned for the rest. The jar of jelly tipped and fell against the brandy bottle with a loud clink, and she heard sounds of motion behind the bedcurtains.

Hastily filling the tumbler with water, she opened them. Dominic looked much more alert than before, his eyes lighting eagerly on the tumbler. She helped him drink, since he was unable to sit up, and only spilled a little.

"How…did I…."

"Just rest now. You will over-tire yourself," Ardhuin protested, and scrambled for the beef jelly and the spoon. "Here. It's supposed to be good for you."

He accepted the spoonful of jelly with some confusion, then his eyes bulged and he coughed. "S-strong!" he managed, after several minutes of coughing and two more glasses of water. Feeling guilty, Ardhuin dipped the tip of one finger in the jelly and tasted it. It was rather bland, at least to her. Well, that wasn't going to work as a diversion.

"I suppose you are wondering what happened," she said desperately, seeing him try to talk again. He nodded. "Do you remember searching the hill for the missing boy?"

He nodded again, watching her face closely. She had to be careful. Only tell him what she wanted him to know. "You found him, and the others took him back to Baranton." So how had Dominic ended up here? "After they left, on the way back to your cottage you started acting strangely, and then you collapsed." True enough so far, but now came the delicate part. "You weren't making any sense, almost as if you were delirious. I managed to get you back on your feet, but you were clearly quite ill. I could not take you all the way back to your cottage, but we were not far from my house. With some assistance, you managed to reach this room before you collapsed again."

He'd needed a lot of assistance, because he hadn't been at all concerned with going anywhere. She'd done the relocation for both of them with magic. It was much quicker than using the stairs, and speed had been strangely imperative.

She didn't want to remember now. Not while he was still lying there, so close. Ardhuin stepped away from the bed and fussed with the brandy bottle, dusting it off with her sleeve and wrestling with the cork. The label was faded and peeling, but still bore traces of gilt. She poured out a generous portion and returned.

"Try some of this. It might help."

He took a tiny, cautious sip. She could see his whole body shudder as he swallowed, but he drank again when she offered the glass.

She had to ask. "Do you recall feeling ill?"

Dominic frowned, closing his eyes in concentration. "Remember the hill. Remember finding Alain." His voice was stronger now, and didn't sound so dry. "You used magic." There was a little smile at the corner of his lips.

Ardhuin froze, holding the brandy glass like a shield. "Are you sure about that?" she said faintly, trying for a disbelieving look.

"I can see it," he answered, soft but confident. "Remember?" Definitely a look of mischief in his eyes now.

She'd been so sure he wasn't looking! Fuming, she held the brandy to his lips and tilted it, spilling some. He coughed and she made him drink again. He looked at her reproachfully.

"Is that really a good idea?"

"You are suffering from overexposure to magic. You need stimulants," Ardhuin said firmly. "How do you feel?"

"I can't move and everything hurts," Dominic replied, grimacing. "Although the brandy is helping."

Unfortunately for her plans, it seemed to be making him more alert, not less.

"Perhaps I should let you rest now," she said, edging away.

"Could you help me sit up a little?" he asked, wincing as he tried to move. Ardhuin cautiously adjusted his pillows, but it was no use, she had to get close to him to lift him. Too close. He could look right at her. And she could see the darker shadows around his hooded eyes, how his face seemed more sharply gaunt than before, and feel guilty.

"How could I be overexposed to magic?" he murmured, puzzled. "You didn't use that much, did you? I felt fine on the hill. Wonderful, in fact. Such a clear, pleasant night, and so much light."

Ardhuin frowned. "It was rather dark on the hill. The trees blocked the moon." Dominic hadn't had a problem, though. She remembered that. "Do you recall anything else strange?"

Dominic looked up at the top of the canopy, eyes unfocused in thought. "Everything felt alive, intense. Smells, and sounds. And I saw light."

She gasped, suddenly understanding. "It was the ley lines. I should have thought of that—but nobody's ever mentioned it before! Your sensitivity to magic," she explained, seeing his puzzled expression. "The power in the ley lines overwhelmed you. I should never have let you go there."

"But I felt fine even after we returned," protested Dominic. "I can remember walking back with you, and thinking if you carried a gun you were afraid of something and I should—"

"How did you know I had a gun?" Ardhuin interrupted, feeling cold. He remembered too much, knew too much.

Dominic closed his eyes. "I could smell it," he whispered. He opened his eyes again, and with a visible effort turned his head and looked up at her. Ardhuin, standing at the edge of the bed, suddenly had difficulty breathing. He stared at her intently. "You have to help me remember. It's so confusing at the end. The roses, and the magic all over your house. Then the moon is floating over me and it's so beautiful but I'm sad because I can't see you." His voice faltered for a moment. "Maybe I was feverish then, because the next thing I remember, the moon had turned into your face, above me just like you are now. I didn't even wonder at it. Just like the moon, beautiful and too far away."

Ardhuin knew she should leave, but his words had shocked her into immobility. So he hadn't confused her with someone else—he'd simply been delirious with magic. Still, it was quite gratifying. She must always remember what he said.

His forehead was creased with effort, and she offered the brandy glass as a distraction. There was just a little at the bottom, and she had to hold it cupped in her hand to let him drink. Her hand just touched his cheek, and she felt the reaction, heard the sudden sharp intake of breath.

"It was just a dream," she said quickly, before he could say anything. "It wasn't real."

"How do you know what was in my dream?" Dominic said softly.

Quick. She had to think quickly!

"You were raving. Talking about fire and silk and rose petals," Ardhuin babbled. She felt the sudden heat in her face and quickly turned away. "Now get some sleep."

She heard a faint keening noise behind her before she reached the door, and she knew she had failed.

"It wasn't a dream, was it?" she heard him whisper. "Ardhuin! Tell me the truth! Was it a dream, you and I?"

More practice lying. How many times had she promised herself she would? She knew she wasn't good enough to fool Dominic. She didn't trust her voice, didn't dare face him. She shook her head.

There was a long silence in the darkening room. At last she could no longer stand the suspense and turned to look at him. His eyes were closed, and tears trickled from the corners.

"How can you be so kind to me now? I deserve to suffer."

Ardhuin set her jaw and turned back to him.

"If anyone is to blame, I am. *I* wasn't out of my mind with the effects of the ley lines. You couldn't even stand up without help! Do you really think you could force me to do anything against my will? I even had a gun!"

"And magic," Dominic said. "A gun and magic, and I knew about both and I didn't care. I abused your friendship and your trust in an unforgivable way." Another tear slid down his cheek.

Ardhuin sighed. "You were drunk with magic. How can you be responsible for your actions? It's my fault for not stopping you. I know —" she had to stop for a moment to regain control of her voice. He was so miserable, and now she was, too. "I know it was wrong. You…you don't remember everything."

"I remember enough," Dominic said bleakly. "But why didn't you stop me?"

"I didn't want to." Ardhuin glared at him, arms folded. And if that didn't convince him of her depravity, nothing would. Why was he so eager to claim all the blame for himself?

Dominic gave her a weary look, but did not pursue the subject. "I should not be here," he said finally. "You should move me to my cottage. You can do that, can't you? The same way you moved me before, in the library."

Even in pain and half dead he could figure things out. What had she done to deserve this? She had enough trouble.

"Well, I can, but not now. I tried to move you, after…" she felt herself go red in the face again, but kept on stubbornly, "when you were sleeping. You cried out in pain as soon as the magical field got near. You're too sensitized to magic right now. I can't do anything until you recover."

He digested this for a moment, looking drowsy.

"You need to sleep. Talking tires you." She was certainly exhausted. Was that an expected consequence of what she had done? She knew so little, really.

He sighed. "Listening doesn't tire me," he said quietly. "Tell me how you became a magician."

"Only if you lie still and don't talk."

He nodded. Ardhuin pulled a chair up to the side of the bed and sat down. In a way, it was a relief he knew. A relief to finally have someone to talk to.

"My great-uncle taught me. We visited, my family and I, when I was very young, and I did something that caught his attention. He said nothing, but remembered. Then, when I was sent to school in Rennes, he invited me to come and stay whenever I had holidays."

She still didn't understand why her mother had insisted on the fashionable Metan Seminary. It was not in Atlantea, and it was clearly intended to prepare one for a life of social events, parties, and the inevitable dazzling marriage—none of which would ever apply to her. Even before sending her to school, her mother had always dragged her along for social visits and other boring events her brothers were never subjected to.

"He gave me lessons during my visits, and he also gave me books I could take back with me. The book you have, that was the first." His eyes lit up with sudden understanding. "I have to be careful, you see. I don't have a license to practice magic, and what if someone reported me?"

Dominic looked at her with half-closed eyes, smiling a little. "I would challenge them to a duel." Then he frowned, saying, "No, that wouldn't work either, would it? My head hurts; I can't think."

Ardhuin got up, putting her hands on the edges of the bedcurtains. "I really think you had better sleep now," she said. Ignoring his protests, she closed them and walked away.

Something told her the most difficult part was yet to come. She should have thought about the consequences. Of course he would ask questions. She should have thought of that.

"Here's *Drakon Atlantea*, by MacCrimmon. My father says it's the best basic reference he knows. Oh, and this has an account of the survivors of the wreck of the *Mhaire Dhu* that might be interesting." Ardhuin laid the volumes down on the coverlet. Dominic picked up one with an effort and opened it. After two days of rest he claimed he was feeling much better. Ardhuin had only noticed slight improvement and great boredom. He was certainly complaining about getting behind with his writing.

Feeling guilty, she had offered him books to read for research. She'd also unearthed an old quilted silk dressing gown that had belonged to her great-uncle and had somehow remained hidden in a clothes press. Since Yves Morlais had been very slender, it did not close in front as completely as it should, something she tried not to notice with indifferent success.

"It's no use," he sighed, letting the book fall from his hands. "I can't read more than a few lines before my eyes start to hurt. What am I going to do?" His fingers moved restlessly over the open pages.

Why was he so impatient? Hadn't he said he had earned enough to get through the winter? "Wait until you are stronger," Ardhuin said, already knowing he wouldn't listen to her. "I'll leave the book here." She reached for it, but his hands closed on the cover.

"You could read it to me."

She could, except that she was trying desperately to stay away as much as possible. She'd already proved her judgment was poor where he was concerned. If she read to him, though, he would probably fall asleep and she could escape without him noticing. She'd always found being read to rather stupefying, herself.

Ardhuin sighed. "Very well." She adjusted the chair so the curtains hid him from view, claiming she needed the light from the lamp to read and that it would hurt his eyes. Besides, she could make herself comfortable in the armchair—meaning unladylike—without his seeing. She picked up the book on dragons and tucked one leg under herself on the seat.

Ardhuin read two chapters before a dry throat and coughing made her unable to continue.

"I can recommend the brandy," Dominic said helpfully from the shadows of the bed.

"Good idea," coughed Ardhuin, and poured a small drop in the glass. It burned all the way down when she swallowed, but it stopped the coughing. Most likely because she couldn't feel her throat at all anymore.

"Oh my," she wheezed. "Is it supposed to do that? Make your blood feel molten?"

He chuckled. "The better variety, yes. And that is the best I've ever had the pleasure of drinking. What kind is it?"

Ardhuin peered at the dusty, faded label. "It says, 'Eau de Vie, 1809,'" she said, and nearly dropped the bottle when he yelled, "What?!"

She scrambled to her feet, looking in at him. He stared back at her with horror.

"Are you quite sure you read that right?" he whispered.

She held up the bottle. "See for yourself. Why? Is it bad?"

He closed his eyes, and she worried anew until she saw he was shaking with laughter. "Ardhuin, Eau de Vie brandy is considered an appropriate gift between royal houses. People like me don't even get to see the bottle, much less taste the contents. That's a very old year, too. You could have sold it for an ungodly sum! Where did you get it?"

"I just found it in the cellar," Ardhuin said numbly. "My great-uncle must have—" she gave him a suspicious look. "How do you know my first name?"

"It was on a letter Michel delivered to you. That," he said, grinning, "was how I discovered how your clever cupboard in the port-cochère works. Quite useful, unless you happen to be an unsuspecting traveler with luggage."

It just kept getting worse and worse. How could she stop him from discovering the rest? Anything she could do, he would notice. She'd trained him to notice.

"Ardhuin." The amusement had left his face. "I was just teasing you."

She tried to smile. Make it seem unimportant. "I just…you must be careful. If you mention it to anyone, if word got to the authorities…."

"I will say nothing. Not even in jest." He hesitated. "Does anyone else know you are a magician? Your parents, I assume. I am surprised they do not object to your living here alone, even with your defenses."

Ardhuin felt her stomach knot, and she wandered to the table to set down the bottle of brandy. "They…ah, don't know."

"Don't know you are a magician?"

The heat was radiating from her now. She must be completely red, hair and face together. "They think I'm still at school," she mumbled. "At least, I haven't told them I'm not."

She *had* gone so far as to suggest that some of her mother's letters had gone missing, especially the ones with awkward questions. Her brothers wrote to her here and did not seem to notice the discrepancy, but the school forwarded the rest. She had told the headmistress she still had complex business with her great-uncle's estate, and so far the excuse had held. Eventually, though, her charade would collapse.

She'd just have to hope her parents wouldn't return until she'd solved her problem here. And then…and then it would be over. Her mother would make her go home and insist on her going to parties and dancing and she would be miserable again.

"Why haven't you told them? Are you angry with them for some reason? Do you dislike them?"

She snapped her head up. "No, I love them dearly! It's just that—" how could she explain? "They won't let me live like this. I have to be proper, which as far as I can see means never having any fun. I had a lot of fun on the expeditions," she said wistfully. "When they let me go."

"You went on expeditions?" Dominic asked, eyes lighting up with interest. "Where?"

Ardhuin gestured at the book on dragons. "Well, that dragonscale you saw came from Yunwiya. My father is a biologist, you see, and my mother does very good watercolor illustrations, so they asked her to come as well."

"Yunwiya!" Dominic lay and thought about it for a while. "What is it like?"

Ardhuin smiled, remembering. "Green. Trees everywhere, vines, everything growing and green. The people were very friendly, too. We were out in the mountains, of course. I played with the Yunwiyan children my age and had a wonderful time. I wanted to stay forever."

The children had accepted her without question, flaming hair, lanky legs and all. Maybe they thought all foreigners looked like her. They had taught her to track, and to hunt using a sling. She'd even wrestled with them and helped them steal honey from wild bee nests. None of them had called her ugly.

Then, one day, she had killed a rabbit with her sling. Her very first kill. Yunwiyans considered that an important milestone, to be commemorated with dark marks permanently drawn on the body and other ceremonies. She'd asked her mother if she could get the markings too, and that's when everything had changed. She was no longer allowed to play with the children. She had to sit with her mother every minute for the rest of their stay.

After their return to Atlantea, she was sent to the school in Rennes. No hunting, no wrestling, no running up mountains.

Dominic sighed. "I want to travel there someday." She heard him shifting restlessly. "Do you think you can keep your parents from discovering how long you have been here?"

She collapsed back in the chair, feeling her stomach knot with tension. "I have to. If my mother finds out…."

"What of your father?"

Ardhuin shrugged. "He's much more reasonable, actually. Sometimes I think he forgets I'm not a boy. I have three older brothers, you see, so he became accustomed."

Dominic chuckled. "He didn't notice any difference?"

"Not really. Now, if I had been a Three-toed Lesser Granski's Sloth, he would have been able to write a monograph on the subject." It would have been much better for everyone if she had been a boy. Her magic would not be a problem, and her mother would not constantly be trying to make her behave properly. Her brothers certainly didn't have to put up with what she went through.

"I hope it will not be too much of a shock when I write to him," Dominic said.

Ardhuin froze. "Write to him?" she said faintly, when she could breathe again. "Why?"

"To let him know we're getting married."

She was on her feet and facing him before she realized what she was doing. Anger and humiliation tightened her throat so she could barely speak. She'd thought dancing classes were the worst thing in the world, but no longer. Somehow it was even worse coming from him.

Dominic, seeing her expression, took a deep breath and drew back on the pillows.

"He'll be angry, of course, but I will encourage him to be angry only with me," Dominic said rapidly. "He'll be even more angry if we don't tell him, Ardhuin. I—I won't mention we met here. Where is this school of yours?" he asked, starting to look desperate.

"You don't have to tell him anything," Ardhuin gritted through her teeth. "We're not getting married. It is generous of you, but unnecessary," she muttered. He was being honorable, and it hurt. She just wanted the whole thing to go away, so she could be miserable in peace.

"It is *very* necessary. What if—"

"No one knows except us," Ardhuin insisted.

Dominic looked away, and she could see dark color on his face. "You don't understand," he said, in a strained, uncomfortable voice. "There could be…consequences. For you. I have little to offer, but at least I can do this much."

Now it was her turn to go red. "No consequences. I mean, not that." Seeing him start to speak again, distressed, she plunged ahead. "I know what you mean, and it can't happen. I won't have a child. It's a spell."

Dominic sighed. "How can you be sure you did it correctly? You might have been slightly distracted at the time."

"I didn't do it."

She could see him take this information, examine it, and follow to the logical conclusion. It fascinated her to see how quickly his mind worked. What she did not expect was his growing expression of anger.

"Your great-uncle, I presume? Did he ask your permission to do this, or condescend to give an explanation?"

Why was he so angry? He should be glad there was no need for his chivalric sacrifice.

"He did ask my permission. I suppose it is shocking, but he never cared for convention. I can remove the spell whenever I wish," Ardhuin said. Dominic still had a skeptical expression, and she couldn't tell him *why* her great-uncle had felt the need. She could not convince her great-uncle that she was never going to marry and thus was not at risk of a poorly timed confinement. He had been worried she might be with child when she was required to fulfill her duties as Mage Guardian. Now, of course, she was glad he had taken the precaution. "No one will know," she repeated.

"*I'll* know," Dominic snapped. "How can you even think I would abandon you like that?"

How her jaw hurt! His stubbornness was giving her a headache. "You don't have to marry me. I don't have to marry anybody. And you can't write to my parents. Even I don't know where they are right now! They are traveling on an extended tour of some remote islands. With very irregular mail service," she added pointedly. She picked up the book from where it had fallen and placed it with a thump on the table beside the bed.

"You need to rest," she said, and ran away.

More than a week passed before Dominic was able to leave his bed, and longer before he was able to sit up for more than a few hours. It was better now, since she no longer was required to spend so much time with him. Still, Ardhuin felt something pending in the air between them, like a spell of great power that had been invoked but not activated.

They were very cautious with each other, in conversation and in everything else. The subject of marriage was not even obliquely referenced, but she knew he had not accepted her decision. She couldn't tell what he was thinking, though. And he spent long hours, longer than he should, writing furiously in the library.

She wasn't sure if she liked that or not. It had been her private reserve for so many months it felt odd to see another person there. He did not disturb her studies, though, and she was not about to give up her comfort and go elsewhere.

Ardhuin glanced up from her book to check the fire. It could benefit from another log or two, but there were none in the woodbox. She got up and went as quietly as she could towards the door.

"That spell you have on the woodshed door—it doesn't touch the hinges," Dominic observed without raising his head.

"Magic and iron don't work well together," Ardhuin answered, narrowing her eyes at him. "It can be done, but it puts a great strain on the structure. And you had no business going down there again anyway. You shouldn't be carrying anything up three flights of stairs yet, and if you would simply listen to reason I would not have to use spells to prevent it."

"I'm much better," he said, looking up at her and smiling. "So much so I should probably return to my own lodging. This is too comfortable."

He was absolutely right, of course. Ardhuin struggled with herself, and the almost equal impulses to make him leave and make him stay. She glanced at the fire again.

"It's getting cold now; you'll need a fire. Do you have any firewood there? And what about food? You're starting to eat again. I don't think you are strong enough yet to walk to Baranton and back. Wait a few more days."

"I'm really quite recovered," Dominic murmured.

Rather than continue to loom over him, Ardhuin sat on a corner of the table he was using. "Yes, you are much improved. However, consider for a moment that you have not walked anything near that distance since your illness. I grant you might be able to reach the town, but then you will be tired *and* carrying a burden when you return. Besides, do you really think you can carry everything you need?"

Dominic sighed and leaned back in his chair, wiping his ink-spattered fingers with his handkerchief. "No, I suppose not. Even with my health perfectly restored. I had thought Michel could deliver—"

"Michel?" He'd mentioned that name before, and she hadn't paid attention.

"The carter who delivers your orders. He was with the rescue party, too."

Ardhuin brightened. "An excellent idea. In fact, why not have him take you to Baranton? He'll be coming here soon anyway to make a delivery. You can leave him a note."

"And I can arrange beforehand for what I need as well," Dominic said, nodding with enthusiasm. "Yes, that will work." He reached for a fresh sheet of paper and started composing his message to Michel.

The note, left in the port-cochère, was returned with a crude "yes" scribbled on it in pencil. On the designated day, it was especially cold, so Ardhuin searched the attic and found a heavy greatcoat, smelling strongly of camphor, and a long muffler.

"I am not going to the polar regions," Dominic said with an expression of mock horror. He could just get the coat buttoned, and the bottom edge came down almost to his ankles. "But I believe I could, in this."

She laughed and saw him out the door into the bright, cold day. He had a neat brown paper parcel containing his latest writing and two letters he intended to post, and an eager expression in his eyes. His face was still more gaunt than she liked, but it was starting to fill out again.

Well, it would be hard for anyone to be cooped up for as long as he had been, and he *was* feeling better. Ardhuin frowned at the suddenly empty house and decided she needed a cup of tea. Now she could sit in the library, prop her feet up, and think. Dominic's illness had diverted her attention, but the larger problem remained. Someone with powerful magic at their disposal had attempted to destroy the mage Oron, and herself as well.

As she waited for the kettle to steam, a soft, slithery thump came from the large cupboard magically connected to the port-cochère. Michel must have delivered something for her, but what?

It was a letter. Her heart raced, terrified it was from her parents and that Dominic might have seen the superscription. Then she saw the stamp, and the strange, heavy lettering she didn't recognize. For her great-uncle? No, it was addressed to her. And directed to Peran. How strange.

She made her tea and took letter and cup to the library, to puzzle it out in comfort before the fire. She curled up in one of the large leather chairs and studied the envelope. From Preusa? Who did she know in Preusa?

The letter was only a single sheet, but closely written in a clear, angular hand.

My dear Miss Andrews—perhaps you may recall me from our shared time at the Metan Seminary. I am now in Baerlen. The von Kitren family has always had a member serve at court, and I have been given permission to do so in my brother's stead. I hope you will forgive the imposition, but I believe you may be able to help the government I now serve. I have reason to think you may know something of a powerful mage, a mage using the name Oron. We have need of his help. If you are in contact with him, I beg you tell him this: his Majesty has invoked the compact of the Guardians.

She took a sip of tea numbly, reading the rest of the letter without comprehension. It was signed "Gutrune." Gutrune von Kitren. There had been a Preusan girl at the school a few years older than Ardhuin, memorable because she was also a foreigner and not actively malicious. By comparison to the others, that made her a friend. They had talked on occasion, but Gutrune had not been outgoing by nature. Now she remembered that Gutrune had mentioned her parents were attached to the Preusan legation at Rennes.

Ardhuin read the letter again, slowly, forcing herself to understand. And then she did. Distantly, she heard something fragile fall and break on the floor. She didn't care.

I can't do this. I'm not ready.

It had begun. The Mage Guardians were real. They knew, or would know soon. They had invoked the compact, and she had to respond.

Dominic walked carefully up the path from his cottage, exhausted but quite pleased with his outing. He had everything he needed now, and as soon as he let Ardhuin know he was back safely he was going to collapse. He wouldn't tell her she had been right, of course, but he would never have made it without Michel's assistance.

She wasn't visible in the library window. He was going to have to go all the way around to the front, then, unless by some chance she was in the kitchen. He peered in the glass panes of the door.

His hand touched the surface. Dominic moved back, and saw the wards flow back in place. He reached for the handle, and like a soap bubble, the wards opened for him. Something was wrong.

He yanked the door open and ran inside, calling her name. "Ardhuin! Where are you?"

No response. Fear propelled him up the stairs, fatigue forgotten. At first he thought the library was empty, but then he saw a fold of indigo silk, the color of the dress she had been wearing earlier that day, hanging from the edge of one of the large chairs.

Ardhuin was curled up in the chair, face hidden in her arms, her bright red hair streaming down her shoulders. The fire had gone out, and the room was chilly. She clutched a crumpled letter in one hand.

"Ardhuin! Speak to me, tell me what's wrong! I went right through the wards!"

She looked up at that, blinking at him, and his terror abated. At least she appeared to be unhurt. He saw a tendril of magic leap up and away from her.

"Y-you were inside when I l-last cast the wards," she managed to say. "They recognize you. They are still there." She stared at him. "You were not gone very long."

Dominic pointed to the library window, where the light was starting to fade. He stepped closer, still concerned, and heard the crunch of china under his feet. Shards of a teacup were scattered in a pool of tea.

"Did you receive bad news?" he asked hesitantly, indicating the letter. She shook her head, then nodded, her face crumpling. She dropped her head into her hands.

"Ardhuin, please talk to me." He grasped her shoulders, shaking her, and she looked up again, her storm-colored eyes red. The misery he saw there was more than he could stand, and without thinking, he found himself holding her close, smoothing her hair and saying inanely, "It will be all right, don't worry."

It seemed to work, at least to the point that she gave a shuddering sigh and relaxed against him. He let the jolt of happiness go unquestioned for a moment, then went back to the matter at hand.

"What happened?"

Ardhuin shifted her head on his shoulder. "It's a letter that…I have to help someone. A promise I inherited from my great-uncle. But he was supposed to explain to them before I—"

"This is a magical obligation?"

He felt her nod.

"I can imagine it will be difficult to convince them you are a magician. It took a lot to convince me." He pulled back just enough so he could see her face and smiled reassuringly. "Can't you simply tell them that you are a woman and see if they still hold you to this promise?"

Ardhuin shook her head. "It's a very serious promise. I can't tell you all of it. It's not my secret, and I don't know what I can tell you that won't put you in danger too."

He stiffened and stared at her. "Danger? How?"

"I think…someone is trying to kill me," she said, reluctantly. She winced, and he released his suddenly intense grip with a muttered oath.

"They want to kill you because you are a woman magician? Why? Who would do such a thing?"

"I don't *know* who, Dominic! That's why I try to hide my magic, why I did all those things to you. I was afraid you worked for them and were trying to find me. As long as they think I can't do any magic, I'm safe."

He shook his head sharply, trying to think his way through. "I don't understand. They are looking for someone, but they don't know who it is? How do you know they are looking for you?"

Ardhuin sighed. "There have been severe magical attacks against this house. That's why I have such strong wards. They are trying to kill the heir of Oron. My great-uncle tried to warn me, before he died…but even he didn't know who they were."

"Why not go to the police? Get help?"

She laughed, sharply and without humor. "And how would I convince them I had any notion of what I was talking about, save by doing magic? I don't have a license! Not to mention word would get out that I have the ability, which I dare not allow. Besides, they don't have any royal magicians in Baranton; they'd have to send for help. I'd know more about it than any of them, anyway."

Dominic thought for a moment. "Is your letter connected to this?"

"To the attacks? I don't think so," she said, looking doubtful. "It's from someone I knew at school. She's with the Preusan court now, and she somehow knows about…the thing I am. What my great-uncle was. She doesn't know I'm the heir—at least I think she doesn't. It was always hard to tell what she was thinking," Ardhuin added, frowning. "But she invoked the…said Oron had to do something, which means I have to do something. I don't even speak Preusan!" She threw up her hands, and Dominic rocked back on his heels. "How can I go there? They won't believe I'm the heir. And what if Mother finds out? She'll put me in a *convent,* or make me stay with Aunt Sophronia, or—"

Dominic kissed her. Ardhuin stared at him, stunned and unable to speak.

"If she puts you in a convent, I am sure you can levitate above the walls and turn the Mother Superior into a frog if needed," he said, smiling at her with affection. As she continued to stare, he could feel his face heat. "You were becoming somewhat agitated."

"That is your idea of a calming gesture?" Ardhuin sputtered. "And animal transformations are incredibly difficult, despite what people think. You have to change everything at once," she added. "Correctly. Or they die."

"Oh." He rubbed his chin. "No frogs, then."

"No frogs," she agreed, with a shaky laugh.

"You know, if you need the help of magicians, perhaps your friend can assist you," Dominic said, indicating the letter. "She appears to know about your great-uncle's abilities and connections."

Ardhuin's face cleared, and she started to look more cheerful. Dominic clasped her hands firmly in his own and stood up. "I'll return shortly, just as soon as I get my things together. I'm staying here," he explained when she gave him a puzzled look.

"But…I thought you were going back to your house," Ardhuin said slowly.

"That was before you told me someone was trying to kill you," Dominic said, feeling grim. "I'll stay in the cellar if you want, but I'm not leaving unless you force me to."

"Ah, it's the brandy you are worried about," Ardhuin said, trying to smile.

"Write to your friend—or better yet, send a telegraph. That will be quicker. We'll have to wait for morning anyway." He looked out the window to the darkness.

A troubled expression crossed her face. "You never considered that I might just be imagining things."

"I could tell from the moment I met you that you were very afraid of something," Dominic said. If she, with all her magic, was afraid, he ought to be terrified. Somehow, that was unimportant.

CHAPTER 6

Dominic crunched his way over the snow-crusted ground, wishing that the late Yves Morlais had left some sturdy boots in the attic along with the overcoat. It wasn't as cold as it had been, but now there was snow thanks to the previous day's storm. It had delayed the planned trip to town by a day.

Ardhuin had been not been happy about the storm, or his decision to send the telegram himself. Strangely, she had not argued—but he could sense her unhappiness, revealed in little flashes of irritability.

He felt for the message she had given him, cryptic enough to have meaning only for the friend who had written to her. He certainly didn't understand it. The slip of paper was still in his coat pocket, and he relaxed.

The morning was beautiful, with frost and snow glinting in the pale light and mist like the breath of the earth rising from the white ground. Dominic saw hoofprints but no sign of a cart on the road's snowy surface. Taking the road was longer than traveling across the fields, but he didn't want to risk the shorter route when he had no idea how much snow would impede him.

How unreal the mist was, winding through the bare trees. Dominic took a deep breath, enjoying the sharp coldness of the air.

A light breeze ruffled a dead leaf on the ground and disturbed the mist that obscured the road ahead. A stab of fear made Dominic stop. Now he could see faint strands of magic crossing the road like a spiderweb between two stands of trees.

He moved a few steps closer. The web completely blocked the road, but he could easily bypass it by stepping off the road itself. *He* could, because he could see it. Anyone else would go through.

And what would happen then? What was the web's purpose? If he were doing such a thing, invisible to all but himself, it would not be to block the road. That would make no sense. It might, however, be a way to tell if someone had passed.

The hoofprints continued on down the road, past the web. Either the horse and rider had gone through before it was put up, or the web was looking for someone in particular. Dominic considered going through himself, just to see what would happen, but decided against it. After his recent indisposition, he did not know what his sensitivity was.

He glanced to either side of the road. The bare trees did not offer much in the way of concealment. Whoever built the web must have some other way of knowing when the trap was sprung.

Dominic turned and retraced his steps. He would try the other, longer road to Baranton. Trap. Why had he used that term? Well, what other purpose could such a thing be put to? Perhaps he was unreasonably paranoid after Ardhuin's letter and revelation of danger.

The other road also had a web. It had to use a fencepost on one side and was more uneven, but it still blocked the road. A vehicle could not leave her house without meeting one of the webs.

Half-running, Dominic made a tour of the path to his cottage, and around the garden walls and carriage house. No webs.

He went inside the house, still marveling at how the wards flowed around him, and found Ardhuin.

She heard him out with a thoughtful frown. "Were they there when you went with Michel?"

He shook his head. "I could have gone around them, but I didn't know what else might be ahead. It's strange they didn't place them closer to your house, though, if they are looking for you."

"It is considered very dangerous to work offensive magic on a magician's home ground," Ardhuin said in a quiet voice. "They usually have many defenses in place, and attempting to find them could also alert the magician. I've set some traps myself," she added, with a quick grin. "They haven't been stupid enough to trigger them, though."

"A pity," Dominic said. "I wonder why are they doing this now? They suspect this house, clearly, but why have they waited to take direct action?"

Ardhuin collapsed into a chair, slouching down in her favorite thinking position. "It must be connected to the reason Gutrune wrote to me. Preusa's worried about something, and these people don't want me interfering with it." She sat up with a jerk, looking frightened. "The letter arrived only two days ago! Can they have known Gutrune was sending it?"

"It is possible," Dominic said, trying to evaluate the ramifications of Ardhuin's careless expression *Preusa's worried about something*. It made it sound as if this were a problem with political origins. No wonder she was distressed. "We really don't have enough information. If this problem came up suddenly, both sides could have taken action at the same time without knowing the other's plans."

"Coincidence, you mean." She sat back again and gave him a

thoughtful glance. "Very well, we can't know if they are connected. My unknown adversaries appear to wish to keep me from going to Preusa. What do they think I would find there that would hinder them?"

Dominic held up the telegram message. "What you were seeking with this. More information, and assistance. Perhaps we should go to Preusa in person. If they are watching, any message we send might be intercepted."

Ardhuin shrank down in her chair, looking unhappy. "Go there?"

"Yes, of course. It is a long way to a cold place, but I don't see much alternative, do you?"

Her long fingers wrapped and twisted around each other. "I can't—I don't like to travel. They will all be strangers there except for Gutrune, and besides, I don't speak any Preusan. It would be better for them to come here, anyway, and—"

"I speak Preusan," Dominic interrupted. "Benefit of a university education. Pray make use of it."

"You're not coming with me!" Ardhuin cried, her face full of horror. "But—"

"They're only after me! You have no reason to be concerned in *any* of this."

"If they are after you, I have a very good reason to be concerned," Dominic protested. "And I'm already involved," he pointed out, seeing her still-troubled expression. "For all we know, they've seen me here. I can help you. Why won't you let me?"

"I have already harmed you enough," Ardhuin said so faintly he could barely hear her. "If—if I go to Preusa and get help, will that content you? Will you leave then? It would be too dangerous here without someone to renew the wards."

"No, I am not going to abandon you when you are still being threatened," Dominic said, irritated. "Do you really have such a low opinion of me? That I would run away just when you need help?"

Ardhuin clasped her hands together and gazed down at them. "I'm afraid for you. I'd feel terrible if anything happened to you because of me." She was silent for a moment, then continued with great reluctance, as if the words were dragged out of her. "I know you are already involved. I just didn't want to…make you do anything you didn't want to do."

"I understand, and I do want to help you—so now that we've taken care of that little formality, what do we do next? How are we going to get to Preusa without alerting anyone?"

Ardhuin sighed and rubbed at her face. "There are mules less stubborn than you," she grumbled. Dominic said nothing, suspecting that she had acquiesced to the idea of the trip and his company. He did not want to change this promising beginning. "The road to town is too busy for the spells to be looking at everything. I imagine regular baggage would escape notice. We can have Michel pick up anything too heavy for us to carry and take it to the station ahead of time."

"And we can go on foot across the fields, avoiding the detection spells."

Ardhuin shifted. "I can. You should go the way you usually do. The farther I get from the house, the more likely they can detect me. I will go another way, over Ankou's Bones. We can meet in town."

Dominic suppressed a shudder, thinking of the dark hill. "Why?"

She stared at him. "You saw how magic works there. No detection web would last a minute in that environment, and any scrying strong enough to get through, I would notice. They won't be that careless. I'll go at night, too. They'll never see me, even if they are watching."

"No." Dominic found himself standing in front of her, glaring down. "Absolutely not. It's too dangerous."

"But any other way they could find me," Ardhuin protested.

"You are not going up there alone, especially at night."

Now she was standing too, and since she was taller she was glaring down at him. "Are you mad? It took over a month for you to recover from your last visit!"

"The point to this exercise is to get *both* of us, alive, to Preusa," Dominic said, temper fraying. "How do you think I would feel if you fell in one of those open pits and hit your head, with no one about to even know you needed help? We should stay together."

Ardhuin compressed her lips together, breathing heavily, then turned and went to the library window. She stood there for some time, saying nothing, looking out at the garden. Dominic walked over to her.

"I don't understand how you can even consider exposing yourself to the ley lines again," she said. She didn't sound angry, and he felt a surge of relief. She sounded simply puzzled.

"It is a risk," admitted Dominic. It puzzled him that he was so adamant. "We were up on the hill almost two hours, as I recall."

"More," Ardhuin said, grimacing. "You were not noticing things very well at the end."

Dominic waved this away. "My point being, I was exposed for a considerable time. If we move quickly over the shortest path, how long would it take?"

A quick flash of a smile. "Less than two hours. But we'll have to skip the picnic," she said mournfully.

Dominic laughed. "Another time, perhaps. Do you agree?"

Ardhuin looked out the window again and sighed. "I still don't like it. But I suppose there are no good choices here."

They packed. Dominic had very little, but Ardhuin had several books, and leather cases in strange shapes. They pulled down two big trunks from the storage room. After a careful scrying, Ardhuin used magic to move them to the port-cochère.

She insisted on waiting another two days, which brought them to the dark of the moon. They left the house well after midnight, carrying the luggage Ardhuin deemed too valuable or magical to risk to the carter.

"This way," Ardhuin whispered. She led the way in the darkness past the now-empty plinths of the marble statues and into the circular enclosure beyond.

She put down her bag and stepped over to the strange sundial in the middle.

"What are you doing?" he asked, in the same low tone she had used.

"If I can get this to work, it will make things much easier for you. It's a ley line observatory."

Dominic looked down at the barely visible stone circle. The crystal posts glinted faintly in the dark.

"I thought ley lines were everywhere," he whispered.

"The strong ones aren't," Ardhuin whispered back. "And they move. Usually with the moon, which is another reason I wanted to wait."

With his other sight, Dominic saw the magic start to flow from Ardhuin about the stone dial, looking as if it were probing for entry. Then it was in, and the crystals glowed with contained magic.

"That should do it. Look up," Ardhuin said softly.

The enclosure now had a dome of magic, and across the surface he could just make out faint lines, rough and wide, that converged in the same direction as the hill.

The magic faded, and darkness returned.

"It's a good thing I checked," Ardhuin said, leading the way out. "That big strong line is right over the path I was going to use. You would have been heavily exposed. This way," she said softly, as they clambered up the steep hill. The path was different from the one they had used to find the boy.

The darkness was thick, like felt, absorbing even the slightest light. Sometimes Ardhuin had to summon tiny little glowing lights, magical fireflies, that skimmed the ground before them so they could see their way.

"Won't this take more time?" Dominic asked, panting. They seemed to be going almost over the top, and he was already tiring.

"It's the clearest way. Any other path would bring us across a ley line. Are you feeling the effects?"

He could see the darker shadow ahead of him, could tell her head was turned towards him.

"I can see more," he said. "It's starting." The magical light actually helped; Ardhuin no longer needed to conjure fireflies for him. Any fatigue he felt was overcome by fear and the need to get away from the hill as soon as he could.

So many rocks, so many steep inclines. They had to lift their bags ahead, then clamber after them. Every time he took Ardhuin's hand, he steeled himself against any overwhelming sensation, but it remained bearable. For now. No doubt it helped that they both wore gloves. The touch of skin would—no, he shouldn't think of that.

How long had they been climbing? At last the slope changed, but now it was steeply downhill instead of up, and Dominic discovered this simply made it easier to fall. He had to climb backwards, chafing at the slowness of their progress, but he could not risk injury.

His hands were cold even through his gloves, and the length of the greatcoat kept getting in his way. Every spare moment, he strained to see Ardhuin. He could hear her, her labored breathing, the slip of her foot on loose gravel, the thump of the valise she carried when she shifted it to climb.

What was driving her? What secret could force her to undertake such a dangerous journey, when even she did not know what waited at the other end?

His foothold shifted as he transferred his weight, and before he could shift, he found himself falling, slamming hard against a boulder before coming to rest against a bush with hard, sharp twigs.

"Dominic!" Ardhuin screamed in a whisper. "Where are you? Are you hurt?"

He moved cautiously. "Just bruised, I think. Where…oh." He could see her outline against the sky, even some strands of curling hair that had escaped from her exertions. Of course she was wearing that damnable hat, so he couldn't see the curve of her cheek, the….

Dominic drew a sharp breath, his heart hammering. "Perhaps you should stay there. It isn't light yet, is it?"

"No, it's still pitch dark."

He got gingerly to his feet, wincing when he put his full weight on them. His right leg did not feel at all well. "I need to get off this hill *immediately*," he gritted through clenched teeth, hobbling forward. He carefully bent to pick up his bag.

"It's not much farther. Let me help you, you're limping."

"No!" He stumbled backwards, away from her approach, and nearly fell again. "That…would not be a good idea."

"Oh." Ardhuin hesitated, shifting her feet, then started down the hill again, looking behind her every few steps to see if he was following. He wasn't sure if she could see anything, but she stopped after only a short distance. "If you don't move, I'll come and get you," she said.

Dominic forced himself into motion, ignoring the small voice that urged him to stay still and wait for her, to let her get closer. Instead, he used it to motivate himself to follow as quickly as he could.

His leg was stiff and sore, making it excruciatingly painful to climb down. He almost collapsed with relief when Ardhuin found a real path the rest of the way. It still hurt to walk, but he was not in constant danger of falling again.

The path eventually led to open countryside and fields edged in hedgerows. He realized there was a distinct brightening on one edge of the horizon. It wasn't entirely magic he was seeing by, now.

Dominic took a deep breath. The air was cool and clear but not intoxicating, carrying the scent of the outdoors and nothing else. Perhaps he had escaped the worst effects.

Ardhuin was waiting for him, the veiling of the hated hat pulled back. He realized he was staring at her and decided he had not escaped the effects of the ley lines as completely as he had thought. Every detail of her face, the line of her jaw, the way her lips curved, fascinated him. He could gaze forever and never tire.

She was looking at him with an expression of concern.

"How do you feel?"

"Very well," Dominic lied, his voice constrained. "My leg is a trifle sore, but nothing to signify."

"I'm going to try some magic," she said. "You must tell me if you have any adverse reaction to it."

He closed his eyes, resolved not to say a word even if it was agony, but he couldn't help twitching when he felt the power touch him. It did feel uncomfortable, in a too-tight, wool-on-skin itchy way, but it was bearable.

He opened his eyes and saw a little old country woman in front of him, shoulders bent with age. Her face was as wrinkled as a withered apple and what he could see of her hair under a black bonnet was snow white, but her eyes were bright and sky blue. She carried a large wicker basket covered by a checkered napkin.

That was what his regular sight told him was there. In the same place, hidden by magic, was the greater height of Ardhuin, as straight as the old woman was bent. He glanced down, staring in wonder. Instead of the greatcoat he wore a patched wool jacket. He extended his arms and saw rough, twisted hands, one holding a hamper that had exactly the same weight as his bag. He touched one hand with the other and felt his own smooth skin.

"How do you do that?" Dominic asked in awe.

"I've always been able to do illusion," Ardhuin croaked. The old woman's face creased deeper with a smile. "It comes naturally to me. We should keep moving. Now that it is light, they might notice us standing here and become suspicious."

Well. If they were being watched, they should act their parts. Dominic took a deep breath and offered the old woman the support of his own aged arm.

Ardhuin took it, carefully, and they continued on to Baranton, just visible in the distance.

"I hope you do not mind the inconvenience," she said in her creaky old-woman's voice.

"I have always wanted adventure," Dominic replied. His voice sounded the same as always to him.

Ardhuin smothered a laugh.

The next stage of their trip, by train, was decidedly more ordinary.

Dominic was glad to be able to sit and let his injured leg rest, although Ardhuin had mentioned his limp added an authentic touch to his illusioned appearance as an old man.

The illusions were dropped once they were on the train to Rennes and unobserved.

"Too much iron about," Ardhuin said with a grimace when he asked why. "I could do it if I had to, but it would take a great deal of effort to no purpose." She spoke very low, and Dominic did not dare ask any of the remaining questions he had. To conserve funds, they traveled in the second class compartment, which became more and more crowded the closer the train got to the capital.

When they got to Rennes they visited Ardhuin's bank, then started on the journey to Gaul. They still needed to get visas for travel to Preusa, but they decided it would be safer to obtain them in Parys.

At the border between Gaul and Bretagne, Ardhuin performed another minor illusion, on their passports, to support the story of their assumed identities as cousins traveling for pleasure. After making sure Dominic did not show up in the list of licensed magicians, the officials examining the passports did not raise any objections. Considering the soldiers on both sides of the border, Dominic was quite glad.

"You could do the same for the visas," Dominic murmured when they were back on the train and their compartment was temporarily empty. "We wouldn't have to risk going to the consulate."

"I have to know what they look like first," she pointed out. She seemed worried. "Are there always so many soldiers at the border?"

Dominic had never had the means to travel before, so he could not say. "I imagine every country with a border with Gaul guards it well, considering their history," Dominic pointed out. She nodded, but looked even more worried.

More people returned and could be seen in the corridor, and she lowered the veil on the shadow hat. Dominic sighed. She was right to be cautious, he knew. But he had the feeling she would have done the same thing if her life were not in danger.

Their compartment filled up again, restricting their conversation. Ardhuin seemed disinclined to talk, so he looked out the window at the dreary winter countryside. Occasionally, the ruins of a war-torn town interrupted the view. One still had a pale, flickering glow of magic about the shattered walls, and Dominic shuddered, feeling ill. This had been the scene of some of the major battles of the Mage War, and Gaul still had not completely recovered. He wondered what the spell had been, and how it could possibly still be active more than thirty years after the war had ended.

Wrenching his gaze away, Dominic took out his writing materials and got to work. It would take his mind away from the depressing view outside.

More importantly, he needed to be productive—and to produce

something more profitable than his previous stories if he were ever to hope to support a wife. Undoubtedly, that would be the first question her father would ask. He'd already sent a letter to an acquaintance at the Université Dinan, asking if he knew a biologist named Andrews who had worked in Yunwiya and how to contact him. It wasn't much, but it was a start.

The trip was long. They arrived in Parys too late to attempt any business. In fact, they were lucky to find rooms at a tiny, unpretentious hotel near the station.

The noise of arriving and departing travelers and a lumpy mattress prevented Dominic from getting much sleep, but eventually he dozed off. He woke with a start, suddenly aware that light was visible behind the age-browned paper shades of his window.

He rushed to get dressed, wondering why Ardhuin had not woken him. He tapped at the door of her room, but there was no response. He began to really worry. What if something had happened to her? He went back to his room, wondering what he should do, and saw a piece of paper on the floor inside just as he stepped on it.

I must run an errand, the note said. *Wait for me. A.*

The handwriting was familiar; the same he had seen in his gardening instructions. Waiting, he had time enough to come up with a number of horrific possibilities for her sudden departure, and since he dared not leave for fear of missing her return, hunger was soon added to his difficulties. The minutes dragged by. At least she had left a note.

A soft knock on his door propelled him from his chair to open it, and he sagged in relief to see Ardhuin standing there.

"Where did you go?" he said in an urgent undervoice. "I would have been glad to go with you."

She shrugged. "I wanted to go early, before the crowds start. Just… something I wanted to get here." Dominic could not see her face because of the magical shadows, but he had learned enough of her voice to make him suspect she was not being completely truthful. "I found a directory listing the consulates at the hotel desk," she said. "Are you ready?"

Parys, being the capital, was in better repair than the towns they had passed through on the way. Dominic took it in with delight. His primary worry now relieved, he could revel in the unaccustomed sensation of being a traveler. With every recognized landmark or famous building, his satisfaction increased. A small stall on their way provided him with breakfast in the form of a sweet roll, as well as a newspaper.

Ardhuin was less interested, even though she, too, had never been to Parys before. She seemed tense, especially if they encountered people on their way.

"You are concerned they may have followed us?" he asked in a quiet tone. "They would have to be desperate indeed to attack in daylight, in public, especially here. The laws against unsanctioned magic are quite severe."

"A pity they didn't have those laws before Guedoc came to power," Ardhuin said, but his words appeared to have cheered her a little. "Look, there's the consulate. They don't really require a sign, do they? Those uniforms are identification enough."

The guards were indeed resplendently uniformed in the bright blue of Preusa. Although not many sought entry, the limited hours meant that several individuals waited with them.

Dominic checked his documents to make sure Ardhuin's earlier illusion had been removed, and waited. They retained the 'cousin' story, despite Ardhuin's foreign last name. Dominic claimed to be escorting her on an impulsive side trip to visit an old school friend. The consular official asked an impressive list of questions, the answers to which were carefully noted down.

Visas were reluctantly granted, although they were stringently warned about the consequences of violating any of the numerous regulations concerning the importation of forbidden devices or substances.

"I wonder why they were so nervous, not to mention suspicious," said Ardhuin after they had left the consulate. "Bretagne and Preusa have always been friendly, and they were *allied* with Atlantea during our Liberation."

"There are rumors of tensions between Preusa and Ostri," Dominic said, indicating the newspaper. "They are probably worried that Gaul may try to take advantage of any trouble. I doubt they were concerned about us."

It was a fine, clear day, but a chill breeze kept all but the hardiest indoors. With the delay in getting their visas, they would not be able to leave for Preusa until the next morning. As they wandered about the city, Dominic tried in vain to interest Ardhuin in any of the couturier's establishments they encountered. The only shops he could persuade her to enter were those selling books.

He stifled a small sigh, abandoning his never-robust first plan for the removal of the shadow hat, but soon forgot his disappointment scanning the shelves.

He looked up and found Ardhuin absorbed in a thick, leather-bound book with color plates.

"It's a new translation of *La Travaille de Fayre*, with illustrations by Monterillo," she said, showing him. "This was my favorite book when I was small; I must have read it fifty times. We would take turns playing the Mortal Champion beset by the monsters of Elfhame, my brothers and I. We had a large dog named Wiggins that was coal black, too, and would have been just like the hellhounds if he had not been friendly to a fault. A pity I must conserve my funds for the trip," she said regretfully, and replaced the book on the shelf.

She stepped to view the next section and Dominic moved back to make room, bumping into a tall, thin man with a handlebar moustache standing behind him. Dominic apologized, but the man merely nodded and left the store without saying anything.

When they left the shop, it was already beginning to get dark. Dominic looked at his watch. "Why don't we have dinner at one of the cafés? There was one not too far from the hotel, if I recall."

Ardhuin sighed. "I've had enough of crowds for a while. Let's go back to our rooms instead."

"There won't be that many people this early. At least give it a try— they might even have music."

Reluctantly, Ardhuin agreed.

The food was excellent, and the music lively and well played. This was somewhat unfortunate, in Dominic's view, because the café was thus quite popular and began to fill up shortly after their arrival. Despite his care in choosing a table in a sheltered nook, out of view of most of the room, he could see Ardhuin getting more and more tense and unhappy as the lively crowd increased. Finally, he realized this was only increasing her dislike of being around people, and they made their way out into the night.

"I think that street leads to our hotel. Through the park, there." She tugged at his arm.

He smiled a bit ruefully. "You really are eager to get away, aren't you?" When she did not immediately reply, he said, "I'm sorry. I thought you would like it."

"It was just the people," she said carefully. "It isn't—"

Out of a pool of darkness beside them, a figure suddenly appeared. He lunged out at Ardhuin, grabbing her from behind and jamming a pistol under her chin. "Hold it there, mage!" the man snarled at Dominic, holding Ardhuin as a shield between them. "Twitch a finger and she gets it!"

Dominic froze, more in utter confusion than in obedience. *He thinks I'm the mage,* he realized, just as a bright flash of magic settled over their attacker and he froze, mouth open to give some new command that never came.

"What was that?" Dominic said, once the shock of realizing the weapon and the attacker were real had worn off. Ardhuin made hushing motions and looked about the park. With the exception of themselves and the immobilized man, the park was deserted and dark. Struggling to extricate herself from the man's rigid grasp, she dislodged something that fell from his pocket. Ardhuin picked it up and glanced at it curiously. It was a false handlebar moustache.

Dominic stared at it, the connections forming rapidly in his mind. The man from the bookshop. He could see the resemblance now. But why had he been following them?

Ardhuin took his arm and continued walking as if nothing had occurred to interrupt them. When they reached the park gate, she said, "He can still hear and see in that state, and the less he knows about me the better. For all he knows, there was a second magician behind him that he didn't notice."

Dominic decided he did not like the sound of this. "So why are we just leaving, instead of going to the police? What did you do to him, anyway? It isn't permanent, is it?"

"A kind of vital stasis. It will last long enough for someone to find him standing there with a pistol, and that will be sufficient for the police to be summoned without involving us. Besides the inevitable delay, it would create precisely the type of attention we need to avoid."

"What if he gets away before the police come?"

"We should be well on our way by then, and I doubt he will be looking for us. The after-effects of vital stasis can last for days if no special precautions are taken."

"There's bound to be some interest in a magical incident like that. Especially here."

"I know." She sighed. "We'll just have to hope it won't attract the wrong kind of notice—and that he was working alone."

Dominic didn't believe that any more than Ardhuin seemed to. Her instinct of avoiding crowds now appeared to make excellent sense to him.

"We need to talk," Dominic said as quietly as he could. The Parys Champs de Nord station was not very crowded at this early hour, but the swirling mist and pools of shadow cast by the bright philogiston lights were perfect for hiding in. For once, he had no objection to Ardhuin wearing the magical hat.

She nodded, a sharp, quick motion of her head that did not interrupt her careful watch as they waited. "On the train," she said. "Take the first empty compartment."

She took her seat on the end nearest the corridor, and glancing quickly up and down, cast her spell. Dominic watched, fascinated, as the illusion took form. He had not seen her cast his own illusion earlier, just felt it. Now their compartment appeared almost completely full, including the master stroke of a woman with two small children. Every passenger who looked in quickly went further down the corridor of the carriage.

"You are quite good at this," Dominic said, impressed.

She ducked her head, waving her hand to dismiss his praise.

"I would do it sometimes when I had to travel. It's an old trick."

"What are you going to do when the conductor comes for the tickets?" he asked.

She laughed. "They won't be there anymore. All the real passengers will have taken their seats, so we won't need the illusion. It's harder to keep it going when the train picks up speed, anyway."

He was intrigued. "Why is that?"

Ardhuin tilted her head to one side. "I'm not sure. I think it has something to do with the iron in the wheels rotating. The closer you get to the engine, the stronger the effect, which makes me suspect the mechanical motion creates an interfering force."

Dominic examined his illusionary companions more carefully when the train began to move. They were not as sharply delineated as they had been at first; he could see very small vibrations, like little shivers, in the illusion's magic. The fat man sitting next to him was immersed in a newspaper, but he could not read anything other than the title.

Ardhuin dissolved the illusion as soon as she glimpsed the conductor in the passage, and when he had gone, she shifted her place to be opposite Dominic, next to the window.

She sat stiffly in her seat, her gloved hands clasping each other tightly, twisting. While the shadow-hat hid her face, the veiling was drawn tight enough to show her distinctive jawline and to let one bright red tendril escape. He took a deep breath. "I need more information about what's going on. What you know, what you can tell me," he added hastily, seeing her hands start to twist even more with agitation. "There is something about seeing a weapon pointed in one's direction that makes one nervous. I expected any attack to be magical. But this is in some ways worse. Despite all our efforts, your enemies have been able to make another attempt on you. Either we were followed, or they have people watching places such as the stations and the consulate. Both possibilities suggest whatever is going on is not some personal vendetta between mages, but…politics." He had not forgotten her casual mention of Preusa itself as a concerned party, and he could see his words had an effect. Her hands had stilled.

Ardhuin sighed, as if resigned. "I'm not certain, but I think it has to do with the Mage War," she said quietly.

Yes, that would qualify as politics. "That was thirty years ago—before you were born! Why on earth would anyone want to kill you now? Was your great-uncle involved?"

"Extensively." Her voice was dry. "We were very close, but there were some things about that time he would not tell me. We forget, I think, what a horrific shock it was when war magic was used so heavily. And what the Gaulan mages did at Guedoc's direction—no one wants to think about that, even now."

"No." Dominic shuddered. So many dead, and some worse than that. Enslaved by magic.

She sighed again, and her whole body seemed to slump. "From what he *did* tell me, it was much, much worse than is commonly known. You must promise never to speak of what I am about to tell you, or even hint about it in your stories."

Dominic nodded slowly. "I promise."

She looked out the window at the passing scenery for a while, then continued. "The Allies came very close to losing," she said bluntly. "Very close. The only reason for their success was the concerted efforts of a group of mages, the best of their respective countries. Mages tend to be reluctant to work together; such close cooperation was unprecedented. It was the only thing that saved them, and the governments involved, who knew what could have happened if they had failed, were determined a danger like Guedoc would never happen again. The temporary arrangement was made permanent, and a compact made between all of what were then called the 'Mage Guardians.' If any similar threat appeared, they or their heirs would come together and stop it." She looked at him. "My great-uncle was one of those mages—under the name Oron."

He closed his eyes, thinking furiously. "And you inherited more than the house at Peran from him, is that it?"

"Precisely. Everyone in the family knew he was a magician, but only a few knew to what extent. None of them know I am his heir-magical."

"Well, it's usually more ceremonial, isn't it? Who gets to use what device on banners, and so on. Or finishing obligations of a magical nature."

She nodded. "Yes. The obligation of the compact is *in aeturnam*, binding on yourself and your heir. The letter that Gutrune sent me said she had urgent need to contact the heir of the mage Oron, and she thought I might know who that might be. How she figured that out—" she shook her head, puzzled. "Of course, she didn't say what the problem was, but given the nature of the compact, it isn't likely to be pleasant."

He felt himself growing cold. "Preusa has plenty of their own magicians, even mage level. The best *ars magica* university is in Baerlen. Why do they want you?"

"They may send me back as soon as I get there," she said in a resigned voice, shrugging. "There will be at least four other high-level mages showing up. When they realize the heir of Oron is female, they may refuse to let me do anything."

It was plausible, and he felt himself relax. Ardhuin would not be placed in any more danger and would be surrounded by people who could deal with the threat to her life. Once it was taken care of, they could return to Bretagne. The frozen landscape flashed by the window. "The person who wrote you, Gutrune? How well do you know her?" he asked, finally.

Ardhuin seemed relieved at the change of topic. "We went to the same school. She is Preusan, and went into the government after she left. The others didn't like her much either, so we were natural allies. Not only did they take exception to my appearance, but many Aeropans think Atlanteans are barely civilized. Gutrune is very intelligent and observant —but she didn't advertise this at school." Ardhuin frowned. "I suppose I should send a telegram when we stop in Koeln. A real visitor would do that, letting her know when to expect me."

"Do you think she will be surprised that you are coming? That is, does she know you are the heir?"

Ardhuin shook her head. "I never could tell how much she knew. She never gave anything away."

They arrived in Koeln without incident and proceeded on their journey early the next day. After several hours they crossed a dark, ice-rimmed river, and the train pulled into a busy station.

"Haagen," said Dominic, reading from the schedule. "A number of the rail lines intersect here."

Ardhuin was unimpressed. "More people wanting to get on and off, and more delay. We should have left fifteen minutes ago." She glanced casually at the platform, then gasped. "They've unloaded our luggage!"

"What?"

"Look—that green trunk. And your portmanteau beside it."

He reached for the compartment door's handle. "There must have been a mistake with all the changes. I'll go and tell them." No sooner had he opened the door than a conductor accompanied by three soldiers appeared in the corridor, blocking his way.

"Herr Kermarec, Fraülein Andrews? Come with me."

"What is going on?" protested Dominic. "Why is our luggage being taken off?"

"If you will come, all will be explained. You must leave the train."

Dominic's first fear was that the man in the park had been found and traced to them. Ardhuin gave him a worried look, but he dared not say anything in front of the soldiers. He and Ardhuin gathered their belongings and left the compartment.

They were barely a moment on the platform, which was partly obscured by clouds of steam, when the train pulled away. They waited in silence, the soldiers alert beside them, and then another train took its place. Unlike the one they had arrived on, it had no lettering denoting the line or placard indicating the destination. There were only two carriages behind the locomotive.

One of the soldiers swung himself up to the cabin of the locomotive; the others remained behind Dominic and Ardhuin as the conductor indicated they should board. Exchanging speculative glances, they did so, followed by the remaining soldier, who closed the carriage door and stood outside on guard.

The interior was furnished as a sitting room, and in luxurious style. Thick carpets, carefully selected to harmonize with the wall hangings, covered the floor, and crystal lustres hung from the central light. They swayed gently as the train moved away from the station and steadily increased its speed.

A door at the rear of the parlor opened to admit a tall, stern-visaged Preusan officer. "*Grüssen,* Herr Magus Kermarec. I am Major von der Kleist," he said, in accented Gaulan. He glanced at Ardhuin. "If the lady would retire to her compartment, there is sensitive information that must be discussed."

Dominic and Ardhuin exchanged glances.

"Er, I am not…that is, I believe Mademoiselle Andrews is the proper person for you to speak with," Dominic said, hesitating at von der Kleist's stony expression.

"This is to be amusing, yes? I am told your predecessor also did not have always proper behavior."

A choked snort came from Ardhuin, who was carefully pulling back the veil of her hat.

She bit her lip, then said in a halting voice, "I should explain—my great-uncle made me—"

The major interrupted her. "Please to leave at once! These are matters of the most importance. I do not understand why you bring her here, she is an inconvenience." He turned an increasingly deep shade of red and glared at Dominic.

Seeing her distress, Dominic gave Ardhuin a reassuring smile. "It was going to happen sooner or later," he said to her. "Once he's convinced, there will be much less trouble." She gave a tremulous nod, looking very unhappy. Dominic sized up the irate Preusan officer and wondered if this could have been any worse.

"Major von der Kleist, I assure you we are not having a joke at your expense. The situation is a serious one, is it not? Despite the apparent irregularity, I must insist you conduct your business with Mademoiselle Andrews."

The major's jaw became even more pronounced, but he said nothing. He extended a folder to Dominic that had a large, multicolored seal on it, bright with magic.

"Please believe me, Major. I can't open that," Dominic said, grasping for patience.

"Do you mean to say you gave misleading information, saying you were—" the major, with an effort, changed what he was going to say, "a mage of great power?"

"I have *never* given anyone to understand I was a magician of any sort or degree," Dominic snapped. "*She,* however, *is.*"

The major's eyes bulged, and he strode angrily towards the carriage door. Dominic was in his path, and when he refused to move, the major raised his fist.

Dominic tensed, but a flash of magic froze the major in place before the blow fell. Dominic raised his eyebrows at Ardhuin, who went red with embarrassment.

"He wasn't listening," she said helplessly. "You did try."

"Yes, I tried." Dominic sighed.

Ardhuin went up to the enraged, frozen major and gingerly took the folder from his hand. She studied the seal, then lightly ran her fingers over it. "Hmm. They did an impressive job on this. Take a look—you won't see this very often."

The magic was intricately crafted, different types woven through one another in a way that told Dominic that undoing the protections without activating the overlaying spell of destruction would be quite difficult.

He watched as she laid the folder on the table, then carefully began to deactivate the seal. It was precise, delicate work, and several minutes passed before she let out a breath and sat down on one of the upholstered seats to examine the contents.

"I presume your telegram was responsible for all this," Dominic said.

She looked up. "I certainly hope so. It had better not be the incident in the park! I doubt we would get the royal treatment for unlicensed magical discharge within city limits, however." She thumbed through the papers. "Current political situation? Initial schedule? What is this, and why did he make such a fuss about it? It looks just like what you read in the newspaper."

"Is there some way you can let him talk, at least? He may know more."

Ardhuin looked at the major, face immobile in eye-bulging fury, and frowned thoughtfully. "I suppose I'll have to."

She did not remove the immobility from anywhere but his head, which Dominic considered a very wise decision. Released from stasis, the Major gave vent to a stream of extremely impolite Preusan, which a quick, worried glance at Ardhuin's face told Dominic she fortunately did not understand. When at last the major had calmed himself to the point where he could rant in Gaulan, he seemed to have accepted the reality of the situation. At least to the point of refraining from profanity.

"She really is the proper person to read those documents," Dominic assured him, seeing him still looking furious.

"Then how is it you are here?" asked the major, determined to get to the bottom of everything.

"I am her assistant," Dominic improvised. The major appeared to mull this over.

"What is so important in all this that justified such a powerful seal?" asked Ardhuin, puzzled, holding up the papers. "The increase in tension between Preusa and Ostri is common knowledge, and the rest of it...." She shrugged dismissively.

"I was told nothing, but ordered to deliver the packet to the mage traveling from Bretagne, and to give any assistance necessary," he said stolidly.

Ardhuin rolled her eyes. "How very helpful," she said dryly.

CHAPTER 7

Ardhuin shivered and hoped this trip by water would not be a long one. Ice in the black river bobbed and swirled about the muffled oars. Their boat hugged the edge of the high embankment, hiding in the deep shadow cast by the philogiston lamps of the street above. There were few potential onlookers, due to the bitter cold and the lateness of the hour, but the Preusans were not taking any chances.

Their transfer from the train on arrival at Baerlen had been equally secretive. Major von der Kleist disembarked like an ordinary traveler, but she and Dominic had left from the back of the train and were whisked through the station on carts with luggage piled artfully around them.

Sitting so close to him on the hard seat, Ardhuin could feel the tension in Dominic's body. She didn't dare ask him anything; the silence was absolute and the smallest sound would have been noticeable. Far from reassuring her, these stringent precautions were making her extremely nervous. Something was very wrong.

The boat came to a halt at a series of stone steps that descended into the river from an imposing building, which she assumed must be the Imperial Palace. Ardhuin, Dominic, and Major von der Kleist disembarked in silence, and the boat moved away and vanished into the dark. A door opened, but no light was visible within. A hand gestured them on.

Once inside, light flared about them. Gutrune von Kitren was waiting for them, looking exactly the same as Ardhuin had last seen her—severe yet beautiful, like a statue of Justice. Outwardly, her expression revealed nothing, but from the gleam in her pale blue eyes Ardhuin suspected she was glad to see them. Gutrune wore a formal, close-fitted dress of watered dark blue silk with a small jeweled royal eagle insignia pinned to one shoulder. It echoed the uniform worn by von der Kleist, but remained graceful and elegant. Her honey-blonde hair, which Ardhuin had always envied, was in a braided chignon at the nape of her neck.

Beside her were several guards, and two men clad entirely in black who were watching them closely. One of these black-clad individuals looked distinctly non-Aeropan, with his heavy jet-black hair and bronze skin. Ardhuin felt her heart skip a beat. Was it possible? A Yunwiyan, here?

Von der Kleist launched into a staccato burst of Preusan she could not follow. No doubt he was complaining about what had happened on the train. She glanced at Dominic, and the twitch at the corner of his mouth confirmed it.

"He's reporting in, having made an end…sorry, having completed his assignment. Strong hint of washing his hands of the entire affair. He delivered the documents but cannot be sure the seal worked correctly since you were the one who opened them."

At this, the two black-clad men reacted visibly, looking startled and unsure. Gutrune permitted herself a small smile. "I was warned of his… what is the word? Eccentricity?" she said in Gaulan. "Even beyond the grave, it is evident. Thank you for coming so quickly. I am greatly relieved."

Ardhuin hesitated, then lifted the veiling from her hat. As much as she would have liked to remain hidden, matters had progressed to the point where she would have to reveal herself sooner or later. "I doubt your relief will be universal," she said, stumbling over her words. "I hope my…that is, I hope this will not cause you too much trouble. He—he didn't always think things through."

Gutrune barely raised one hand, and Ardhuin understood. They could not talk freely, even here.

"You are to come immediately to the Council chamber. Major von der Kleist, thank you for your assistance." The major bowed punctiliously, but did not look at all sad to see them go. He refused to even glance at Ardhuin.

As they followed Gutrune from the antechamber through the polished marble and wood of the palace proper, Dominic murmured under his voice, "This is the friend you spoke of?" Ardhuin nodded. They passed another brace of soldiers at a doorway, and he added, "They like to have guards, don't they? I wonder why she is our only escort, though. What happened to the two—" he glanced over his shoulder and blinked. "Oh. Still there, but illusioned. They illusioned the boat, too, you know."

Ardhuin just nodded, too nervous to speak. She was profoundly grateful for Dominic's presence. Besides his talent for seeing magic and knowledge of Preusan, he seemed to regard this as a grand adventure. It made it just slightly less terrifying.

It was going to be bad. She started to feel sick just thinking about it. There would be people. Strangers, and she would have to talk to them. *Argue* with them. Prove what they would consider two impossible things —that she was a mage, and the heir of Oron.

When they reached the imposing doors of the Council chambers, Ardhuin had to force herself to breathe deeply. Dominic looked at her, concerned, and she tried to smile.

The door opened. It was not a large room, but was furnished with the same richness as the rest of the palace. Seeing the elegant splendor of the people gathered about the table, she was conscious of feeling distinctly shabby.

"The Mage Guardian of Bretagne, Fraülein Andrews, and her assistant, Herr Kermarec," announced Gutrune von Kitren.

Ardhuin stifled a gasp. How like Gutrune to simply state the whole, complicated truth from the very beginning. She wished she were one-tenth that brave.

The councilors stared, petrified into silence. Then a swell of outraged muttering grew until one apoplectic gentleman sputtered something she didn't understand. Gutrune had spoken in Gaulan, but the Council refused to take the hint.

Ardhuin could tell what the general topic of conversation was without Dominic's whispered translation. She was a woman, and therefore could not be a mage.

Gutrune replied to the shouted imprecations calmly, but the angry voices were having their effect. Ardhuin stepped back, desperately wanting to escape. There were more of the black-clad men here, including the one who looked Yunwiyan, some between her and the door.

"They ask if you have any proof of what you claim," Gutrune said, looking as if she were merely discussing the weather.

What had her great-uncle told her? *A tedious formality, the* gloire, *but it has its uses. It is essentially a sigil that cannot be written, for it is power incarnate.* A formality between mages, he had said, that she should know.

Ardhuin swallowed, gathering the magic thickly close to her, reassured by the silky feel of it. Unlike other spells, this one had words. Just like in fairy tales. Dominic sensed the magic and turned his head sharply to look at her, his mouth open in shock.

"Plaestutiis karon ote Oron hai!"

Dominic cried out and flung up his arm. She should have warned him, and she felt a stab of guilt. The gloire burst around her, a slowly fading golden shimmer that surrounded her like a cloud. Suddenly all the black-clad men were standing between her and the Council, looking angry and intent. She found herself gathering magic for defense instinctively, but Gutrune placed a hand on her arm and shook her head emphatically. She looked startled and a little frightened.

"Ein gloire," someone said, sounding shaken. *"Können sie falsch gemacht werden?"*

This started another angry argument between an elderly councilor with muttonchop whiskers and a man in resplendent military uniform.

"Rühe." The word was said quietly, but with an undercurrent of power

that silenced the argument completely. All eyes turned to the figure at the head of the table, whose face bore an expression of grim weariness. Ardhuin blinked, recognizing that face. It was on many of the Preusan coins and was featured prominently in newspaper illustrations. The King of Preusa looked up from his clasped hands and regarded her steadily. "We thank you for your prompt and swift response to our request for aid," he said in Gaulan.

A ripple of reaction went over the faces of the councilors. Emotion was carefully submerged, and none ventured to speak. The King's words apparently had more meaning than she understood. His acceptance made her even more terrified. Ardhuin realized she had been hoping they would reject her, but the King was not going to let her go.

He looked so tired.

Ardhuin swallowed again, trying to overcome the sudden dryness of her mouth. "They are right, really, they didn't know—I mean, my great-uncle intended to introduce me himself before it was necessary to..." she mumbled, feeling her face go hot and red. Again. "I have no wish to intrude if I am not needed. The other Mage Guardians will doubtless be able to manage without my assistance." The silence in the room deepened, and the councilors were still, looking away or down at the table. "You have contacted the others?" Ardhuin felt a stab of fear. There *had* to be others. Who would help her with *her* problem?

"Tell her," said the King, with a hint of a snarl in his voice.

A grey-whiskered councilor said nervously, in accented Gaulan, "Well, the mage from the Low Countries, Schulyer Colfax, he had a debilitating stroke two years ago. Died not long thereafter. Couldn't speak, didn't name an heir."

Ardhuin thought for a moment. "The Alban Mage Guardian can't be that old; he isn't one of the originals like Colfax. Where is he?"

"MacCrimmon vanished into some godforsaken corner of Asea called the Tian Shan eight months ago and hasn't been heard of since. And we weren't the only ones searching for him, either," said a lanky man in uniform, considerably younger than the others in the room. "Looking for dragons, supposedly."

"MacCrimmon of the dragon book? He is a Mage Guardian?" asked Dominic in a whisper. Ardhuin just nodded.

"And the mages of Preusa and Ostri?" she asked.

"The nature of the difficulty makes us very reluctant to ask Ostri for help," said the King flatly.

"And I am afraid Professor Siebert met with an accident...let me see, it was three weeks ago. In his laboratory. If he had an heir, we are unaware of it," said the whiskered one.

"Do you...." Ardhuin took a shaky breath, and continued, "Do you mean to say I am the only Mage Guardian you have?"

"Yes," said the King. "That is precisely what we mean."

Dominic picked his way carefully around the scattered trunks and boxes. All of them were open, and many had their contents strewn about. The rooms they cluttered had been provided for Ardhuin's use, once she had recovered from her shock at the Council's news and requested them.

He'd never seen her so terrified, and he couldn't blame her. This was a trifle more adventure than he had been looking for.

"Blast and damn! I can't have forgotten to pack them!" Ardhuin sat back on her heels, looking red and flustered, and gave the trunk she had been searching a scowl.

"You haven't looked in that one," said Dominic quietly, pointing.

She glanced at the trunk in question and dove into the contents. Ardhuin gave a triumphant cry, pulling out a heavy wooden box with metal clasps. "Now we can get something done," she said. She sounded much less frantic, and Dominic felt relieved.

She set the box down on a table and opened it. Dominic came up beside her to observe. The box contained pieces of a beautiful silvery material in a variety of shapes and sizes, each in a padded hollow.

Ardhuin picked up one of the silvery objects and looked about the room. It was a good-sized space, somewhat bare of its usual furnishings, but the walls still had the gilt ornamentation he'd seen throughout the palace. It was interior, which meant it had no windows, and instead of a fireplace it had a beautiful cobalt-blue ceramic cylinder stove.

There were guards outside. Everywhere Ardhuin went now there were soldiers, and the men all in black. They were only alone now because she had convinced them, with unusual vehemence, that setting up a workroom that no one but her assistant and herself would be able to enter was, in fact, increasing her safety.

At last Dominic's curiosity overcame his concern. "What are you doing?"

"Setting up for the warding," she said absently, fingering another of the silvery pieces. "These are channels—made of specially tempered chryselectrum. Sometimes it is also called silverglass. The channels shape the field to fit the room."

"When you set wards before you didn't use them."

"Ah." She looked at him and gave a shaky smile. "Those were simple wards of force, cast from within. This will be a ward of intent and defense. It will be permanent, and we will be able to enter and leave without lowering it. The kind of ward I have at home for my workroom."

"Oh." He thought for a while. He remembered that workroom, or at least the door of it. Even when he was just beginning to see magic it had made an impression on him. "Do you have to do it now? You look tired."

"I'm tired because I was up half the night setting minor shielding and detection spells. If they hadn't played games with our luggage I would have set up wards last night," she snapped. Then, more evenly, she continued, "I'll feel better when I get the wards up."

"You could have set up a ward of force."

"You were in a different room, far away." She shuddered. "If I set a ward of force I would have been unable to detect any attempt on you."

He helped her place the channels at all the corners of the room, and several on the ceiling for good measure. Ardhuin took a deep breath and nodded.

"Right," she said softly to herself. She looked over at Dominic. "I'm going to need to concentrate now. Don't distract me."

She closed her eyes, standing tall and straight. No longer did she seem flustered and hesitant; her chin jutted out stubbornly. At first, nothing seemed to happen, even though he could see power building and roiling about her. Her eyes opened, wild and stormy, and the table beside him rose a few inches in the air. Soon all the luggage, furniture, he, and Ardhuin were no longer in contact with the floor. Lines of strain were visible on Ardhuin's face, and power built to a blinding intensity.

Suddenly Dominic could see a wall of magic that enclosed them completely, like a bubble. The bubble expanded, and where it met the channels it flattened and deformed from its original spherical shape. It seemed slightly thick and elastic, and the sheer density of power it contained made him shiver. He had never seen her perform such powerful magic before.

At last the bubble fully conformed to the interior of the room, and Ardhuin let the floating furniture back down. The floor felt as if it had been covered by a thin layer of rubber when Dominic's feet made contact again. Ardhuin collapsed into a chair, looking completely exhausted but relieved.

Dominic paced as best he could for the scattered luggage. "We still don't know what happened to make them summon you. Unless they think the accidents involving the other Mage Guardians weren't accidents."

"Why do you think I was so desperate to get the wards up?" asked Ardhuin wearily. "It sounded like there was some other problem, though, and they only found out about the other Mage Guardians when they tried to invoke the compact. It could just be coincidence and bad luck. But if it isn't...."

Dominic felt himself growing colder as she spoke. "And if it isn't?"

Her narrow face was pale. "Few people know of the compact's existence. Even fewer know who the Mage Guardians are. It is the kind of information governments like to keep secret, you understand. Then, who has the ability to remove such powerful magicians without being detected? The person doing so would have to be a powerful mage in their own right. If the Mage Guardians *are* being deliberately removed, it must be because of something they would otherwise have prevented. And that," she sighed, "means something very, very nasty."

"You think the attacks on Peran are connected to this," Dominic said.

Her forehead wrinkled in thought, and she shifted restlessly. "It's hard to tell. My great-uncle died naturally, so I don't think…but he was suspicious of something. If they are connected, whatever it is has been planned some time in advance."

"Did he tell anyone else you were his heir?" Ardhuin shook her head, looking sad. Dominic felt his stomach knot. She would have been safer if they had just stayed in Bretagne. No one else knew her secret. Now she had come to Baerlen and identified herself to the Council. If the person behind the plot had known the identities of the other Mage Guardians, what were the chances he could find out what the Council now knew?

Ardhuin was in terrible danger, and he could do nothing to protect her. It was all magic. He would only be able to see it happen.

A muffled thumping came from the direction of the door. He and Ardhuin looked at each other for a moment, then he went to open it. He could feel a slight resistance as he passed through the ward.

Gutrune von Kitren and the foreign-looking black-clad man from the previous night were waiting in the hall. "If Fraülein Andrews is free, we would like to speak with her," said von Kitren.

Dominic relayed the message.

"It was decided you should have some personal protection," Gutrune said when Ardhuin appeared. She indicated the man who stood beside her. "This is Markus Asgaya, a defensive magician of the King's guard. He or another will be with you at all times."

Dominic glanced at Ardhuin. Knowing her dislike of close contact with strangers, he was surprised to see her looking pleased. She glanced at the other magician and said carefully, *"O'siyo. Tse' salagi?"*

A smile flashed across the man's dark face. "I would answer, but my accent would shame me. I have not spoken Yunwiyan for many years. How do you come to know it?"

She had an answering smile when she replied. "I spent several seasons with my parents on Duno Elutani when I was young."

"At the ruins, then?" Asgaya was clearly interested.

Ardhuin nodded. "Have you been in Preusa long?"

He made a deprecating gesture. "Most of my life, in fact. My mother is Preusan. When my father died, we returned to Aerope."

"Yes…of course."

Gutrune cleared her throat, and Ardhuin returned her attention to her former schoolmate. "It was also decided you should be given the full details of the situation as soon as possible. It has been arranged, but I am afraid Herr Kermarec will not be allowed to attend. The matter is extremely sensitive."

Ardhuin frowned. "He is my assistant. He will be with me when I deal with…with whatever it is, so why can't he know now? Besides, I need his help. I understand barely five words of Preusan."

Gutrune smiled slightly but shook her head. "It is not completely sensible, I agree—but those are the orders I was given. As for translating, I will be happy to assist you. Given our connection, I will be the liaison with the Preusan government in any case."

Ardhuin scowled, glancing at Dominic. He shook his head. The two of them would not be able to defy the entire Council, as much as he would like to. She turned back to Gutrune. "How many of these meetings are planned? Will we be staying here?"

"At the Imperial Palace, and also at the *Kriegszauberkollegium*. It will likely take most of the day, and tomorrow as well."

Muttering under her breath, Ardhuin motioned Dominic to follow her back into the workroom, with the excuse that she needed to fetch something inside.

"Unbelievable. Something has them so bothered they are desperate even for a female Mage Guardian, and now that I am here they want to talk me to death!" She snorted.

He forced a smile. "They like to be thorough. It appears they have accepted your magical ability, however. Perhaps they are not so biased as you fear. Your friend clearly has a high place here, despite being a woman. Is there anything I can do for you while you're engaged with these meetings?"

She hesitated, then said, "I'd like to know more about what happened to this Professor Siebert. Go to the university and see if there was anything at all suspicious. Try not to let them know that's what you're looking for, though. After all, we have no proof this was anything other than an accident."

He looked at her skeptically. "You don't believe it is an accident, do you?"

"No," she said soberly. "You should be discreet in case it isn't. Just… be careful."

"You be careful as well," he said as they returned to where Gutrune and Markus were waiting. He tried not to feel desolate as he watched them leave. *It's only for a little while, and I have work to do.*

One of the functionaries of the palace gave him directions to the university. Dominic declined the offer of a carriage, thinking it best to find his own way. It was not far from the Imperial Palace.

He wandered the grounds for some time after his arrival, looking for the *ars magica* department. The university was of sufficient antiquity that many of its buildings were formed from the accretions of several centuries, producing a bewildering series of corridors, stairways, and halls connecting the older section to the new. Dominic began to think he had achieved something significant when he found the correct building.

Dominic rubbed his chin and looked about the corridor, seeking inspiration. It seemed that the morning lecture had recently ended and students were crowding the halls. A small group descended the stairs, cheerfully arguing.

"Of course I missed some lectures! Nobody can listen to that venerable fossil every day without risking brain fever. He's usually half asleep himself, anyway," said a short, sandy-haired student.

"He was awake enough to notice your absence," observed one of his companions.

"Pardon me," Dominic said as they came near. "I am here to see Professor Siebert. Could you perhaps tell me where I might find him?" Siebert's death had been recent enough an obvious foreigner like himself might not have heard about it, and it would be better to pretend he did not know. Besides, it would make it easier to come up with a believable excuse for trying to find out more about the accident. Seeing the astonishment in the faces of the students, he ventured, "This is the College of Thaumurgic Science, yes?"

"Ah, you want the Theology department now," said the short one. He was promptly punched in the arm by another in the group, a fellow with dark hair and a stormy, intense expression.

"Show a little respect, Jens-Peter, it won't hurt you and it would be a welcome novelty. He could be a friend of the professor's." Jens-Peter's assailant turned to Dominic. "I regret to say Dr. Siebert is recently deceased."

A tall, grave student who had previously remained silent added, "There was an accident with some equipment in his laboratory. Are you perhaps Dr. Gavreche? He had mentioned—"

"No, not at all. My name is Dominic Kermarec. I had never met the professor, but he was recommended to me by an acquaintance as an expert on some questions I have in my research."

The remaining member of the group, who had been looking about in a genial, myopic fashion during the discussion, suddenly perked up and gazed at Dominic with great interest, pushing up his steel-rimmed glasses for a better view. "Do you also work on levitation magic, then? I had not been aware…but of course, there is the group at the Université Rhames…."

"I'm not a magician," said Dominic hurriedly, "I merely have an interest—I'm a writer."

All the students, with the exception of the one with spectacles, stared at him in amazement.

Jens-Peter laughed with frank amusement. "*Quatsch!* A writer, interested in magic? What do you take us for? Here is boring utility and dull theory, not missing heirs, beautiful ladies, ancient castles, and the rest of the lot."

Dominic could only hope they had not noticed his start of surprise at how close they had come to describing Ardhuin. "No, the fables…" he struggled for the correct Preusan word "…the stories I write are of amazing things, but things that could really happen. So if I wish to write a tale of someone who makes a magical device to rise to the top of a mountain, I look for those who work on similar things so they may tell me how my idea could be made more believable."

"Are you…did you write 'Secret World' in *The Family Museum?*" asked the dark-haired student, frowning thoughtfully.

"Is it out already? Yes, I am the author." Dominic was astounded that a Preusan student had read it. "Are they translating the magazine now?"

The dark-haired student grinned. "No, more's the pity. I have a subscription. To improve my fluency in Gaulan." His comrades made rude noises indicative of disbelief. "I thought your name sounded familiar! Look, we're just on our way to meet a friend of ours, Dieter Theusen, and get a meal. He was Professor Siebert's assistant. Why don't you join us?"

Jens-Peter enthusiastically seconded the invitation, with the rider, "If he doesn't mind being seen with university students in public!"

"It wasn't so long since I was one myself," retorted Dominic. "I would be honored."

"What university?" asked the tall one as they descended the stairs.

"Université Dinan."

"Do you still remember how to throw bread rolls?" asked Jens-Peter.

The other students introduced themselves as they walked to the restaurant where they would rendezvous with Dieter. The dark, stormy one was Wolfgang Maurer, the tall one gave his name as Stefan Arendt, and the bespectacled student was Jochim Weiskopf.

"Dieter and Jochim are studying magic, as am I," said Stefan.

"It is the theory of magic only, for me," said Jochim, apologetically. "My ability is itself not good."

"I have none at all, so I'm stuck with mechanical arts," said Jens-Peter. "And since Maurer has ambitions to learn as much as possible without actually making himself useful, he studies both classics and literature."

Maurer rolled his eyes at this but said nothing.

Dieter Theusen was an earnest, enthusiastic young man with an unruly shock of blond hair and one arm in a sling. "I was in the next room when it happened," he said between mouthfuls. "There was this tremendous explosion, and the whole building shook. Some of the equipment cabinets fell over—that's what got me." He indicated his arm with his fork.

"What was he working on that was so dangerous?" asked Dominic.

"Levitation ships," Dieter said thickly, and took a deep drink from his stein.

"But levitation doesn't create explosions," Dominic protested, thinking of the countless times Ardhuin had levitated objects, including himself, without the slightest hazard.

"Not by itself, no. But by itself it doesn't make a self-propelled ship, either. We were using a motor to actually move it. The dangerous part is mixing the magical and mechanical devices in such a close space—too much chance of a large enough piece of iron moving through a magical field and building up a discharge, and then the fuel can ignite." Dieter shrugged. "One of the fields must have become misaligned or something. Siebert was usually very careful about that, though. He knew how dangerous it was."

"Are there any others working on levitation ships?"

"Not in Baerlen," Dieter answered, then thought for a minute. "He'd mentioned something about the Gaulans, and I think the Atlanteans are trying something too. There aren't many that have the right combination of abilities. It's pretty unconventional, mixing magic and engineering like that."

Dominic frowned. "If it is so dangerous and difficult, why do it? Isn't there a purely magical or purely mechanical way? It doesn't seem very practical."

"It will be very practical once we get it to work," said Dieter a trifle defensively, and Dominic suspected he had been asked this question before. "We don't have anything close to a mechanical equivalent of levitation. Some say it just can't be done. Magical methods of propulsion are pretty weak, and in any case require a magician to do them—not like the levitation, which can be set as a static spell. He wanted to make something anyone could use."

"Why?"

"Wouldn't you like to fly like a bird?" asked Jens-Peter, eyes brightening at the thought. "Think of the things you could see, the places you could go!"

"I know the army is very interested," added Stefan. "My brother is at the *Kriegszauberkollegium*, and they have been pursuing their own investigations as well as following Professor Siebert's efforts."

Dieter turned to him. "Yes, in fact there was a military magician who visited the day before the explosion." He grinned. "I wasn't there, but the professor told me he was impressed. The fellow seemed to know what he was talking about, and even asked a few intelligent questions!"

"He'll never get far at that rate," observed Maurer. "They don't like you to think in the army. They also don't have a high opinion of magicians, even their own. How were you intending to use levitation ships in your writing?" he asked.

Dominic thought furiously, casting about for a suitably fantastic plot. "Oh, I thought perhaps a competition to reach the Northern Pole. It would be easier to reach if you could rise in the air, closer to the sun and therefore warmer."

Jochim cleared his throat. "In fact the upper air is colder than that at the surface. It is thought it is because the air is thinner, also."

"Well then, thick coats. It would still be easier than going on the surface, dealing with ice and snow."

"We would have to improve our design quite a bit to make it work," confessed Dieter. "The most ours could have carried was one man, and he couldn't have been very heavy, either. Not to mention the range was less than a hundred leagues."

Dominic sighed. "You see? This is the information that I need. It will take more work to make it believable. I wish I could have seen it."

"You can see what's left of it, if you like," shrugged Dieter. "There isn't much, but we do have some drawings and a scale model."

"That would do admirably."

They made their way back out into the street and towards the university quarter. "When does your next story appear? Will you be writing about levitation ships then?" Maurer wanted to know.

"That will have to wait until I return to Bretagne, I think," smiled Dominic.

"Are you making a long visit to Baerlen?"

"I hardly know. I am here on business that has no certain end at present." Dominic suppressed a shiver.

"Well, if you are still here tomorrow evening, perhaps you would come to a small party at my chambers. A friend is becoming a barbarian —"

"That means graduation," added Stefan, seeing Dominic's startled look.

"—and he would be honored to have a real author as a guest. He also has aspirations in that direction."

It was Dominic's first inclination to refuse outright, but then he recalled how Ardhuin's time would very likely be taken up. Anything would be better than staring at the walls in the palace workroom, wondering what she was doing. Maurer seemed pleased by his acceptance, and gave him the directions to his chambers. He, Stefan, and Jochim said their goodbyes and left for their afternoon lecture, while Jens-Peter accompanied Dominic and Dieter to the late professor's workrooms.

"Don't you have classes as well?" asked Dominic.

"I'm on my *Praktikum,*" said Dieter. "I finished classes last year."

"I have a class, but it will have to live without me." Jens-Peter grinned unapologetically. "This is much more interesting than railroad bridges, with or without buttresses."

"You think anything is more interesting than lectures. It's a wonder they haven't asked you to demonstrate the use of the front gate one last time," Dieter said, shaking his head.

They had by now reached a series of outbuildings in the more utilitarian quarter of the university, and Dieter led the way to a long shed attached to what seemed to be an old carriage house. With a bit of effort he unlocked the door with the unaccustomed hand and motioned Dominic inside.

"I've started tidying up, but it still is a mess," he said. Indeed, several of the equipment cabinets had glass-fronted doors that were shattered or were missing entirely, and on tables and counters were dented and damaged objects. "Here are the design drawings, and...oh, there it is. This is the model."

The model looked so fragile Dominic felt it would crumple in his hand from its own weight, such as it was. Made of splinters of wood, scraps of cloth, and a few lopsided but artistic swirls in ink, it looked like the standing, bleached skeleton of a four-legged spider. "This is a levitation ship?" he asked incredulously.

"It's just a prototype, see? To show that it works. This was Professor Siebert's clever idea, having four separate levitation sources, each on the end of one arm. To control the height, the operator would move this lever here and the arms would move down and in, concentrating the field. Of course, the field had to be precisely aligned and the arms move smoothly, or the whole thing would tip."

"What is the fan for?" asked Dominic, pointing to the back of the model spider.

Dieter was shocked. "That's not a fan, that's the aerial propeller. That's what makes it move once it is off the ground. The engine is under the seat."

This puzzled Dominic until he looked at the drawings, which had in one corner an illustration of the levitation ship with a pilot. "Wouldn't it have been better to put the seat somewhere else? In front of the engine, perhaps?"

Dieter shook his head. "It was most crucial to keep the mechanical engine as far from the levitation field as possible, and the field had to be symmetric about the pilot, which was hard enough to accomplish. We had some of the largest levitators ever made."

"Was that what limited the amount of weight?"

"Yes. The material would simply break apart under the force of the field if we made them any larger."

Dominic considered further. "Could you use chryselectrum to shield the engine?"

Dieter looked at him strangely. "Too close to the engine, and the heat would shatter it; too close to the levitators, and the field would force any shield away," he said after a while.

"I see." Dominic looked at the model again and sighed. "It must have been impressive. Will you attempt to fix it?"

"There is nothing left to fix," said Dieter sadly. "Come and see."

The next room was larger, with less furniture, and a total shambles. Twisted, blackened wreckage lay strewn about, and it took Dominic some time to mentally piece together the remains to identify their original shape. "Dear God," he whispered. There was one lump larger than the rest, looking a little like a loaf that had been split lengthwise and spread apart. "The engine...that must have been where it exploded." It was strangely hard to look closely at it, as if it were akin to a corpse, but a sense of duty compelled him. What he saw made him glance suddenly at Dieter, startled. "I thought you said there weren't any magical devices near the engine."

"There aren't. There can't have been."

"By the end of the shaft." Dominic pointed. "That's a stasis field—small, but powerful. You could hold twenty kilos with that."

A silence fell over the room, and Dominic turned to find Jens-Peter and Dieter staring at him. "I thought you said you weren't a magician," said Jens-Peter.

"I'm not," said Dominic shortly. "I can see thaumurgic fields, that's all."

"That's all!" Dieter laughed incredulously. "What I wouldn't give… but how do you know the difference between a stasis and a levitation field? And chryselectrum? It's not precisely common knowledge, even among magic students."

"I've worked with a mage, a time or two."

"You have." Dieter stood looking at him thoughtfully for a minute. "Look, there is simply no possible way for a stasis field to be anywhere in the structure. We didn't use one! And any fragments of the levitators would be up there," he said, pointing to the high ceiling where a few clumps of what looked like stone were drifting like dust motes.

"I know what I saw," insisted Dominic.

Dieter left the room, returning after a moment with a long wooden wand. He placed a sealed glass tube filled with a pale blue liquid into a fitting at the end. "We even had the stasis detector head, for a miracle. Now we'll see." He slowly began to move the tip of the wand around the remains of the engine. "There, you see? Noth—"

The tip, nearing the area Dominic had indicated, began to glow. Carefully and slowly, as if he feared to set off another explosion, Dieter placed the wand on the floor and picked up something caught in the engine casing. He stared at it for a moment, his expression stunned, then held it out to Dominic.

"The light from the wand caught it," he said.

It was a half-melted shard of chryselectrum.

The wards muffled sound, so all Ardhuin heard at first were indistinct voices outside, and she pushed them to the back of her mind. She'd returned to the workroom after the first meeting, the information she'd been given making her feel numb with dread. She'd hoped to find Dominic there, but he was still out. They'd given her some items they'd found, to examine, but she couldn't concentrate. Papers in Preusan that she couldn't read, even a scrap with Yunwiyan characters on it. Did Markus know about it? Would it get him in trouble if she told the Council what it was?

The King had been right to invoke the compact. Someone was trying to plunge Aerope into war. Again. And the Council expected her to stop it.

Something—the tone, the rhythm of the words—made her certain one of the voices outside was Dominic's, and she ran and snatched the door open.

Markus Asgaya, seated in a chair outside the workroom, was arguing with Dominic.

"We can't simply let her go everywhere to see things for herself, especially if what you say is true," Markus said patiently.

Dominic was furious. His deep-set eyes snapped in anger, and he had run his hands through his black, springy hair so many times he looked deranged. "It is true, and if you won't let her go, send someone else!"

"What's wrong?"

Both men looked up at her.

"Siebert was assassinated," Dominic snapped, glaring at Markus. "His assistant and I found a sabotage device in the machine that exploded. A strong field encased in a shell of chryselectrum, placed near the mechanical engine. When the engine heated up, the shell cracked and the field was exposed to the moving parts."

She felt herself sag, as if her legs had lost strength to support her, and she clutched at the door. "We'll need to prove it," she said finally.

"The field is still quite strong, and we found a piece of the chryselectrum. Any magician should be convinced. And the assistant swears they used neither stasis field nor chryselectrum in the construction. It has to be sabotage."

"This assistant…what did you tell him? Does anyone else know of this?" asked Markus.

"One other was there when we discovered this, but I think both can be trusted. I left them to watch the evidence, just in case."

Markus narrowed his eyes, frowning. "I should notify the Council." He went and spoke to one of the guards, who left immediately. Ardhuin went back inside the workroom. Dominic followed her, and she noticed the expression of pain in his eyes.

"I'm sorry I ever persuaded you to come here," he said, his voice tight. "They can't possibly expect you to do this on your own, especially when they won't even let you leave the Imperial Palace."

She put her hand on his arm. "It's too late, Dominic. Whoever did it will try to find me wherever I go. Better to face them here, where I have the resources of the Preusan Empire at my disposal. Besides—" she hesitated. They might be angry that had she told him, but what could they do about it? They needed her help too badly. "Things are worse than I thought. Aerope has been on the brink of war more than once in recent years, largely due to the huge military buildup of the Preusans under the previous King. This King has been doing his utmost to reduce the threat, but he has been hampered by the intransigence of the senior military officials who would like nothing better than a war. And it looks like someone has been trying to provoke one. They almost succeeded, too."

"I hope this isn't your idea of cheering me up," said Dominic, looking grim. "Is this what they've been telling you in all those meetings?"

"Among other things."

Markus' muffled voice made itself heard through the door, saying something about the Council.

They left the workroom and found Markus waiting for them in the hall. "They want to talk to you," he said, looking at Ardhuin with amusement.

"He needs to come with us," Ardhuin said, indicating Dominic. "He is the one who saw what happened." Markus shrugged and led the way.

Predictably, there was argument when they arrived at the Council chamber entrance. One minor official bristled at Markus, who reacted by looking bored and detached.

"How could you permit this…this irregularity!" he said, outraged and glaring at Dominic, the source of the problem. "He is not permitted. The instructions could not have been more clear, and—"

"I am responsible only for the Mage Guardian's personal safety. His Majesty's instructions were explicit. I do not presume to make policy decisions, or dictate her actions," Markus interrupted, a slight edge to his voice.

The official was turning a strange shade of red and stuttering incoherently with rage when Markus finally said, "Wait here," and entered the Council chambers. Ardhuin heard nothing for a while, then a series of raised voices, followed by a short silence. The door opened, and Markus glanced out and motioned them in.

She recognized many of the faces from the first encounter, the night they had arrived in Baerlen. The King, looking even more haggard and tired than before, did not look up as they approached, but stared at a pen he held in his hand. At the Council's request, Dominic recounted everything he had learned that day, concluding with the discovery of the sabotage to the flying machine.

"I beg your pardon, perhaps I was not attending…how was it that you knew to test the device?" asked an old, white-haired gentleman whose gentle demeanor was belied by a keen gaze.

"I am…I have the ability to see thaumurgic fields," said Dominic. Ardhuin couldn't help smiling. He sounded almost apologetic.

This created a stir in the Council. "How—"

"Oh, don't be so backward, von Gering. It isn't a common ability, certainly, but not unheard-of."

"I am aware," von Gering answered in a glacial tone. "Perhaps my colleague would be so kind as to tell me why he is certain this man has the ability in question. I myself doubt that someone with that talent would be attached to an unrecognized female magician."

Ardhuin felt a stab of anger at the undisguised contempt in the man's voice and his casual dismissal of Dominic's talent. Before she could defend him, one of the younger soldiers asked, "Well, why can't we have him give a demonstration? The defensive magician can—"

"Not in the presence of the King; you know that. Not even illusion is permitted." Ah. That explained the reaction to her *gloire*. Of course, no one had seen fit to mention this error of protocol afterward. She wondered why. Had the King intervened, or were Mage Guardians exempt?

"But…there is an illusion on the King," blurted Dominic. Ardhuin stared at him, startled. The room went completely silent, and the tension was almost palpable.

"Ah…what was that again?" asked the white-haired councilor.

The King held up a hand. "What do you see? Where?" He locked gazes with Dominic.

Self-consciously, Dominic traced a line along his own angular cheek down to the jaw. "All I see is…illusion. Very complex, and not a large area…" his voice trailed off.

After a brief period of stunned silence, the Council erupted into argument.

"He should never have been allowed to—"

"We cannot permit this to continue. Security is—"

The King's voice rose over the Council, speaking with finality. "That is proof enough for me. Someone is to go immediately to the university. Ask permission of the Provost as required, but secure that workshop. Find out who is responsible with all possible speed."

An officer standing against the wall saluted and left. One of the councilors said, soberly, "It would be wise to look into the others as well. The other Mage Guardians who are dead or missing."

The argument went on for some time before one of the more realistic councilors noticed the Mage Guardian herself would not be needed until they decided the next step. Another chimed in with a suggestion for additional protection for the Mage Guardian. Ardhuin raised her head at this.

"There is also the matter of protection for my assistant," she interrupted, startling herself with her own bluntness. That seemed to be the only way to get anything done around here, and while it still made her uncomfortable, it was getting easier to do. Practice really was the key. "You have seen how useful he is. Any threat directed at me will also threaten him. I want him guarded as well."

"I agree," said the King, cutting off another incipient debate. "They show a remarkable degree of ruthlessness and cunning, whoever they are." He looked at Dominic and smiled without humor. "This illusion conceals evidence of an assassination attempt."

Back at the palace wing, Dominic watched Markus unpack a small valise and arrange a cot at the foot of his bed. Although he was surprised and pleased Ardhuin had made such a point of it, he wished the defensive magician assigned to his protection had been someone else. He wasn't sure what the problem was. Markus was pleasant and courteous, and Dominic suspected he also had a low opinion of the Council's intelligence. That should have made them instant friends.

Perhaps it was the way he always moved with a supple, catlike grace, or the expression of faint amusement that was never far from his eyes. Or, he confessed, Ardhuin's instant acceptance of Markus. It had taken weeks before she had voluntarily even talked to him, back in Peran.

She was changing. They both were. Ardhuin was changing the most, and he smiled to himself, recalling how fiercely she had argued for his protection. She wasn't wearing the shadow hat, either. It would look strange indoors, but that wouldn't have stopped her before. Perhaps there was hope.

Having settled himself and ascertained Dominic was going to retire, Markus set up the defensive wards.

"Why did you do it like that?" asked Dominic, when Markus had finished.

Markus flashed him a glance. "What do you mean?"

Dominic gestured. "You did it in sections, not all at once."

"Is that how Fraülein Andrews does it? In one action?" Dominic nodded, and Markus raised both eyebrows in astonishment. "She must have formidable control."

Markus sat on his cot, seeming quite comfortable and relaxed, more so now that the wards were set. He regarded Dominic with frank curiosity. "How long have you been working for her?"

"Less than a year."

"What made you choose that position rather than one with some… more well-established magician?"

Dominic knew what he was trying to say, and despite himself he found himself admiring the diplomatic phrasing of the question. For some reason it was even more annoying that Markus was likeable and intelligent. "She was the one who discovered my ability, and trained me in how to use it."

The defensive magician leaned forward, looking at him even more intently. "Now, how did that come about? From something Fraülein von Kitren said, I had the impression the Lady Magus is not fond of company."

Dominic began to feel uncomfortable, wondering where this line of inquiry was headed and why. He was beginning to suspect Markus had a more than casual interest in Ardhuin. He knew he did not have the conversational adroitness Markus exhibited, and it would be entirely too easy to let fall information of a compromising nature.

"She travels on rare occasions. She visited Dinan when I was a student there." He decided that going to sleep would be an effective way to cut off further questions, and made his own preparations.

Markus stretched out on the cot, hands behind his head, and regarded the ceiling. "Thaumatic scryer…and a superb one, too. You could practically name your price, work wherever you wished, with the most influential and well-connected magicians in Aerope. Magical talent can overcome any number of obstacles, as I can attest." He flashed a grin, and Dominic realized Markus knew very well how much he stood out in Preusa, and that was what amused him.

"I have no intention of leaving her," said Dominic, realizing as he did so it sounded more forceful than he intended.

Markus looked at him thoughtfully and asked no more questions.

CHAPTER 8

Markus was gone when Dominic woke the next morning, and the wards had disappeared as well. He could hear voices and footsteps in the hallway, so presumably his guard was somewhere about. Dominic dressed in haste and rushed out of his room, barely avoiding an official-looking person who was running down the hall. The man held a sheaf of papers and a dispatch case. Looking about, Dominic noticed a number of regular soldiers who hadn't been there the previous night.

It appeared something had been decided, but the precise nature of the decision remained unclear. A black-clad defensive magician followed him when he headed for Ardhuin's workroom. Unlike Markus, this man was silent and stolid, but still conscientious about his work. Even here, inside the Imperial Palace, his eyes constantly shifted about, looking for signs of magical attack. He was not, however, a great conversationalist. Despite repeated attempts, all Dominic's questions elicited only "Yes, sir," "No, sir," and "I couldn't say, sir," which seemed to be his entire repertoire.

When he found her, Ardhuin was not in the workroom, but in an antechamber nearby. She wore a plain, dark blue dress and was looking out one of the windows at the park below, two defensive magicians on either side. One looked bewildered that he was guarding her but determined to do it, and the other appeared to be debating whether or not to forcibly move her away from such an exposed location.

"We're not to even leave the wing," said Ardhuin when Dominic came up and joined her. "Nobody seems to know anything except for the decision to add more guards."

Dominic grimaced. "This could be a slow morning."

She gave a perfunctory smile, still looking out the window. Her long fingers tapped restlessly at the windowpane for a moment, then she turned to him. "Come with me to the workroom."

Their respective escorts were not pleased at having to wait outside. Dominic felt a twinge of satisfaction, knowing they were excluded and he was not.

Somehow, Ardhuin had found the time to unpack and arrange her equipment. The room showed little sign of its earlier disorder. She went to a secretary cabinet and opened one of the drawers, taking out a small, dark green box.

"This is for you," she said without preamble, thrusting it at him. Her long, intent face showed nothing—he couldn't read her face, or tell what she was thinking. She watched him warily as he took it from her.

Thin, graceful gold letters on the box formed the words "de Cusac, Parys." Inside was a gold stickpin. The top was an emerald rosebud, delicately held in place by small gold leaves. It took him a moment to find his voice, suddenly overcome by emotion. So that was the secret errand that had taken her out, alone.

"You had this set when we were in Parys," Dominic said finally, incredulous. There was a faint sheen of magic to the stickpin, and he turned it in his fingers, admiring it.

She nodded. Her face was flushed. "It isn't just...it has another use. I've tuned the natural magical signature of the rose just enough that I could search for it. I...I'd like you to keep it with you. It doesn't have to be visible to work, just away from iron," she said earnestly. "I keep telling them you are in danger too, but they don't listen to me, and they won't let me do anything! But just in case something *does* happen...I want to be able to find you." Her voice trailed off, her face creased with worry.

The only other piece of jewelry Dominic still owned was his father's pocket watch, whose greatest value was sentimental. He had never thought he would own something as beautiful and rare as this, and Ardhuin seemed worried he would refuse it.

"The style of dress here is in general beyond my touch," he said lightly, trying to insert the pin by feel and by dint of tucking in his chin. "Now I shall look a little more the thing. I don't suppose there is a mirror anywhere?"

The beginnings of a smile on Ardhuin's face vanished. "I don't like mirrors." Then she turned bright red and mumbled, "I am sorry. You should not be inconvenienced by my habits."

She held up her hands, thumbs and forefingers touching each other. The magic flared sharp and bright—painfully so. Through watering eyes, Dominic saw a smooth, silvery surface framed by her fingers.

"Does that work well enough?" Ardhuin asked, glancing at him.

"Oh yes, perfectly," Dominic lied. With the glare of the magic he could barely see anything more than a blur. "What spell is that?" Some instinct made him look away when he saw the magic begin to flow back toward her hands.

Ardhuin looked guilty. "It's, um...the encasement field for a fire shell." His shock must have shown, for she hurried on, "I remembered thinking how shiny it was when I did them before, and—"

"When did you cast fire shells?" That was war magic even he knew about. He had a sudden flash of recollection of Professor Botrel in his office in Dinan, recounting the destruction of Fougéres.

"My great-uncle insisted I learn," Ardhuin whispered. "He said—he said I might need to use it someday, and theoretical knowledge was not enough."

She sat down on one of the remaining couches and drew her feet up underneath her, clasping her knees with her arms. She looked miserable.

Well, why was he so shocked? She had told him she had been taught by one of the top mages of the War, trained to prevent a recurrence of that war. Of course she would need to know such things.

"I am glad he did. It would appear he was quite correct," Dominic said, and smiled to see her relieved expression. "I only wish I could be of more assistance in defending you myself."

Ardhuin sighed. "You have helped me simply by being here. If I were by myself, I think I would go mad."

Hearing the shaky tone in her voice, Dominic set himself to distracting her. "I wouldn't, if I were you. Preusan medicine is woefully primitive when it comes to the treatment of mental imbalance. A great deal of cold water and simple food, interspersed with voltaic shocks."

She shook her head, adding a few more fiery strands of hair to the tendrils that had already escaped. "No, that does not sound appealing."

Dominic sat down on the couch beside her. She remained in her unconventional pose, and he remembered now that she would do so at Peran if she felt either particularly at ease or distressed. Her choice of attire, too, was a signal of her mood. Were they at home and she were wearing the same dull, plain dress, he would say she was extremely annoyed.

"I have no means of improving my wardrobe, but I know you have dresses that would suit the court," he commented. "Why don't you wear them?"

Ardhuin widened her eyes. "I don't want to be noticed—I was hoping I would look somewhat older in this." She flicked at a fold of the dark blue dress. "Besides the obvious objections to my being female, I am considered far too young for the responsibility of being a Mage Guardian. They say I can't possibly know mage-level spells at my age, so how could I have mastered the magics only Mage Guardians are permitted to know? No doubt that is causing at least half of the frenzied discussions taking place. The compact is quite explicit on the subject of heirs, and with everyone else dead or missing, they have little choice." She frowned. "Perhaps I should have illusioned myself to look older? Or put some powder in my hair, as they did in olden days."

"It wouldn't have worked," Dominic said, grinning. "They would have found the illusion eventually, and powder would not make you look older. If you had mirrors about, you would know this. I don't understand why you dislike them," he added. "All the beautiful ladies I've met were incapable of staying away from a mirror for more than five minutes."

Ardhuin laughed, then choked, staring at him. She said nothing, remaining silent for so long he finally had to ask if something was wrong. She gave a curious half-smile, a little wistful, and said, "Until I find a mirror that sees what you see, I will retain my aversion to them."

The day dragged on, and still no word from the Council on any decision. Ardhuin was conscious of a terrible restlessness that only aggravated the tension of waiting. Since nobody would tell her anything, she stayed in her workroom the entire time, demonstrating various war magics for Dominic's edification.

She could not understand the man, could never predict his reactions. Somehow she had taken to thinking of him as being like her great-uncle, or as another magician. Then something would occur, such as her mention of fire shells, and his response would startle her. It forced her to remember that most of what he knew of magic she had taught him—and it might not be enough for what they faced.

So she had suggested the demonstration, partly to address his lack of knowledge and partly, she had to admit, to introduce a less uncomfortable topic of conversation. Sometimes she thought it would be better to avoid Dominic Kermarec and his peculiar preference for her company—but when she did, it made her even more irritable.

"Dieter used a kind of detector to find the stasis field," Dominic commented as she got ready. "Can't they do something like that for these spells, too?"

Ardhuin concentrated on building the sticky magic-threads that formed the spell, then answered. "First, detectors like that are very crude and only exist for a small number of very common spells. Second, war magic like this is usually extremely powerful and…unstable. Introducing more magic to find it could set it off. Like this," she said, and snapped the magic free from its constraints.

"I hope that wasn't valuable," Dominic said, watching as a coy porcelain shepherdess disintegrated into a fine dust on the inlaid table where it had stood.

Ardhuin scowled. "The King specifically told me I could do as I pleased with these rooms. I am quite certain he would prefer I demonstrate the Crystalline Polythrenode attack on a small ornament than the walls of the Imperial Palace."

Dominic grinned and gestured acknowledgment. "Put that way, it makes perfect sense. But why the figurine and not…oh, a wineglass?" He indicated the remains of their luncheon, brought to them when requested.

"It doesn't work on glass, for some reason. No one really knows why. It has best effect on stone, but brick and porcelain also are—"

Pock. Pock. Pock.

The comforting background vibration of the wards was disturbed sharply. A glance at Dominic's startled face told her he had sensed it too, in his own way.

He pointed. "The door. It didn't look very strong, though."

Ardhuin gathered hard, dense power before her as a shield, and opened the door. Outside were two defensive magicians—one who had been with her earlier in the morning, and Markus Asgaya. Markus had an amused gleam in his eye as he turned to the other defensive magician, who sighed and gave him a gold coin, saying something resigned in Preusan before leaving.

Markus bowed. Ardhuin felt a thick-headed cloud of confusion for a moment, seeing him, so clearly Yunwiyan yet also Aeropan, and her mind tried to see long black hair with clan insignia instead of a Preusan military crop. It disoriented her, but only temporarily. Markus was by far the most friendly of the Preusans she had met.

"Good afternoon, Lady Magus. I merely wished to inform you that I had come on duty." He smiled.

Lady Magus? Somehow she doubted that was the official term.

"What were you doing?" Dominic asked with a disapproving expression. "That was you disturbing the wards, wasn't it?"

Markus nodded and grinned. "A small matter of a wager only. My comrade did not believe I could get your attention from outside the wards. Just a few light probes," he added.

"You deliberately attacked the wards?" Ardhuin asked, anger building and overwhelming her initial shock. "What if I had set a response?"

"And what if you had distracted her?" asked Dominic, folding his arms. "She was casting dangerous spells in there." Markus raised a questioning eyebrow, and Dominic added, "Crystalline Polythrenode."

Markus paled. "My profound apologies. It did not occur to me—"

"That I would know the spell?" Fury replaced her anger.

"That you would have any cause to cast it here," the defensive magician said, holding up his hands. "Perhaps there was a wall you wished removed?"

"Just a figurine," Dominic murmured, the corner of his lip twitching.

Ardhuin scowled at him. "I thought it wise that Monsieur Kermarec be able to recognize any war magics we might encounter," she told Markus. "I was merely demonstrating them."

"Ah." Markus Asgaya rubbed his chin thoughtfully. "You raise an important point," he said, nodding to Dominic. "How are we to contact you inside the wards? They are…formidably powerful. We tried calling to you for five minutes before I made my attempt."

The wards did deaden sound, especially further away from the door, which was the only real contact point.

"I'll think of something. Do you have any news from the Council?" Ardhuin asked hopefully. If only they could *do* something. It was maddening to be kept in the dark as they were.

Markus shook his head. "Nothing yet. I will be here or in one of the antechambers, if you should need me." He smiled again and left.

Ardhuin followed Dominic back inside and closed the door, looking at it thoughtfully.

"We need more information," she said. "I have the feeling he might tell us something."

"Perhaps." Dominic did not look convinced. "I suspect they have been ordered to remain silent. My guard this morning barely spoke to me."

Now that was remarkable. Dominic could get anyone to talk to him, even her.

"We could persuade him, I think, if the others couldn't hear," Ardhuin began.

Dominic interrupted, looking shocked and angry. "You aren't thinking of letting him in *here*, are you?"

Ardhuin blinked. "No, of course not. I'd have to completely redo the wards." Sometimes Dominic made absolutely no sense. "I have something that will disguise what we are saying. Would you find him and tell him we want to speak with him? I will join you shortly."

Dominic sighed, then nodded and left the workroom. Ardhuin rummaged through the equipment she had brought with her until she found what she was looking for—a small, leather-covered box with a handle that looked like an ordinary travel case. Until now she had not understood why the obscurer had been given such a bland container, especially given the maker's predilection for ornate ornamentation. Now, however, she knew. If the obscurer was being used, it could not draw attention to itself.

Then the small scrap of what appeared to be paper that she had been given earlier by the defensive magicians. The writing was familiar, and she wanted to question Markus about it.

She left the workroom carrying the box. Dominic and Markus Asgaya sat at a table in an alcove off the main hallway. It was a good location. The other defensive magicians would be able to see them and would not be suspicious.

Markus was relaxed and at ease, and stood courteously when she arrived. Dominic radiated a stiff prickliness that made her wonder if Markus had said something to offend him—or did Dominic object to Markus, to his Yunwiyan parentage? It seemed very unlike him.

Ardhuin sat down and opened the case. "This will make our conversation private," she said as she took out the ivory pedestal, decorated by a twining gold vine. The pendular came next— gold on one end, clouded crystal on the other, and a long, narrow pin that rested on a cupped crystal at the top of the ivory pedestal. She set it in motion, watching it sway and spin in a way that always seemed like it was going to fall, but never did.

"What is that?" Markus asked, fascinated. "I've never seen anything like it."

Ardhuin shrugged uncomfortably. "Schuyler Colfax made them for all the Mage Guardians. It was my great-uncle's."

"And what does it do?"

"Within a ten-foot radius, we cannot be overheard. Magic is blocked, and anyone listening by ordinary means would hear only murmured voices, with no words being distinguishable."

Markus leaned back and crossed his long legs. "One might wonder what the Lady Magus would wish to discuss with me that the others could not hear." He looked at her blandly.

How many times had she made the resolution to learn to tell convincing lies? Markus Asgaya was a magician at a major Aeropan court. Of course he would be suspicious.

Perhaps she should just abandon any pretense and tell the truth. It usually surprised people so much they did the same.

"They won't tell me anything, and they won't let me leave, either. If I'm supposed to uphold the compact all by myself, I need information."

Markus drew back a little at her vehemence and did not look so relaxed any more. Ardhuin was somewhat surprised that her face didn't feel at all hot and flushed. Usually arguing with people made her red as a beet.

"What do you want to know?" Markus said, raising his hands. "There's quite a bit going on here, most of which is secret or confidential to some degree. I sympathize with your predicament, truly, but I am not in the Council's confidence."

Dominic shifted. "The assassination attempt. When did it happen? Why is such an effort being made to cover it up? We already know it happened, so you may as well tell us the rest."

Markus glanced at Dominic and then at her, the lurking smile flitting over his face as if to appeal for mercy, but Ardhuin did not relent. He released a deep breath, then, and ran his hand over his chin.

"At first, because it was damn near successful. Then we started finding out more about it, and nothing made sense. The attempt took place when the King was riding in the park. At the very instant the shot was fired, the King inclined his head to better hear what someone was saying, so the bullet missed its mark and instead grazed his cheek, as you saw." He nodded to Dominic. "After assuring his Majesty's safety, the guard immediately sealed off and searched the park—and found a known anarchist hiding in the shrubbery with a pistol that had recently been fired."

He stopped and seemed to be at a loss how to proceed. "That sounds rather straightforward," said Ardhuin. "Where was the difficulty?"

"It simply didn't add up," he said, striking the edge of one hand into the palm of the other to emphasize each word. "The pistol was a very cheap, poor quality weapon. It could not have been fired with any degree of accuracy, when you take into account the distance between the King and the nearest available hiding place. Some said perhaps he had just gotten lucky." Markus grinned. "Then, *we* got lucky—after a lot of work.

We searched the entire area, crawling over every centimeter of ground. Someone found the bullet that had hit the King. We knew it was the right one when we did the spell to test for wounding, but the pyrometric spells said it had been fired five hours before. The bullet had suffered very little damage, and it was easy to tell it was the wrong type for that gun."

Dominic leaned forward. He was curious now, and seemed to have forgotten his earlier unfriendliness. "How could you tell?"

"It had a metal casing. The anarchist's gun was cheap, as I said. A favorite weapon of the criminal class, and it is intended also for cheap ammunition, which uses cardboard or wax paper for casing instead of metal. The bullet that struck the King could not have been fired from that gun."

"Another gun, then."

Markus frowned. "Clearly there must have been one, but we found no trace of it there, and the anarchist was captured immediately. No one else in the park was even in range. And there is one thing more. When we did the wounding spell, we noticed some interference, and we cut the bullet open. We found grains of lodestone mixed in the lead."

Ardhuin drew a sharp breath. "That would only be useful in a magical field—it would not affect the firing of the weapon."

"Precisely." He sighed and ran his fingers along the edge of the table. "After a lot of work, we think we know what happened. Another gun was indeed fired earlier, by someone else, and into a specially prepared stasis field. The bullet was released from stasis when the King went by."

Ardhuin regarded him thoughtfully for a while. "You still aren't telling us everything. That would not have been enough. The bullet had to be aimed at one particular target, and he could have been anywhere on the path. They could not have known in advance. I think the release of the field, and the aim of the bullet, were linked to something on the King's person. Something planted there." Markus' eyes narrowed, but he remained silent. "And the number of people who would have the necessary access is…not large. Probably politically sensitive, as well."

Markus still had said nothing, but he didn't need to. Confirmation of what she had said was written on his face.

"What of your anarchist?" asked Dominic. "Did he have something to do with it, or was he just unfortunate?"

"He did, and he didn't," responded Markus, a puzzled and unquiet look in his eyes. "He had some magical ability, but it was barely enough to give him work as a lamplighter—and he wasn't very good at that. He was even worse after a philogiston explosion at the lampworks that employed him. He recovered to some extent, but the accident seemed to have addled his wits and he couldn't light lamps any more. Even before the accident he would not have been able to set up a highly complex stasis field. And when we tried to question him," he continued slowly, "we could get nothing. Not even lies. He simply could not speak. After finding the lodestone we did some investigation and discovered he has a *geas* on him."

The word hit her like a blow. First she wondered, in horror, who would be casting *geasi*. Then she remembered *she* had. On Dominic.

"What is a *geas*?" he asked, and she flinched.

"A magical compulsion," Markus answered.

"It is forbidden," she managed to say.

"Yes, to all but a few extremely high-placed and trusted mages. The Mage Guardians, for example," Markus said, bowing slightly in her direction. "It is even forbidden to teach it without permission."

So her great-uncle had broken the law to teach her, but Oron was beyond their reach now. A Mage Guardian was allowed to cast a *geas*, but was she a real Mage Guardian? Would they even consider her a magician? Even if what she had done wasn't illegal, would Dominic understand?

Talk of something else. Anything.

"Does anyone know what has become of the Gaulan mages who were not executed? Have they been kept track of?"

"Do you think they would have done it?" Markus looked horrified. "They had *geasi* on *them,* specifically to prevent this sort of thing from happening. Besides, most of them must be in their eighties, if they are even still alive."

"It was the older, senior mages who were executed at the end of the war. The younger ones had not committed the same crimes, but that doesn't mean they didn't have the knowledge."

"I still don't understand why you called on the compact," said Dominic. "Of course now you know someone has apparently been killing the Mage Guardians, but you didn't know that at the time. Assassination is a serious thing, but you seem to be dealing with it well enough. How is it on the same level of the Mage War?"

Markus looked grim again, but he said nothing.

"They hinted at something more in the meetings I attended," said Ardhuin. "He is right. If you have invoked the compact, I have a right to know the threat."

"They will have my head for this," he muttered, then made a sharp gesture of resignation. "It isn't just the assassination attempt. If we had not been obscenely lucky, we would be at war now."

"With Ostri?" asked Dominic, and Ardhuin remembered the newspaper accounts.

"Yes." Markus sighed and gave a sardonic smile. "Our interminable bureaucracy saved us. One incompetent clerk was all that was needed. A message was put in the wrong box in the central mail facility, and the person who received it in error was an unimaginative, stuffy martinet who wanted to make an example of the unfortunate mail clerk. So instead of sending it on to the intended recipient, he raised a hue and cry and had it delivered to the purported sender, along with a masterpiece of pompous self-righteous verbiage in his own hand."

"Something tells me you don't have a high opinion of this fellow," observed Dominic.

Markus grinned. "An opinion shared by everyone who has to deal with him. Or so I have heard," he added hastily. "That's when things got interesting. If the original message had gone to the right place and the orders in it had been acted on, troops would have been mobilized and moved into a restricted area near the border. That may not sound like a matter of much importance, but it would have been a direct contravention of several important treaties—more than enough to start a war, especially when the Ostri government had been told in advance this movement would occur."

Dominic frowned. "I don't understand why the orders were given, then. Unless Preusa wanted to start a war."

"Of course we don't want a war! The orders were forged. Someone introduced those orders into the central mail facility—on the proper stationery, written in the proper language. It would not surprise me if the same person, or group, told the Ostri government. It was very well planned, and it would have been difficult to discover and stop if things had worked as intended."

Ardhuin glanced at the other defensive magicians still about. They were talking amongst themselves and paying no particular attention to the group at the table. It was probably safe to speak, and she should warn Markus that he was personally threatened by this plot.

"I knew a message had gone astray, but I had not realized how this was all connected. It is more important than ever, then, that I show you this," she said, drawing the odd piece of paper from her pocket. "You know they discovered the courier who had put the message in the box?" she asked Markus. He shook his head. "They searched his rooms and belongings and found a few unusual items that they handed to me. This is one of them." She offered the strange paper to Markus, who looked at it. His face froze in shock.

"But I don't…I can't even…."

Ardhuin nodded vigorously. "I know. They either didn't look at it closely, or didn't recognize the language." Seeing Dominic's puzzled expression, she added, "It is written in Yunwiyan. That would seem to indicate you were intended as a scapegoat. *I* know you didn't write it. You can't. I also know you would have no motive to conspire with Yunwiya against Preusa."

Dominic shifted uneasily. "I am not saying he would, but it might appear…that is, if he has not been accepted in Preusa, they might think he would be angry enough to want to do something for Yunwiya, maybe to gain prestige when he returned."

Ardhuin smiled sadly. "But he can't. Any more than you or I could. By Yunwiyan custom, he is considered full-blooded Preusan."

Dominic looked puzzled. "His father was Yunwiyan, correct?"

"They count only relations on the female side. To them, he has no blood connection."

Dominic considered this. "So…whoever planned this does not know much about Yunwiyan custom."

Markus snorted. "That does not eliminate many people from the list. I would be doubly unwelcome in Yunwiya as a magician," he added. "They regard Aeropan magic as unnatural, especially the magic of war."

Ardhuin regarded him. "You must have enemies here."

He spread his hands wide, still staring at the strange piece of paper lying on the table before him. It now had the look of polished wood. "Enemies…yes, but nothing on this scale! Only those who disliked my foreign blood, who wanted me to leave, but their dislike was open and easily dealt with."

"The paper is illusioned!" Dominic burst out. "It takes on the appearance of whatever it touches."

Ardhuin nodded. She looked at it more carefully. "Only on the one side, too. A very clever piece of work."

Dominic took it in turn, staring at it in fascination, then turned it over. "There is illusion here, too," he said, puzzled. "But where? It looks only like paper with writing."

"Let me see." She stared at it for a while, flattening it on the table. Making a circle of her hands, she let a very delicate haze of magic form, the antithesis of her usual illusion to cancel what was there. It caused the illusion on the paper to fade and disappear, and Aeropan letters replaced the Yunwiyan symbols. Holding her circled hands over the letter, she shifted so the others could view it. "Highly revealing, don't you agree?" Markus and Dominic peered over her shoulders. "What does it say?" she asked impatiently. "I can't hold the spell, decipher the writing *and* puzzle out the Preusan."

"It is addressed to 'L,' " said Markus promptly. "It says, 'We can still turn the park to our advantage. Give this letter to R to use against the mongrel—it will have its effect, and he will be further indebted to us. Remove this layer as a precaution, however.' The next paragraph…" Ardhuin shifted her hands. " 'Send as many new "friends" as you can discover. The first blow is approaching quickly, and if Oron's heir is not found, strength will be crucial. I will deal with any questions of sincerity in your candidates in my own fashion.' It is signed with a sigil I do not recognize," he added in a voice devoid of emotion.

Ardhuin slowly flattened her hands together, thinking hard and feeling very cold. The message mentioned Oron by name, and her by reference. "A sigil. One magician to another. What a great deal of confirmation. This must have been sent shortly after the assassination attempt."

Markus nodded slowly. "Which they wanted to have me blamed for."

"Any of your enemies match this?"

"Evidently, at least one…no, none that make sense. There is one on the Council, von Rügen, who would give a great deal to be rid of me."

"The initial matches," pointed out Dominic.

Markus shook his head. "He hates me, but he is a rabid monarchist who lost several members of his family in the Mage War. I find it very hard to credit he would conspire to assassinate the King or the Mage Guardians."

"A point." Ardhuin conceded.

"It could have been used against me without connection to the assassination attempt. Simply finding a hidden message like that could end my career. They would never be entirely sure of me." He looked at Ardhuin impassively. "I realize it will be necessary for you to disclose this information to the Council."

She looked at the letter, thinking furiously. It was information, and information was power. Right now she had little of either. She returned it to her pocket. "I am not certain that is the best course. Clearly, these plotters want you out of the way; this leads one to think you are not one of them. This letter, and other evidence, *does* lead one to think that these people are either highly placed in the military or government, or have contacts there. I see no advantage in advertising how much we have discovered."

"I should probably argue against it," said Markus softly, "but I lack the will. I swear to you on my honor I am guilty of no conspiracy, and I will do anything in my power to help you uncover this one."

Dominic did not look overly impressed. "Can you get us out of the Imperial Palace? We aren't going to uncover much in our current situation."

Markus steepled his fingers, eyes narrowing in thought. "We'd need a believable destination, one that would require the Mage Guardian's personal attention...." He suddenly sat up. "I suppose your training covered the removal of *geasi* as well as their creation?" he asked, tilting his head at Ardhuin.

"W-well, yes, of course, but—" She hoped her face did not reveal her trepidation. Where was this going, and how could she stop it?

"Excellent." Markus rubbed his hands together. "Let me see if I can persuade them to take you to our assassin-substitute." He got out of his seat. "They are so desperate for information it may overcome their reluctance to let you travel." He bowed and left.

"Do you dislike the idea?" Dominic asked after a short silence.

She should tell him. It was only about the roses. He would understand. Wouldn't he?

"I dislike the entire affair," Ardhuin snapped. How she wanted to just go home—except her unknown enemy would still attack her there. She had to continue. "My preferences are unimportant. We need to know more and this appears to be the only means by which we can obtain information."

"The man they caught, the anarchist. Will you be able to help him? It must be horrible to have that kind of spell on you. He will undoubtedly be grateful, and more willing to answer your questions."

She had to tell him. "He may not even be aware of the spell. They aren't…if the *geas* isn't forcing him to do something he dislikes, it is possible he doesn't even know it is there." Ardhuin swallowed, smoothing the fabric of her skirt with a shaking hand. "In fact—"

A stir of motion in the hallway caught her eye. A dark shape joined the other defensive magicians, but it wasn't Markus. He was accompanied by a tall man in civilian clothes. One of the defensive magicians pointed their direction, and the two newcomers headed their way.

The defensive magician was someone she had not seen before, but the other man Ardhuin recognized as being a Council member, von Mittern. He was the one who had first objected to her youth. She didn't like him or his profuse muttonchop whiskers.

She stopped the obscurer and placed the pieces back in their case, to forestall questions. Part of her was glad von Mittern had interrupted her confession, but another part was filled with dread. What did he want? He was smiling at her in what he probably thought was a fatherly way, an effort that lacked the necessary skill to be convincing.

"My dear Fraülein Andrews," he began, in heavily accented Gaulan. "Will you permit me to introduce *Schutzmagus* von Pelow?" He indicated the defensive magician standing beside him.

Ardhuin nodded, feeling awkward. Von Pelow was a handsome, fair-haired young man with pale grey eyes. He had a carefully neutral expression as he bowed to her, but she had seen the faint flicker of revulsion when he looked at her. Something about him seemed familiar, besides his reaction. Most people in the Imperial Palace were better at hiding their opinion of her appearance, or perhaps they had merely become accustomed.

She glanced at Dominic. He didn't seem to like von Pelow any more than von Pelow liked her.

"His Majesty has made clear your protection is of the highest importance. *Schutzmagus* von Pelow is one of our finest defensive magicians, and comes from a distinguished family that has long served the royal house. He would make a fine addition to your guard."

Ardhuin blinked, astonished. It would appear von Mittern had accepted that the King was not going to make her leave and was now trying to curry favor—or perhaps he wanted von Pelow, for whatever reason, to have the prestige of being one of the defensive magicians guarding her.

She sighed. Court politics made her head hurt.

"I believe there is no need for any additional assistance, and if there is, I am not the one who selects the…*Schutzmagus*," Ardhuin said, stumbling over the Preusan word.

Von Mittern waved away her objections. "A request from you would carry weight, I assure you, and he could replace a less able man. I understand Asgaya has been assigned," he said, his tone conveying that he did *not* understand why such a mistake had been made. "I don't see him here. I suppose he does not consider desertion of his post to be a serious matter, but what can you expect of such a one? Perhaps you don't understand, my dear, but to a soldier that is a grave offense."

Ardhuin found herself on her feet, hands clenched in fists. Von Mittern was tall, but she was gratified to find she could stare him directly in the eyes. "But I do understand. My brother is an officer in the Atlantean navy. I understand that making an unfounded accusation of that nature is a grave offense, as well." Von Mittern started to sputter, but she continued, aghast at her own boldness. "*Schutzmagus* Asgaya is running an errand at my request. I have no complaint of his performance of his duties, and no interest in replacing him with anyone." Her knees shook, and she dropped down on the sofa again to hide it.

Von Mittern was not giving up so easily. "You show a very unbecoming streak of independence, young woman. You should pay greater heed to the wisdom of your elders," he said with a disapproving look.

"Is there a problem?" Gutrune von Kitren's calm, quiet voice said unexpectedly.

Von Pelow turned his head sharply to look at her. Ardhuin drew a breath. Seeing them together, the resemblance was strong. Strangely, von Pelow looked angry—the first time he had allowed himself to openly show emotion.

Von Mittern didn't look very happy either.

"We were discussing some needed changes in Fraülein Andrews' guard," he said.

"Do you wish any changes?" Gutrune asked Ardhuin in a mildly interested tone.

"No, I do not," Ardhuin gritted.

"This is a matter of gravest importance to the security and defense of Preusa. We cannot risk having a foreigner in such a delicate position of trust," von Mittern growled, his face growing darker.

"Foreigner? Are you referring to the Mage Guardian?" Dominic asked blandly. Ardhuin choked back a laugh.

Gutrune interrupted von Mittern's convoluted apology and explanation. "If Fraülein Andrews has no complaint, there is no need to change the arrangements already made," she said.

Von Mittern gave her a fulminating glare, a barely adequate bow, and left, followed by von Pelow with a set jaw.

Ardhuin looked up at Gutrune and gave her a grateful smile. "Thank you. I don't know why he was so determined."

Gutrune joined her on the sofa. "*Schutzmagus* von Pelow is his protegé. Serving on your guard could bring him to the notice of the King."

That made sense. Von Pelow might not like her, but the position could bring the advancement he wanted.

"Is he related to you?" Ardhuin asked.

"My cousin," Gutrune replied. Her face became even more expressionless. "He is very ambitious."

"I am surprised Herr von Mittern did not argue with you," Dominic commented.

Gutrune permitted herself a small smile. "I serve the King directly," she said, indicating the small jeweled eagle pinned to one shoulder. "Herr von Mittern will not offend me if he can help it."

Another piece of the puzzle fell into place. No wonder her cousin seemed so resentful. Ardhuin sighed and wished once again for the uncomplicated life she had led at Peran. So many things to remember, so many people with conflicting schemes.

"Have they decided yet what they want me to do?" she asked.

Gutrune shook her head. "You must understand the news of the deliberate murders of the Mage Guardians came as a shock. It changes many plans that had already been made."

Down at the end of the hall, Markus Asgaya became visible, walking towards them with an energetic step. When he reached the alcove, he said, "Everything is arranged. They are most eager for your assistance. The Lady Magus is going to help with the prisoner," Markus explained, seeing Gutrune's questioning look.

Ardhuin felt her heart pound. She had forgotten about the purpose of his errand.

"I recommend that you use one of the side gates," Gutrune remarked, rising. "A mob has formed in the square."

Markus sighed. "What now?"

"They found another body outside the Closure," Gutrune said, nodding farewell.

CHAPTER 9

Dominic turned to ask Markus why "another body" would precipitate a mob at the Imperial Palace, but he had already left. Ardhuin went to the workroom with the magical listening shield. When she returned she would not sit down, but paced impatiently, refusing to be drawn into conversation.

His frustration had several layers, really. Ardhuin had been on edge since Parys, and the more people she had to deal with the worse it got. The strict, formal setting of the Preusan court was very different from Peran and the Bretagne countryside, not to mention more populated. She was even more impatient with him, and he'd thought things were improving in that regard. Now, however, she wouldn't even tell him what was wrong.

This wasn't the first time he'd seen her become stubbornly silent and evasive. Even regaining consciousness after the ley lines, confused and in pain, he could tell she was trying to hide something from him. Then, it had been the knowledge of his shameful actions. Had he done something else to embarrass her? Was she angry with him?

He glanced down at the emerald rosebud stickpin and smiled. No, she was not angry with him. It had to be something else. He wished she would trust him with it, whatever it was.

Their departure from the palace was hurried and confused. Markus rushed them, surrounded by defensive magicians and soldiers, down the stairs and out to a waiting carriage. Dominic was pleased when Markus did not join them in the carriage, but rode beside it.

As they left the grounds of the Imperial Palace he could not see the mob Gutrune von Kitren had mentioned, but he could hear it. People were shouting something he could barely make out—something about blood. He was glad they had taken a side gate.

The carriage swayed as they went around a corner, and Dominic remarked, "They seem to be in a hurry."

Ardhuin merely nodded and did not look at him. She wore the shadow hat, so he could not see her face.

Dominic sighed. There had to be *something* she was willing to talk about. "I did not tell you…I was invited to a gathering being held tonight by some of the students I spoke to, the ones I met at Siebert's lab. If there are disturbances in the street, however, it would probably be best not to go."

"I think we should," Ardhuin said. "This could be useful."

Surprised, Dominic blurted, "You want to go? I'm not sure—it might be awkward. Most student lodgings don't permit women visitors." Then he shook his head in annoyance at his own stupidity. She didn't have to look like a woman if she didn't want to, and what on earth was he doing discouraging her? "But with illusion, of course, it will not be a problem. Why do you want to attend this party?"

"The students won't know I'm not supposed to be told anything." Ardhuin hunched a shoulder. "Besides, I don't like it at the palace."

Ah. Maybe this was the problem. "What's wrong?"

Her gloved hands twisted together. "I think the only person who wants me here is the King. Everyone on the Council has some objection. I'm too young, I'm female, and how can I possibly be the Mage Guardian of Bretagne when I'm Atlantean? So of course they don't want to let me do anything. They just sit and talk."

"I don't think that's unique to your situation," Dominic remarked dryly. "Councils are famous for it."

"But they are *frightened,*" Ardhuin said softly, shaking her head in disbelief. "Very frightened. Why won't they let me help them?"

Their entourage reached the entrance of what at first looked like one of the numerous military barracks of Baerlen, but Dominic caught a glimpse of the sign that read *"Kaiserliche Kriegszauberkollegium"* on the gate. Imperial War Magic College. The building was impressive in an austere way, with vast sweeps of unornamented granite and a front of tall, square columns.

Dominic helped Ardhuin out of the carriage, and he felt her hand trembling when she saw the entrance. He was not surprised to see a swirling cloud of black avoidance magic begin to surround her. This was the spell on the book of magic that had first gotten him in trouble, and he shook his head, remembering. It was obvious to him, but for everyone else it made Ardhuin very difficult to look at directly—and they would not notice that they were looking away.

It was another way of hiding, but this time he did not object. The presence of Preusan military magicians made it all the more likely they would try to prevent her from even entering—if they saw her.

Markus Asgaya was looking about, worried, until Dominic gave him a discreet nod.

"The Mage Guardian is here to examine the prisoner," Markus informed the uniformed magician who had come to greet their arrival.

The magician gave Dominic a stiff bow.

Dominic stifled the urge to correct his misapprehension. It would only complicate matters, and this way Ardhuin would be protected from notice. They followed the military magician up the stone stairs and through an echoing entry hall, then down a corridor illuminated by magically frozen flames. Dominic stared, wondering how it had been done and resolving to ask Ardhuin at the earliest opportunity.

Down a series of rough stone stairs they went, with guards at the head and foot. At the bottom was a large door completely encased in iron. Markus produced a document, which the guard carefully examined before the door was opened.

"I did not know there would be a prison in a war magic college," Dominic murmured to the shadow beside him. Ardhuin's hand tightened on his arm. The door closed behind them with a deep clang he could feel through the flagstone floor.

No one had accompanied them through the door, which surprised him until he saw that there were guards within the prison as well. He saw Ardhuin glance at them and then leave the avoidance magic in place.

The failed assassin was a sad figure of a man, bony and haggard with wisps of hair in patches on his scalp. His prison clothes were thin. There was a chair placed for him, but the prisoner made no attempt to use it. He huddled against the wall, his chains clanking as he shook, and slowly slid to the floor. Pale, watery eyes watched them with abject terror.

"This is the man you found in the park? The anarchist?" Ardhuin asked in amazement. "How could he stand up long enough to shoot anybody?"

Markus grimaced. "This is the one. Hans Krieder." At the mention of his name, the prisoner cowered even further, raising horribly scarred hands to hide his face. His right hand was missing portions of the fingers. The scars were old ones, and Dominic recalled Markus Asgaya saying the man had been in a philogiston explosion.

"Look me," Ardhuin said in slow Preusan. The man whimpered and slowly lowered his hands, looking about fearfully. She lifted the veil of her hat. "I help." This seemed to calm him a little.

Ardhuin stared at him, biting her lip, then slowly moved forward. The prisoner whimpered again, shrinking away as far as the chains would permit.

"Are you sure you need to be so close to him?" Markus asked, and Dominic could see his long brown fingers curling with suppressed intent to pull her back, away from potential danger.

"He's chained with iron," Ardhuin said in a choked voice. "I must examine him carefully if we are to remove the *geas*."

Ardhuin knelt beside the terrified prisoner. Dominic saw power build around her hands, and she carefully touched Krieder's head. The effect was sudden, and remarkable. Hans Krieder stopped trembling and stared unblinking into midair with a slack expression on his face. Ardhuin changed the position of her hands and the magic changed too, continuously, more quickly than Dominic could follow.

Krieder started to breathe more quickly, and sweat beaded on his brow. Again Ardhuin shifted, and the prisoner showed increasing agitation, making mewling noises in the back of his throat, but he seemed strangely unable to move.

Dominic drew a sharp breath. He could see something now. Magic, like lavender mist, faint but visible on the assassin's head, where the man's scalp showed through his thin hair. Ardhuin must have brought it up from where it was hidden. Dominic shuddered. To have magic *embedded* in you like that....

Ardhuin bent her head and spoke into the man's ear, words soft but intense, and Dominic saw she was focusing power.

Krieder's eyes bulged, and he screamed. Screamed as if his heart were being ripped out of his chest, his body arced and rigid.

"No!" Ardhuin desperately grabbed his head in both hands, power streaming from her fingers. Krieder spasmed and collapsed in a limp heap, and she let go.

Ardhuin scrambled back, then hesitantly reached out to shake Krieder's shoulder. He did not respond; his head lolled from one side to the other without any change of expression.

The iron door scraped open, and the other defensive magicians of Ardhuin's guard came in. They cast a quick look around the cell, then stepped back, alert and wary. Markus had interposed himself between Ardhuin and the assassin and was examining him.

"Is he dead?" asked Dominic.

"There is a pulse," Markus said, and shrugged. "Not much else."

Ardhuin looked pale, swaying on her feet, and Dominic hastened to support her. "His body lives, but his mind—" she gagged and swallowed, hard. "He has no mind anymore. There was a trap attached to the *geas*. Mage work," she said, glancing at Markus. "The same kind the Gaulans used during the War."

Footsteps pounded in the hall, and this time soldiers of the Kollegium came through the door. Ardhuin hastily let down her hat's veiling as they entered.

"What happened?" one snapped in rapid Preusan.

Markus Asgaya turned to face them. "A remnant spell to prevent interrogation," he said. He spoke calmly, but Dominic could see the tension in his body. "It has been dealt with, I believe."

Ardhuin gave a minute nod, and Dominic looked carefully and could see no trace of magic on the prisoner.

"The *geas* is gone," he said, and grimaced. Ardhuin was right. There was nothing left of the man but his still-breathing body. "You should send for a doctor."

Markus sighed, shaking his head. "There is nothing else to be done, I suppose. A pity. Well, at least we learned something."

Something in his voice made Dominic look up, disturbed. The Preusans weren't going to blame Ardhuin for that, were they?

There were more people in the hallway of the prison section when they left the cell, some in the semi-civilian dress of military magicians. More were waiting for them outside the iron door. Dominic glanced at Markus. His face was a mask.

The military magicians were distantly polite. Procedure must be followed. A report of what had happened was needed, since the prisoner was their responsibility and they must be able to answer any questions as to his condition. They were shown to a room bare of any furnishings except for a wooden bench and a framed engraving of the Siege of Andaluz.

Dominic started to speak, only to be stopped by a warning glance from Markus. Ardhuin gestured, and a thin fog of magic filled the room.

"Our voices are muffled now," she said. "Do you think they are trying to listen?"

"I didn't see any magic until you cast the spell," Dominic commented. "Is there a problem?"

Markus let out a pent-up breath. "Please understand I trust the Lady Magus and her abilities implicitly. But do you see how this will appear to the Council?"

Ardhuin sank down on the hard wooden bench. "A failed attempt to lift the *geas*." Her voice was dull with despair. "And I did fail. That poor man…."

"But the *geas* is gone—I saw it disappear!" Dominic protested.

"However, the prisoner is now even less communicative than when it was present," Markus pointed out. "You must be aware that there are those on the Council who would prefer to decline the assistance of the Lady Magus, and this incident will give them an excuse to do just that."

"What can we do?"

Markus grinned. "I don't suppose you could discover the plot, the plotters, and a tidy solution to everything before dawn tomorrow? That would be very helpful. I don't wish to appear unreasonable, though. Any new information would be…not precisely a distraction, but a different bone for the Council to chew. They are more tenacious than intelligent."

Just when he was most infuriating, Markus would reveal a side Dominic could not help but sympathize with.

"They wouldn't let us find out anything before," Ardhuin said bitterly. "Why would they change now? As soon as we return they will refuse to let me leave again."

"Then we should not return until we have discovered something," Dominic replied. He had no idea how they were to do this, but anything was better than seeing the look of despair in her eyes.

"You are aware that the general feeling at the *Kriegszauberkollegium* is also…not precisely friendly to you," Markus said. "In fact, I believe they will try to make mischief for you, and use this incident to do it. They will not help in any way."

Ardhuin sighed. "Then we need to leave without being detected."

Markus gave her a sidelong glance. When he spoke, his voice did not have the usual undercurrent of amusement, and Dominic felt his curiosity spike. Markus seemed *wary* of her. "From what I have just observed, you have no need of my assistance in that matter."

"Not for that, no. But I am quite certain the *Kriegszauberkollegium* has other protections, possibly even regular Argus castings. I am not asking you to tell me," Ardhuin said hurriedly, holding up a hand to stop his protest. "But I would rather simply avoid such things, instead of using my own methods to…eliminate them."

Dominic hid a smile at Markus' expression, which was a combination of horror and fascination. "Tempting as it is to find out what you would do, my tiresome conscience will not permit me," he said finally. "But do you have some destination in mind? Or is this just a stroll for exercise?"

"The party tonight," Ardhuin said, glowering at him.

"A *party?*" Markus asked, incredulous.

"Students that I met at Professor Siebert's laboratory," Dominic explained, grinning. "She wants to talk to them herself."

"The military has already sealed off the laboratory, and I am quite sure they have been questioning everybody with great enthusiasm. No doubt their magicians have scoured the place."

Military magicians. Dominic blinked, trying to remember why that phrase had sudden meaning. Then he had it, and a wave of cold washed over him.

"Dominic? What's wrong?" Ardhuin was staring at him.

"Perhaps it is nothing, but…I remembered something Siebert's student told me. A military magician visited the laboratory just before the accident."

Markus Asgaya raised an eyebrow. "And you think they might be connected?"

Dominic shrugged. "I don't know. But if they are, I would not rely on that investigation."

"We already know someone in the government is involved," Ardhuin pointed out. "I'm beginning to think that's why the Council wouldn't let me do anything. And now that they have an excuse to get rid of me, how long do you think it will be before they do? We need you not only for dealing with the magic here, but because you know more about the political situation."

Markus folded his arms, leaning against the wall. "So you want to leave without telling anyone and you want me to assist? Do you have any idea how much trouble I would be in?"

"Only if you get caught," Dominic muttered. Markus gave him a fulminating look.

"You could be in trouble anyway," Ardhuin said. "Remember that illusioned letter? They could try again to make you look like a conspirator."

The defensive magician sighed and shook his head, running his fingers through his short dark hair. "Yes, very true. Forgive me. When I think of court intrigue, I usually do not imagine having such a close view of the proceedings." He glanced at Dominic. The glint of amusement returned. "Now you only need to come up with an explanation of why you are bringing two uninvited guests."

Dominic snorted. "This is a student party. All we need to do is bring food. No questions asked."

"You are determined?" Markus glanced at Ardhuin, then Dominic. "Then I will attempt to find a way out that will not tempt the Lady Magus to destroy Imperial property or endanger anyone." He opened the door to their room, and with a quick glance about to make sure he was not observed, he left.

"I could have illusioned him," Ardhuin muttered.

"There is no need. By himself he will occasion no comment, and he can move more quickly. Besides, I think you should rest a little."

He noticed her hands twisting and knotting together, and since they were alone, he permitted himself to take them in his own.

She started, but before he could move away she had recovered enough to grip his hand tightly.

"You tried your best," Dominic said, trying to comfort her. She was shaking, but he could not read her face because of the shadow hat. "It must have been a very powerful *geas*."

Her grip on his hand tightened. "Dominic, whoever did that wouldn't even let him scream! And then left that…that final spell. They must have known magicians would try to remove it."

"The incident with the prisoner was very distressing to you. Are you quite certain you wish to go to the party?"

"I'm fine." Her tone was curt, and did not invite further inquiry.

"Are you? I am not convinced," Dominic said, folding his arms.

She threw up her hands. "Well, what *would* convince you? Perhaps you neglected to notice, but someone is killing Mage Guardians and using forbidden war magic all over the place, and—" she gulped. "It has to be stopped. It doesn't matter how I feel about it."

"Yes, it matters. To me, at least." Perhaps that was of little importance to her, he thought bitterly.

Ardhuin glanced at him, the dark veiling of the hat obscuring all but the outline of her face. Before she could stop him—or he could stop himself—Dominic took the bottom edge of the veil and snapped it over her head.

A sharp, startled intake of breath and one upraised hand were her only reactions. They stared at each other, Dominic cursing his sudden impulse. The expression in Ardhuin's sea-colored, reddened eyes held a noticeable trace of fear.

Dominic dropped his gaze, rubbing a hand across his forehead. They were both on edge, it seemed.

"Please forgive me. I am afraid my dislike of that thing is approaching the level of mania."

"But I need it," Ardhuin said softly. "It's dangerous for me to be noticed. Especially now."

Dominic sighed, then smiled at her worried face. "I know. I just wish it wasn't necessary." One tendril of red hair hung free, and he reached up to tuck it behind her ear. Ardhuin froze for an instant, then turned her head so his hand cupped her face. He could feel her breath on his skin, short and quick.

Then he heard the door open, and Ardhuin spun away.

"Well, that wasn't as hard as I thought it would be," Markus said cheerfully. "Perhaps more exertion than I would prefer, but—" he gave Dominic a puzzled look. "Now, why are you glaring at me?"

It was good to have something to do, something that demanded her attention. What else could go wrong? Ardhuin strengthened the intensity of the avoidance spell around herself and Dominic, hoping the additional power would not be noticed. Markus was taking care of his own shielding magic. That was only proper. He knew the best course of action for his own safety.

They waited, hidden, for what seemed like hours. When the halls were empty, Markus led them on a strange path. First down one main hallway, past a throng of uniformed magicians. Then down a servant's stair, rough underfoot and plain in color, out a side door and then up a narrow marble staircase to a large balcony beyond glass-paned doors. She could see a carriage court and gates beyond, where several sentries stood guard.

"I'll just make sure it's clear," Markus said softly, opening the glass doors with care and slipping outside.

Ardhuin shivered. The wind was sharp and cold, and she wanted to be anywhere but here. To distract herself, she examined an old painting hanging on the wall. It was a battle piece, but unusual for the fact that no weapons were depicted. It was all magicians and magic. The painter had added a ribbon over the scene, on which were gold sigils. She recognized the sigil of Oron, as well as a few others that had appeared in his correspondence. At the bottom of the painting, where crushed and defeated mages of the Grand Armeé cringed, was what looked like a tattered paper. It had sigils too, but only one looked familiar to her.

"Dominic. Isn't that the sigil that was on the illusioned letter?" she asked, pointing.

He came over to her and stared at the painting. "Yes, that's it! What is this?"

"It's a scene from the Mage War. Look, the allies are here. That must be the Gaulan mage who sent that letter. But how? They were so sure they had caught or killed them all."

Just then, a tapping at the window alerted them to the return of

Markus.

"You must go over the balustrade," Markus whispered. "Do you need assistance?"

She looked over the edge. There was a section of flat roof, perhaps two feet wide, that paralleled the upper section of the building. If she kept her back to the wall it wouldn't be too bad. Getting over the balustrade with her skirts was another matter. Markus had warned her not to use levitation anywhere in the *Kriegszauberkollegium*. There were several different detection spells set for that.

Well, at least it was dark. Nobody could see her clumsiness, or her face red from effort. And she couldn't complain, since she had insisted on going.

The path on the roof connected to one of the stables by a stone archway. Ardhuin saw the glint of ice in the shadows, and added that to her list of fears. What would she do if she fell?

The ice seemed to be concentrated in the ridges between the stones. Carefully, she inched her way across the arch. Her knees were weak when they finally made it across to the relative safety of the stable roof. But they were not finished yet.

"How are we going to get down?" Ardhuin whispered to the shadows, hoping one of them was Markus. There was a sharp drop to the stone pavement from where they were, and she couldn't see any way to descend safely.

No reply. She started to worry, then Dominic said softly, "He's bringing a ladder. There, it's in place. Right by that broken slate."

She felt her way to the magically shadowed ladder and fumbled with her feet for the rungs. Her skirts got caught, necessitating a furious, silent struggle that ripped something, but she was free. She'd have to fix it herself later, though. It would cause comment if the servants found out.

Now they had to cross back almost the entire length of the *Kriegszauberkollegium* to find the gate Markus wanted to use. At least they were on the ground now. The gate was guarded, but Markus removed his avoidance spell and the guard let him through, pausing while the defensive magician asked some question Ardhuin didn't understand. It was enough of a distraction to let her and Dominic go through undetected.

Once through, Markus led them through the shadows until she could no longer see the *Kriegszauberkollegium* walls. They crossed the street to an alley. "Now would be a good time for the illusions, milady," he said quietly, glancing out at the street. It was deserted.

"Are you sure?"

He smiled. "We can find a cab on the Opferstrasse, but it will be easier if we aren't invisible. And I don't want to be recognized just now."

Ardhuin wanted to ask about the guard at the gate, but was afraid her shaking voice would betray her. Markus must think the risk acceptable.

Dominic had to appear as himself; that couldn't be helped. She knew what illusion would suit her, but for Markus....

There had been a young, gawky, and eager magician in the crowd at the *Kriegszauberkollegium*, with hair so blond it was almost white. That would work, especially if she replaced the uniform with clothing a student would wear.

It was hard to focus—with the icy wind, her jittery nerves, and fatigue, there was always something to disturb her concentration. Three attempts, and still nothing. She could not complete the delicate bubble of magic that created the illusion. Dominic was looking at her with concern. He knew it shouldn't be that difficult for her.

Ardhuin took a deep breath. She remembered how pleased her great-uncle had been when he found her out, how astonished she had been that she was not going to be punished for "disappearing" the hated asparagus on her plate. At the age of seven, she had not understood what she was doing was magic. And eleven years later, she still did not understand why other magicians found illusion so difficult. It was *fun*.

She smiled, closed her eyes, and summoned up a wave of power, shaping it to her will by not even allowing the possibility it would fail. She heard a stifled gasp from Dominic and felt the internal snap in the flow of her power that told her the spell had closed itself, completed. She opened her eyes.

A gangly, white-blond student stood before her with a lopsided grin on his face. Dominic was struggling to contain his amusement.

"Now, you look very familiar," the student said with Markus' voice. "Although I prefer your true form, I can see a definite resemblance. Don't you agree?" He turned to Dominic.

Dominic squinted at her. "It's hard for me to tell. I can see both the real thing and the illusion, and the light is poor," he said apologetically.

"This is what my brother Brian looks like," Ardhuin mumbled, confused. She'd picked him because he was the youngest, most likely to pass for a student. All her brothers were handsome, but he was the best-looking of them. Which, of course, meant that she and the other brothers had to tease him mercilessly about it. This was probably Fate's revenge, telling her if she'd only been born male she would have been considered handsome, too. "We should go."

The street was not as empty now. A sleek black carriage with a device on the panel went by as they left the alley, and a man in a heavy coat and muffler was hurrying away on the other side of the road.

Markus-the-student led the way to the philogiston-lit street ahead, which was much wider and had even more traffic. Ardhuin presumed it was the Opferstrasse, and hoped it would be easy to find transportation. The wind was making her fingers numb.

She scanned the traffic, wondering how one discerned a carriage-for-hire in Baerlen. How strange—there was the black carriage with the device again. Hadn't it been going the other way earlier?

Even stranger, it was coming towards them. And stopping. The door opened. Gutrune von Kitren was inside, calm and imperturbable as ever. She wore a dark pelisse trimmed with black fur, making her pale face appear detached in darkness.

"I am on my way home. May I take you anywhere?"

Ardhuin gaped. Then a strong hand in the small of her back propelled her forward.

"Get in!" hissed Markus.

Somehow she got in the carriage without tripping. Her skirts were illusioned to look like trousers, but the *reality* was still there. She should have thought of that. Dominic was propelled in after her, and then Markus leapt in and closed the door. Gutrune took one hand out of her large fur muff to open a compartment next to her seat, on the wall. She spoke into a small, dark opening revealed there, and Ardhuin felt the carriage start to move.

She turned a reproachful look at Markus. It was hard to tell through the illusion, but the tone of his voice made it clear he was furious.

"There's no point in continuing if even *she* can find us so easily," he said, with a suggestion of a snarl. In his own voice, too, since she had not added anything to disguise it.

Gutrune von Kitren raised an eyebrow. "That is uncalled for, Herr Asgaya. However, I am glad you had the good sense to insist on accompanying them."

"Insist? Good sense?" Markus sputtered. "I wasn't given a choice!"

"Well, you were," Dominic pointed out. "Not a very pleasant one, I agree, but that was hardly our fault. How did you find us?" he asked Gutrune.

"And where are we going?" added Ardhuin. Her voice was disguised, but it didn't seem to confuse Gutrune. It was all very strange, but for some reason she did not doubt Gutrune could be trusted.

"I had my men watching all possible exits from the *Kriegsa* as I circled in the carriage. It is not uncommon for drivers to take their carriages in a roundabout path while waiting for their passengers to arrive, especially when the weather is too cold to leave horses standing for very long. One of my men recognized you leaving. When he saw you go into a blind alley and then *three* people come out, none of them you, he decided that was unusual and flagged me down. We are still circling, until you tell me where you would like to go," she added, nodding to Ardhuin.

Still, she had to be careful. "You haven't explained why you were watching for us to leave," Ardhuin said. "Or how you know who I am."

Gutrune was silent for a moment. "I heard about what happened. I was also…made aware of certain plans regarding the Mage Guardian, and ordered to secretly assist her in any way possible," she said quietly.

Ardhuin felt a small spark of hope. Gutrune von Kitren served the King directly. The King was only person who could order her to do anything. He knew—of course he knew. He was counting on her to uncover the plot, and even though he could not assist her openly, he didn't expect her to do it on her own.

"I cannot be completely certain you are the Mage Guardian," Gutrune continued, "but given your company, the circumstances, and the phenomenal illusion on Herr Asgaya, it seems a reasonable conclusion. Also," she said, turning her head to give Dominic a small smile, "it is not usual for a man to attempt to assist another man into a carriage. Or for that assisted man to try to pick up his invisible skirts while doing so."

"Oh dear." She shouldn't have said that, either. Brian would have cursed. "Blast."

Dominic laughed. He seemed to be in a much better mood for some reason. "With all due respect, Fraülein von Kitren, your carriage is rather noticeable for errands of some subtlety. And you seem to be aware that we must avoid being noticed."

"I have other, less elegant means of transportation I can place at your disposal, if you wish." Gutrune looked at Ardhuin, inquiringly.

Ardhuin glanced at Dominic, who nodded after a brief hesitation, and then at Markus.

"I am resigned to death," he said, sighing and throwing up his hands. "It only remains to choose the manner of my going. I do hope it isn't a firing squad, though. It lacks style."

Taking that as agreement, Ardhuin said, "We need to go to the Student Quarter."

CHAPTER 10

Dominic followed Markus out of the carriage and looked around. Shabby wooden buildings surrounded a small, cobbled courtyard. The windows looking in on it were opaque with grime in the lamplight. The driver was closing the gate behind them, a huge, iron-bound thing in much better shape than the building it was attached to.

"I wonder what else she uses this for?" Ardhuin said, behind him. He turned back, reaching up to help her out of the carriage. He stopped, realizing his error, just as she remembered herself and drew back her hand. Both the illusion and her real face smiled at him. "Poor Dominic. This will be a trial for you, I fear." She jumped lightly down.

"It would be easier if I could only see the illusion," he agreed. "I might have a chance of remembering what everybody else sees."

"I need to remember the illusion too," Ardhuin said, sighing. "Perhaps I can use some twine to solve the skirt problem. If I don't do something, I'll either trip or reveal the illusion again."

Across the courtyard, Markus was nearly invisible in the shadows. He made a complete, careful circuit, then returned.

"Excellent. There is another gate to a different street; that will be very useful. This is your home?" Markus asked Gutrune, eyes bright with mischief. It hadn't taken him long to recover from his earlier ill humor, Dominic noticed.

"Don't be absurd," Gutrune said, in a quelling tone. The driver, a huge man in a caped greatcoat, stood before her. "*Wir brauchen den Lampekart, Stoller.*"

"*Jawohl,*" he answered, standing at attention before turning and unhitching the horses from the carriage.

"What about him?" Dominic asked. "Can he be trusted?"

"Stoller was one of my father's soldiers," Gutrune said. "When my father was killed, he went into service with my family. I trust him completely."

Stoller produced a battered cart, long and covered like a baker's van, except it had a ladder to the roof next to the driver's seat, and brass pipes and fittings along one side that led to the roof as well, ending in a prosaic pump handle. Hitched to it was a shaggy, elderly horse.

"A lamplighter's cart," Gutrune explained, opening the door in the back and preparing to enter. "They are seen all over the city, and people pay no attention to them."

"One moment," Markus said. "While your assistance is greatly appreciated, do you really think your presence will be of any use? That is, I cannot imagine you would enjoy staying in the cart, waiting for us. The student quarter is entirely too near the Closure, as well. It's too dangerous."

Gutrune listened to him politely, then reached into her fur muff and took out a pistol with a long, narrow barrel that gleamed palely in the dim light.

The defensive magician looked startled, then laughed. "Behold, you are a treasure of the nation! Is that a Kreisheim?"

"Yes. One of their custom marksman's pistols."

He raised an eyebrow. "I would like to know how you come to be carrying such a thing tonight. Is it a habit of yours?"

A small smile curved the corners of her mouth. "It helps the drape of the furs."

Ardhuin choked back a laugh.

"Still, you agree discretion is of the essence," Markus said, persevering with a tinge of desperation. "Perhaps I am overly imaginative, but I can't help but suspect in that area a woman with a pistol would be even more noticeable than a woman without one."

Gutrune glanced at Ardhuin, who shook her head regretfully. "I have already done two very complex illusion castings, and I was tired before that. They are very intricate—it takes a great deal of control to make something that will pass close inspection."

"And I could not even begin to match Fraülein Andrew's skill fully rested, so I cannot be of assistance either," Markus said, apparently serious.

Was Ardhuin truly that powerful? Dominic realized he had no basis for comparison until now; he'd simply accepted her ability with no thought of what other magicians could do. It could be important to know, but how would he find out?

With unchanged calm, Gutrune stepped down from the cart door. "Wait," Ardhuin said, holding up a hand. "I think…it won't get you inside the room with us, but I can do a visual avoidance spell. If there is somewhere you can stand that is out of the way, it would work."

Markus sighed but made no further objection.

In a few moments they were leaving the decrepit warehouse. The cart was much less comfortable than the carriage. It had wooden benches on either side, and it appeared springs were considered an unnecessary luxury. Evidently philogiston was not as unstable as many people thought. Besides the door in the rear of the cart, there was an opening to the driver's seat but no windows. Dominic could only catch glimpses of the outside over Stoller's broad shoulders.

The jolting grew a degree smoother as they got nearer to the university. Dominic could see the great stone walls that surrounded it. Gutrune murmured something to Stoller, and he drove the cart a little further and turned into a narrow, dark alleyway.

"We'll walk from here," she said, sliding a small shutter open and peering out before opening the door in the back of the cart. In silence, Ardhuin cast the avoidance spell on Gutrune. He had seen her do this same casting many times, but it seemed to Dominic it took longer than usual.

He also didn't know the limits of Ardhuin's strength. Another thing to worry about.

Wolfgang Maurer's quarters were only a few streets away. A tiny baker's shop reminded Dominic of the need for provisions, and he purchased a good meat pastry.

"Is that really suitable?" Ardhuin asked doubtfully when they had left the shop. "It is a party, correct?"

"Student party," Dominic said, grinning. "They are always hungry, and sweet things do not satisfy as well. You will see."

"Hey, you came!"

Markus spun around, alert and wary. Jens-Peter Oberacker was behind them, his cheerful freckled face beaming at them.

Dominic relaxed. "Er, yes, of course. These are some friends of mine. Do you think there would be any objection if they—"

"No, of course not! It could be a bit thin of company, actually. The trouble on the streets is making many stay within doors. That's why I was surprised to see you," Jens-Peter added. "Come, don't just stand in the street, you'll freeze."

Dominic, Markus, Ardhuin, and the dark shadow containing Gutrune followed Jens-Peter up the creaking wooden stairs to the third floor. By gestures, Gutrune indicated she would remain on the landing, which had an odd corner where she would be out of the way of any other visitors.

"Ah, this brings back memories," Dominic said, looking around the cramped room.

Shelves had been put up on every surface available, full of books or odd bric-a-brac. Besides the two beds, pressed into service for seating, the room boasted a plain wooden table, an armchair upholstered in cracked brown leather, and a once-elegant chaise now leaking horsehair from its lower regions in an embarrassing manner. A loaf of bread, a knife, cheese, some sausages, and a pot of mustard graced a small desk.

Only a handful of other people were there, just as Jens-Peter had predicted. Wolfgang, the host; Stefan Arendt; and the small bespectacled student he'd met with them—what was his name? Jochim something.

Wolfgang introduced them to the others: the guest of honor Karl Hoffberg and his roommate Arne from Noverige.

"Help yourself. Karl is feeling generous, so we at least have some good beer," Wolfgang said, waving his hand at a small wooden barrel and a collection of battered steins. "I am surprised you were able to make it. Was it very bad?"

Dominic was at a loss, and looked helplessly at Ardhuin and Markus. "We went through the Marktstrasse and the brickmaker's quarter," Markus said smoothly. "The streets were empty there."

"Ach, what a long way to go. Poor Jochim, he'd had his head in a book for the last two days and didn't even know. He's been staying with us until it's safe for him to go out."

"I thought he lived over the bookseller's on Eisengare," Jens-Peter said, wandering up with a slice of meat pastry in one hand and a stein in the other.

"He does, but his parents are in the Closure and he's worried. He hasn't been able to get any word of them."

"What is the Closure?" Ardhuin asked.

Wolfgang blinked at her. "Are you from Bretagne, too?"

"No, Atlantea." Ardhuin looked like she wanted to fade into the shadows again. Dominic gave her a meaningful glance. "I, ah, had met Kermarec in Bretagne, and when I heard he was visiting Baerlen too, I looked him up."

"The Closure is the Adaran quarter in Baerlen. It used to be the only place they could live, until the current King came to the throne." Wolfgang started asking interested questions about Atlantea, and although he wanted to listen, Dominic decided to find another conversation. They needed to find out something that could help Ardhuin with the Council.

"Was Dieter going to come tonight?" he asked Stefan Arendt.

Stefan shrugged. "He was planning to." Jochim, trying to read the titles of some books by tilting his head to one side, instead tilted his entire body and fell to the floor. Stefan bent down and helped him up. "Do be careful, you owl! Hey, who gave him more beer? You know he can't handle very much."

"I gave to myself," Jochim said, swaying slightly but with great dignity. "You prefer that I cry, maybe?"

"No, no, that's even worse. Oh, just try to aim for the beds, all right? Otherwise you'll break something."

"Maybe I should tell him one of my stories," said Karl, the would-be author. He was about the same age as Dominic, with a friendly, open face.

Jens-Peter inhaled some of his beer and coughed uncontrollably. "Why? We don't want to make him cry, remember? Every one of your stories I've read is enough to drain the sunshine from one's life. Why is it that they always end unhappily for the lovers, eh? Do you think people enjoy reading that sort of thing?"

Karl gestured airily. "Alas, love escapes me! And if I cannot have *my* love, I'll be damned if I give any paper creation the satisfaction I am denied."

"If she does not satisfy you, simply pay her less," teased Arne, to the laughter of the others.

Karl shook his head in mock sorrow. "Is that what you frozen Northerners call love? Or is that all you can find in a civilized country?"

Dominic could not help glancing towards Ardhuin, to see if she had heard any of this highly improper conversation. She was still talking with Mauer, and appeared unaware. She didn't seem frightened at all, now; instead, it was as if she were interested and had forgotten to be afraid. It was incredible.

"Besides," Karl continued, "my latest story is about a cursed diamond that can trap your soul. No lovers of any kind."

Karl and Jens-Peter continued to argue about the need for happiness in fiction, with Jochim weaving around them, picking up things from the shelves and looking at them with complete, if drunken, absorption. Dominic wondered what the fascination was. It looked like junk to him. He glanced at the contents of the shelf nearest him, and amended that to *magical* junk.

Dominic looked around for Markus. The door opened, and Dieter and a tall man came in, snow dusting their coats.

"Hans won't be coming," Dieter told Wolfgang Mauer over the noise of everyone greeting the new arrivals. "His friend came off the worse in a duel a few hours ago and is not expected to live. I just found out."

"A duel!" Stefan got up from his unconventional seat, a stack of books on one of the beds. "Who was it? Who did he fight?"

Dieter shrugged. "I didn't hear. I only know it was a duel, and he's badly hurt."

"There've been an awful lot of duels at the *Kriegsa* lately," Wolfgang observed, and took a deep drink. "What's going on, Ermut?" This was addressed to the tall man, who had a definite resemblance to Stefan Arendt. This must be the brother at the *Kriegszauberkollegium*.

"I don't know everything that happens there," Ermut said good-naturedly. "I work more than I listen to gossip. Now that you mention it, though, we've had some unexpected deaths in the ranks of the juniors. None of my friends, but people I knew. It could have been duels, I suppose, but they would try to hide that. It's not like it used to be. You can get in a lot of trouble dueling."

Not to mention dead, thought Dominic. Curious, but not what they were interested in. He went over to Dieter, who was loading up a thick slab of bread with mustard and beef as best he could with one hand. Small ice crystals were slowly melting in his thick blond hair. For such a thin man, he had a tremendous appetite.

"Oh, good! You were able to come after all," Dieter said, just before attacking his sandwich.

"Yes, we were able to find a safe route," Dominic replied. "What is all the trouble about, anyway? Is there a rebellion?"

Dieter swallowed his mouthful with a blissful smile, then shrugged. "Might be one, if they don't stop the bodies showing up. I forgot, you haven't been in Baerlen that long. They're probably trying to keep it out of the papers, too. About three months ago, a dead body was found outside the gates of the Closure. Poor fellow's throat had been cut. Not a drop of blood in him, which was strange since no blood was anywhere around him either. A few weeks later, another one showed up, same place, same condition. This is the sixth so far, and the police have not found the culprit. People are getting angry, and they think the Adarans are to blame."

Dominic glanced at Jochim, suddenly understanding his fear and worry, now drowned in drink. He was Adaran, and dared not go out in the street for fear of the mob. Jochim had worked his way around the room and was now examining some of the strange objects on the corner shelves.

"Did anyone come and talk to you about what happened in Siebert's lab?" Dominic asked.

"Well, there was this rather unpleasant fellow who came and warned us to say nothing," Dieter said, looking doubtful. "I suppose I can tell you about it, since you found the damn thing. He didn't ask me questions. Just took away all the wreckage and the designs. Well, he did ask if I had been there the previous afternoon, when the Professor had his visitor, but when I said I hadn't he had no further interest in me. He wouldn't tell me anything, either. *He*'s not going to find out who killed Professor Siebert," he added angrily.

A shimmer of magic from the corner of his eye told him Ardhuin had come up to join the conversation. "Did he just say he had not been questioned?" she asked, in Gaulan.

"That is what he said. It is very strange," Dominic replied.

"It was deliberate sabotage! Can't they be bothered to try and find out who did it?"

"You appear to be familiar with this," Dieter said in heavily accented Gaulan, looking worried. "You are perhaps the mage Herr Kermarec has spoken of working with?"

"Er, yes. That is, we have worked together before. I am very much concerned with what happened to Professor Siebert." Now Markus had joined the conversation as well, overhearing the name.

"We should be discreet," he said softly, glancing about the room.

Now Dieter was showing signs of distress. "We were warned…most strongly. To say nothing." He stared at Ardhuin. "You said sabotage. You know, then? And you?" Markus smiled. "I don't understand why they told us to be silent, if everybody knows about it."

"Not quite everybody. Yet." Markus sighed. "You know, this makes me a trifle concerned. What if the, ah, instigators decide to clean up lose ends? That means you," he added with a grin to Dieter.

"This is your idea of discretion?" Ardhuin said, her eyes wide.

"It can't be too bad," Dominic said, noticing who was still present at the party. "The only ones here who don't know anything are Karl, Arne, and Stefan's brother, and he works at the *Kriegszauberkollegium*."

"Karl and Arne are all right," Dieter said immediately. "They can keep their mouths shut if it's important."

"The Council has made no real effort to investigate, so I will have little patience with any complaints about our attempt," Ardhuin said, folding her arms. "So, what is this about a military magician visiting Siebert before the accident?"

"He came while I was away," Dieter said, looking confused. "Siebert told me about him, just before he went back to the work area and…and it happened. I almost missed it. I was in early that day."

"So you didn't see him? Did Siebert describe him to you?" Markus asked.

Dieter thought for a moment. "Said he seemed to know what he was talking about, which would be unusual where Siebert's work was concerned. Asked intelligent questions."

"Is that it?" Dominic couldn't help asking. "It doesn't narrow down the field very much."

"It narrows it completely," Markus said with a sardonic smile. "Intelligent questions? Such a person does not exist in the entire *Kriegszauberkollegium*."

Jochim had managed to pick up a large chunk of a slightly silvery, glassy material. It appeared to be heavy and awkward, and there was a tense moment while Jochim struggled to hold it and his stein, finally solving the problem by balancing the chunk on the stein's mouth and holding the stein with both hands. Jochim lifted it up to the light, and then at various things around the room. For some reason, Ardhuin's illusioned form held a special fascination to him.

"There must be *something* more you remember," she was saying to Dieter. "Did Siebert mention his unusual height? Noticeable limp? Pet parrot?"

Dieter grinned. "If he left his calling card, it must have burned up in the explosion. Let me think—"

Now Jochim was looking at Ardhuin through the glassy lump, then without it. His jaw was hanging open. Dominic felt a cold stab of fear, and quickly stepped between her and Jochim.

"Who's th' lady?" said a bewildered Jochim. "Is she in here?" He peered at the lump suspiciously.

"Let me look," Dominic offered, walking quickly over and taking it away. The view was distorted by the rough surface of the glass, but he could see enough. The illusion was just a nebulous cloud around the very clear vision of Ardhuin. "I don't see anything," he lied, firmly retaining his grasp of the thing. Jochim blinked, looking confused, then continued his investigation of the shelves with a huge yawn.

"What is this?" Dominic asked Wolfgang Maurer, hefting the chunk of glass in his hand.

"Oh, that's something Arne was given. He has a relative who is a chryselectrum maker—I don't know exactly what it is, but magicians use it. That was a defective batch, but he keeps it as a curiosity."

Well. It wasn't completely silvery, like chryselectrum ought to be. He could see through it. Evidently it blocked enough of the magical effects —what had Ardhuin said? It shaped magical fields. This appeared to shape the magic away from the eye.

"Curious," he said, and put it back on a shelf, hiding it behind a battered brass telescope. He should warn Ardhuin, but how could he in the crowded room? Besides, they hadn't gotten what they came for yet, and nobody was paying any attention to what Jochim was saying since he was clearly the worse for drink. Hopefully he would forget his dangerous vision, or at least not understand what it meant.

Dieter's forehead was still wrinkled with effort, trying to remember. "Well, the Professor did mention the *Kollegium* must at least pay the senior members well. I didn't understand why, exactly. Something about a bazaar ring, which makes no sense."

Markus looked up sharply. "Was it perhaps, instead…a bezoar ring?"

"Oh." Dieter gave a slow nod. "Yes, I think you are right. I thought it sounded strange. What's that?"

"A very rare and extremely expensive stone with magical properties. It is found in the skulls of a species of toad that seeks thaumatic influences." Markus had a very grim expression on his face. "It is so rare, I have only seen one. It was in a ring worn by the second-most powerful mage of the *Kollegium*. Horst von Stangen."

"That must be him, then," Dominic observed.

Markus grimaced. "There is one slight difficulty. Von Stangen was not in Baerlen when the explosion took place."

"If he were planning an assassination, he would take pains to conceal his true location," Ardhuin said dryly. "Perhaps he forgot his gloves and came back for them, pausing to visit Professor Siebert on the way. How can we find out the truth of the matter?"

"Ermut might have an idea," Dieter said around the last bite of sandwich before turning and shouting, "Hey, Ermut!"

Dominic felt a tug at his elbow. Markus was urging him and Ardhuin back into a corner, a little further away from the general conversation. "This is not a good idea," he said, his voice low and tense. "You know the dangers. Why do you risk everything with these well-intentioned but ignorant students? How do we know we can trust them?"

"We don't," Ardhuin said softly, after a long pause. "But what choice do we have? It's pretty clear we can't trust the Council. They're trying to cover this up. How else are we to find what we need to know?"

Markus sighed, shaking his head, but before he could say anything more a voice intruded.

"Von Stangen? I try to stay away from him as much as possible," Ermut Arendt was saying. "Why do you want to know about him?"

"I don't, they do," Dieter said, pointing. "They think he was Siebert's mysterious visitor."

"Oh." Ermut looked at Dominic and Ardhuin, puzzled. "Your pardon, but...I don't understand why foreigners are involved in this. That is, my superiors would *definitely* not understand why foreigners were involved, or why I would be talking to them about any of this. I mean no offense."

"I am going to regret this," muttered Markus, reaching into a coat pocket. The object he held was shielded by illusion until he dropped it into Ermut's hand. As soon as Ermut saw what it was, he gasped and closed his hand around it, returning it to Markus.

"I was sure you were...I thought I had seen you around the *Kriegsa*. I must have confused you with someone else."

Ardhuin coughed. "You may well have seen someone like him. His appearance is...borrowed for the occasion."

Ermut gave a low whistle. "*Ausgezeichnet!* I had no idea that the... those like you paid much attention to concealment. Well, I thought you had very good control just now to hide your badge, but—"

Markus looked like he was going to object, but Ardhuin shook her head at him with a slight smile, and he subsided. "Yes, we have a number of secrets we choose not to share with the world. Now, about von Stangen...."

"He's very political," Ermut said, his brow wrinkling. "He takes offense easily, too. Most find it easier to simply stay out of his way. If you want to ask questions about him, I would suggest his aide, instead: Lars von Gerling."

"Where does von Gerling live?" asked Ardhuin.

"If he isn't married, he'd be in the *Kriegsa* barracks," observed Markus.

Dominic was distracted by the sound of Jochim's voice, growing louder and more insistent by the minute.

"It was a *lady!* Inna crystal. Show you!" He got up from the ratty armchair he had been sitting in and swayed on his feet, ignoring Arne's efforts to get him to sit down again.

"Why don't you let me find this crystal," Arne said in a soothing voice. He glared at Kurt. "It's all your fault. If you hadn't been telling your fairy tales he would never have gotten the idea. Possessed diamonds, is it?"

Arne wasn't drunk. If he found the chunk of flawed chryselectrum, Ardhuin's illusion would be uncovered.

"Why don't we go and see this aide?" Dominic suggested quickly.

Ermut frowned. "Could it not wait for morning? Oh, I suppose this would cause less official notice."

"Yes. Exactly. Let's go now, before it gets too late," Dominic said, trying to urge the others with grimaces and nudges.

Ardhuin and Markus picked up on his signals readily, but now the others were causing delay. Wolfgang Maurer objected they were leaving too soon. Dieter wanted to accompany them. Dominic felt the tension in his body increase. Arne was searching the shelves now for Jochim's crystal. He should have thrown the damn thing in the stove.

"It won't take long," Stefan consoled Wolfgang, who looked depressed. "We'll be back, as long as you don't let Jochim drink all the beer."

Out the door, finally, and Dominic did not bother to object to how many were going with them. Just as the door closed behind them he heard Arne's voice saying, "Oh, here it is, Jochim. Show me the lady!"

Ardhuin sighed. She had really only exchanged one problem for another. Her skirts were held up now, but that meant she could feel every icy breeze on her ankles. If illusioned adventures were going to be a habit, she needed to devise an alternate costume.

"Where's Gutrune?" she whispered to Dominic, walking beside her. It had been decided the destination was close enough they could go on foot. She suspected the students were mostly interested in saving money on cab fare.

"Following in the cart," he whispered back. "She knows where we are going."

It wouldn't be that hard to track them. The streets were almost empty, and they were the only large group she'd seen. Besides herself, Dominic, and Markus Asgaya, four of the others had decided to come along. She had expected Stefan to accompany his brother, and Dieter seemed to have a slow, burning grudge against whoever had killed his professor, but Jens-Peter had joined them purely for the fun of adventure.

It was strange. At first, meeting so many strangers at once had terrified her, but now she liked them all. If it weren't for the danger hanging over her (and the cold, she had to admit) she would be enjoying the adventure too.

She glanced at Dominic. He'd been unusually insistent on leaving, and she could tell he was worried about something. Now, however, he looked much more relaxed.

A gust of wind, bitterly cold, rushed down the street. Ardhuin shivered and wished for Gutrune's thick fur muff, or at least some good wool socks. She was sure her nose was red—her real nose. The illusion wouldn't change.

Stefan's brother Ermut was in the lead. He turned to them, saying, "We can take this street, it's more direct."

"But the barracks entrance is on the other side," objected Markus.

"Von Gerling rated quarters with a private entrance," Ermut said with an expressive grimace. "Important aide, don't you know. In fact, he—"

A shout came from up ahead, and the sound of running feet. In the pool of light from a philogiston lamp Ardhuin saw a man, his collar askew and his coat torn, running with a desperation born of fear. He turned to look behind him and tripped on an uneven cobblestone, landing hard with a grunt of pain.

His pursuers were now visible, a crowd of men with crude weapons in their hands.

"Get back, out of sight!" Markus was in front of her, dragging her by main force into a doorway.

"They're going to kill him!" she protested.

"My instructions only specify preventing anyone from killing *you,*" Markus snapped. "Kindly note the lead thug has a large iron chain, and there are far more of them than us. If they see us we'll be in trouble. I can't handle that many. Can you?"

Fully rested, she could. But it wouldn't be pleasant, since the only spells that would work were very destructive. Right now she wasn't sure she could do anything, and if she failed, they would all be in danger.

The man had scrambled to his feet, but the crowd had caught up with him and he was soon on the ground again. The man with the iron chain kicked him hard, yelling "*Schmutziger Adarar!*"

There had to be something she could do, even as weak as she was. They were going to kill that man right in front of her. Desperately, she ran through the spells her great-uncle had taught her, trying to find something that would work. Spells of power, of control—perhaps a distension of the cobblestones to make a protective shell?

"Close your eyes!" Stefan said in an urgent whisper. Ardhuin did, just in time. A flash of light so intense it leaked through her eyelids burst over the mob. A chorus of screams and moans forced her eyes open again. The man with the chain was clawing at his face and stumbling blindly away, as were the rest of them. Their victim was left lying in the street, curled up and moaning. Stefan and Jens-Peter darted out and carried the man to safety in the dark doorway.

Ardhuin couldn't follow the rapid Preusan conversation that followed. The man was grateful, but still terrified. Blood streaked his face from a cut on his head.

"He says he can walk, and he has a friend only a few streets over," Dominic translated, seeing her lack of comprehension.

With great dignity, despite his disheveled appearance, the man shook hands with everyone and limped away, glancing nervously to each side until he reached the shadows on the opposite side.

"Is this what is happening with the riots you mentioned?" Ardhuin asked Dieter.

He shrugged, his usually cheerful face sad. "Usually it's worse."

"Let's go before the glare-flash wears off," Markus said.

They walked quickly away down the side street. Ardhuin glanced back, hoping the man would be all right and wondering if there was any way she could find out.

"Was that a special spell he used?" Dominic asked her under his breath. "I couldn't tell if it was just him, or…nobody seems to cast magic like you do."

What was that supposed to mean? "It's a very basic spell," Ardhuin said, feeling tired and stupid. "I should have thought of it myself." Instead, she'd been thinking of all the advanced attacks her great-uncle had taught her, trying to find one that she still had the strength to do. It wasn't a good excuse. She should have done something. What kind of a Mage Guardian was she? So useless even the desperate Preusans didn't want her.

"There. That row of brick fronts. It's one of them," Ermut pointed. Ardhuin noted a shabby lamplighter's cart on the street ahead and felt a little better.

The third door in the row had a small brass nameplate with "v. Gerling" on it. The front window was dark, but Ardhuin thought she could see faint light reflected down a hallway.

Ermut rang the bell. From her vantage point, Ardhuin saw a darker shadow cross the zone of grey light, and the door opened.

She had a brief impression of a handsome, narrow face, the paleness accentuated by a precisely trimmed beard. Von Gerling looked at Ermut with a polite lack of enthusiasm while he explained the reason for the late visit. A certain hard expression entered von Gerling's eyes when Ermut said the name "von Stangen."

Von Gerling let his gaze travel over the others. He passed over her with no reaction; a brief flicker of recognition when he looked at Dominic. Then he saw Markus, and Ardhuin saw his eyes widen with shock and, strangely, horror.

Dominic yelled, "Watch out!" and shoved Markus away, hard. The blast of power made a familiar icy tingling in her skin. Before she even knew what she was doing, power instinctively gathered with painful strength and she loosed it in rapid, javelin bursts. Just as she had been taught, as she had practiced countless times with her great-uncle.

Sawtooth cloud is powerful, but it takes time to recover. Be quick in response, and never let your opponent gain the initiative again, he had said.

She thought the first bolt had caught him, but she wasn't sure. They were all weaker than they should be, but still the rest shattered the door as he tried to slam it shut.

Ardhuin ran up the steps, dodging the grasping hand of Markus. This was her job—she wasn't going to let them down again. She had to be cautious. Von Gerling didn't know how weak she was. She tried to smooth her ragged breathing, terrified that he would hear and find her.

Von Gerling must be involved with the plot somehow. Her mind was numb, unable to think beyond the basic need for action, but her body was paralyzed by fear. The front room was dark, and she heard noises in the rooms beyond. Shouting from the entry told her the others were on their way. She had to move.

A deflective shield to the front, Ardhuin darted to the hallway, wondering at how gathering power had felt like a thousand tiny knives. It had felt like that when she had attacked, too. Was it something von Gerling was doing? She peered around the corner of the first doorway. It appeared to be a study, with bookshelves and a small desk before a window. A shadowy figure was frantically stuffing papers into a valise.

She felt her shield shrivel and pop as soon as she tried to cross the threshold. Ardhuin jerked back, terrified, and fell. *Devourer Gate. He knows Devourer Gate.* Another blast of power from von Gerling just missed her. If he hadn't been taken by surprise by her clumsiness, it would have killed her.

A cry from Dominic made her twist around where she had fallen. He was sagging against the wall, hands over his eyes. Alive. He was alive. He had seen the magic and avoided it. But now?

Power surged within her and she grasped it despite the stabbing pain, not daring to wonder where it was coming from. Ardhuin used a quick bit of levitation to get to her feet, cold fury crowding out her fear. No one was going to hurt Dominic. The power came from every atom of her being, a raw flood that ripped out the spell on the doorway and incorporated it, throwing it back at the man who had cast it. The pain was so intense that darkness started to crowd the edges of her vision.

Von Gerling shouted, and there was fear in his voice. His own shielding was starting to ravel at the edges; she could tell by the way the power was leaking around him.

"You can't be doing this!" he gasped, panting with effort. "Denais said you were dead! We're the only ones who—"

Suddenly the window shattered from the magical stress, melting in midair and freezing into a cloud of small spheres. Von Gerling grabbed the valise and leaped out the empty window frame.

She darted for the window, just catching a glimpse of von Gerling's coat as he went around the corner to the front street. Ardhuin clutched the window frame, fighting a wave of dizziness now that the pain was gone. She couldn't get there fast enough—he was going to get away.

"Gutrune! Don't let him escape!" Ardhuin yelled at the top of her lungs.

Suddenly, she was so tired she could barely stand. She staggered, and caught herself on the back of a chair. A gun fired in the street outside, then again.

"Good," Ardhuin gasped. Her voice sounded higher with fatigue. "Gutrune must have got him."

She looked up at the doorway. Stefan Arendt was staring at her in horror, as was Dominic. Markus had his face in his hands and was shaking his head.

A sinking feeling washed over her, and she looked down. The illusion was gone. "Oh, damnation," said Ardhuin, and collapsed.

CHAPTER 11

The sheen of magic covered everything Dominic saw like frost. How much of it was from the fight and how much was normally there, he could not tell. Chunks of plaster and pieces of broken furniture littered the floor. He dropped to his knees beside Ardhuin's unconscious form.

Her face was pale as marble, the lack of color even more noticeable since her fiery hair was now loose and framed it. For a terrible second he thought she was not breathing, then he saw her chest barely rise and fall. He took one hand in his, gasping when her dark gloves shattered into flakes of ash at his touch.

"Her hands are like ice," he said, even more frightened than before. His heart was beating so hard and fast it felt as if it would jump into his mouth.

"Not surprising, given that an entire window has gone missing," Markus said absently, searching the room cautiously.

Dominic glanced over to where the window had been. Draperies hung at a lopsided angle, one end wrenched loose. He jumped to his feet and pulled a section free, returning to tuck the fabric carefully around Ardhuin. His hands were shaking.

"*Gott im Himmel.*" That was Jens-Peter, for once unable to make a joke. "What happened? Who is *she?*"

"I think she used to be Herr Andrews, or he used to be her, or… something. It's not quite clear," Ermut said slowly, as if he were still figuring it out. "That is, I saw Herr Andrews fighting von Gerling, and then von Gerling escaped out the window, and then she was standing where Herr Andrews had been."

Jens-Peter's mouth hung open. He shut it and moaned, "I *missed* it?"

"I asked for discretion. I distinctly remember saying the words." Markus Asgaya addressed the ceiling, arms outspread. "Where did I go wrong? Does this," he said to the group gaping in the doorway, gesturing at the wreckage of the study, "look like discretion to you?"

"Not in the slightest." Gutrune von Kitren stepped into the room, gracefully avoiding the debris on the floor. She was still holding her pistol. "In fact, you have attracted notice from the neighboring houses. They will be here soon."

Jens-Peter, Stefan, and Ermut glanced respectfully at her weapon and edged slightly closer to the wall.

Dominic returned his attention to Ardhuin, only dimly registering the sound of voices around him. Jens-Peter was arguing about something, and Gutrune von Kitren was responding in a calm, reasonable tone. He took Ardhuin's hands in his own, trying to warm them. What had happened to her? He hadn't seen any attack from von Gerling when her illusion had vanished, or when she had collapsed.

"Ardhuin. Please wake up," Dominic pleaded, his voice breaking. "You're frightening me. *Ardhuin.*"

Still no response. Was it his imagination, or was her breathing more even now?

A scrap of torn wallpaper fluttered in an icy breeze that came from the shattered window. The floor was becoming quite cold. Dominic lifted Ardhuin's shoulders, cradling her head against his chest while holding her close to give her what warmth he had. A strand of fire-red hair partially covered her face, and he brushed it away.

Moonlight. The scent of roses. Confusion, desperate need, his hands wrapped in thick, silky warmth....

Dominic snapped out of the sudden, overwhelming memory with a gasp. Ardhuin's hair was not warm now, and his fear gave him unexpected strength.

Somehow he managed to stand, carrying her. The next room down the narrow corridor was a small dining room. It was warmer, but there was no place for Ardhuin to rest. The kitchen wouldn't be any better, so he turned carefully to go back to the front parlor.

Markus was there without his illusion, dark and lithe. He was lighting one of the lamps, and talking to Gutrune. The students were gone.

"It's gone too far to be concealed now. I was merely hoping to keep them out of it, if possible," he said.

"But all of them?"

The lamp flared and glowed as the match caught, casting Markus' face in planes of light and shadow. Dominic was suddenly reminded of an illustration he had seen of Loka, the Teuton god of trickery.

Markus shook his head. "Ermut Arendt felt it was his duty to report, and I could not persuade him otherwise. I only hope von Stangen—" He looked up and saw Dominic. "Where are you going? You don't mean to leave us to explain what happened, do you?"

"It's too cold in the study," Dominic said, trying to ignore the sudden, hot spurt of irritation at Markus' attempt at humor. "She will be more comfortable on the sofa."

Markus came around the marble-topped table that held the lamp. "Here, let me help you."

He reached for Ardhuin, and Dominic snapped. "Get away from her!" he shouted, clutching her even more tightly. She shifted with a small sigh, a promising sign he barely noticed through his rage.

Markus froze, then slowly and carefully moved back, his face without expression. Dominic breathed deeply, suddenly shaken. Over the rage came a cold wave of fear. What was wrong with him? Markus had never endangered Ardhuin, so why was he acting as if he were a threat?

It's not her he's a threat to, a small voice in his mind said slyly.

Dominic shook his head sharply, and with an effort lay Ardhuin on the green velvet sofa near the lamp. His arms ached, and his sudden strength deserted him. He dropped to his knees beside the sofa.

For a moment, his voice deserted him too. "Forgive me. She is…she is in need of a physician."

A hand on his shoulder made him look up. Gutrune von Kitren was looking at him with compassion in her pale blue eyes. "The attendance of a physician would be wise, but the case is not desperate. Look, her color is better already. Do not take offense, Herr Kermarec, but your talents are needed elsewhere. We have but a few moments to search this place unencumbered, and Herr von Gerling will undoubtedly have magical protections about anything of importance." Dominic hesitated, and she added softly, "I will remain with her and alert you if there are any unfavorable changes. Make haste. I was unable to stop von Gerling, and he might have allies in the *Kriegsa* still."

Dominic got stiffly to his feet. "But I thought you shot him."

Gutrune's lips thinned. "He was only wounded."

"Wounded? Where was he when you hit him?" Markus sounded eager.

Dominic thought Gutrune was as puzzled as he was. "He had just reached the opposite side of the street. Near the post box."

Markus cast a quick, undecided look around the room, threw a sudden, bright bubble of magic that made Dominic twitch, and ran out the door.

Dominic exchanged a puzzled glance with Gutrune. "Start searching!" she whispered. There were voices outside, ones he did not recognize.

"He's put some kind of triggered perimeter about us," Dominic replied in similar low tones. "I don't know what will happen if I cross it, and it's hard to see anything through the magic there."

Gutrune sighed. "It is to be hoped Herr Asgaya does not intend a lengthy errand. Is there anything you can do?"

Dominic walked to the edge of the bubble. It enclosed most of the end of the parlor, centered on the sofa. The walls were out of reach, but two brocade armchairs, a plant stand, and a small wooden cabinet with a glass front were inside.

He discovered that one of the armchairs was missing a spring, that the fern on the plant stand needed watering, and something was odd about the cabinet.

Dominic stared at it, wondering what had caught his eye. The cabinet couldn't be hiding anything; the glass door showed the entire interior. The shelves held two carved meerschaum pipes, a delicate porcelain floral decoration with the inscription "Souvenir de la Parys," two mismatched jet buttons, and a copy of a Baerlen racetrack schedule from the previous year. All of them completely devoid of magic.

He shook his head, then caught his breath. There it was again! Just a tiny glimmer, from the joint between the right front leg and the carved front of the bottom edge of the cabinet. The edge was quite deep, at least four inches.

Dominic pulled gently at the edge of the carving. To his surprise, it came out smoothly, revealing a simple drawer. Inside were some of the infamous Parysan postcards of cabaret dancers in various scandalous stages of undress and imaginative poses.

"Have you found anything?" asked Gutrune.

Dominic experienced a moment of pure panic. "Er, nothing of interest." He stuffed the postcards back, hoping his shocked expression had not been noticed.

There it was again! Only this time the glimmer of magic was stronger, and underneath the last of the postcards. Dominic lifted them away. On the bottom of the drawer was a complex magical seal. Now that he was looking more carefully, the depth of the drawer did not match the depth of the piece of carving. There was a second hidden compartment.

Quick steps in the hallway made him look up sharply, but it was only Markus, returning with a bloodstained handkerchief held up like a trophy.

"Got it!" he said, grinning.

Dominic expected to feel irritation at the sight of him, but it was not as strong as before. Perhaps he was getting more accustomed. "What did you find?"

"His blood," Markus said with satisfaction. "I had to hurry before the crowds trampled all over it. Why aren't you looking in the study? That's where he'd be more likely to hide something," he told Dominic, carefully tucking the handkerchief away.

No, he was still irritated. "You cast a perimeter before you left. Don't you remember?"

Markus made a sound of disbelief. "You could cross it, you know. It's only set for anyone trying to get *in*."

Dominic gritted his teeth. "That piece of information would have been very useful to know before you left. Besides, I found something."

Eyebrows raised, Markus went over to the cabinet. He cast a very amused look at Dominic when he saw the postcards, and Dominic felt his face go hot.

"Not those. There's a magical seal on a secret compartment

underneath. It looks similar to the one I saw on the document packet from the Council. I think it is set to destroy the contents if the seal is not opened correctly."

"The people from the neighboring quarters are remaining outside," Gutrune observed calmly, her pistol in one hand as she checked Ardhuin's pulse with the other. "Why is that?"

Markus grinned again, the glint of mischief strong in his eyes. "Perhaps they took to heart my offhand comments about needing to disable the many magical traps we've found," he said. "And lo, I spoke the truth without knowing!"

"A common occurrence, I think," muttered Dominic under his breath.

"It will not buy us much time. One of the brighter individuals will undoubtedly realize the *Kriegszauberkollegium* must have someone equally capable of dealing with traps, and send for them. Describe this seal to me," he said, looking at Dominic.

His amused, mocking manner was gone. Markus Asgaya was all business dealing with the magical seal, asking precise, knowledgeable questions. Despite himself, Dominic felt a grudging respect. It was very different from working with Ardhuin. Markus was slower, making it easier for Dominic to see the separate steps involved. Ardhuin's fluid style was more impressive, but this was still interesting.

"Ah, that should do it. Is it engaged?" Markus asked. Dominic checked. All the overlayers were precisely matched to the ones on the seal, and he nodded.

He blinked at the flare of bright magic released by the seal. Apparently even Markus had sensed something, for he whistled.

"That would have been nasty. Now, let's see what we have here." Markus delicately lifted the false bottom out of place and reached inside. "Looks like letters. So why the elaborate concealment? Hmm." Only the pages had been preserved; the covers were missing. Markus skimmed one, and suddenly sucked in his breath.

"What is it?" Dominic asked, seeing his frozen expression.

"Oh, merely a scandal of monumental proportions," Markus said in a faint voice. "Herr von Gerling appears to be having a most imprudent affair with a certain well-connected woman." He tucked the letters in an inner pocket of his coat, shuddering.

"Why are you so shocked?" Dominic asked. "I had not thought your morality so strict."

"Oh, it isn't," Markus agreed without offense. "Court scandal usually amuses me, but this…no one would benefit if this came to light. Her husband is vindictive and powerful. The King's interests," he said carefully, "would be badly hurt if this were known."

Gutrune looked up from her station by the sofa. "I exist to serve."

"I dare not, forgive me. Even you should not know." Markus appeared genuinely distressed. "*I* should not know. These should go directly to the King or into the fire."

"Seal them in a packet, and I will deliver them to the King. You cannot do it yourself without attracting notice," Gutrune pointed out, stepping closer. "Decide quickly. I believe they have decided to enter despite the danger." Her gaze alighted on the highly improper postcards, and her eyebrows went up.

Dominic and Markus both made a desperate effort to conceal them, but it was too late. Gutrune gave them an enigmatic look, then commented, "An excellent decoy. Anyone searching would assume the pictures were the only items concealed. I am surprised, though, that some are of quite recent date. I do not think Herr von Gerling was granted permission to travel, considering the current situation."

"I cannot believe that you are conversant with this type of thing," Markus said, his eyes wide with shock. Dominic was equally dumbfounded.

A small smile curved the corner of Gutrune's lips. "I have seen one of these dancers before. The one with the fan," she said blandly. One of the cards did feature a picture of a dancer with a fan—and no other concealment for her charms. "She was more warmly dressed when I had occasion to see her, on her debut three months ago at the Chien Vert cabaret in Parys. Also, I believe I saw the name Trezabel on another. That establishment, I am informed, opened its doors a mere five weeks ago."

She turned her head to the entrance. The sound of feet stumbling over pieces of broken door could be clearly heard. "They are coming in. Go to the study—I will attempt to delay them."

Markus quickly closed the hidden compartment and left the parlor. Dominic followed, dazed by all the sudden revelations. Gutrune had been right about one thing, though. Ardhuin was looking better.

The wash of magic over the chilly study was beginning to fade, fortunately. Dominic started searching, while Markus took the scandalous letters and folded them in a sheet of paper. Dominic saw magic as well as molten wax go into the seal.

"What luck?" Markus asked, tucking the packet back in his inner pocket.

"You have decided to give them to her?" Dominic asked.

Markus scowled. "She's right, damn her. I have no choice. They are too dangerous. Well?"

"Avoidance spell on the bookend that looks like a gargoyle. Sloppy stasis lock on the second drawer of the big bookcase. Something hit the corner of the desk; I can't see anything past that. Pieces of glass with magic, but that's from the fight."

He could hear voices from the shattered window as he continued to point out magic to Markus. They should conceal their presence as long as possible. They were lucky that the study window did not front the street, but it would probably be wise to draw the one remaining drape to hide the light.

Dominic went to the window, kicking aside the larger globes of glass from his path. A folded paper was lodged between the drape and the sill, and he picked it up. Leaning out, he saw two other papers, one torn, on the flagstones outside. Carefully avoiding the glass remaining in the frame, he eased himself out the window and dropped to the ground.

"What on earth are you doing?" hissed Markus. "They are coming!"

"Looks like he dropped them," Dominic said softly, holding the papers in his hand. Seeing the door to the study open behind Markus, he whispered, "I'll come in the front! Be surprised!"

He dropped down out of sight, waiting for a clear chance to leave the side alley and get back inside unobserved. Behind him, he heard Markus dealing with the *Kriegszauberkollegium* officials. Creeping away, he realized it was a very good thing that Markus Asgaya was an accomplished liar.

Someone was beating on her head with padded mallets. Ardhuin wished they would stop. The sensations became a little more distinct, and she realized they were voices, not mallets, but they still made her head throb. She moaned and tried to wrap her head in her arms, but something was making it hard to move them.

"Do you need anything?" It was like being hit with a pillow. This voice was low and much quieter than the others, but it was so close it seemed her whole body vibrated. Ardhuin opened her eyes. Gutrune von Kitren looked down at her, and the ceiling behind her swirled in a way that made Ardhuin's eyes twist. She shut them again.

"So…loud…" Ardhuin managed, her head aching anew with her own voice.

She felt a firm, strong grip on her hand that released, followed by a cloud of rustling noises. Somewhere in the distance Gutrune spoke, and was answered by chastened booming voices that faded and then disappeared. The relief of silence was so great it brought tears to her eyes.

Rustling and a cool hand on her forehead told her Gutrune had returned. "Do you feel able to sit up?" she asked, so softly it didn't even hurt. Ardhuin nodded, surprised that her head didn't fall off. It did swim unpleasantly, though, and a cloud of dust made her sneeze. It sounded like a cannon going off.

She drank the water Gutrune put to her lips, which helped with the dust. After a moment she dared to open her eyes. "What happened?" she croaked.

Gutrune gave her a quick summary, apologizing for being unable to stop von Gerling. "At present we have officers of the *Kriegszauberkollegium* investigating with Herr Asgaya and Herr Kermarec," she added. A certain restraint in her voice told Ardhuin there was more to the story.

"Dominic…Herr Kermarec is unharmed?"

"Yes. You are the only one who has suffered any ill effects. He was quite concerned for you."

Again that slight restraint in Gutrune's voice.

"Is something wrong?"

Gutrune hesitated. "He did not approve of Herr Asgaya's attempt to assist you," she said. "You should be aware—we have not told the officials anything about you, merely indicating you were attacked by von Gerling. They have not asked any awkward questions yet, but they will if given the chance. Do you think you can stand?"

Her head felt much better now, but attempting to stand brought on another severe dizzy spell. If Gutrune had not been there, she would have fallen.

"No matter; you must rest until you feel more able." Gutrune took a seat in a chair nearby, taking her pistol from the table and tucking it into her fur muff.

Ardhuin frowned. Little memories were coming back.

"Do you remember what Markus Asgaya said to you, when you first showed him that?" she asked.

Gutrune looked at her inquiringly. "Why, yes. It seemed an unusual thing for him to say."

"That's because it wasn't him," Ardhuin said, feeling awkward. "I mean, it's a saying. Among the Yunwiyans, "treasure of the nation" is another way to refer to a woman warrior. They have them, you know, and they are held in the highest esteem. Any Yunwiyan man would be proud to marry one," she said, her voice trailing off uncomfortably. "I just…thought you should know."

It was impossible to tell what Gutrune's reaction to this piece of information was. Her expression remained one of calm politeness as she gravely thanked Ardhuin, then asked if she was feeling better.

"I think so," Ardhuin said cautiously. The dizziness had abated, certainly. She tugged at the swath of heavy fabric surrounding her, releasing a cloud of dust. She sneezed, her head throbbing again, and looked more closely at what she was wrapped in. "Why a curtain?" she managed when she could talk again. A lock of hair fell free over her forehead. She reached up. As she feared, her hair was half undone. She must look like she had been dragged backwards through a thicket.

"Herr Kermarec was concerned that you were not warm enough. The curtain, I believe, was already torn down during—" Gutrune stopped. Another group of people had entered, one of whom Ardhuin recognized. Ermut Arendt.

"I am glad to see you are better," he said, coming forward and giving a polite bow. Ardhuin tried not to wince at his voice. It was also depressing to see him treat her with such formal courtesy, after his easy friendliness at the party.

Ardhuin was painfully aware of her disheveled appearance, wrapped in a dusty curtain. Of course she could not be as friendly and relaxed as when she was hiding behind an illusion, and she stammered a greeting. Then it occurred to her that Ermut himself seemed more than a little confused and off-balance. The other men with him continued down the hall, ignoring the two women as unimportant.

"I should apologize for imposing on your friends as I did," Ardhuin said, as loudly as she could without making her head pound, "but it was the most agreeable part of the evening."

Ermut smiled and relaxed a little. "The illusion on you was completely convincing," he said. "As was the one on the *schutzmagus*. I was going to ask him—but it occurred to me, having seen—" he waved in the direction of the study, "perhaps you are the correct person to ask." He took out a small photograph. "Can you tell me why he was illusioned to look like this man?"

Ardhuin took the photograph. It was, in fact, the eager young magician she had seen at the *Kriegszauberkollegium*. "No particular reason, save that it is easier to cast that level of illusion using a model instead of imagination." There, she had been truthful without admitting anything. "Why do you ask?"

Ermut looked uncomfortable again. "He was the one I mentioned, the friend of Hans. He was killed in a duel earlier today."

Ardhuin froze, suddenly making some disturbing connections. Hans' friend, the one killed, was a *Kriegsa* magician. Von Gerling had not shown any suspicion until he saw Markus, illusioned as the dead man. When he did, he panicked.

Why? Von Gerling must have known about the duel and expected a certain person to die—and if that person *hadn't* died, then he knew something von Gerling desperately wanted to keep secret.

"Fraülein...." Ermut still had something on his mind.

"Andrews." Ardhuin smiled at him, feeling tired. "That much was true."

"Good, it will save me learning another name." His answering smile was perfunctory. "I must ask. How did you do it? I could never fight von Gerling and win...and he ran from you. I think...I think the illusion was yours, too. It only vanished when you were on the point of collapse."

Gutrune had stiffened in her chair, but there was nothing she could say to undo the damage. Ermut was a magician, and confident in what he had seen. Fortunately, he was the only one who had.

Ardhuin twisted her hands together, wondering what to do. "Women don't do magic. Everyone knows this."

"But—"

"It is a matter of grave importance that this impression is not corrected in Fraülein Andrews' case," Gutrune said quietly. "*State* importance."

Ermut looked at her, then at the jeweled eagle pin on her pelisse. His eyes widened. "I see. I will say nothing. The *schutzmagus*...?"

"He knows."

"Ah." Ermut scratched his head. "May I be of help in any way? It would be a privilege, and if you—" he stopped and corrected himself carefully, "if *a mage* needed temporary magical assistance while recovering from the *kraftdampung*, I would be glad to provide it."

"The…kraft-what?" Ardhuin asked. He'd called her a mage. What did he mean by that?

"*Kraftdampung*. It can happen when a mage overextends his abilities, but usually only in the heat of battle. There is a collapse, then, and limited power for a period of time. If done to extremes," Ermut said, looking serious, "it can kill. All war magicians are warned of this, from the beginning of their training."

Well. Useful information, Ardhuin supposed, not that it would have changed much if she had known.

"Is there any way to treat this condition?" she asked.

"I have heard that milk can help," Ermut offered.

It was very late by the time Ardhuin, Dominic, and Markus returned to the Imperial Palace in a carriage borrowed from the *Kriegszauberkollegium*. Ardhuin wasn't completely certain because of her limited Preusan, but it appeared the Council had changed its attitude regarding her presence. Presumably von Gerling had left enough incriminating evidence to convince the officials of his guilt in *something*. She wished she knew what.

Perhaps it had something to do with the packet Markus had slipped to Gutrune, which she immediately tucked into her muff. Markus had made sure none of the *Kriegsa* magicians were in sight before he did, though. Gutrune had left when they did, but alone, to complete her mysterious errand with Stoller and the lamplighter's cart.

So tired. It was hard to think, to concentrate. Maybe the milk would help with that, if she could get some. She didn't like milk. Ardhuin frowned with the effort of remembering. Had Ermut said to drink it?

"Ardhuin. We're here." Dominic had a worried expression on his face, and she struggled to appear awake and alert. "Can you get out without assistance?"

She could, just barely. For the rest, however, she had to lean rather heavily on Dominic. "I am sorry," Ardhuin gasped, stopping to catch her breath. "There are too many grand staircases for me right now." Fortunately, it was past three o'clock, and only the palace guards were in evidence.

"Would you like to rest?" Dominic asked, laying a hand on her arm.

Ardhuin studied the path remaining. Red figured carpeting extended up another flight, and then there was a hallway before reaching their wing. She could do that, couldn't she?

"Standing is tiring also," she said, sighing. "I just want to get to my room and sleep."

"If need be, we can carry you," Markus said cheerfully, flicking a glance at Dominic.

She felt Dominic's grasp tighten and his whole body stiffen. "No doubt," Dominic said, his voice cold and unenthusiastic. Markus appeared amused.

Ardhuin sighed. The last thing she needed was more mysteries. Her head hurt. She started wearily up the last flight of stairs.

"I know you are very tired, but there is something I need to tell you. In your workroom," Dominic said softly. Ardhuin started to object, but she recognized the stubborn look in his eyes. It would take effort to argue with him—easier to agree and get it over with.

Slowly, slowly down the hall. There was the door to the workroom. Ardhuin turned once they reached it.

"There is one last thing," she told Markus. "It won't take long." If Dominic's message was too lengthy, she would just fall asleep there. *Her* problem would be taken care of.

Markus hesitated. "Are you sure that's wise?" He looked at Dominic. "You will try to prevent her from overexertion, won't you? I must write up what we have found for the Council, so I will leave you here."

"Finally," muttered Dominic as they stepped through the wards.

"You seem annoyed with him," Ardhuin ventured, gratefully sinking down on the sofa inside. "Has he offended you?"

"Offended? Well, I suppose not," Dominic admitted. "I find his habit of smirking at you and making snide comments to me tiresome, that's all. Everything is a joke to him. I am concerned he is trying to amuse himself with you as well."

It was strange how the sudden understanding flooded her mind, how it felt as if she had always known. Dominic was jealous of Markus.

Because of her.

It didn't make any sense, but then wasn't that one of the most noticeable things about love? At least, that's what she had observed in all the stories. It didn't make any sense that Dominic would be in love with her, either, but why else would he be acting as he had been?

She had to say something. Her mother would have known exactly the right thing to reassure him.

"That's simply his nature, I think," Ardhuin said, hoping her voice didn't wobble too much. "He's not making fun of you, or…or me to be cruel. He's just teasing. My brothers are the same way—well, maybe not Chris, but even he does it sometimes," she stopped, realizing she was babbling. "They only do it to people they really like." Ardhuin winced as soon as the words left her mouth. Now Dominic would take what she had said as proof of intent on the part of Markus.

Instead, Dominic looked thoughtful. "He reminds you of your brothers? What a trial that must have been. And I think you said you had three of them, too." He shook his head. "Perhaps you are right, but I do not think he regards you in light of a sister. He is entirely too friendly for that."

"The novelty of my magic, perhaps, combined with my familiarity with Yunwiya. Truly, I believe his…his interest lies elsewhere," Ardhuin said, thinking of Gutrune. That made no sense either, except that Markus clearly loved a challenge. It might be interesting to watch, at least from a safe distance.

Dominic brightened. "Really?"

"Really," Ardhuin said, smothering a laugh. She felt as if little bubbles of happiness were flowing through her. "Now what is it that you had to tell me?"

His face grew serious. "At the party…Mauer's roommate had a large piece of chryselectrum from a bad batch. His uncle makes it or something like that. Jochim Weiskopf found it, and was looking through it. He saw you—without your illusion."

"What? That's impossible." Iron could distort an illusion, and a more powerful magical field could overpower it, but nothing she knew of could see *through* it, leaving the illusion intact.

Dominic shook his head. "He said he saw a lady, and you were the only one there. Fortunately, he was quite drunk and nobody took him seriously. I looked through it too. You appeared in your real form, only slightly shadowed. What if someone else knows about this?"

"Hmm. I suspect this may be a property only of the flawed chryselectrum, possibly unique to that piece. Really, Dominic, it is used so often with higher-level magic it would be remarkable if no one else had noticed."

Dominic looked unconvinced. "I need some chryselectrum to check. Where are the channels you didn't use for the ward?"

Ardhuin pointed to the cabinet. He opened it and brought out the case with the remaining channels in it, removing an angular piece splayed like a tripod.

"No good—I can't see anything; it's too narrow." He examined the contents again. "This should be better."

It was an oval, slightly concave. "You are right—I can't see anything at all through this. It's like a mirror—"

Dominic's face was a pale mask of horror.

"What's wrong?" Ardhuin felt her heart start to pound.

"I felt something, but I didn't know he had done anything…what is it making me do?" he whispered.

"What? Who did this? What are you talking about?" Ardhuin got painfully to her feet. Was Dominic still obsessing about Markus Asgaya?

He stared at her. "Von Gerling, in the fight. He put a *geas* on me. I can *see* it."

There was no air in her lungs, no strength in her legs. She sat down hard, a voice screaming in her mind. *Not now. Please not now. He is going to ask questions, you know he is. And you still do not know how to lie.*

"He did not put a *geas* on you," a calm, distant voice said. It seemed to be her own. "You must touch the person to set it, and he never touched you. Besides, with your training you would know if something like that had been done."

"But—" Dominic rubbed his hand frantically through his black hair. "I can *see* it."

Maybe she could avoid it a little longer. "How do you know it is a *geas?*"

"It looks like what the prisoner had. It is not exactly the same, but very close."

No, it was over. She had to tell him; she had been intending to anyway. Now she knew she had been avoiding it because there would be no happy ending to this story. He knew what *geasi* could do now, and he would know she had cast one. On him. It was not possible he could forgive her.

"That must be why I was acting so strangely," Dominic added, looking dazed. "I don't understand. If I would have known it was done to me when it was cast, who did it? What does it do?"

Say it. Get it over with. She was so tired.

Ardhuin took a deep breath. "It was done before you were trained to see magic, so you noticed something but didn't understand what had happened. And all it does," she forced herself to say the words, "is prevent you from telling anyone about my roses."

The silence lengthened, spread through the room. Ardhuin looked down at her clenched hands and waited for the explosion.

"You did this." His voice was only a whisper. Ardhuin nodded, not daring to look at him. "Why?"

She could hear the pain; it echoed her own. "Because I was being attacked. Because you walked through my defenses as if they weren't there. Because you saw the roses of Oron, that no other mage has been able to duplicate, that would tell my enemies they had found me. Because I was afraid."

"But why haven't you removed it? Don't you trust me?"

This was not the explosion she had been expecting. Ardhuin looked up at him. "Of course I trust you!" she blurted. "You wouldn't be in here if I didn't."

He gave her a look. "You can't set a *geas* for that?"

Ardhuin shook her head. "A *geas* can't make someone trustworthy, and it can't change what they think or believe. It only affects outward actions, like talking, or avoiding a certain place, or…or firing a gun, like the anarchist did. He had no objection to shooting the King. All the *geas* did was make him do it at a certain time and place." Dominic still looked skeptical, and worried. "Look. The more a *geas* goes against someone's convictions, the harder it is to set. Also, it is obvious they are under constraint."

"But you didn't take it off."

"I couldn't! By the time I knew I could trust you, you had learned enough of your gift to be able to tell I was doing something to you. I was afraid you would be angry if you found out. I was afraid," Ardhuin said, her throat so tight she could barely speak, "that you would leave." She dropped her head to her knees, wrapping her arms around them.

"Ardhuin…."

She refused to raise her head. It hurt too much already, and if she had to look at him when he spoke it would hurt more. She heard footsteps, the sounds of him before her. His hands touched hers and she started, but he grasped her wrists and did not let go.

"Remove it. Now."

At this, she did look up. He was crouched in front of her, his expression grim.

"You would let me? After I—"

His mouth twisted. "Who better?" Dominic closed his eyes. "I remember noticing you were frightened, and wondering why. I think… just remove it. Then I will know what I think."

The question was, could she? It was trivial compared to setting it; hardly any power was used. In her current condition, however, it still might be too much.

Ermut Arendt had warned of the dangers of overtaxing her magic. Well, did it matter if it did kill her? Right now life did not hold much attraction.

She raised her hands to his head; his grip shifted but did not loosen. Ardhuin fought to keep from crying as soon as her fingers touched his face, realizing she had lost what she only now realized she had. The planes of his face, the angled cheekbones, were even more sharply delineated by pain, and seeing that, her eyes welled up. She had hurt him. The only thing she could do now was set him free.

First, the resonance. As soon as she tried to summon power, pain flared through her as if her blood had turned to fire. She gasped, lost the thread of the resonance, then gritted her teeth and forced it back.

Her hands shook with the strain; tears flowed freely down her face. Just a little more, a small counter-resonance that would break the pattern and set him free. The agony was a white-hot roar in her mind.

A quick pulse was all that was needed to break the *geas*. She felt it dissolve under her hands.

"It's gone."

Dominic did not shift his position, did not release her hands. Then, slowly, he lowered them and stared at her. His dark eyes looked haunted.

"I don't feel any different."

"It was just for the roses," Ardhuin whispered. "I'm sorry, Dominic."

He looked at her for a long moment. Then he suddenly leaned forward, gave her a hard, passionate kiss, and got up and left the workroom without saying a word.

Ardhuin found she lacked the strength to even stand, but doing magic hadn't killed her after all. She wondered if that was a good thing.

CHAPTER 12

Dominic tossed and turned for what seemed like hours, his troubled thoughts keeping him awake despite his exhaustion. Too tired to sleep, perhaps...and then, with Ardhuin's painful revelations so recent...she would be troubled too, he knew, and was probably awake as well. Thinking of her unhappiness drove sleep even further away.

Twice he decided to go and find her—whether to resolve his own conflicted feelings or to comfort her he wasn't sure. But then he would hesitate and change his mind, too tired to make the effort. All he could think of, round and round, was that he loved her and she had put a *geas* on him.

She could do it again, and even if he knew about it, how could he stop her? He was beginning to realize how powerful she was. And yet... he could not forget the look on her face when she had said, *I was afraid you would leave.*

He felt ashamed of his fear. When had she ever hurt him, even when he deserved it? When she was terrified, thinking he had been sent by the enemy trying to kill her, the most she had done was bind and question him. Even then, she could have added to her earlier *geas* with one more restrictive and forced him to leave. She hadn't. Somehow, he knew she never would. Still, she had the power. It would always be there.

Dominic managed to doze off, but there was no refuge in sleep. He dreamed of the stone cells of the *Kriegszauberkollegium* and the imprisoned anarchist, screaming in mortal agony as Ardhuin removed the *geas* from him. Her hands were red with blood when she released the man, and Dominic realized it was *her* blood, that it poured from her palms in a torrent. She fell to her knees, looking to him with a soundless plea for help, but he could not move, he was frozen, watching helplessly as she fell unconscious on the bloody stone floor.

He woke with a gasp, feeling nauseous, heart pounding. It was useless to think of sleeping now, and his watch told him it was almost morning anyway. He needed to see Ardhuin, to make sure she was all right. He should not have left her as he did.

A vigorous wash with cold water cleared his mind a little, and he dressed, taking care not to wake the defensive magician still asleep within the wards. Shaking out his coat, he heard a rustling. The papers from von Gerling's study—with everything that had happened, he had forgotten to give them to Markus. Should he find him now, despite the early hour? It was worth a try, in any event, and would be better than sitting in his room with his troubled thoughts.

The defensive magicians on duty outside his room disclaimed any knowledge of Markus Asgaya's location or activities, and seemed glad to say so. Dominic cast a look at the closed door to Ardhuin's room. A maid came by with a tray containing a teapot and a dish of sweet rolls, leaving it on a table nearby after consulting with the guard. If Ardhuin was still sleeping, it would be better not to disturb her.

Dominic went down to the main level of the Imperial Palace. The corridors were mostly empty, but he passed one door where he could hear the sounds of angry argument. No one he passed could tell him where Markus was. He found a settee in a corner, out of general view, and took the papers from his coat pocket.

The first was a list of names, with notations. Some of the names had been crossed out. Dominic read the comments and started to feel a chill. "Mentioned as potential by v.R, approached and showed interest. Ambitious, ties to *Echtkraftgemein*." "Resents military, was held back for promotion twice due to political opinions." "Promising, intelligent and quite skilled. Family commoners, no patron so advancement limited. Suspicious, asking questions."

The name next to that comment had been crossed out.

The next piece of paper was small, a half-sheet that had been folded many times. For concealment? It was covered closely with writing, but Dominic could not puzzle out the meaning or even the language it was written in. A code! There had been an article in *The Family Museum* about codes. He would have to try to see if he remembered any of the techniques for deciphering them.

A torn scrap of paper was all that remained of the third piece he had rescued. He had found that one in the alley, so the remainder was probably still in von Gerling's valise. It must have some importance.

"... begin the next phase. We will...at need. Be certain to contact...place articles a week before...delay required...timed to match Feast of Sacrifice, and...common belief, and their own tradition will make the event credible and sure of success."

It was signed with the same glyph he had seen on the illusioned message Ardhuin had shown him, and he thought he could see the faint remnants of magic on this paper as well.

Dominic got up, more determined than ever to find Markus. There were more people about now, but the angry meeting was still going on when he passed that door again. He reached the upper level and had only enough time to notice the tray outside Ardhuin's door remained untouched when he heard Markus himself hailing him.

"Well, at least I found one of you," the defensive magician said. He looked tired and irritable. "Where have you been hiding, anyway?"

"I was trying to find you," Dominic answered, surprised. "What is wrong?"

"My most immediate problem is locating Fraülein Andrews. She's not in her room. The fool guard didn't even check for himself when he relieved the man before him, just assumed she was there. Where do they get such idiots?"

"The workroom?" Dominic blurted and started to run down the hall.

"Yes, that's why I was looking for you. I tried my usual method, but no response," Markus said with a trace of his customary grin. "I don't think she likes it. But what happened? I thought you were going to see that she got some rest. She could barely stand, and you let her stay up working?"

Dominic bit back an angry response, feeling guilty. He could hardly explain to Markus, of all people, what had happened last night. The door to the workroom was before him, the ward undisturbed. He reached for the door handle, but the door opened before he could grasp it.

Ardhuin stood in the doorway, still wearing the simple dark outfit she had worn the previous day, only now it was creased and rumpled. If she had slept, it had not rested her. She looked at Dominic, then at Markus and the group of defensive magicians that had been clustered around the hall.

Markus breathed a sigh of relief. "Excellent. If we had managed to mislay you, the King would have had us all execute each other."

Ardhuin blinked. "I was inside," she said, gesturing. Her voice was rough. "I didn't...I slept there. I didn't want to cast wards."

Now Dominic really felt ashamed. "You mean, you were too tired to cast wards." At least she'd had the sense to stay in the workroom, with its permanent defenses. "If you were so tired, why did you—" he stopped, remembering Markus stood next to him.

"It was important," Ardhuin said, her voice so faint he could barely hear it. "Don't you agree?"

"I admire your dedication, but if you could keep us informed of your whereabouts at all times, it would reduce the number of headaches I must suffer. No one mentioned it to you, I am sure, but half of the *Kriegsa* wants to arrest the other half, the Council wants to arrest the whole, and the army is strongly suggesting the imposition of martial law until the situation is cleared up." Markus closed his eyes, clearly struggling to regain his calm.

"I see. Is this because of von Gerling?" Ardhuin asked, after a pause.

Markus nodded, looking even more tired. "He was in a powerful position, and if *his* loyalty is suspect...." He gave Ardhuin a critical glance. "Forgive me, but you do not appear to enjoy your customary good health. May I suggest a visit by a physician is in order? We can't afford to lose you, you know. Especially not now."

Ardhuin scowled. "I'm just tired, that's all."

"You did collapse yesterday," Dominic said, wishing Markus and the others were not there so he could say more. Wishing they were back at Peran, and safe. "Please. Let them send for a doctor."

She gave him a long look, her face unreadable. Finally, she just nodded and slowly made her way down the corridor.

"And why aren't you catching up on your sleep as well?" Markus wanted to know, cheerfully oblivious to his earlier impatience at Dominic's absence.

Dominic glanced around, then handed Markus the papers. "I forgot to give you these. One I think is a code, but the others—they smell like a plot to me."

Markus scanned them quickly. The list of names held his attention the longest. "Yes, I think you are correct," he said. His expression was serious. "Did you recognize any names?" Dominic shook his head. "I did, two of them. They were from the *Kriegsa*. They both died in duels."

The doctor sent to her was a quiet little man with a bald head and a full beard. He did not seem at all surprised that his patient was a woman; presumably someone had warned him ahead of time. It was hard for her to pay attention to his questions, to think about what he was asking her. She felt numb, as if a thick cloud separated her from everything around her.

She just wanted it all to go away. Forget Preusa, forget the politics. Forget the wary expression in Dominic's eyes when he looked at her, which hurt more than anything she'd felt in her life. There was little hope of improvement that she could see. She wanted oblivion.

Ardhuin had never been examined by a thaumatic physician before, so she had no idea if he was doing anything unusual. Among other things, he had her hold a sheet of paper, which he carefully sanded with what looked like powdered pearl, and then asked her to summon power. The sharp stabbing pain did not return, to her relief. The little granules shifted in a pattern, which he duly noted with a thoughtful expression and informed her there did not seem to be any permanent damage to her abilities. He ended by prescribing a sleeping draft, and left.

Her first emotion when she woke, later in the afternoon, was disappointment. Sleep had only deferred her problems for a little while. She did feel better, though. With an effort, she forced herself to leave the comfortable safety of her room. The sooner she solved Preusa's problems, the sooner they would let her leave.

Markus Asgaya found her shortly after she emerged. Dominic was nowhere in sight.

"How charming!" Markus said, giving her an admiring glance. "You will enliven the gloom of the company simply by your presence."

Ardhuin looked down. She wore a cream-colored tea gown, the only article of clothing both she and her mother approved of—she because of the comfort, her mother because of the cut and style. She hadn't even been aware of what she had chosen when she put it on.

"Should I wear something else?"

Markus shook his head emphatically. "Absolutely not. I admit the protocol for female Mage Guardians has not yet been established, but that simply means you will be the standard against which all others will be judged. A weighty task, but you have begun admirably. Besides, you are the heir of Oron. A certain eccentricity is expected."

What had her great-uncle done to earn this reputation? Shown up without a shirt?

"Come," Markus said, offering his arm. "They want to hear your version of last night's events. I delayed them as long as I could, but now that you are awake they will insist on your presence."

He bore her irresistibly along, talking in a cheerful, inconsequential way the entire time. Ardhuin heard him as if he were talking from a distance. The same remote feeling as before surrounded her like a fog. She wanted to ask about Dominic, but she was afraid of the answer.

There were a handful of men in the room when they entered. One she recognized from the Council meetings, Dr. Roemer. He was an *ars magica* professor from the university, advanced in years but still possessing a sharp mind hidden behind a gentle manner. The others were mage-level magicians from various departments. She forgot the names as soon as Markus introduced them; she was still having a great deal of trouble paying attention.

"...and this is the head of the *Kriegszauberkollegium*, Magus-Kommandant von Koller. Herr Magus, this is—"

"I have no wish to be introduced to this...person." Von Koller rose to his feet and glared at Ardhuin, undisguised hatred in his eyes. He was a large, muscular man with a thick moustache and short-clipped salt-and-pepper hair. He wore the usual *Kriegsa* uniform, but with additions that made it look more than a little military.

The fog around her mind burned suddenly away. Ardhuin felt the old sick feeling of apprehension return, and she had a sudden impulse to turn and run.

"Are you trying to destroy us? Your vapid imaginings have ruined a proud and loyal institution, but that is nothing to you, in your deluded belief of power. How *dare* you!"

It was hard to breathe, to think. "I was asked to come here," she stammered. "I had an obligation." How she wished that were not true. Von Koller could not possibly want her to leave more than she did.

His eyes narrowed. "We asked for a *mage*, and you are no *mage*, girl! Now get out!" He strode up to her, his face working. Ardhuin was too paralyzed by terror to move, but Markus quickly stepped in front of her.

"I must object, sir. Fraülein Andrews is here at the King's request, and I can personally attest to her abilities."

Von Koller scowled at Markus. "And it is a sign of our decay that a mongrel like yourself is even allowed within the palace. You are not worthy of the uniform you wear," he said in an even, implacable tone. Markus stiffened and went as pale as his brown skin would allow.

"The Magus-Kommandant is no doubt aware I am forbidden to accept or give challenges, which is why he feels so free to speak in such a manner," Markus replied in the coldest voice Ardhuin had ever heard him use.

Von Koller stiffened in turn, but before he could speak, Dr. Roemer interrupted gently. "There is no need for such behavior before a lady, von Koller. She does not deserve your anger." His tone was one of reproof, and von Koller's face grew noticeably more red, but he refrained from any reply. "Now, my dear, I understand you were present at the recent unfortunate event, and I am told you confronted von Gerling by yourself. What can you tell us of that?"

"Impossible," sputtered von Koller. "Von Gerling is the victim of a vendetta. What could he possibly fear from her?"

The gentle, encouraging expression on the old professor's face, ignoring von Koller's angry comments, made it possible for Ardhuin to take a deep breath and speak.

"I suggest, sir, that you ask Herr von Gerling why he attacked us with no provocation—if you can find him." Her knees shook, but she didn't dare sit down. "I would also like to know who taught him the Devourer Gate spell. It was cast on the doorway of his study."

There was a deep silence, broken by sotto voce queries that seemed to be about the Preusan translation of the spell's name.

"You have no idea what you are talking about," von Koller snapped. "How could you possibly recognize that? It is forbidden, Mage War magic."

"A Mage Guardian is required to know such things," Ardhuin said. Her voice shook too, but only a little.

"Did I understand you correctly? Von Gerling attacked you?" Dr. Roemer asked.

"Not me, but my assistant. I returned the attack, and von Gerling fled inside the house. I followed and found him in his study. I attacked again, but he was able to escape through a broken window." And if she had not been so spent, she could have followed him.

"You can't even tell a consistent lie," von Koller said with contempt. "Have you forgotten the Devourer Gate you said was guarding him? Or do such things not affect you?"

"I forced it back on him," Ardhuin blurted. She had forgotten the anger that had made it possible; even she found it incredible now as she recounted the story.

One of the other magicians gave an astonished snort of laughter. Von

Koller relaxed a little. "No doubt. Did you then call down lightning, or summon a dragon? We have wasted enough time with you. These are serious matters, and we cannot humor you and your fairy tales. Go and attend to more suitable things for young ladies. You will find dancing lessons much more enjoyable."

The rage did not build; it was present in an instant. It consumed her. The power was gathered before she was even conscious of her plan.

Ardhuin stepped away from Markus before he could realize what she was doing, and raised her hands. "I do not choose to dance," she hissed. And let the full force of her power go.

Dominic took out his watch yet again, shook his head, and put it back in his waistcoat pocket.

"Isn't there anything we can be doing?"

"Very little, I am afraid." Gutrune von Kitren examined the selection of little pastries on the plate, finally selecting a chocolate macaroon. She wore a light blue ensemble corded with black *passementerie* like a cavalry uniform. "Your assistance will not be welcome. They will be at pains to conceal any weakness from foreigners at such a time." She inclined her head in a graceful half-apology.

"But we were the ones who uncovered it!"

"True, and they will never forgive you for doing so. Only consider, Herr Kermarec. This is a scandal that has shaken the *Kriegszauberkollegium* at the highest levels. It is a very important part of our defenses. If they did not know Herr von Gerling was, at the very least, plotting for personal gain, what else has been hidden from them?"

The more public search of von Gerling's quarters had uncovered a set of bank books with a startling total, completely unsupported by his official income.

"It is also disturbing that no one has been able to contact Herr von Stangen. He is…not where he was expected to be."

Dominic saw her austere expression and realized there was even more going on than she was telling him, at least explicitly. Von Stangen was the second-ranking magician at the *Kriegsa*. That would indeed be a scandal if he were also involved, and everyone there would be under suspicion to some degree.

He took a sip of his tea. It had grown cold. The door opened and a harried-looking man looked in, apologized for intruding, and closed it again. Outside, he heard the sound of running feet and urgent voices. Another man came in, this time in the black uniform of a *schutzmagus,* and quickly scanned the room before turning to go.

"Is something wrong?" Gutrune asked in a tone that meant tell-me-or-else.

"The, ah, that is, Fraülein Andrews is needed urgently." His eyes darted to and fro and he swallowed nervously.

"I had thought she was in discussions with the senior magicians,"

Dominic said, frowning.

"Yes sir. She was." The *schutzmagus* looked even more nervous. "Your pardons, Fraülein, sir." He darted away.

Now Dominic was really worried. "If they won't tell you, it must be serious," he said, getting up from his seat. "But what are they searching for? A lost canary? He was looking up at the ceiling!"

He had a sick feeling in the pit of his stomach. He'd left a message for Ardhuin. She either hadn't gotten it or didn't want to talk to him. Something was wrong.

He heard Markus shouting outside in the hallway, arguing. "Well? What manner of fool insults another mage like that? It's not as if he wasn't warned! Von Koller got his just rewards for being an idiot, and I hope he learns his lesson."

"Yes, but he can't learn it in his current condition," the other man pointed out. "Look, Asgaya, it doesn't matter if she was justified in doing it. We can't get him out and we've tried everything! Find her, for God's sake!"

"If she doesn't want to be found, neither you nor I will find her. What we need is—" Markus caught sight of Dominic and his expression changed. "Come, quickly. We have a problem."

"Where is Ardhuin? What have you done to her?" Dominic was in no mood to do anything but make sure she was safe.

Markus had taken him by the arm and was propelling him into the next room, which was full of agitated magicians. His face was haggard. "Von Koller was being even more offensive than usual, and she did... that."

He dragged Dominic through the crowd and pointed. A man in a *Kriegsa* uniform was literally embedded in the wall. His arms and feet stuck out from the otherwise undisturbed surface. His face was purple with suppressed fury, no doubt exacerbated by the fact he could not speak. He had no mouth.

"What did he say to her?" Dominic asked, awed and a little frightened.

Markus shook his head, looking confused. "Oh, the usual sort of nonsense. Nothing she has not heard before, actually, perhaps not as crudely expressed, but still! He refused to believe what she said about what happened with von Gerling. The next thing I know he's flying into the wall and she's nowhere to be seen."

"I find it hard to believe she would lose her temper to such a degree for that," Gutrune remarked, behind them. She looked at von Koller coolly, then returned her attention to Markus. "Are you sure that is all he said?"

"It was all of a piece, rude and deliberately offensive. He even made sure to insult me as well. I had thought, though, the worst was over. He had decided she was simply making it up and was treating her like an over-imaginative child. Told her to go back to her dancing lessons."

Gutrune gasped. The look of shock on her usually calm face surprised Dominic as much as if she had screamed.

"Oh. I see." She took a deep breath.

"See what?" Markus asked, perplexed. "What's wrong with dancing lessons?"

Gutrune had regained control of her expression, and she shook her head. "It is not for me to say. However, I most strongly urge you never to mention them to her. As you can see, the associations are painful." She gestured to the imprisoned von Koller.

"Well, whatever her feelings, we can't leave him like that." Markus sighed, running a hand through his hair. "Tempting though it is. Can you look for her? She can't hide from your talent," he said, turning to Dominic.

Dominic was not so sure, but since he also desperately wanted to find her, he agreed. Ardhuin was not in the workroom, or anywhere else he would expect her to be.

"We may have to search the entire palace," he sighed. "I don't think she has left. Her cloak is still here." Dominic fingered the emerald rosebud stickpin in his cravat, wishing the magic worked both ways so he could find her. "Is it really so urgent to find her? She will likely return when her temper has cooled."

"Unfortunately, yes. We can't figure out how to release von Koller. She's transformed him into the wall itself. We have to reverse it correctly or it will kill him. And that, by the way, would reverse any improvements we have only now managed to introduce," he added, giving Dominic a significant look.

Dominic stared at Markus, incredulous. "What? All these magicians, and you can't do anything?"

Markus shrugged. "Everything we've tried doesn't work. I don't understand it."

"Well, maybe I can help. I'm not much good finding her," Dominic said.

Back in the room with the imprisoned von Koller, Dominic examined the magic carefully. As he understood what Ardhuin had done, he had to fight the impulse to laugh. It would only make the situation worse. At last he had to gesture to Markus to follow him outside, where he could grin unseen by von Koller.

"It's an illusion," Dominic said, snickering.

Markus gaped. "What?"

"There's no transformation; that's why your spells weren't attaching. She's used an extremely strong stasis field along the entire wall, anchored at the far corners. There's another on his mouth. Everything else is illusion." He felt a great relief. Even though she had been very angry, Ardhuin had acted with enough restraint to not harm her tormentor—just humiliate him and demonstrate to everyone else what she could do. The illusion was a masterful touch. If he had not pointed it out, the other magicians would have tried for days to lift a spell that wasn't there.

After thinking about it for a moment, Markus started chuckling too. "Superb. Now, how long do you think we should leave him like that? He doesn't look very repentant to me."

"That's entirely your affair," Dominic replied, his worry returning full force. Ardhuin was angry, hurt, and alone. "I'm going to look for Ardhuin."

The room she'd found to hide in was small by palace standards but it still had several sofas and chairs. All Ardhuin cared about were the windows, and of course none of the sofas faced that direction. She fixed that. Then she curled up and stared out at the grey sky above the rooftops of Baerlen, wishing she could blow something up.

Everything had gone wrong. The Preusans hated her, Dominic was afraid of her, and she still didn't know why she had been attacked in Peran. The only thing that could make it worse would be if her mother found out what she had been doing.

Even though she was still furious, she had to admit some of her problems were her own fault. If she'd known what being a Mage Guardian was like, she would have refused. Had her great-uncle known? Was that why he hadn't told her much about what she must do?

Ardhuin thought for a moment, anger slowly dying, and reluctantly decided Oron would not have deliberately put her at such a disadvantage. He might have avoided it because he disliked it, until it was too late for him to rectify the omission. He hadn't told anybody about her, again likely because he did not want to be embroiled in an argument. And then he had died.

A tear rolled down her cheek. He hadn't planned that either. Still, here she was. It had been his responsibility to prepare her, and that preparation had been incomplete. What had he been thinking? Was she really the only choice he had?

She sat in the gloom and wondered what to do next. They weren't going to forgive what she had done. The best thing would be to leave without anybody knowing. But how?

Ardhuin considered and discarded plans, her tragic mood deepening the more she thought about the trouble she was in. Her gear was in the workroom; she'd have to get it out, and then get herself and the trunks out of the Imperial Palace without detection. And what about Dominic? She winced. He had followed her here out of a misplaced chivalry. Well, she'd cured that. It wasn't his fault, though, and he didn't deserve to be abandoned here.

If she told Dominic, he would try to stop her. He couldn't do it himself, but he could tell others. Miserable, Ardhuin realized she would have to choose between escape and honor. He would be all right. They didn't hate him like they hated her. He might even be asked to stay by one of the mages here, for his talents. She'd already lost his love and his trust. It didn't matter anymore what he thought of her.

But it does matter! her treacherous heart protested. Ardhuin clenched her jaw. She was being soft. She could not afford to hope.

How long had she been sitting here? Her stomach was starting to growl and the light outside was getting dim. She had to move quickly. Take only what she could carry herself, leave everything else behind. She stood stiffly and went to the windows to see if she could see a likely escape route.

There were people in the courtyard, and she drew back out of sight. The shadow spell should be enough to avoid notice. She drew it about her and went to the window again.

A hand suddenly appeared, scrabbling for purchase on the edge of the ornamental balcony before the window, joined soon after by a matching hand. The fingers tightened, and Dominic's face appeared. He was looking directly at her and shouting something.

She'd put up wards, of course, and they dampened the sound. Her chest tightened with fear. She couldn't hide from Dominic; he could see through everything she could do. Fear and indecision paralyzed Ardhuin. What did he want to say to her? Did she even want to hear it?

The expression on his face changed, eyes widening. His fingers were slipping from the stone balustrade. Ardhuin wrenched the window open and cast the levitation spell just as he began to fall.

Dominic hung in midair before her, staring at her in astonishment. Ardhuin didn't know what to say either. He wasn't wearing a coat, and the cold was making his teeth chatter.

"M-may I come in?"

She had never once been able to make him leave when he wanted to stay. And she couldn't just leave him to freeze. Ardhuin nodded jerkily and moved him inside. She turned away as soon as she set him down, ostensibly to fuss with the window fastening, but really to avoid seeing him. While she had been planning on running away without him, he had been searching for her, and she felt her face heat with shame.

"How did you find me?" She had to know. There were countless windows in the Imperial Palace, and she doubted he'd been looking at them all. Not without freezing to death.

"A *schutzmagus* reported a room he couldn't open, even with a key. We could get in to all the others in the wing, and I saw magic from the outside. Markus Asgaya helped me up to get a look. They were desperate to find where you were." He still shivered, but he made no move towards the ceramic stove in the corner.

"I suppose they sent you," Ardhuin said in a tight voice, angry and hurt.

"There was no need. I would have tried to find you earlier, but they insisted I help free von Koller first. They didn't know how you had done it. They were afraid he would die."

Ardhuin turned around at this, stung. "I wouldn't have *killed* him!"

Dominic's expression was serious. "But you could do it. Couldn't you?"

Certainly she had the ability. She had even had, for an incandescent second, the desire. When it came to the deed itself, however, she'd found herself curiously reluctant to even harm von Koller.

"They want you to come back," Dominic said gently.

No word on *his* feelings on the matter, Ardhuin thought resentfully. "No they don't," she snapped. "If they do, it is only for the opportunity to rant at me. They can send me a letter if that's all they want. Why aren't they here? Why are you running their errands?"

Dominic hesitated, running a hand through his hair then glancing at her. "They are afraid of you, Ardhuin."

To have him so close, in the same room, and yet so distant was more painful than she could ever have imagined. He hadn't moved since she'd brought him in, his eyes never leaving her for an instant. And she couldn't move away.

She forced herself to speak around the tightness in her throat. "Are you afraid of me?"

Dominic closed his eyes, his face drawn and white as if he were in pain. "Sometimes," he whispered. Then his eyes flew open again. "Sometimes I forget to be afraid. And sometimes…sometimes I think you have a right to punish me for what I did to you."

He was looking at the floor now, color tingeing his prominent cheekbones. It took Ardhuin a moment to understand what he was referring to, and then she felt her own face go hot. She had almost forgotten his view of what had happened that night. It didn't make sense. Hadn't his illness been more than enough punishment?

"That was entirely my fault!" Ardhuin protested. "I was strong enough to stop you, and I didn't. Don't you understand that?"

In a few quick steps he was standing directly in front of her, his face inches from hers. His dark eyes blazed with anger. "I refuse to accept that I have no blame at all in the matter. How can you possibly know what I was thinking? Why can't *you* understand *that?*" he yelled.

Ardhuin stared at him dumbly, taken aback by his intensity. She still thought he bore no responsibility for anything he had done while intoxicated by the effects of the ley lines, but clearly he disagreed with her, and she wasn't even listening to him. Of course he would be angry.

She took a deep breath, and in a small voice said, "Very well."

Dominic's furious expression changed to one of surprise. The absurdity of the situation struck them both and they started to laugh.

A rapping noise came from the direction of the door. Ardhuin was startled, until she remembered she had dropped the wards to bring Dominic inside.

Dominic swore. "What impeccable timing," he muttered. "Well, I suppose they are getting impatient. Shall we?"

Ardhuin backed away, glancing at the window and wondering if she could escape that way. All of her earlier fear had returned full force.

"What's wrong?"

"I don't want to go," Ardhuin said in a shaky voice. "They are angry with me."

Dominic held out his hand. "They still need you to help them with their problem. Remember, they are afraid of you. If they are angry, they will do their best to conceal it."

She'd still be able to tell, and it would terrify her. Worse, she might do something even more unforgivable than pin a very important government official to a wall.

She felt her hand taken in a firm grasp. Dominic gave a gentle pull. She resisted it, but did not let go. It was too much of a comfort.

The rapping repeated.

"That's Markus," Dominic said. "He's probably worried something's wrong. You don't think *he's* angry with you, do you?"

Ardhuin frowned, feeling irritable. "I still don't want to talk to him. I don't want to talk to anybody." She just wanted to go home. With Dominic.

"But—" Dominic looked puzzled. "You are talking to me."

"You are different," Ardhuin said without thinking, and felt her face go red again.

"I'll stay with you," he said, smiling. Ardhuin felt a wave of guilt, and when he tugged again she followed reluctantly.

Outside the door, waiting, were Markus and Gutrune. Ardhuin had only a moment to notice that Gutrune seemed ill at ease, when she said, "The King wishes to speak with you. Alone."

CHAPTER 13

Ardhuin followed Gutrune, wishing she had yielded to her impulse to jump out the window. They were in the King's private wing. Dominic had not been allowed to accompany her. The refusal was phrased firmly but politely. There was no reason for anybody to be angry with him.

"Do you know why the King wishes to see me?" Ardhuin ventured. Gutrune shook her head, and she sunk further into gloom. Her friend looked worried, and that was a bad sign as well.

Ardhuin was escorted by three *schutzmagi* into a large room fitted up as an office. It was notable for the complete lack of the gilded plaster trim and ornate furnishings found everywhere else in the palace. Behind the large double-fronted desk was the King.

He wore a plain uniform without insignia, and he looked even more tired than he had before. The desk was covered with papers and half-rolled maps.

"Fraülein Andrews, your Majesty."

The King looked at her for a moment without expression, and Ardhuin felt her stomach twist. "Thank you, Adler. You may go."

Her escorts were so startled one of them broke discipline and protested.

"But...your Majesty! She is—"

Now he looked angry. "Out! I do not wish to be disturbed. See to it."

The door shut with a solid click behind her. Ardhuin swallowed, her mouth suddenly dry.

"They wish to protect you, your Majesty," she said, amazed at herself for speaking at all. She was as surprised as the *schutzmagi* had been that the King had sent them away, and wished they would come back. She didn't know if she trusted herself right now.

The King sighed, resting his forehead on his clasped hands. "They do. I have no complaint with their service. From what I am told, however, if you truly wished to harm me, three would not be at all sufficient to stop you." He raised his head and gestured to a chair near the desk. "Please be seated."

Ardhuin sat. She was only an arm's length away from him, and she could see the grey in his hair and the fine lines on his face. This was not at all what she had been expecting. His tone was brusque, but it felt more like it was his natural way of expressing himself, unconnected to her misbehavior.

She thought about suggesting more than three defensive magicians but decided it would be better not to argue. The King had enough reasons to be annoyed with her.

He leaned back in his chair, regarding her for a moment. "Do you know how I came to my present state?"

Ardhuin blinked. What did that have to do with her? She shook her head.

"I was not intended to inherit the throne. My father was the younger son. I was nineteen years of age when the Mage Wars began. My uncle was killed and my father badly wounded in a magical attack on Fortress Gruneiden. My grandfather, advanced in years, died just before the end of the war. My coronation took place on my twenty-first birthday, and I was almost completely ignorant of everything I needed to know to rule."

The beginnings of understanding filtered through her mind. "Did anyone say you could not be King?" she asked. Strange, how this felt nothing like a conversation between King and commoner, but more like one between equals. She looked down, seeing a litter of papers on the floor behind him, and smiled to herself. It seemed the King of Preusa did not hold tidiness in much account.

"Yes." There was a glimmer of amusement in his pale eyes. "For one thing, my father was still, barely, alive. There were factions opposed to me, including those of my grandfather, the late Emperor. It was known that he had not been pleased at the prospect of my inheriting, and that I held quite different views on the desirability of expanding the reach of the Teuton empire by military conquest."

Ardhuin sat up. She remembered reading about this at school, and the discussions of whether the Preusans had really changed. It also reminded her of a question that had bothered her since her arrival.

"Is that why you are only the King, even though this is the Imperial Palace?"

"No." His face had a hard, forbidding aspect for a moment, which softened when he took a small oval frame from where it stood on the corner of the blotter. He turned it so Ardhuin could see it. It held a photograph of a woman who at first glance did not even appear to be pretty. As Ardhuin looked more closely, she saw the firm line of the jaw and the tiny curves at the corners of her mouth that made her look as if she had just thought of something amusing. "By law, the Emperor of the Teuton Nations must take as consort one of royal blood. My wife is of a noble, but not a royal, house. Every year the Assembly petitions that the King of Preusa take his customary title, and every year I ask if the law has been changed."

The poor man had troubles everywhere he turned. Ardhuin felt guilty all over again, thinking that she had added to them.

"About what I did to Herr von Koller. I am sorry for—"

The King held up a hand, and she stopped, astonished.

"You did what needed to be done."

"I did?" Ardhuin gasped.

"The circles in which you move have been, until your arrival, exclusively male. The code of honor applies and any insults must be addressed to retain your status." He ticked off points on his fingers. "Firstly, he challenged your abilities before important and influential people that you must deal with, who must respect you. Secondly, he refused to hear any refutation from those who had seen what you can do. Thirdly, he challenged *my* word as to who and what you are. If you had not acted, I would have been forced to do so, and given the delicacy of the situation I am relieved the necessity has been removed."

Her brain was moving too slowly to understand everything he said. It felt like the world had been turned upside down and given a good shake. "It was the right thing to do?" she repeated, dazed.

The King permitted himself a small smile. "No one present in that room will ever question your ability again—at least, not where you can hear. That is an improvement. Von Koller will resent that you shamed him before his colleagues, however. Be aware that he will now be your determined enemy."

Well, that was no surprise.

"Was there any other way for me to prove myself that—that wouldn't make him angry?" she asked.

The King shook his head. "The two are inextricably connected. Your mere existence is an affront to him. Moreover, he blames you, rightly or wrongly, for the difficulties the *Kriegszauberkollegium* finds itself in. No, you must simply be aware that he is angry, and that doing such things when you are angry yourself can make others angry too. You will want to limit the number of enemies you make, if you can." He sighed. "It becomes difficult to keep them straight after a point."

There was a lot to think about here. Ardhuin felt herself relax, finally accepting that if the King was angry, it was not with her. Still, she had created an uncomfortable situation.

"Should I apologize to Herr von Koller?"

The King raised an eyebrow. "For what? He insulted you. It is for him to apologize. No," he said, as she started to object, "I understand what you mean. I will say that I reprimanded you, as I reprimanded him —reminding you both of the danger we are in and the grave need for cooperation. So, officially, don't do it again." He shook his finger at her, frowning sternly.

Ardhuin stifled a laugh, got up and curtseyed. "I will not do it again, your Majesty. I'll think of something different," she muttered under her breath as she sat down again.

The King affected not to hear.

"I did not know there was so much to being a Mage Guardian," Ardhuin said, the overwhelming feeling of being out of her depth returning. "My great-uncle did not mention this sort of thing at all."

"Oron never paid much attention to politics or diplomacy, so he probably thought it was not important," the King observed dryly. "I was privileged to meet him at the signing of the Armistice in Parys. He publicly refused to teach a spell of power to Prince Ranalt of Alba, saying the prince lacked the mental strength. He declined an invitation to the Duchess of Hevard's ball, offering as his excuse that he would prefer to be spending his evening among the booksellers. Those are only the incidents I personally witnessed; I daresay there are hundreds more. I am told he could always be relied on to vanish magically when he found a party dull or company trying. So you see, I was not entirely surprised by you."

Sensing the audience was over, Ardhuin rose. "I would prefer…that is, I fear I may make enemies that I don't intend, since I am a stranger here and do not know the…the customs."

The King gave her an enigmatic look. "You may confide in Gutrune von Kitren," he said after a pause. "Her family has served mine since both came into existence. There is very little concerning the court and its intrigues she does not know."

❧

"They could be there for hours. Must you wait here?"

Dominic clenched his hands. "Yes. I must." Why Markus felt he needed to stay as well was unclear to him.

"What did she do, put a compulsion on you?"

Dominic turned on him, suddenly furious. "How dare you say that!"

Markus held up both hands, eyes wide. "It was only an attempt to lighten your thunderous mood, I assure you."

"I do not care for your humor," Dominic said through gritted teeth. "If my mood offends you, go somewhere else."

Markus shrugged, grinning. "What, and miss all the fun? I haven't heard any explosions this half-hour. I hope Fraülein Andrews is not feeling unwell."

Dominic was already worried that Ardhuin might do something to get in even more trouble, and Markus' casual comment reminded him that she had been unwell earlier. Some of this must have shown on his face, because Markus added, in a more serious tone than he usually used, "I am certain all is well. The King has far better manners than Herr von Koller. I merely wondered if we might more profitably use our time elsewhere. You recall that I recognized some of the names on the list you gave me?"

Dominic nodded.

"I sent a message to Ermut Arendt, asking him to list all those who had died in duels lately. His reply matches the crossed-out names exactly."

"Someone has been using duels to get rid of them?" Dominic asked. "But why?"

Markus rubbed his chin, eyes narrowing in thought. "It looked like a list of potential plotters. If I were to guess, the ones killed were found unsatisfactory in some way but knew too much to be left to their own devices. As you recall, von Gerling attacked me when I was illusioned with the appearance of one who had a duel that day. What if he had survived? Von Gerling would assume he had reported whatever this secret plan is and we had come to arrest him. No wonder he panicked."

"I am not familiar with magical duels," Dominic confessed. "Is it possible to be so certain that you will win every time?"

"It is not likely the same opponent killed them all," Markus pointed out. "That would be too noticeable, and everyone would be at pains not to offend him. You are right, though. Especially a duel to the death would be subject to chance. They could not guarantee the outcome…and yet clearly they did."

"What of the other papers?" Dominic asked.

"If we had the code book, or a longer text, we might be able to puzzle out the cypher," Markus said. "The most it tells us is something was going on that required secret communication. In the interest of time, I suggest we give it in."

"Won't they wonder why we didn't give it to them earlier?" Dominic asked, doubtful.

"Oh, not to the *Kriegsa*. To the military. They'll be so delighted to have something that could make the *Kriegsa* look even worse they might actually tell us if they find anything." Dominic looked at Markus, wondering if he was joking, but the defensive magician was not smiling. Were matters really at such a pass that the different institutions would not help defend their own country? "Now that scrap, that could be interesting. How did it get torn?"

"I found it in the branches of the bush just outside the window he escaped from," Dominic replied. "The other half must still be with him. It sounds like they are going to take decisive action, doesn't it?"

"Yeesss." Markus took out the scrap of paper and studied it, frowning. "I am afraid we have the same difficulty. We simply don't have enough of it to understand. I mean, we don't even know what objects the 'articles' refers to. It could be anything. And what on earth is the Feast of Sacrifice?"

Something Markus had said made Dominic's mind race. Something out of place, that didn't make sense. He reviewed the conversation several times before he understood.

"Not things. Articles in a journal or newspaper," Dominic burst out.

"Otherwise they would say something about the location. They have to send the articles a week before to make sure they are published in time."

Markus considered the idea. "Well, and what would these articles be about, and why would it be so important? After all, the—" he broke off, staring down the hallway to the private wing. Dominic followed his gaze and saw Ardhuin and Gutrune walking towards them, deep in conversation.

Neither appeared terribly concerned, and Dominic let himself relax a little.

"Have you been waiting all this time?" enquired Gutrune. "It is well past the dinner hour."

"He would not let me leave," Markus said, his mobile face becoming suddenly mournful. "Asking questions, one after the other." Dominic's jaw dropped with indignation. Then Ardhuin, surprisingly, laughed.

"He does that very well. It is a formidable talent," she agreed, smiling. He had not seen her smile for much too long. What had happened? "What were these questions?"

Markus froze, but managed to recover. "Well, he wanted to know what the Feast of Sacrifice was."

"One of the holy days of the Adaran religion," Gutrune said. "Why do you ask?"

Markus glanced casually around the hallway before answering. "It was mentioned in something we found at von Gerling's quarters."

Dominic watched Ardhuin carefully. She seemed rather pale to him, and the brief flash of humor was gone.

"Adarans. Again." Markus thought for a moment. "You recall the bodies they have been finding, completely bloodless. It is a common superstition that Adarans use human blood in their rituals."

"You don't think they are responsible for the killings, do you?" Ardhuin looked shocked.

"No, I do not." Markus gestured in a dismissive way. "I know very little about their customs, but every Adaran I am acquainted with is sufficiently intelligent to realize leaving a body on your front doorstep attracts attention. I think someone is using that superstition to cast suspicion on them." He hesitated. "There is one other thing. This is not generally known, and has been suppressed in the newspapers. Each one of those killed had some degree of magical talent—three lamplighters, a minor jobbing magician, and a man who did advertising simulacra."

"Is there any way we could search for unusual newspaper articles concerning the Adarans…and perhaps this blood superstition?" Dominic asked.

Markus sighed. "Again with the articles. You don't even have a good idea of what you are looking for."

"I will make inquiries," Gutrune said in her calm way. "There are services that do precisely what you describe," she said to Dominic, giving Markus an enigmatic look as she left.

Dominic wondered how quickly these services could produce results, and if it would be in time. Now he had other concerns.

"When did you last eat?" he asked Ardhuin. She gave a wan smile that was not convincing.

"Sometime this morning," she confessed. "I was hungry, but…I did not wish to talk to anyone."

"Then you shall be fed, in our select company," Markus stated with a sweeping bow. "I am sure Herr Kermarec is as in need of sustenance as I. You keep us very busy, you know."

Ardhuin ducked her head, face crimson. Dominic scowled furiously at Markus, who grimaced in silent apology.

Markus found a room and sent servants for food. He made no further awkward comments, and Ardhuin gradually regained her composure and joined in the conversation.

"There is something I have been trying to recall," Dominic said when the meal had finished. "Is there any connection between blood and magic? I read a curious passage once, about ancient priests drinking a cup of their mingled blood to share power." He felt his own face heat, remembering where he had read it. A book in Ardhuin's library, just before he was trapped by the magical protections of another volume.

She looked surprised. Dominic noted that her face had regained some of its natural color. "I am not aware of any connection—but then little is known of how a magician uses magic. The thaumatic physician who examined me might be better informed."

Gutrune von Kitren entered the room with a quick step. She was breathing deeply and held a sheaf of papers in her hand.

Markus got to his feet, tense and alert. "You have found something." It was a statement, not a question.

"In what context did the reference to the Feast of Sacrifice occur?" she asked abruptly. Markus said nothing, but handed her the scrap of paper. Gutrune drew in her breath as she read. "This is most alarming. I have disturbing news."

"You were able to find what I described?" Dominic asked, incredulous. "So quickly?"

"Unfortunately, yes. They knew precisely where to look, because they had seen the articles earlier and remarked on them. Here are two of them. They were published in a working-man's newspaper and a radical political magazine."

Gutrune placed the clippings on the table. Dominic craned his head to read them. They were full of cold hatred for the Adaran people, ascribing every possible vice to them and blaming them for the troops now seen in the streets. The reason, it seemed, was their treasonous intent to destroy Preusa and put it under their control. Much was made of the bodies found outside the Closure and a purported connection between the Feast of Sacrifice and human blood.

While the two articles differed in many details, there was one phrase repeated in both. *The rats should be destroyed in their holes, the wasps-nest burned.*

"When is this Feast of Sacrifice?" Dominic asked, numbly trying to comprehend. Was someone trying to start a war here, in Baerlen?

Gutrune spread her hands. "The Feast lasts four days. It ends tomorrow."

Ardhuin looked up from the newspaper clippings. "Perhaps their plans were disrupted when von Gerling was discovered."

"Perhaps, but I will point out the articles date a week from tomorrow," Gutrune said.

"What can be done?" Markus said, his dark face looking very grim. Gutrune merely shook her head.

"But…the danger is clear," Dominic said, puzzled. "The police, the military—you have alerted them, have you not?"

Markus grimaced. "There is a good deal of animosity towards the Adarans right now. These articles are only remarkable for the level of hatred and the specific threats, unfortunately. The police may not take part in the attack, but they won't stop it, either. The military is engaged in keeping the general peace of the city."

"And the *Kriegsa* is not a possibility either," Ardhuin added bitterly.

"Not through official channels, no," Markus agreed, flashing a smile. "But I've never liked that method anyway. Don't mope. You are not the only one von Koller has irritated. I think some of the younger magicians might be willing to lend quiet assistance."

What they really needed were people who felt well-disposed towards the Adarans, if they existed. Dominic drew in a sharp breath. "The students! Jochim Weiskopf is their friend. I think they might be able to help—or know of those who will. I will go find them and enquire." Besides the need for action, he also felt a strong desire to be alone with his thoughts for a while. He could not resolve what he felt concerning Ardhuin when she was present.

"The university gates will be closed by now," Markus pointed out. "Even the *Kriegsa* will not be very lively at this hour."

"What if they attack tonight?" Ardhuin asked. "We can't be sure that they will hold to exactly one week's time from the publication of the articles."

In the discussion that followed, Markus persuaded Ardhuin to let him arrange for watchers on the Closure, in exchange for her promise to go to sleep. Gutrune remained silent but watchful.

"I can set watchers as well," she said when Ardhuin still hesitated. "I can also arrange for a warning to be sent to those in authority in the Closure. They likely have their own defensive measures. It has been attacked before."

No alert came through the night. Once again on the grounds of the university the next day, Dominic was at a loss. He didn't know where to find the students he knew. The lecture halls he found were empty. Then he remembered that Dieter was no longer taking classes, and he *did* know where his workroom was.

The large laboratory was locked up, but Dominic's pounding on the door brought Dieter out from a side office, hair as tousled as ever. He listened attentively to Dominic's explanation.

"That's bad," Dieter agreed. "Of course we want to help, but I don't know how much good I'll be," he said wryly, indicating his broken arm.

"Your friends, perhaps?"

"Yes, and…we have a fencing club. Here, I'll give you my key. It's right by the gate, with a gabled slate roof. You go and wait there, and I'll start finding people. It might take a while. We've got a half-holiday."

Over the next few hours, students straggled into the club. When Jochim arrived, he was very upset and argued with the club president about opening the cupboard where the foils were kept.

"I must go and defend my family!" Jochim wailed, his eyes brimming.

"Jochim. We will *all* go. Don't you remember what happened the last time you fenced? You stabbed yourself in the foot so bad Stefan had to pull the foil out of the floor to free you," Wolfgang Mauer said, rough but affectionate. "How will it help them for you to hurt yourself and no-one else?"

One of the other students, one Dominic didn't know, shifted his feet. "But…what if it is true?" He glanced at them in turn, then looked down. "I mean, of course I don't think Jochim would ever do such a thing, but there could be other Adarans who—"

Poor Jochim looked completely bewildered. "You are thinking we would kill these people? When we only now may go safely among you, we would throw this all away for nothing?"

The other student was unable to meet Jochim's eyes. "People say it, alright? That Adarans think human blood will give them special power, and they put it in their food."

None of the students spoke, silently watching Jochim. He raised his head, then shook it. "How many times must we say? *We eat no meat.* Human blood would be a hundred times forbidden to us."

Dieter pushed forward, between Jochim and the accuser. "Come on, you lot. Don't you remember how hard a time he has ordering a meal in a restaurant when he eats with us? Not much that doesn't have meat somewhere."

Small, reluctant nods. The accuser wasn't giving up, though.

"That's just because he doesn't like it. I wouldn't eat Adaran food," he muttered.

"Oh, yes you did," Wolfgang said with scorn. "Remember that chocolate torte two weeks ago? You had a big piece and said it was the best thing you'd ever had."

Dieter perked up. "The torte? The one with the little chocolate curls on top?"

Jochim jerked his head, once, twice. "My mother. For my birthday."

The mood of the room suddenly changed. Dominic watched, with amusement tinged with sadness, how the students eagerly rallied to defend a lady and her people because of her culinary skills. Her religion, the reason for the threat, was simply not mentioned again.

He reminded himself the goal was to protect the Adarans, not completely remove the prejudice against them. Not in a single day, at least.

"Hey, I know!" It was the club president again. "Let's do a call-out!"

Mauer blinked. "Will they do it?"

"Sure! It's been a long time since we have, you know. Everybody is bored with studying."

Suddenly the students were rushing around, some to the recently-opened cupboard to gather foils in their arms, others running to the door with excited shouts.

"What's going on?" Dominic called to Wolfgang Mauer. Wolfgang gave him a crooked smile.

"They are calling out the entire university."

Through the diamond panes Dominic saw the crowd of students grow. They were shouting.

"*Bursch! Geh raus! Geh raus!*"

Ardhuin leaned forward to stare out the carriage window at the crowd of young men outside. They were laughing and smiling. Most held some kind of weapon.

"Are we too late?" she asked, even as she realized this was not anything like an angry mob.

Gutrune smiled. "It would seem the gentlemen were successful in finding allies."

The carriage stopped at the entrance to the Closure. A great curving stone arch was carved with Adaran letters, and marked with signs of battering. Some of the stones were newer, others were cracked but left in place.

Ardhuin got out, stumbling slightly in her haste, and looked about. At last the crowd parted enough for her to see Dominic, who was talking to an elderly man in white robes edged in red. His face brightened when he saw her, but he also glanced at the shadow hat she wore and sighed.

"Permit me to introduce *Sofon* Gedchi. He is the religious leader of the Adarans here. *Sofon* Gedchi, Mademoiselle Andrews."

When she took his offered hand, Ardhuin first felt the expected touch of warm skin, but she also had a fleeting sensation of cool, polished stone. *Sofon* Gedchi looked at her with an astonished expression she was sure her own face echoed. She also noticed he was not looking away, as the avoidance spell would encourage.

"Now how is this?" the old man said, in heavily accented Preusan. "Is all this power your own?"

Ardhuin gasped. She glanced at Dominic, who immediately shook his head. He looked shocked as well. If he had not told him, how did he know?

"Yes sir, it is. I have come to help you."

The *sofon* simply said, "Yes." The word encompassed her ability and intent, but she did not know how she knew this. "The children shelter within the temple. I go to them now." He inclined his head and made his way into the Closure.

"How did he—" Dominic asked softly.

Ardhuin shook her head. "He has some kind of magical ability of his own, akin to yours, perhaps. Where did all these people come from?"

He grinned. "You know I went to see the students. Well, they managed to convince the entire university! It's some kind of custom they have. If the leaders decide to do a call-out, every student must obey or risk social ostracism."

"And Herr Asgaya?" Gutrune asked in her cool voice. "I do not see him here."

"He is disposing the magicians who agreed to help at the other entrances, with the rest of the students."

The rest of them. Meaning there were even more. Ardhuin looked at the boisterous crowd, clearly spoiling for action, and became aware of a sinking feeling.

"I fear we may have been too successful," she ventured, quailing at Dominic's downcast reaction. She indicated a quiet corner, and Dominic and Gutrune went with her. Satisfied that they were less likely to be overheard, she continued. "If the instigator of this plot sees such strong defenses, it will be clear to him the Adarans were warned. He must be led to think he can attack. Only then will we see the face of the enemy."

"Do you think this plotter will appear in person?" Gutrune inquired.

"I don't know—but it seems strange to me that they would rely entirely on an unguided mob. Someone will be present to make sure that their true intent is carried out."

Dominic frowned. "We told the *sofon* that we would not enter the Closure. They are understandably worried about any large group of outsiders among them."

"The defenders would only need to go far enough inside to conceal themselves," Gutrune pointed out. "Perhaps that would be permissible."

"Let us ask him," said Dominic. "I, too, would prefer we solve this mystery as soon as possible."

Gutrune declined an invitation to join them, saying she would wait there in the event Markus Asgaya returned before they did.

Ardhuin and Dominic walked down the narrow, twisting streets of the Closure, occasionally asking directions. The light was leaving the sky, and in a few hours it would be dark. At last they came to an unexpectedly open area, and in the center was the temple.

It was a large, round building, made of boulders cemented together in such a way it seemed more like a natural pile of rocks than a wall. The entrance led down a gentle slope to two immense hammered copper doors.

Inside, a man wearing a black robe embroidered with white went to summon the *sofon* at their request.

"I thought the children were here," Ardhuin remarked softly. "I don't see them anywhere." They stood in a sort of foyer, with numerous carved wooden pillars blocking the view of what seemed to be a large room beyond them. The walls were wood too, with faint golden symbols scattered over them.

The man in the embroidered robe reappeared and gestured for them to follow him. They went past the pillars to a wide-open space filled with simple wooden benches. The benches ranged in a circular pattern around an immense column, made to look like the trunk of an ancient tree. It had branches as well, springing up to the top of the temple's dome and the stained glass inset in the center, and from these branches hung leaves of glass.

Ardhuin stared at it, amazed. Each leaf hung from its own wire, and even the tiny breezes within the temple produced a faint chiming noise. The overall color was a rich, clear green, but there were flashes and streaks of slightly different colors, and the whole shimmered with reflected light.

She recollected herself and continued forward. Dominic had been similarly astounded. The *sofon* waited for them near the base of the tree, and as she came closer she saw that there were doors in the trunk, as if it held a cabinet.

"It's so beautiful," she breathed.

"Yes," said the old *sofon*, the lines at the corners of his eyes deepening. Once again she had the feeling he was responding on more than one level. "It represents Zanathil, the Tree of Life, the center of all that we are. Look up. Tell me what you see."

Ardhuin tilted her head back, lifting her veil to see better. Now light was shining through the leaves, and there were patterns. Shapes.

"Two birds, flying over a mountain," she said. The *sofon* nodded, looking thoughtful.

"And you?" he said, looking at Dominic.

"A hand, placed on the blade of a sword." Dominic looked puzzled. "Where are the birds?"

"Each person sees what is needed to draw closer to wisdom," the *sofon* said, smiling gently. "These are symbols of our belief. It is said that all but one of the hundred are shown somewhere in the leaves—but we do not know which one is missing. No one has ever seen them all." He was silent for a moment, apparently lost in contemplation. "You wished to speak with me."

Dominic explained their plan to conceal the defenders within the Closure.

The *sofon* raised his eyebrows. "This would encourage conflict and violence that might be otherwise avoided," he replied, with a note of disapproval. "Is there a reason to permit this?" He looked steadily at Ardhuin.

"I am afraid this is but one battle in a larger war," she said hesitantly. "We believe the attack on your people is being used as a pretext to create cover for a greater attack on Preusa, and perhaps beyond. You will be protected as best we can in either case, but if we can trick this enemy into thinking he is not expected, we may be able to defeat him." She felt guilty, knowing that what she was asking for was more likely to end with people getting hurt, but the larger responsibility weighing down on her gave her little choice.

"The people will be fearful," the *sofon* said. "I hear what you are saying, but they are in my care." He thought for a moment. "I will send one or two of my people to remain by each group, to reassure any who may fear. Let them wait until my people come, and then they may come within."

With that Ardhuin had to be content, although she was starting to worry that there would not be enough time to arrange things as the *sofon* wished.

She went outside with Dominic. An old woman came by with a pot of some kind of hot mulled drink, and Ardhuin was glad to have it. The night was clear, the half-full moon visible in the sky, and it was very cold. A messenger informed them the defenders were now inside the gate, and as the hours went by she began to worry that nothing was going to happen. Had the defenses been discovered? Had they never intended to attack the Closure at all?

And then there was Dominic, always nearby. She was too tense and nervous for anything more than ordinary conversation, but she was glad he was here. Just his presence gave her confidence. Alone, she would have left long ago.

She heard quick, energetic footsteps on the cobbled street, and Markus appeared.

"There you are! Waiting is dull work, is it not? A pity we do not have more precise information, but that is the nature of war."

The word sent a chill up Ardhuin's spine. War. Yes, that was what was going on here, only they did not know who their enemy was.

"Speaking of which—did you ever make use of the blood you found from von Gerling?" Dominic asked. "I assume you intended to do a location spell."

"Exactly right, and I did so. Unfortunately, he had already run beyond the range of the spell when I cast it. If he comes back, I'll know."

"Is it possible to make the spell itself seek him out?" Dominic wondered, and both he and Markus looked at Ardhuin.

She considered for a moment, intrigued by the idea. Something was distracting her, and she concentrated until she recognized what it was.

Shouting.

"Do you hear that?" she asked. Markus nodded, his face suddenly serious. "Where is it coming from?"

"It's hard to tell. I think the main entrance," Markus said. He left at a run. Ardhuin followed with Dominic. They caught up with the defensive magician a few minutes later. He was speaking with Gutrune von Kitren. "A mob has attacked the main entrance, but it is being handled quite well by the students. No more than a hundred of them."

"I wonder if Jochim has injured himself yet," commented Dominic. "It would have been different if they had any firearms, I suppose."

Markus gave a sardonic smile. "Students are not permitted firearms. In fact, they are generally not permitted in the city, with the exception of the army and a few individuals," he said, grinning at Gutrune.

A young man ran their direction, shouting. As he got closer, Ardhuin could hear him saying, "Herr Asgaya! Herr Asgaya!"

"Here!" Markus shouted. The young man skidded to a stop.

"Grunbaum sends…magical attack. Fleischerstrasse." He gasped and continued. "He said…saw something…north too."

Multiple attacks. Magical. Ardhuin's blood ran cold. The war had begun in earnest, and it was coming here.

"Go find out what that is. I will go to Fleischerstrasse," Ardhuin said, surprised at her own decisiveness. "Take me there," she ordered the young man, who gaped at her, then turned and started running again.

She followed as quickly as she could. There was a strange, metallic scent in the air as she got closer, and a flickering orange glow ahead. Fire.

The shouting was turning to screams. Now she could see a line of people forming a bucket brigade, and others scattering and running. Something rumbled, making the ground shake, and the metallic smell grew stronger.

"Ardhuin! Look up!" Dominic yelled. He pointed to something she couldn't see. "It's a fire shell!"

For a dangerous second she wondered how he knew what one was, and then she reacted. Fire shells were most dangerous if they made contact. Dissolve the field holding the power and it dissipated. Dominic was still pointing, so she aimed her counterspell that way.

"Any more?" He shook his head, scanning the sky again.

More salvos of fire shells came, one after the other. In the dark she relied entirely on Dominic's magical sight. From the corner of her eye she could see one house completely ablaze, and the crowd desperately trying to keep the fire from spreading.

The rumbling grew louder. She heard a shot, then another. Hadn't Markus said firearms were rare in the city?

Gutrune had a gun.

"Keep looking!" she shouted to Dominic, and took him by the elbow. Which way had the shots come from?

She ran down the street with Dominic beside her. There was

Gutrune, a smear of soot down one side of her face and a strand of pale hair falling over her eyes, calmly reloading her pistol while crouched down behind a well. In the road ahead, slowly rolling in a flowing, molten way, was a ball of flame.

The heat that radiated from it was like a blow. Anything close to it caught fire within seconds.

There was a well….

"Gutrune! Get away!"

All the water she could move, as fast as possible, everywhere it would go. Surrounding the molten ball, putting out the fires. Ardhuin felt the sweat sting her eyes.

Something tugged her sleeve. "More shells! Coming in low!"

She could feel the strain now, the familiar tingle of overload. How long had she been fighting? Just enough power to disable the fire shells while keeping the pool of water surrounding the molten ball. One of the fire shells got through, but the ball remained motionless. She couldn't do both again, though.

She saw Markus and called to him. "Keep the water in place!" He nodded, and she let her power withdraw. The water pooled down for a minute, but Markus, face working with effort, managed to bring it up again.

There were two more fire shell attacks. She had no strength to wonder at them any more. She could barely stand. Then she realized they had stopped, and with Dominic supporting her, they went through the Closure. Fires could be contained with stasis fields, smothering in their own smoke. She did as many as she could, and then directed any magician who was at hand.

She found herself staring at the sky, wondering if the whole world had caught fire, then realized. It was dawn. And someone was telling her the fight was over. They had won.

Dominic wearily went up the stairs of the Imperial Palace. His clothes reeked of smoke, and he was sure he presented a frightening appearance. The servants were well trained, however, and showed nothing when they encountered him. He saw Ardhuin go into her rooms, and combined relief and fatigue nearly buckled his knees.

Sleep. There was his bed, and there was the defensive magician assigned to guard him. First, though, he had to wash the soot off his face and out of his hair.

The cold water felt wonderful, even though he found more than one cinder burn when he dried his face.

The defensive magician still stood by the door. Dominic wondered for a moment why he seemed different. There was magic, of course, but wouldn't there be magic if he had just cast the wards, and….

There were no wards.

Illusion.

He spun around, but not fast enough. The blow caught him on the side of the head, and he fell into darkness.

CHAPTER 14

Ardhuin brushed her hair vigorously, sighing when she saw the ash and cinders that fell from her brush, and trying to ignore the beginnings of a headache. It hardly felt like she had slept at all. "I wish I had time to wash it," she complained. "I was even wearing my hat. How did all that get in?"

"You did not notice the wind caused by the fires," Gutrune said, handing her a hairpin. "They will understand any deviation from perfect grooming, given the situation. Matters are still urgent." She sat up a little straighter on the bed. "Von Stangen was found outside the Closure."

Ardhuin dropped her hands from her head, and her hair escaped from its arrangement. "Well then! We suspected he was behind this. Is that why Herr Asgaya left in such a hurry?"

Gutrune took the hairpin back from her, stood, and started arranging Ardhuin's hair herself. It was a much more elegant look than Ardhuin had ever been able to create. "He was behind some of it, but not all. I do not know all the details, but they found that much early this morning. It was the blood-seeking spell that uncovered him," she said, placing another hairpin with precision.

"I had thought that was for von Gerling," she said, hesitantly.

In the mirror, she saw Gutrune's face tighten momentarily. "It was. More precisely, for the rest of von Gerling's blood. There was a splash of it on von Stangen's boots."

Ardhuin sat frozen while Gutrune completed her coiffure. It was unlikely that a man of von Stangen's stature would be wearing the same dirty boots for days on end. If the blood was fresh, it implied von Gerling had bled from a more recent wound. She shivered. *They must have been very angry with him.*

"How do they know von Stangen is not the main conspirator?" she asked finally.

"I was not told," Gutrune said. "It was mentioned to me just before I was sent to bring you."

Ardhuin took another look in the mirror, sighed, and decided there was no point in delaying. It was depressing to think they had not solved the problem, but then, perhaps they were mistaken and von Stangen really was the source of all the attacks. She would have to see for herself.

Two defensive magicians waited outside. She didn't recognize either of them. They looked annoyed. One complained in a rapid spate of Preusan Ardhuin could not follow. Gutrune turned to look at her, her usual cool, noncommittal expression on her face.

"Have you sent Herr Kermarec on any errand? They complain that he has left without notifying them. Again."

Ardhuin shook her head, staring at the magicians wordlessly. Her denial seemed to dismay them.

"Where is the one who stayed with him last night?" she asked.

The question made the defensive magicians even more agitated and incomprehensible.

"They cannot find his guard. It is against procedure. The *schutzmagus* is required to notify his relief if…that is why they thought you had sent Herr Kermarec outside the palace. Neither he nor his guard were in the room when these gentlemen arrived."

Frowning, Ardhuin went down the hallway to Dominic's rooms. The door was ajar, but likely the others had left it so. She went in.

The room was orderly and empty. The brushes and shaving gear on the washstand were arranged precisely. She felt them; they were dry. Ardhuin turned slowly, searching for something she could not name. Her heart was pounding, her knees weak.

A glimpse of color, half-hidden under the bed caught her attention. She stooped quickly and picked it up: a book with a blue leather binding. The pages were creased, as if the book had been dropped while open. One page was even torn.

Sudden, unreasoning terror filled her mind, overwhelming any thought but that Dominic would never, ever treat a book in this way. And he was missing.

She gathered her power and sent it streaming away, more than she had ever used at once before, seeking the emerald rose pin she had given him.

She could not find it.

Dominic realized he was awake because his head hurt. He had no idea where he was—it was pitch dark, chilly, and the air had a smell that reminded him of the cells below the *Kriegszauberkollegium*. Metallic.

He was lying down on some kind of bed. When he made an effort to rise, he had to collapse again from weakness. There was a clinking noise when he did. Chains?

Where was he? What had happened? He had flashes of memory,

sensations that he couldn't patch together. Cold, but a chilly, damp kind of cold not at all like the freezing air outside. Swaying, being carried, and icy drops of water landing on his face. Sharp, lancing pain in his forearm.

Where had he been last? The Closure. Fighting an attack with Ardhuin. He drew a sharp breath, fear driving out the last of his mental confusion. No, he hadn't been captured there. They'd gone back to the palace. She was safe.

Wasn't she?

Someone had attacked him there. He strained to remember what had happened for some time in the cold and dark, until a scraping noise caught his attention. A line of light appeared—a door. And a human shape in that light.

The sudden contrast of light and dark blinded Dominic for a moment. He blinked as his eyes adjusted. Now he could tell he was in a small, strangely dark room with no furniture save the bed he lay on. The figure entered, and strong, impersonal hands lifted his arm, the same one that had felt the pain before. With movement the pain returned. The same hands turned his face one way, then the other. Dominic had no strength to resist, or even talk.

"It is too cold," the figure said in a resonant voice, speaking Gaulan as a native of Parys would. "Henri, a brazier this instant. Has he eaten?"

"No, my lord. He was not awake." This was said by someone outside, in a shaky, thin voice.

"He is awake now. Some bouillon at first. He will not be able to keep anything more down at present."

"Yes, my lord." Footsteps faded away.

"I must give you credit for your efforts against me, even though I cannot permit them to continue," said the Parysan voice softly. "Your talents are wasted with the tattered remnants of the Alliance. Fortunately, you have provided me with a means to repair my losses. Pray do not take it personally. Although I am your adversary, I hold you in great respect. We will talk when you are more recovered."

Dominic heard sounds of movement, and the light from the open door disappeared with a solid clunk. Despite his fear and confusion, his fatigue was strong enough that he dozed again, only to be awakened as the door scraped open.

Either he was stronger, or the light was better. An older man, dressed as an upper servant, brought in a charcoal brazier with both hands. He placed it on the floor near the head of the bed, left, and returned with a lamp and a bowl. He assisted Dominic to sit up, and then proceeded to feed him a spoonful at a time, never looking him in the eyes or speaking.

The bouillon was good, and Dominic was starving. He did wonder why he was being so well cared for. He felt much better, and looked more carefully at the man holding the bowl—Henri? The man had a long, drawn face with lines of worry, and something about him….

Dominic gasped, and Henri's gaze flicked up to his face. A *geas*, strong and powerful, was visible in a light haze over the man's head. Still silent, Henri gathered up the bowl and lamp and turned to leave.

As he shut the door, he gave Dominic a sudden, burning look of mingled pain and reproach. His lips trembled.

Dominic shifted and heard the chains again. He felt at his wrists, and found that thick metal bands encased them. A chain was attached to the shackles, and from that chain another went to the wall.

Why was he a prisoner? He had been captured by the enemy Ardhuin had been fighting all this time, but why had they not tried to capture her? Fear spiked through him. Perhaps they had. Or perhaps they thought to use him in some way against her.

The brazier made the little room much more comfortable, and he fell asleep, wondering why Henri had looked at him with such reproach.

Dominic awoke much later, still in total darkness. He had no way of telling exactly how long he had been asleep, or how long he had been imprisoned, but his stomach indicated the bowl of bouillon had been some time ago.

He was able to sit up now, and he did so. Searching the room by feel, he discovered the bed he was on was only a metal frame with a thin mattress. The walls and floor of his prison were metal, too, and he shook his head, puzzled. He explored the dull ache in his left forearm. The cuff of his shirt was unfastened, and his arm was bandaged just above his wrist. His head had a painful bump on the back, too, but that had not been bandaged. He appeared to be wearing the same clothes from the night of the Closure attack.

How long had it been? He felt his face. Rough, but no more than a day or two of growth. He let his hand fall with relief, and his sleeve snagged on something rough on his chest.

For a moment he was startled, then he remembered. The emerald rosebud stickpin Ardhuin had given him—for just such a situation as this. She would find him. Was that what the enemy wanted? Was that why he was still alive?

He had to warn her.

Dominic racked his brain, but before he could come up with a solution, the door to his prison opened. Henri appeared, bearing a tray on a stand that contained a lamp, a folded neckcloth, shaving gear, a bowl of something that smelled delicious, and a mug. He set them down and bowed.

"His lordship's compliments, and he requests the favor of your company when you are ready," Henri said, glancing at him quickly and then looking down.

"Who is this lordship?" Dominic asked. Henri jerked, his face working and eyes wide. His mouth was open as if he would speak, but not a sound came out. It looked frighteningly familiar.

"No, please…never mind. Don't try to answer. I know you cannot."

Henri drew a shuddering gasp of air, eyes closing for a moment.

"Thank you, sir." He looked at Dominic directly for the first time, and his earlier hostility seemed to have diminished. "I regret that it is not possible to offer you any other fresh linen, but his lordship will not permit your bonds to be removed for any reason." He seemed ashamed.

His bonds. The shackles. Dominic lifted one hand and raised his eyebrows. The shackles were quite thick, but they were not entirely metal. He looked more closely. Each one was lined in silvery chryselectrum.

Dominic picked up the bowl of food and started to eat, both from hunger and from a desire to hide the startled reaction on his face. Iron, chryselectrum—and his prison was entirely iron as well. It would only make sense if he were a magician.

A chill thought went through him. Magic was affected by iron; he remembered Ardhuin mentioning this to him. He, and the emerald stickpin, were completely encased in iron. She would probably be unable to find him.

Well, he had been summoned to meet this mysterious lordship. Presumably there would be less iron about then. He could not be sure, however, that the conversation would last long enough for her magic to locate him. He would have to arrange for the pin to stay outside, unless he decided it was a trap.

The bowl was full of minced chicken in broth, well-seasoned. The mug held porter. Food for an invalid, not a prisoner.

"Do you wish me to shave you, sir?" Henri asked. Dominic shook his head. Even if he still felt a little weak, he could not be sure of the full nature of the *geas* on Henri.

It was awkward shaving in chains, but he felt much better cleaned up. He left the stickpin out when rearranging the fresh neckcloth, and tucked it in his pocket when Henri was busy removing the tray.

"Shall I tell his lordship you are ready?" Henri asked hesitantly.

"I am quite eager to speak with him," Dominic said.

❧

"They found Giessen. Dead."

Ardhuin looked up at Gutrune, the words barely penetrating the fog of pain, wondering why this was important. Then she remembered. Giessen, the defensive magician who should have been guarding Dominic that night.

"Nothing else?"

Gutrune shook her head. "He was found in a dustman's cart. From what they were able to discover from the dustman and the condition of the body, he was killed before the attack on the Closure."

It was a small piece of good news, made large from the absence of any other. The substitution had been made in advance, not in revenge. However, it did not absolve her of the ultimate guilt of putting Dominic in danger in the first place.

"Still no messages," Ardhuin said, her voice rough with disuse. "Not in two days time. It would appear they do not intend to use him as a

197

hostage." Her stomach tightened. "What other purpose could they have?" And did that purpose require him to still be alive?

She'd stayed in the palace too long. At first from shock, and then at the urging of the King and Council, for her safety. Staying here wasn't finding Dominic, though. She'd tried.

"May I use your carriage?" Ardhuin asked, getting stiffly to her feet. "Perhaps if I conduct the search outside the city—"

Gutrune stood and held up both hands, stopping her. "That would not be wise. What if they did this to lure you out?"

"It is not *wise* to wait and wait." Ardhuin snapped. "I have to do something!"

"It is always best to fight on ground of your own choosing—not the enemy's," Gutrune replied, still calm. "If you rush out without any information, you will be at a great disadvantage."

Ardhuin fought to keep her temper, or at least not to burst into tears. "But there *is* no information. I must go to find it," she said, her throat so tight she could barely speak. "There is no time...."

They might already be too late. That was the horrible thought that kept her from sleeping at night, that made her want to lash and tear.

Hands gripped her shoulders, squeezed in a comforting way. "I know he is dear to you," Gutrune said in a voice so soft Ardhuin could barely make out the words.

He is my world. Tears brimmed and fell down her cheeks. "He only came here because of me. This is all my fault."

Gutrune gave her a quick shake. "Nonsense. From my observation, Herr Kermarec is well able to speak his own mind and make his own decisions. He knew there would be danger here before he came, did he not? You cannot afford any mistakes now. You may be his only hope."

"But we don't *know* anything!" wailed Ardhuin. "What are we doing to help him?"

Gutrune gave a small smile. "We know he was here in the palace when he was taken, and it was night. Soldiers are enforcing the curfew, and there is a tight perimeter around the palace itself. Each of the bridges has a full guard. It is possible that this kidnapper was able to gain entry in the confusion of our return from the Closure, but it would have been very difficult to escape unseen. The King has ordered a search of the area," she said. "Have hope, and be patient. If he is in the perimeter, we will find him."

Not long after Henri had left his cell, two rough-looking men came in. Like Henri, they had *geasi* and were silent. One pointed a pistol at Dominic while the other unfastened the long chain from his manacles. The two manacles were still chained to each other, but not closely.

Outside the iron cell was a narrow passageway paved with rough flagstones. They passed another door, similar to his but ajar, and then the passage opened to a wider area, more reminiscent of the cellar of a large house. This cellar, however, did not have barrels and rough stores like coal. Instead, it was swept bare to accommodate a table and a bench with a rack of glass chemical apparatus.

His guides jerked him forward, but not before he saw the restraints on the four corners of the table. There was a raw, sour smell he associated with medical examining rooms, as well. He was very glad to leave.

When he finally arrived at the living area, his legs shook with fatigue and it was an effort to stand upright. Far too many stairs had been employed, in his opinion.

It looked like it had been a rich house once, with marble tile floors and marble columns in the entryway. The floor was covered in undisturbed dust that had a hint of magic to it. Dominic glanced back the way they had come and saw the marks of their feet slowly being erased. Someone wanted this house to look unused.

There were other signs of careful deception as they continued. Heavy curtains over old tattered ones, thick enough to block any stray light yet deliberately stained and ripped to match. A grand staircase that appeared to be completely unsafe, a few nails keeping it from collapsing entirely, but Dominic noticed discreet metal brackets and illusion that made it appear some of the treads were missing.

He was nudged up the "falling" staircase. Beyond was an area more clearly lived in, the carpet clean and fresh. His escort stopped in a large parlor that had an attached glass-framed conservatory to one side, the panes opaque with grime. The thug with the pistol pointed it at him again while the other left the room.

As he waited, Dominic became aware of motion in the conservatory. Henri was there, busy about some task. It seemed a pleasant place, green plants and statuary scattered throughout.

"Ah, there you are. How kind of you to come."

Dominic turned sharply, then winced at the sudden wave of dizziness. A man stood in the double doorway of a connecting room. He had a taut, lean look that could have placed his age anywhere between forty and sixty. Tall and loose-limbed, he was dressed in a slightly old-fashioned suit. As he came closer, Dominic saw a scattering of small scars along one side of his thin face.

The man made a slight dismissive gesture, and the two thugs left silently.

"I was not aware I had any choice in the matter," Dominic replied, wondering at the man's air of casual courtesy and unconscious command. It was not arrogance, which would have included some recognition of others, even if that recognition was pure contempt.

"There is a certain regrettable degree of constraint, it is true," the man said, nodding. "I beg you regard it as a compliment. I have taken my own measures, which should render you powerless for the moment, but I have no notion of how quickly you can recover. Thus—" He indicated the manacles and gave a wry smile. "But you should not be standing like this, so soon after the procedure. Please come in, and be seated. Henri! Bring refreshment."

Henri froze in the act of arranging a tendril of ivy about a statue of an undraped woman making a gesture of surprise. Dominic could see him trying to fight the compulsion, even as he turned to go.

Two observations jostled in Dominic's mind as he followed his captor into an exotically furnished office. The statue was not of a graceful, perfect nymph, but an ordinary woman—and the statue was full of magic, of a kind he had never seen before.

Dominic sank down gratefully on a large, soft ottoman, richly upholstered in gold-laced brocade. "I do not have the honor of your name," he said cautiously.

The man laughed. "You know, I have almost forgotten it myself. In any event I have not used it since the war, and that young man no longer exists. Dead, if you believe the records. I have taken the mage-name Denais. And what name has Oron's heir taken?"

For a brief moment there was utter confusion, and then Dominic found it hard to breathe. Denais was looking at him with interest, waiting.

He had to think, to focus. Of course Denais thought he, Dominic, was the Mage Guardian. He'd put him in an iron cell, after all. To protect Ardhuin, Dominic would have to pretend he was. Fortunately, Denais would not expect him to be able to do any magic in his current condition. Now, how would the heir of Oron reply?

"I have not yet decided," he said, hoping he sounded careless and casual. "Besides, it amuses me to have them refer to me, as you did, as the heir of Oron. It reminds them of things they would rather forget."

It then occurred to Dominic that perhaps Denais, apparently a Gaulan mage, would also rather forget Oron, but no change of expression was apparent in Denais' face.

Time for some questions of his own. "How did you escape the impoundment at the end of the War?" Dominic asked. Denais did not have a *geas* now, if he had ever had one.

"Ah." Denais took a seat in a deep leather chair. "Well, I was fortunate enough to be so badly wounded I was left for dead, and a truly dead man was mistaken for me—with, I admit, some assistance on my part. I looked even younger than I was at the time, so no one who saw me thought I could possibly be a mage's assistant. I left Aerope as soon as I could travel, which was also of great use in remaining at liberty."

Henri entered, carrying a heavy tray, and proceeded to lay out tea and pastries. After pouring, he left as silently as he had come, closing the big double doors behind him.

The exotic tea matched the room, rich and heavy. Dominic sipped carefully, trying to keep his cup from rattling against the saucer, or his chains from touching any of the delicate china.

"You mentioned a procedure. Is it connected to this?" he asked, raising the arm with the bandage.

Denais leaned back and regarded Dominic over the edge of his teacup. "Of course. For many years I had nothing to do but research. My remote location was awkward, but it had other advantages. In Anatoli, life is cheap. I discovered from my own experience and some half-remembered tales that a magician's strength—his power, if you will—is carried in his blood."

"You bled me to make me weak?" Dominic asked, surprised.

Denais gave a mocking smile. "That is a useful side-effect, but no. I learned after many years of effort how to *remove* the power from a magician's blood—and to use that power myself."

"The bodies left by the Closure. That was your doing," Dominic said slowly. All magicians of one kind or another, all drained of blood.

"I do try not to be wasteful," Denais said, nodding and taking a chocolate-dipped madeleine from the tray. "I needed the essence, of course, and there is always the problem of disposal. Creating fear and unrest was also useful to me."

"Are you trying to start another war?" Dominic asked, feeling very cold. "Was the first not horrible enough?"

"I am finishing one," Denais snapped, his eyes narrowing. "*I* did not surrender. Have you seen what the Alliance did to Gaul? Even now, thirty years later, it is broken and humiliated! We who were the pinnacle of Aerope reduced to cringing servitude, forced every day to apologize for daring to dream of glory!"

That this glory had consisted of conquering and humiliating the *other* countries of Aerope seemed to escape Denais.

"So you assassinated the…the other Mage Guardians. How long have you been working on this?"

Denais smiled, his earlier ill humor vanishing. "Long enough, and you have caused me significant delay. How fortunate you have provided me with means to make up the deficiency. Magicians of your level are not common." He leaned forward. "You are still somewhat pale. We must not risk your health, even though I have enjoyed this conversation and indeed, hope to have more. As long as I feel confident that you are under control, who knows how long our acquaintance will last?" Denais gave him another mocking smile, and rose. "Come. The laboratory will interest you."

Dominic followed him outside. There was just enough time for him to glance at the conservatory. Henri was there again, still attending the magical statue, trying to arrange the ivy to conceal more of the undraped woman, whose expression now seemed frightened rather than surprised. He caught a glimpse of gold on one of the statue's hands before the conservatory was out of view.

It was easier going down stairs, but still tiring. Dominic was beginning to stumble by the time they reached the cellar.

Denais went over to the table and apparatus and motioned Dominic to join him.

"You see, I have designed a most efficient method. The source is connected here, and the essence is collected in a stasis vial. Unfortunately, even that does not permit long-term storage, since the nature of the essence affects the stasis spell."

"Of course." Dominic looked at him in fascinated horror. That table where the "source"—a human being—was fastened and drained of blood, was just another piece of equipment to Denais. If what Denais had said was true, Dominic had himself been tied down there and bled for power.

"It is a nuisance, but the essence cannot be contained more than two weeks without losing its effectiveness," Denais commented, unlocking a carved wooden cabinet with a bright flash of magic. On a shelf were a physician's hypodermic, a length of cord, and some sticking plaster and bandages. Above the shelf, in velvet-lined niches, were five bottles labeled with a name and a date on each. They contained a clear liquid that glowed to Dominic's vision. That must be the essence, then. One of the five bottles was only partly filled, and the fluid did not glow. The name on the bottle was his.

"I could not obtain a full measure of essence without killing you," Denais said, seeing the direction of his gaze. "With luck, I can repeat the procedure several times. And your essence is, of course, much stronger than any of the others, so less is needed."

Dominic thought furiously as the rough servants were summoned to return him to his cell. He had at most two weeks before Denais discovered the essence derived from his blood was worthless, and when he did, both he and Ardhuin would be in danger. If Denais considered his essence more powerful, he would probably save it for a special occasion, or only use it if he had no other.

As Dominic got closer to the door of his cell, he desperately tried to think of some way to get the emerald rose stickpin out of his pocket and hidden unobtrusively, but the thugs were too watchful. There had been no opportunity upstairs, either. He would have to think of something else.

Ardhuin pushed up the stray strands of hair that had escaped and stared at the document again. Gutrune von Kitren had been translating it for her, but she wanted to look at it herself. Markus Asgaya lounged in a chair nearby, outwardly relaxed, but with shadows under his eyes showing the long hours he had been at work.

"So, we still don't know who this mysterious individual 'K' is, other than that he is powerful and telling von Stangen what to do."

Markus stirred. "Not exactly. It appears K and von Stangen were allies, but sometimes reluctant ones. K wanted to use some of the army in the Closure attack but von Stangen refused."

"What does von Stangen say about that?" Ardhuin asked.

Gutrune shook her head. "He is refusing to answer questions. Despite these documents, he maintains that even to respond to the accusations is a stain on his honor, that he has never endangered the safety of the King or of Preusa. It is true, we have no proof but what we found in his quarters, and that is murky at best."

"I heard something interesting about von Stangen," Markus said, sitting up with a stifled groan. "He was with the detachment that worked with the impounding process at the end of the war. He met most of the Gaulan mages and knew about their magic. Something of an expert on it, in fact."

"He was also an adherent of Marderian," Gutrune said. "A political leader who objected to the present King's views on empire," she explained, seeing Ardhuin's puzzled look. "Marderian firmly believed in the purpose of Preusa being conquest."

A knowledge of Gaulan mages, and perhaps their magic, in combination with an opposition to the King's policy of non-aggression, made von Stangen very suspicious indeed. The documents were further indication, but sparse on information she could use. Von Stangen's quarters had been thoroughly searched, once by her. Dominic was not there, and probably had never been.

"Didn't you say the reason he was away was to visit his estates?" Ardhuin asked abruptly. "Where are they?"

Gutrune and Markus exchanged a glance. "In the south. Near Bad Gluckshof," Gutrune said. "A little more than a day's travel."

"You think they managed to evade the perimeter?" Markus asked.

"We've searched almost every building inside," Ardhuin said. "They must have gotten him out somehow. And in three days he could be anywhere."

Gutrune thought for a moment, then reluctantly nodded. "I will make the arrangements to leave at first light tomorrow."

Dominic explored his cell in the darkness, feeling every inch he could reach. With the chain in place, he could just place one hand on the surface of the door. He continued down, straining to reach, and at the limit of the chain felt a gap at the bottom of the door, no more than an inch high. He could not tell if the gap went all the way through to the hallway.

More substantial meals were brought to him now; once by one of the rough servants, once by Henri. They both waited until he was finished, then removed the plates and utensils.

"The statue in the conservatory—it's a real woman, isn't it?" Dominic asked Henri, while he was waiting.

The older man stared at Dominic with wide, astonished eyes. His mouth worked, and finally he pantomimed putting a hand over it.

"You have been forbidden to talk. I understand." Henri nodded. "Is she…is she perhaps your wife?" The woman appeared the right age, and Dominic remembered the gold ring. While Henri could not speak, the tears sliding down his cheeks were confirmation enough. "I'm sorry. I would help you if I could."

Behind Henri in the open doorway, a large orange-and-white cat wandered by. Seeing the newly opened door, it stopped to investigate. Giving Henri a casual lean as it walked by, it sniffed Dominic and looked at him expectantly.

Dominic took a scrap of chicken from his plate and offered it to the cat, who took it with delicate grace.

The beginnings of an idea started to form in his mind. He gave the cat another small bit of food, and it started to purr. Asking Henri for more water, he quickly hid a handful of chicken from his plate while the man's head was turned.

The meal over, Henri shooed the cat out of the cell and closed the door. Dominic waited until the sound of footsteps faded down the passageway, and then carefully shoved a scrap of food under the door. A small tug told him it had been taken away.

Working quickly, Dominic took out his handkerchief and the emerald rose stickpin and made a small bundle of them, rubbing the bundle vigorously on the floor of his cell to disguise the whiteness. Using a thread pulled from his blanket, he wrapped the bundle further with the remainder of the food he had hidden away.

Carefully, he nudged the bundle under the door. He felt nothing, and had a momentary spurt of panic. Had the cat eaten its fill? But then a tug came — a firm, determined one — and he let go. He could no longer feel it anywhere.

He had to hope it was out in the passageway now, and that it would remain unnoticed. It *had* to work. It was his only chance.

CHAPTER 15

The summons was always the same. The creak of his prison door, the blinding line of light, and Henri's soft, polite voice extending the invitation from Denais. After the initial visit, Dominic had been summoned twice. Each visit was nerve-wracking, especially after Dominic discovered his captor had some level of inside knowledge. It was not complete, however, and Dominic struggled to keep his expression from revealing anything.

He hoped he hadn't revealed anything. It was hard to tell. Denais had a light, casual manner, but Dominic was not fooled. There had been some awkward moments at dinner. It had gone on forever, but he could at least pretend to be busy with his food while he tried to invent an answer. When Denais mentioned that "someone" had told him the Mage Guardian was a woman, his fork dropped from his grasp and he made a great show of being impeded by the manacles while he tried to gather his frightened thoughts.

"Did they really say that? How amusing." He took a deep breath and gestured for Henri to fill his wineglass again. Carefully holding the chain back with one hand, he picked it up and sipped cautiously. "Perhaps you have heard that illusion is a specialty of mine. It is a pity I cannot give you a demonstration," he added, in the absent, careless way he had affected.

The lines about Denais' eyes deepened in amused appreciation, and he raised his glass. "It is indeed a pity. But why? There is also talk that the young lady is some relation to the late Oron, but I find it hard to believe she could be involved in these matters. Yet, there she is."

Dominic shrugged, his heart beating so hard he felt dizzy. "Oron taught her to be his assistant. I find her useful as well. Besides, I do not care to be surrounded by strangers. I have switched our appearances now and then, especially if there was a boring meeting I was required to attend."

Denais laughed and relaxed back in his chair. From his reaction, Dominic judged the immediate danger over.

"I understand completely. Why else do you think I am so eager for your reluctant company? For safety, I keep myself apart as much as possible from my associates, and even if that were not the case, their abilities are not remotely comparable to mine." He made a contemptuous brushing motion. "I have little interest in their conversation. It is enough if they serve me well."

And those like Henri, only there because he was under a *geas*, would be understandably prone to silence if not compelled to talk. Dominic wondered about that afterward, as he was being escorted to his cell by the rough, criminal-looking servants. Why hadn't Denais put a *geas* on him? It added another level of fear to his thoughts. He could do nothing to prevent it. Given that the Gaulan mage used them so casually, there must be a reason he had not.

It had been nearly a day since he had gotten the stickpin out of his cell. He looked as carefully as he could in the flickering lamplight of the corridor when he returned, but he didn't see it anywhere. Had the cat taken it somewhere else that was shielded? Where was Ardhuin?

The next morning, Henri brought the shaving gear again, saying as he poured out the hot water, "His lordship wishes to enquire if there is anything he might do to make your…confinement more comfortable."

Dominic froze, his face half-lathered, thinking furiously. Henri was probably a friend, but was also probably under a compulsion to repeat everything said to him. "It would be a relief to be free of these wretched manacles, but I doubt his concern for me would extend so far." Henri said nothing, but tears welled up at the corner of his eyes. Dominic looked at the manacles, suddenly caught by the close-worked combination of chryselectrum and metal. A dimly remembered article from *The Family Museum* stirred an idea. "But beside that, my great annoyance is boredom. Something to read, to take my mind off my troubles—but perhaps he would not permit a lamp, either."

"I will enquire, sir," Henri said with resolute dignity.

It was still quite dark and bitterly cold outside as Ardhuin went out to the courtyard and the waiting coach. It had no insignia, but the mounted military escort would remove any doubt about it being an ordinary carriage.

"A fine morning for hunting, ladies," Markus Asgaya said cheerfully, assisting Ardhuin and Gutrune into the coach before mounting his own horse.

Ardhuin barely refrained from snapping at him. Mornings were never her best time, and she had hardly slept at all last night. "Is he always like that?" she grumbled.

Gutrune smiled. "I am afraid so. He is relieved to be taking action again. He did not like waiting any more than you did."

He had certainly hidden it better, which was probably what Gutrune was hinting at. Feeling rebuked, Ardhuin stared out the window. She could just make out the black outline of the rooftops against the slightly lighter blackness of the sky.

"How long will it take to get there?" she asked, wincing inwardly when she heard herself sounding even more like a child.

"Tomorrow afternoon, if the weather holds. If it were not so remote we could travel all night."

There were rail lines, but none where they needed to go.

What would she do if they found no sign of Dominic on von Stangen's estates? It would take another day and a half of travel to return, still knowing nothing. He could be dead, and she wouldn't know.

The dark, ice-covered arch of the bridge came into view, and as the coach crossed the broad river, Ardhuin cast the finding spell one last time.

There.

Ardhuin gasped, sitting bolt upright. Gutrune reached for her. "What is wrong?"

"I found him. The location device I mentioned…over there!" Ardhuin pointed across the river, along the bank. "It's so close! Why couldn't I find it before?"

Gutrune gave her a serious look. "Perhaps it wasn't there before. Or it is a trick. Can they be faked?"

"This? No! It is grown. Even I couldn't make one from scratch." Ardhuin gritted her teeth. "And even if it is a trap, they must have gotten it from Dominic—and will know where he is. Tell them to turn the coach."

"They will not permit it. We cannot risk you like that." Gutrune's eyes were wide, and went even wider as Ardhuin reached for the door handle.

She'd wasted too much time already, and Dominic was in danger.

"What are you doing? You'll be killed!"

Ardhuin shook her head sharply. "No I won't. Have you forgotten what I am?" She gathered power around her, preparing to levitate as soon as she was outside the coach, and turned the handle.

"Wait!" Gutrune yanked hard on the check cord. The coach slowed but did not stop.

"*Was ist los herein?*" yelled a voice from the coachman's seat.

Gutrune pulled down the window and called back something clipped in Preusan. Ardhuin had no problem understanding the reply. No.

"Ladies? What's amiss?" Markus rode closer to the coach.

"I found him!" Ardhuin called. Markus' horse broke into a gallop until it was reined back. Markus stared at her.

"You are certain?"

"Yes!" She almost screamed. "They won't turn around! He's over there." Ardhuin pointed. "Make them stop!"

If he hesitated, it was only for a moment. He spurred up to argue with the commander of the escort.

"He's taking too long," grumbled Ardhuin. "We're almost out of the city."

Gutrune bit her lip. "Have patience. Oh, here he comes."

They were still moving, and the expression on Markus' face was not encouraging. Ardhuin yanked the door open, clutching the side and trying to pick a good place to jump. She'd have to get away from the rest of the escort, too, and travel back a good distance. Maybe she could steal one of the trooper's horses?

A rush of horse, and black uniform, and a familiar voice swearing in Preusan at her.

"No! *Gott,* please, what do you want? What do you want me to do?" Markus tried to push her back into the coach one-handed, a look of horror on his face.

Or she could just steal the coach.

"Can you get on the box?" she yelled, pointing. He nodded, uncomprehending, and she leaned out again, clutching the doorjamb, and cast vital stasis on the coachman. "Do it now!"

She had a brief glimpse of him snatching at the rail on the side and swinging off his horse as she stumbled back inside and scrabbled at the window fastenings on the other side. There was an armed guard seated beside the coachman, who was just realizing something was wrong. She cast vital stasis on him too.

Ardhuin frowned. "Any guards on the back?" she asked.

Raising an eyebrow, Gutrune remarked, "Fortunately for them, no. I can see you are in a ruthless mood." She appeared calm again, if breathing a little quickly. "The escort will have noticed what just happened, and will at the very least investigate," she added, as if she were commenting on the weather.

"Oh." Ardhuin leaned out the door again. Sure enough, the troopers behind them were speeding to catch up to the coach, and shouting. It wouldn't be long before the ones in front figured it out as well. "Turn back!" she yelled to Markus, who was awkwardly trying to steer the coach using the reins still frozen in the coachman's hands.

"I expect you to attend it, you know," he shouted back.

"Attend what?"

"Funeral, execution," he yelled, and grinned. "Both!"

Ardhuin shook her head and cast a cloud of deep shadow about the oncoming troopers. More Preusan profanity, and terrified neighing from the horses. "Take that street, before they notice!"

One wheel hit the curb as Markus took the sharp turn, tilting the coach for a dangerous moment. Ardhuin glanced inside. Gutrune was holding onto a strap, looking mildly concerned.

The cloud had only given them a brief respite. The troopers ahead, even in the dark, would have been able to see which way the coach had gone, so it was only a matter of time before they were found again. Realistically, Ardhuin was glad. She had no idea what they would find, and armed soldiers would be welcome, even if they were annoyed with her.

They had to slow their speed more than she liked in the twisting streets, which were not in very good repair. Ardhuin pointed directions, but she only had a sense of where the stickpin was—not which streets to take to get there.

"Stop here," she called.

Markus glanced about. The river was close by, and there were many old, dingy warehouses. "Here?" he asked, looking dubious.

"No, but we're very close. I don't want to attract attention." She stepped down from the coach, followed by Gutrune.

"I am afraid a coach such as this has already attracted attention," Gutrune remarked, looking at its glossy black sides.

"So we send it away," Markus said, eyes gleaming with mischief.

Gutrune regarded him for a moment, expressionless. "You are enjoying this."

He nodded, cheerfulness undiminished. "A grand adventure, with exquisite company, and in a good cause. I will be very surprised if we don't get a splendid fight in as well."

I hope we win. Ardhuin determinedly ignored the conversation and sent out the detection spell again. More focused, less powerful. She blinked. She almost felt as if she could reach out and touch it! She looked about, frowning. It felt *down*.

"I think he's in a cellar. Somewhere below ground level," she said slowly. "This way."

On the river side, in a gap between the warehouses, was an ancient, crumbling mansion. In the pale light of dawn she could see that dead yellow grass filled the front yard almost shoulder-high, hidden behind a rusting, partially collapsed wrought-iron fence. Slates had fallen off the roof in patches, one balcony had completely given way and was lying on the ground, and the windows were coated in grey grime.

Markus whistled softly. "It's immense! What on earth is it doing here? It must be over a hundred years old."

"Approximately two hundred and twenty-five," Gutrune said, just loud enough to hear. She joined them, huddling behind a watchman's shed for concealment. "At that time it was forbidden for any but nobility to build such a large house within the old walls of Baerlen. This area became fashionable among the wealthy commoners."

"I don't want to sound critical, but this house looks quite thoroughly abandoned," Markus said. "In fact, at the point of falling down."

If only Dominic were there, he could see what they were missing. Ardhuin looked more closely, then snorted. She'd lived in Peran by herself, almost abandoned, and yet she'd had plenty of company. Animal company. "I don't see any squirrel or bird nests, or tracks in the grass. By the river would be prime hunting area for mice and rats. If that's real, there's magic keeping the animals out."

Still, it was doubtful anyone went in the front door. Too open and easily observed.

"But how could Herr Kermarec be here? It's on the other side of the river, and all the bridges from the palace were blocked by the curfew."

Ardhuin shrugged. "I don't know. He's here now. This place is going to have considerable magical defenses, and I don't have time to find them all myself. Do you think if we free the coachman, he could go get more magicians?"

Henri brought a small oil lamp and a selection of books with Dominic's breakfast. The lamp was metal, and the usual glass chimney was missing.

"I am to remove it after your midday meal," Henri said, looking apologetic. "Are the books sufficient, or shall I attempt to find others? I am afraid the library is not extensive."

One volume was a tattered collection of classical poetry, another a treatise on migratory sea birds, and the rest parts two and three of a gothic romance.

"I believe these will be satisfactory," Dominic said, wondering if the library were truly that limited or if Denais was having a joke. It was just as well he had no intention of actually reading them.

He pretended to do so at first in case Henri had been ordered to check, loudly rustling the pages when he turned them. He continued to appear fascinated by the hand-colored illustrations of the Gervy's blue-footed tern even after the cell door was closed, but when he heard Henri's footsteps fade, he sat up and quickly got to work.

If he was lucky, he had less than three hours to escape. He took down the oil lamp from the shelf and placed it carefully on the floor. His chains clinked, so he ripped a strip from his blanket and wrapped it around them.

The concept was quite simple, really. Chryselectrum was a form of glass and therefore brittle. The chryselectrum in the shackles was protected by the outer shell of iron, but metal, when heated, expanded more than glass. The article he had read detailed the clever means devised to work around this difficulty, but he was going to make use of it. That is, if he could only ignore that the metal and glass were firmly attached to his wrists.

He held one manacle directly in the lamp's flame, but not so close as to put it out. This was his only chance. Dominic started to feel an uncomfortable warmth on his skin. What if Henri came back early? He'd have to prevent him from alerting Denais. The heat grew painful, then excruciating, and he bit his lip to keep from making any noise.

A tiny *tink* came from the manacle, then another. Wincing at the pain, he quickly took it away from the flame and, covering his arm with the blanket, brought the manacle quick and hard down on the edge of his iron bedframe.

Holding his breath, he listened for any sound in the corridor. There was none. The pain in his wrist had a sharp new component now, and when he took his arm out from under the blanket there was a thin line of red trickling down his hand. The chryselectrum had cracked, but was still either attached to the iron or too large to remove from the manacle. He would have to do it again.

It hurt even more than the first time. Tears of pain ran down his face as he forced himself to hold his wrist over the lamp. More crackling noises, several in a row, and finally he could bear it no longer. He smashed the manacle against the bedframe, gasping at the staggering wave of pain that made him dizzy.

The shards of chryselectrum that came out were bloody, but they did come out. He checked his watch. Over an hour from the time Henri had left him, and he still hadn't even gotten out of his chains. Dominic tugged fiercely, despite the stabbing sensation this caused, and slowly pulled his hand free. A long, deep cut ran along his thumb, dripping blood.

He sacrificed his cravat to tie up his hand, desperately wishing he had water, or anything for the burns. He had to bandage the cuts that were bleeding freely, but even soft cloth touching the burns was agonizing.

Dominic gritted his teeth and started the procedure on the second manacle. He knew what to do now, which made it easier, but now he had one hand throbbing with pain already and the other on its way. Just as he started to hear the cracking noises of the chryselectrum giving way, the rattle of the key in the door made his heart jump.

He had just enough warning to put the lamp on the shelf and wrap his arm in the blanket. He needed Henri to show up again, to open the cell door, but if Denais wanted to talk to him, the two thugs would be outside to escort him.

There was no sign of the thugs. Henri came in with a tray of food containing, in addition, a pitcher of water.

"Oh good," Dominic sighed.

Henri put down the tray, stiffened, then leaned over to pick a shard of chryselectrum off the floor. "Why, what is this?"

Dominic gripped his hands together and swung as hard as he could at the back of Henri's neck. The older man crumpled to the ground.

"I'm sorry, I'm sorry…." Dominic quickly picked him up and laid him carefully on the bed. He smashed the remaining manacle again and again, dragging his hand free with a whimper of pain he could not entirely suppress. More burns, more blood. He poured water over his hands, his breath hissing in when the cold water made contact. It helped, but not enough. He felt unsteady for a moment.

Henri moaned, and Dominic panicked. He couldn't use the manacles —even if he had the key, Henri's wrists were much thinner than his. He ripped up more of the blanket and quickly tied Henri's hands and feet together. Thinking a moment more, he added a gag. It was hard to focus through the pain.

Henri didn't look very good. His face was pale and his skin, when Dominic felt for a pulse, was clammy. He dragged the remaining scrap of blanket over Henri's thin shoulders and tried not to feel guilty. He failed.

He'd had no choice. If he wanted to escape and help both Henri and his wife, this was the only way. He tried not to think that he might have done Henri more harm than could be fixed. Dominic sighed, poured more water on his bandages, and carefully left the cell with the manacles in hand as an improvised weapon.

He kept the door unlocked but closed, just in case. Unhooking a lantern from the hallway, he set off towards the mysterious far end of the corridor. Going back towards the cellar ran the risk of encountering one of Denais' servants.

The stone got rougher as he continued on. The air was cool, and slightly damp. Dominic turned a corner, and stopped short. A web of magic filled the corridor ahead, completely blocking the way. He didn't recognize what it was, nor the complex, multilayered seal-like device on the floor. Were those faint gold markings around it? Why did they seem familiar?

He could walk around the seal without touching it, or jump, but the mesh was a difficulty. Well, didn't magic have a problem with iron? He held one manacle in each hand, spreading the chain wide, and tossed it at the mesh.

The mesh twisted and pulsed, but held. The manacles landed just on the edge of the magical seal, and when they hit, a long piece of chryselectrum fell out. Magic flared along the edge of the silvery glass, warping the intricate symmetry of the seal. The pattern was changing, flowing, becoming…larger. The magic writhed like a living thing in pain, making the gold markings more clearly visible, and he suddenly remembered where he had seen them before—in the Adaran temple. Was the mesh there to block whatever it did?

The seal suddenly vanished in a powerful blast of magic. Dominic felt something like a shudder in the air, and then an orange-and-white furry streak flew by from beyond the darkness, ears flat against its head. The mesh had not impeded the cat at all, and Dominic wondered if he should just go through.

Then he saw the water. It was filling the end of the corridor and brought a strangely familiar smell with it. Well, now he knew what the seal was intended to do. He had just destroyed the spell that kept the water out.

The edge of the water glittered in the lamplight, because it was moving. Towards him. He stared at it resentfully. He was so tired—all he wanted to do was escape. Now he was going to have to go the other way, and he couldn't leave Henri down here. Who knew where the water would stop?

"A slight setback," he whispered to the still-unconscious Henri, lifting him to his shoulders and trying not to gasp when his burns made contact. Fortunately, Henri was thin and not very heavy. "I think I broke something."

If he had to go through the cellar, there was something else he definitely wanted to break on the way. He crept cautiously to the end of the corridor. The main cellar appeared empty. Dominic went as quickly and silently as he could to the cabinet and smashed the door in, remembering the magical lock. Magicians rarely considered more brutal methods of burglary when designing their defenses.

Freezing water was seeping into his shoes and rising higher as he watched. Dominic's heart sank when he saw two of the bottles were missing, but then realized one was his. Denais would not be getting any use from that one. He took the rest and emptied them out, feeling unclean. It was like pouring out someone's life.

Dominic headed to the stairs. Then he heard the shouting, and the sounds of running feet, and wondered where in the mostly-empty cellar he could hide.

In a way, it was fortunate they had been planning to leave the city, Ardhuin mused. Her most crucial equipment had been packed on the carriage. It would have been nice to have everything, of course, but she did not want to leave the ruined mansion, and no one else would be able to enter her workroom. Time was running out.

She looked up from the hollow glass ball she was warming in her hands when Markus approached. It was a cold, grey day and she was having trouble getting the lodestone powder active.

"Did you find it?" she asked.

He nodded. "It took longer than I expected. The one by the north warehouse—two laborers came by, one after the other. At least that's what they looked like. The sound their shoes made did not match their appearance." Markus grinned. "I think that is the entrance."

"Is Colonel Biedermer gone?"

His grin widened. "He saw no need to stay, since he is only setting up the area cordon. It doubtless occurred to him that criticizing you so vehemently was not wise, considering what you did to von Koller. I greatly admired your restraint."

The dust was not floating at all. She needed something warm. "He wasn't afraid of me, and his complaints were quite justified. I can't blame him for being upset with how I dealt with his troops."

"More likely he was upset that you were able to do it. Made him think several entirely new thoughts, and he's not used to that. Where is Fraülein von Kitren?"

Ardhuin pointed down the street. "Diplomatically informing the owner we've taken over his building. Do we have anything to build a fire with?"

Markus frowned. "Wouldn't that be too noticeable? Are you cold?"

"No, it's not for me," Ardhuin said quickly, as he went to take off his caped greatcoat. "It's for this." She held up the scrying ball.

They both turned to look when the sound of hooves rang along the street. "How the devil did Biedermer let anyone through? He's going to alert whoever is in the mansion!" Markus said, looking annoyed. "Oh. It's von Koller. The coachman must have been persuasive. I only asked for him to send any magicians he could find."

"Speak of the devil and he appears," Ardhuin said dryly. He must have ridden as fast as he could when the summons was delivered. His horse's sides were heaving. That gave her an idea, and she started walking towards him.

"I have nothing to say to you," growled the head of the *Kriegszauberkollegium*.

"If I had my way, I would have left you unable to say anything to anyone," Ardhuin snapped back. She pressed the scrying ball against the flank of his steaming horse, and noted with approval the lodestone dust beginning to swirl.

"You are a damned impertinent child who insists on playing with dangerous things. I have nothing but contempt for you."

"And I for you," Ardhuin replied, keeping her gaze focused on the scrying ball. She was amazed at her calm, almost worthy of Gutrune. She didn't even feel her face getting hot. "Unfortunately for both of us, we have a common enemy. I require your aid to defeat this enemy and rescue my assistant. You will need my aid to stop a determined threat to your King and country. The question is, will you be able to overcome your distaste for my company long enough to do your duty?"

Von Koller jerked at the reins, making his horse toss up his head and dance nervously away. Ardhuin didn't mind. The scrying ball was now cloudy with dust, and all she had to do was keep it protected from the wind.

"I do not need any advice from *you* on how to perform my duty," von Koller hissed.

"I am pleased to hear it," Ardhuin said, turning away with the ball carefully cupped in her hands. "We will need a basic scan done when your magicians arrive."

"Is that sort of thing beneath you?" von Koller sneered. "That is a scrying ball, is it not? Do it yourself."

Ardhuin sighed. "Can any of them cast Devourer Gate? If not, they cannot use a scrying ball to find it, can they? We are dealing with a mage who knows the spells of the Grand Armeé. Wouldn't you prefer to know as much as possible where they are?"

Von Koller sat in silence for a moment, his face working. "Very well," he said between clenched teeth, and rode away.

Ardhuin walked to the watchman's shed, the closest point to the mansion that could not be seen from it. She felt depressed and disappointed, and wondered if they could succeed. Yes, she had won an argument with von Koller. Unfortunately, it was barely even a truce, and she had not been able to ask him for advice on which spells to trace.

It wasn't exactly the same as casting the whole spell—just the elements that comprised it. But it still took power, and she had been made painfully aware that she had limits. Use too much with detection, and she would not have enough to fight with. Use too little, and she might not survive to fight at all.

Devourer Gate, of course. Von Gerling had that set up in his quarters. She considered the spells her great-uncle had taught her, narrowed down the list to ones that would be useful here, and then selected five of the most dangerous.

The scans required a great deal of concentration, and she was only distantly aware of the sound of voices, of Markus and Gutrune and the hurrying of feet. The magic revealed itself as patterns in the dust, responding to the magic she cast and the resonances felt by the little activated pebbles she'd had Markus place about the perimeter of the mansion. It was horribly crude, but without Dominic, it was the best she could do.

As she finished the last scan, she felt the scrying ball tremble. Suddenly the dust compressed itself into a tight lump in the very center, and just as suddenly exploded. A crack formed and darted in a jagged line over the surface of the ball, which she nearly dropped in surprise.

"What's wrong?" Both Markus and Gutrune stood in front of her. She must have cried out. "Are you hurt? What happened?"

Ardhuin looked at the broken scrying ball, and then at the mansion. She frowned. "I'm not sure. There was a very powerful event just now. But…but it felt like a release, not a construction."

Markus, being a magician himself, understood what she was trying to say. "You mean a spell was broken? Did you do that?"

"Not with a scrying ball," Ardhuin blurted. "Was someone else casting spells?"

"Will they be able to detect this broken spell?" Gutrune asked, looking worried.

"If it was one of theirs, most likely," Ardhuin said slowly. "I am not sure it was one of theirs. I have never seen anything like it before."

Von Koller was quickly made aware of the situation, and he flatly declared that regardless of the source, the people in the mansion would be alerted and the attack should begin immediately. He delayed only long enough for Ardhuin to indicate where she had found the dangerous spells before ordering his magicians to attack.

She managed to stifle her protest before von Koller heard it; instead, she silently followed the *Kriegsa* magicians. Taking action was a relief even if her knees felt dangerously weak. If she had seen it, the enemy could have seen it too. But it felt wrong. Something told her the powerful burst of magic had not been created by either side. It felt *old.*

Denais' voice shouted something unintelligible. He sounded annoyed, and the shouting was coming closer. Dominic cast about frantically for a hiding place. The water was nearly to his knees, and numbingly cold. The cellar was too open, there was nothing…no. The stairs themselves—behind them, there was a space. Moving as quickly as he could without sloshing, Dominic wedged himself and his burden in the cramped space even as he heard feet descend.

"No, do not reveal yourselves! We have no idea who—*salaude de chien!*" The steps on the stairs halted, then continued. "So that was it! He escaped and destroyed the tunnel behind him. *Piente jeune!*"

Tunnel? A tunnel…under the river? That would explain the smell, then. Dominic could just peek around the edge of the stairs. Denais ran through the water to the cabinet, and when he found it was shattered and empty, he flung the cabinet door shut with a bang and strode back up the stairs, his face furious.

After waiting as long as he could stand it, Dominic carefully went up the stairs again. He could barely feel his feet from the cold. It was unlikely that anyone would come down again, which was good news, but he would be trapped if he remained here, and the water might continue to rise. He had to find another way out of the house.

Each step was an effort. Henri still had not stirred or made a sound, and Dominic worried even more. What if he had struck too hard? His burns throbbed, and his back ached with the strain of carrying Henri for so long. He had to find a hiding place for Henri as well.

He followed the damp trail left by Denais and his men to the ground floor, pleased that his own wet footprints would not be so noticeable by comparison. From the back of the house came sounds of argument.

No one was visible in the foyer, so he decided to risk attempting the front door. His hopes were dashed by the wash of strong magic framing the entrance just inside. It looked slightly familiar, and definitely dangerous. No, the front door was out. He would have to try the back, where the voices were.

Denais was yelling again. His calm, detached attitude was considerably frayed. "No, you fool! If we strike first we reveal our strength, and they could still call for assistance. Lure them in and destroy them utterly. From that beginning we can recover."

Dominic glanced at the door to the cellar stairs, and then at the hallway where the voices came from. He would not be able to reach the door in time, not with the burden he had. He looked at the apparently collapsing staircase to the upper floor and took a deep breath. He had to risk it. There might still be someone up there, but Denais and others were definitely down here.

The uneven stairs made him lose his balance more than once, painfully landing on his knees. Had Denais heard him? Fear gave him strength, and he staggered up in one last burst before collapsing behind a plush settee in a corner.

He took deep, ragged breaths, trying to muffle the sound in the crook of his arm. Henri lay where he had fallen, a thin trickle of blood coming from one nostril. At least he was still alive enough to bleed. Dominic wrenched off his coat and covered him with it.

Now he had to escape. The upper parlor was empty, as he had hoped. There must be a servant's stair somewhere that he could use to reach the ground floor undetected. It would probably be near a rear exit, too. He hesitated, thinking of Henri, but realized he was too tired to carry the man any further. If he was going to escape and rescue them both, it would have to be on his own.

Watching carefully, he passed the conservatory and Henri's petrified wife. Dominic stopped short, staring. Sparks of magic flashed outside the conservatory glass, arcing from the iron framework that held it in place. Amazement held him motionless, until he realized what was happening. Denais was under attack.

"Ardhuin," he breathed. His efforts had been successful, and she had found the emerald stickpin. But did she know about Denais? He had to warn her somehow.

The floor under his feet shook as if the whole mansion had been struck. His skin tingled with the wash of powerful magic, and in the distance he could hear shouting voices. How many people had come with her? Dominic hurried to the conservatory windows, but the glass was so scummy and streaked with dirt he could not make out much in the way of detail. Dark figures moving rapidly, one or two still and prone.

Dominic scrambled for a heavy stoneware pot with a sad-looking miniature palm tree in it, intending to throw it against the glass and call for help, until he heard two familiar voices coming from the direction of the main stairs—Denais, cursing, and Ardhuin.

Peering around the archway of the landing, he couldn't see her, only a sudden bolt of magic so strong he had to look away. Denais was in the foyer in a defensive position, his hair disarranged and one hand reaching for an inner pocket of his jacket. Denais suddenly turned and ran up the stairs, and Dominic dropped down and backed behind the end of a sideboard. He could see what Denais held now—one of the vials of elixir, and it glowed with magic.

He must have used the other vial already, the one that only Dominic knew had no power. This one did, though, and Denais was apparently thinking of using it now. Dominic crept forward and wondered how he could steal the vial.

Someone else was running up the stairs. First he saw the hat of shadows, the veiling tossed over the top, and then the angry and determined face of Ardhuin. In the distance, he could hear Markus Asgaya pleading with her to stay back or wait for him. Dominic couldn't help smiling, even under the circumstances.

Ardhuin was alive but in danger. Dominic saw the explosive magical force building around Denais and shouted a warning. Her head snapped up, stormy eyes wide. Power was building around her, too, but he couldn't tell what kind, and then the stairs disappeared in a thunderclap, and Ardhuin with them.

Dominic stared at the cloud of dust, his blood turned to ice. She wasn't…she couldn't be. Denais turned calmly away and walked towards the archway. The vial was in one hand now, and a syringe in the other. He looked about as if to see where the warning shout had come from, but he did not seem that concerned about it. Ardhuin had been his greatest worry, and she had been dealt with. Dominic wanted to scream.

The cloud of dust was thinning. There was magic in the dust. A bright core moved upward. With a desperate strength he didn't know he had, Dominic put his shoulder to the sideboard and shoved it into Denais as he went through the archway.

The vial fell from his hand. Dominic dove for it and rolled away, expecting any minute to feel a bolt of magic. He scrambled to his feet. Denais stared at Dominic as he stood on the landing, then past him with a stunned expression.

Ardhuin levitated where the missing staircase should have been. Her dark coat was ragged and torn, and her bright red hair streamed about her like the rays of the sun. She looked like a vengeful fire goddess.

"You!" Denais said. "*You* are the mage!"

"I am," Ardhuin replied, biting each word off. She dropped lightly down on the landing.

The two mages wasted no more words on each other. Denais was pale and furious, perhaps just now realizing the danger he was in. Ardhuin looked tired but equally angry.

Power built around Denais, and Dominic recognized the magic from Ardhuin's training back in the palace workroom. "Gesalt's Lance!" he shouted, and Ardhuin parried the attack with a small defensive shield.

Denais narrowed his eyes, glancing at Dominic. Ardhuin stepped between them so her shielding covered him as well.

For every attack Denais came up with, Dominic either named it or gave the closest one he knew. Ardhuin grew even more tired, but she was doing better than Denais. She only had to deflect, and with Dominic's help she wasted none of her power.

He could see when Denais knew he was defeated. The look in his eyes, followed by a desperate shadow spell when he ran. Dominic pointed, and Ardhuin cast her spell.

It was one Dominic had never seen before. It looked *thick,* like syrup. Ardhuin sagged, and he hastened to support her. The spell clearly was draining her last reserves.

Denais had not given up entirely. Ardhuin's spell surrounded him, but he continued to fight, creating his own similar spell, which insulated him and prevented her magic from touching him. He was sweating, and his expression was one of terror.

Ardhuin's spell slowly crept closer. A thud on the floor beside him made Dominic start and glance aside to see a fireman's ladder with hooks grabbing the edge of the landing, and then a dark scramble of Preusan magicians. The first one was Markus, followed by others in *Kriegszauberkollegium* uniforms. Markus alertly put up a shield, but did nothing else.

Dominic caught the glow of magic from the corner of his eye, but not in time to stop it. One of the other magicians loosed a powerful bolt, intending to help, but when it struck the combined magic around Denais, all the magic exploded in a blinding flash that made Dominic cry out.

He could not see. Frightening, groaning noises came from the walls, and the floor shook beneath his feet. Plaster dust rained from the ceiling.

"He's getting away! Frieder, get your men to circle back," called Markus. "We'd better get out. He must have triggered a destructive spell."

"There's a man behind the settee, tied up—and the statue in the conservatory is a transformed woman," Dominic said quickly. His vision was slowly returning. "We have to get them!"

The roof fell into the foyer with a thunderous roar of wood and brick. Debris pelted them.

"Well, we can't go that way," Markus panted. "What now?"

"Get to the conservatory!" Ardhuin said, coughing in the dust. Large chunks of plaster were falling, and the floor was tilting.

Dominic ran to where Henri lay and half-carried, half-dragged him to the conservatory. He had a hard time keeping on his feet as the floor bucked and sagged. He dumped Henri at the foot of the statue. Ardhuin put her back against it and held him, and he clutched her tightly. He had just enough time to see the bubble of shielding begin to take form around them as the house finally collapsed.

CHAPTER 16

With complete lack of consideration, the weather had turned to snow. It was only a light dusting, fortunately. Ardhuin only really became aware of it when she saw the flakes collect in the folds of a dead *Kriegsa* magician's uniform. His face was deeply seamed and ridged, the signs of Devourer Gate. She had warned them, hadn't she?

Everything blurred together. She couldn't remember if she had searched this section of the house before, or if one pile of rubble simply looked very much like another. At least she was no longer finding bodies, which was a blessing. At the thought, she glanced around for Dominic, drawing in her breath sharply when she didn't see him.

Markus, seeing her anxious face, guessed the reason for her concern. "I was finally able to convince him to allow the doctor to see to his hands," he said with a wry grin. Pain made a sharp furrow between his dark brows, but he had retained his sense of humor even with a broken arm and other, less severe, injuries. He also sported a flash of white in his black hair, residue of a dangerous spell. "Of course, I had to promise to keep an eye on you to accomplish this. I expect to be thanked profusely."

"I do thank you. I was afraid he would fall over in a dead faint. He is so stubborn!"

Markus cocked an eyebrow at her. "That must be why you have such a fondness for him. Being so sweetly reasonable yourself," he added hastily, holding up the hand that wasn't in a sling. "Now, are you going to follow his excellent example and come away? We can find no trace of this Denais fellow anywhere. He must have escaped."

Ardhuin took stock, and for the first time realized she was so tired she could barely move. Her coat was ripped and tattered, making any warmth purely accidental, and her hair had completely escaped all hairpins and was streaming down her shoulders in bright red waves. There was no sign of her hat. She must look like a madwoman.

A line of coaches waited along the street. One of them had to contain Dominic. She started towards them, shivering. She stopped short at what looked at first like a pile of overcoats, until she saw the stone face of the transformed woman. Some chivalrous soldiers had covered her undraped form. It was fortunate she could not feel the cold in her current state.

When Ardhuin did find Dominic, she was too tired to step up into the carriage. To her embarrassment, two soldiers had to lift her up. Dominic was slumped in a corner, wrapped in a horse blanket embroidered with the royal crest, his bandaged arms held out awkwardly before him. When he heard her, his eyes flew open. She was shocked at how pale and drawn his face was.

"Are you in much pain?" Ardhuin asked, sitting next to him.

"Dr. Wustel gave me some tincture of morphia," Dominic said, his words slurring a little. "The pain is nothing now." He shifted one hand and winced. "Well, not as bad. Have they taken Henri away?"

"The old man? I believe he was with the first group of wounded."

There was something in Dominic's voice, something she could not name. They had not had an opportunity to talk until now, but she had thought from the instant feeling of connection that any remaining awkwardness between them was gone. Now she was not so sure.

"Is something wrong?"

Before he could answer, the door to the carriage opened. Gutrune von Kitren, covered in plaster dust and cinders but otherwise completely unchanged, looked in. "We will be leaving soon. A few minutes at most."

Ardhuin just nodded, and Gutrune left.

"I should have known you would find me," Dominic whispered. "He was only injured because I tried to escape." He had closed his eyes again.

"Who?"

"Henri. The old man. Because of the *geas*…I knocked him unconscious so he could not call for help. I must have hit him too hard —but what else could I do?"

Without conscious thought, Ardhuin reached for his hand. That part of his fingers left unbandaged gripped hers tightly.

"You were right to try to escape however you could. You could not be sure when I would find you, and I almost didn't. We were on the point of leaving the city when I checked one more time." Her voice faltered, thinking how close she had come to missing him.

He stared at her, agonized. "But now he won't wake up! I meant to save him, not kill him!"

"Sometimes all you have are bad choices," Ardhuin said slowly, understanding at last. "You have to choose anyway, and hope for the best. Fix it if you can afterward. The woman turned into a statue is his wife, you said, correct?"

Dominic nodded.

"Would he have been willing to die to restore her?"

An arrested look came into his eyes. "Yes. He would have done

anything to save her. You are right. I saw him try to fight the *geas*, and…
and I understood. I would have done the same for you."

Ardhuin felt tears spring to her eyes. "Even though I once put a *geas*
on you? Can you understand why I felt I had to do it…and forgive me?"

Dominic nodded slowly, his face working. He raised his bandage-
covered arms towards her, made a sound of mixed pain and frustration,
and lowered them. Ardhuin shifted in her seat and wrapped her arms
around him, horse-blanket and all, and cradled his head against her
shoulder, stroking his hair. She felt more than heard his sigh, and a slight
tug on her hair as his fingers found it and held on.

When Gutrune returned, Ardhuin felt him start to try to sit up but
she did not let go, and he subsided. With one look at them both,
Gutrune took her seat opposite, and as the carriage started to move,
considerately pulled down the window blinds.

Six men already stood around the statue of the transformed woman
when Ardhuin entered the room. She had been expecting Magus von
Westerhof and his colleagues, since they had taken part in the discussions
of how best to attempt the restoration, but von Koller, glowering in the
corner, was a complete and unwelcome surprise. Ardhuin glanced away,
and also saw the little thaumatic physician who had examined her after
the fight with von Gerling.

He bowed, seeing her surprise. "I have some knowledge on the
medical effects of spells and their treatment," he said in a soft, accented
voice. "I trust my presence will not intrude?"

She shook her head and moved to the rough wooden table, covered
with odd-sized cushions to support the awkward shape of the statue in
something like a level position. Looking at the stone woman, she felt a
sinking feeling in her stomach. Under her great-uncle's supervision, she
had once transformed a rabbit to stone and back again, but a full-grown
woman was another matter.

"Are we ready to begin?" Ardhuin asked.

"You could have begun an hour ago," growled von Koller. "We have
been waiting for *you*."

And what possible concern could it be of his? "I was speaking with
her husband to see if he knew anything we should be aware of, and to let
him know we were about to begin," she replied, striving to keep her tone
even. In a softer voice, she asked von Westerhof, "Why is he here? Did
we not agree that extraneous people would only be a distraction?" That
was what they had said about Dominic, and since there was nothing
more he could tell them about the magic of the statue, she had agreed. It
still would have been reassuring to have him there—and now she had
von Koller breathing fire instead.

Von Westerhof shrugged, with an understanding twinkle in his eye.
"He came to hear of what we were attempting, and insisted on being
allowed to observe. How are we to deny the head of the *Kriegsa*, hmm?

This is a rare event."

Ardhuin gave up and resolved to ignore von Koller as much as possible. She held out her arms for one last inspection. No metal, not even so much as a button. Her hair was in a braid tied by a ribbon, and her feet in slippers more suitable for home. The gentlemen were likewise in simple clothing and had left all metal belongings outside. The doctor —she peered more closely and smiled. His spectacles had wooden frames. Clearly he had done this sort of thing before.

With silent agreement they took their pre-arranged places. Ardhuin stood at the head, leaning over to reach towards the woman's feet. She held her position and nodded to the magician facing her. He took a deep breath and lifted his hands to touch the statue's soles.

As soon as Ardhuin saw the flush of pink on the feet, she started her own magic—a variation of vital stasis. It had to match exactly with the progress of the transformation—if it covered the stone portion, the transformation spell would not work; if it delayed too long, any severe damage would be fatal to the living woman. No one knew how well Denais had performed the transformation.

"There is bleeding!" gasped the magician, sweat beading on his face.

The little doctor stepped forward. "It is only surface damage, most likely done when the statue was moved. Do not delay! You have little time to restore her circulation entirely."

That was why they had begun from the feet and moved up. It took time, and even vital stasis could not help if half her body was stone. Ardhuin kept her hands steady even as her eyes stung. She dared not look away for an instant.

There were bloody scrapes on the woman's knees, too. Blood welled the instant the transformation crossed over them, and then slowed and stilled as Ardhuin's magic held it back. It was agonizing. She'd never done such a powerful spell so slowly, with such control. It seemed like time had stopped.

The first mage was looking ragged and spent—fortunately, he had nearly reached the point where the next two would take over, continuing their progress up the body. The little doctor watched alertly, and Ardhuin noticed he held bandages in readiness.

They were almost there…the end was the hardest. All four mages crowded together to transform the heart, lungs, and brain in one final, massive effort. Ardhuin forced herself to wait, to let the scream that had been frozen all this time escape and a new breath be taken before finishing the vital stasis.

She had to grip the edge of the table to support herself, and the other mages were likewise affected. The first mage was still gasping with effort.

"Doctor?" Ardhuin wheezed. "Quickly, please…."

The little doctor rapidly glanced over the transformed woman. "Yes. The immediate prognosis appears good—that is, she is injured but we can therefore see her circulation is intact. Beyond that," he made a fatalistic gesture, "we must watch, and wait. Man proposes, but God disposes. We have done what we can."

"And I venture to say we have done quite well, do you not agree, gentlemen?" said a beaming Magus von Westerhof.

Ardhuin looked at him, surprised and a little hurt. They would not have been able to do the gradual transformation without her, but that appeared to be completely forgotten. Von Westerhof sent a servant off on some errand, and the other mages came up to her and shook her hand, one by one, pouring a torrent of Preusan she did not understand, but it seemed to be congratulatory.

Then von Koller came up, clicked his heels, and gave her a barely perceptible nod of the head. She could not have been more astonished if he had tried to kiss her. What was going on?

"Ah, there you are, Otto! Bring it here. Gentlemen, if you would...." Von Westerhof held out a pen and indicated a sheet of paper, already closely written in thick Preusan script. Von Koller signed, turned on his heel, and left the room. The others took their turns signing, and then felt the need to shake Ardhuin's hand all over again.

"Herr Magus...what is this all about?" Ardhuin finally managed to say.

"Ah yes. It is somewhat unconventional, I agree," von Westerhof said, signing the document with a flourish. "We haven't issued a degree by trial in over a century, but it used to be more common. More wars then," he added, handing the quill to the servant, who then dusted the paper with sand to dry the ink. "However, we decided it would be more discreet to attend to matters this way than making you sit for exams. Students would be bound to talk, you know."

"Degree? You mean...an *ars magica* degree?"

He gave her a grave look. "It is *highly* improper for a Mage Guardian —possibly the *only* Mage Guardian—to lack the correct credentials to practice magic. Perhaps you have noticed that we in Preusa are very fond of credentials. You should show respect for regulations and order, my dear. Now, this was merely the practical requirement. There will also be an investiture ceremony at the university tomorrow. We are fond of ceremonies, too," he said, his face still grave but with a twinkle.

"I would like to offer my congratulations, and also on behalf of the *sofon* of Baerlen," said the little doctor, bowing deeply. "The *sofon* took the liberty of suggesting to the King that this would be a right and proper recognition of what you have done for all of us."

"Yes...indeed! I...thank you, very much," Ardhuin said, feeling dizzy. Now she wouldn't have to worry about breaking the law every time she set up a ward back home. She could do magic in public, with people watching if she wanted to!

The little doctor glanced back at the table where the transformed woman lay, now covered more modestly with a sheet. "I will remain until the regular physicians arrive. From my observation, her injuries are not life-threatening."

"I will inform her husband," Ardhuin said, and escaped the room before more surprises showed up.

"Are you sure you should be up and about?" Dominic asked. "You must consider your own health is not robust at present, and I would not want you at risk of a relapse. How are you feeling now?"

Henri sat up straighter in his chair. "Much better, sir, thank you. May I say it is a relief to be able to speak freely once again. When you were being held captive…." His hands trembled.

"Do not distress yourself, Henri. Neither of us are captive any more," Dominic said, trying to soothe him. One of things that still agitated Henri were the many lapses of good manners forced on him by the *geas*.

"I heard her that once…it didn't sound good," Henri said worriedly. "Now I don't hear anything at all, and that's even worse."

"I'm sure they are doing everything they can," Dominic said, trying to hide his own worry.

The door opened. Ardhuin stood there, looking stunned, and Dominic felt his heart plummet.

Henri stood up stiffly. "Is she…?"

"The transformation is completely reversed," she said, still looking dazed. "Your wife is still recovering, however. The doctors must now attend her." Ardhuin shook herself, seeming to see Henri for the first time. "I…must prepare you a little. You understand that any damage that was done to the statue is reflected in her person?"

Henri nodded, his eyes locked on her face.

"Most of the scrapes will heal with time, although there may be some scarring. Unfortunately, there was also some breakage. Part of one ear, I'm afraid. She is missing the little finger of her right hand entirely, and the first two joints of the finger next to it. Even if we had been able to find the missing pieces, we would not have been able to restore them."

Henri clasped her hand, cheeks wet, and murmured in a broken voice, "Alive! Estelle is alive!" When he could speak again, he said, "Thank you, mademoiselle. If I may say so, I was quite relieved that you were one of the magicians. Not that I would wish to impugn the characters of the others, but it simply would not be proper without another lady present."

Ardhuin stared at him. "Why do you say I am a magician, Henri?"

"I saw you fighting that evil man," Henri said stoutly. "I woke up just enough for that, and it did me good. How many times I wished I could do the same! And no offense, sir, but you didn't seem quite strange enough to be a mage, saving your reverence. I've been in service to magicians all my life, so you could say I've learned their ways, sir."

Ardhuin concealed a smile. As soon as his shock wore off, Dominic grinned himself, feeling a little shaky. Evidently Henri did not have a problem with women magicians, at least not in situations like this. Dominic gripped Ardhuin's shoulder.

"Henri, you must understand Mademoiselle Andrews' talent is…not to be mentioned to anyone. It would occasion comment, and with Denais still at large—and with a grudge against her—it would be dangerous if generally known."

"But of course, sir," Henri said with dignity. "I would in any case refrain from discussing a young lady so freely, and when I owe Mademoiselle Andrews so much, it would be unpardonable!"

"That's all right, then," Ardhuin said, smiling and patting Dominic's hand. "Would you like to see your wife now?"

"After so long…. Thank you. Thank you for Estelle."

"You are welcome, Henri," Ardhuin said softly.

Henri went inside the room where his wife lay. Dominic gave Ardhuin a look before drawing her arm through his own. "You should be more careful, you know. He might forget his good intentions one day, telling someone about the miraculous recovery of his wife."

"Oh, I doubt it," Ardhuin said, giving him a mischievous smile. "Henri is quite old-fashioned in that regard. Didn't you hear him? He doesn't discuss young ladies. Besides, he doesn't know how *much* of a magician I am, and that's the real danger."

Dominic raised an eyebrow, but refrained from arguing. "So…how soon can we leave?"

Ardhuin sighed. "I think the Preusans are done with me for now. The university wants to give me an *ars magica* degree—that is, they've already done it but there is some kind of ceremony at the university tomorrow. After that, I believe we can leave whenever we like."

"Good." Dominic glanced up and down the hall, making sure they were unobserved, and stole a kiss. "I'll start packing immediately."

Ardhuin frowned. "Speaking of that, I have to go shopping for a new coat so I can return the one I'm borrowing from Gutrune. And a hat. I had no idea how hard being a Mage Guardian can be on one's clothes."

"Is it safe to go out?" Dominic asked, feeling a stab of concern. "Can they be sure they found all of Denais' people?"

"Without Denais to give them orders they will do nothing. He used the *geas* extensively. In fact, von Koller caught three of them returning to the old mansion, even though it was destroyed and guards posted. He'd ordered them to go there, you see."

"And von Stangen?"

Ardhuin gave a shudder. "Gutrune said the executions will be carried out in secret, to avoid alarming the population. I think the King was shocked at how many of the *Kriegsa* magicians were involved. Resentment had been building for some time at their lower status compared to the army, and von Stangen exploited that. Don't worry," she said, giving his arm a squeeze and grinning. "Gutrune will be with me."

"Then I withdraw my objections," Dominic said immediately. "Unless you would like me to accompany you?"

Ardhuin grimaced. "It will be quite tedious, I am afraid. I would not subject you to that when I can barely stand it myself."

Dominic saw her and Gutrune off on their expedition and went up to the workroom to begin packing. As he worked, it occurred to him he really ought to go out and visit some shops himself. He had been conscious of a stab of guilt when she mentioned her missing hat. She did not know that he was responsible for destroying it. No one had seen him, in the dust and confusion after the collapse of Denais' mansion, as he carefully nudged it into the watery hole that was the remains of the entrance to the cellar.

He should ask Henri if it was proper for a gentleman to buy a lady a hat.

Dominic finished and Ardhuin had still not returned, so he decided to go out himself. Even without the issue of the hat, he wanted to find some little gift for her. They were back on their earlier friendly footing, and he wanted to improve it. He smiled to himself. They would be able to spend more time together when they left Baerlen, and—he drew in a breath, a sudden fear appearing in his mind. She would stay in Peran, wouldn't she?

He wandered past the shops on the main fashionable boulevard, realizing he could not afford anything he wanted to buy. That was another problem. All the time they had been here he hadn't written anything. He couldn't expect Ardhuin to marry him if he could barely support himself, let alone a wife.

After looking in a few more shops, he noticed a bookstore and his depression lifted. He *could* afford a book. He walked quickly towards the door, nearly running into a man who had his nose in a guidebook.

The man looked up, startled, and Dominic gasped. "Phillipe? Is it you? What are you doing here?"

"Looking for you and freezing to death," Phillipe snapped. "After a week of searching, of course I find you outside a bookstore. I should have started here. Why, oh why Baerlen? You can't find anything decent to eat and the girls look sturdy enough to pull a plow—not that you can see much of them under all the heavy wraps they have to wear in this weather. Are you mad?"

Dominic urged his friend inside the store, smiling. "I'm delighted to see you too, Phillipe. But why do you need to see me so urgently? A letter would not suffice?"

Phillipe tapped his head. "Oh, that reminds me." He went through his pockets, finally pulling out an envelope. "That's for you. That post office fellow, can't remember his name at the moment, gave it to me on the off chance I did find you. Recognized my name, if you can believe it."

"Post office?" Dominic was completely bewildered. "What post office?"

"In Baranton," Phillipe said. "I thought I'd surprise you with a visit to your rural fastness. The locals think you've been turned into a frog, by the way. How do you get yourself mixed up in things like this? And when

I went to Peran, I ran into *her*. This trip was all her idea," he added in bitter accents.

"Who?" Dominic asked, even more confused.

"Madame Andrews," Phillipe said, shuddering.

Dominic gaped at him, not comprehending, and then feeling like a bucket of ice water had been dumped over him. Ardhuin's mother. Had she come to take Ardhuin away?

"You look white as a ghost," Phillipe commented. "You have met the lady, I take it."

"No, never," Dominic stammered. Where could he talk to Phillipe undisturbed? The beer gardens were too noisy and public, and anywhere outside would be too cold. He pulled his friend into the section of the store where the dictionaries and other reference books were kept. Hardly anyone came over there. "Try to remember. What did you tell her about me?"

Phillipe gave him an intrigued look. "Don't tell me. She's looking for her daughter. You found her, eh?"

"Be serious for a moment," Dominic said in an agitated whisper, feeling his face get hot. "Ard—Mademoiselle Andrews is here in Baerlen, too."

"Yes, we knew that. Visiting a school friend. Hence the formidable Madame Andrews. We discussed the coincidence of your trips at some length on the train. You aren't actually staying, ah, together, are you?"

"In a manner of speaking, yes," admitted Dominic. "At the Imperial Palace, though, which is thick with guards and a rather awkward place for a tryst." Phillipe's eyes widened. "It's a long story."

"You. Staying at the Imperial Palace. With Mademoiselle Andrews." Phillipe took a moment to digest this. "No, it does not have the air of scandal, which I also doubt would be encouraged there. Depressingly moral, these people. Besides, I was at pains to convince Madame Andrews that you were the last man on earth to notice, much less seduce, any young lady."

"No doubt that reassured her greatly," Dominic said dryly, trying not to remember that he had essentially done exactly that. "As a matter of fact, I wish very much to marry Mademoiselle Andrews," he said with some difficulty. "It's all a mess. I need your help, Phillipe."

"If you want to marry that woman's daughter, you certainly do," Phillipe agreed. "She talks for hours, and the only thing that will distract her from her goals is fashion. Only consider! You'll go mad inside a month."

Dominic laughed. "Ardhuin is the exact opposite. I'm determined, Phillipe. Come, you said yourself I'm not the type to notice a pretty face, so can't you see she must be something out of the ordinary?"

Phillipe sighed. "Oh, very well. You know your mind; do you know the young lady's? Is she agreeable to your plans for her?"

"Well, I did ask, but...she thought I was not serious. That was some time ago, anyway, and…I think I can convince her, but not if her mother takes her off to Atlantea!"

"Calm yourself," Phillipe soothed. "You are very agitated; it's not like you. Some time ago? How long have you been acquainted with Mademoiselle Andrews?"

"I met her when I came to Baranton. Don't you see? Her mother doesn't know how long she's been there, and mustn't know. But if you've already told her—"

"No, I just said you were renting the cottage from the owner of the house." Phillipe rubbed his chin. "I can see we need to think this out."

Ardhuin looked up sharply as the door opened.

"Found him!" announced Markus triumphantly. "Alive and unharmed."

Dominic followed through the door, going immediately to her. He did appear uninjured, but he had a worried expression. Her terror transformed to anger.

"Where were you? I thought something horrible had happened. How could you do this?"

"We were talking, and I didn't realize what time it was." He glanced at Markus and Gutrune. "I, ah, met up with a friend unexpectedly."

"That does not account for your looking like a hunted deer," observed Markus. "Do you perhaps owe this friend money?"

"No, no." He glanced at the other two again, and it seemed to Ardhuin he was wishing they would leave. "It was my friend Phillipe. I told you of him," he said, giving Ardhuin an earnest look. "He went to Peran to visit me. He found your mother there."

Ardhuin jumped to her feet, a terrible tightness in her stomach. Now she understood why Dominic was disturbed. "Oh no…what does she… is she still there?" Dominic shook his head. "She's *here?*"

A small quiver quirked Gutrune's lips. "She can easily be accommodated at the palace, you know."

"That's not the issue," Ardhuin said, distractedly ramming her fingers into her hair and starting to pace the room. "She doesn't know about *any* of this. She thinks…she thought I was in school all this time."

"She will want to take you back with her, won't she? To Atlantea," Dominic said softly. Ardhuin bit her lip, nodding. She'd be in for a terrible scolding no matter what, but then—parties. Parties without Dominic. She turned to face him, trying not to cry. "I don't want you to go," he said, in a tight, jerky voice.

She tried to speak, but couldn't.

"I am afraid we cannot permit you to go so far at present," Gutrune said in her calm way. "Denais will undoubtedly attempt another return at some point, and you are still the only surviving Mage Guardian we have."

"I can't possibly tell my mother I am responsible for the magical defense of all Aerope," Ardhuin said, aghast.

"That would be best," Markus agreed, a wide grin on his face. "It's not a thing we care to have generally known. Now, what are we going to do? I suppose it would not be very polite to hide from your family forever."

"It wouldn't work anyway. From Phillipe's account, Madame Andrews is a particularly determined woman," Dominic added. "Ardhuin, I...I need to talk to you."

"Oh, don't mind us," Markus said, leaning back in his chair and adjusting his sling. "After all we've been through together, why the need for secrecy?"

"I believe Herr Kermarec has a rather personal question to ask," Gutrune said, the corners of her mouth turning up. Ardhuin was briefly distracted from being embarrassed by the realization that Gutrune was actually *smiling*.

"Splendid idea!" Markus tried to gesture with his broken arm, and drew in his breath with a hiss. "That would solve all our problems. Marrying her might even cure him of constantly glaring at me in that rude manner."

Gutrune held up a hand. "There is a reason these matters are usually discussed in private, Herr Asgaya. You have placed Fraülein Andrews in an awkward position." She sounded annoyed.

Ardhuin stared at Dominic, trying to sort out her tangled thoughts. Somehow she knew the answer to the one question that had troubled her before, that he did love her.

"The difficulty will be in persuading my mother," she managed to say, finally. "I'm not of age, and...and I don't think she will approve."

"But you have no objection yourself?" asked Gutrune. Ardhuin shook her head, not trusting her voice.

Dominic's shoulders sagged in relief. "If it is a question of my ability to support you, Phillipe brought me this. It isn't a fortune by any means, but if it does well, and I write more...." He handed her a letter. She scanned it quickly. *...idea an excellent one, no doubt of your ability to execute it...if terms acceptable, write at once...500 guilders in advance.*

"Your book! How wonderful!" Ardhuin beamed at Dominic. "I don't think she will be as concerned with that as she will with the thought of... of not being as splendid a match as she had hoped. With a big wedding," she said gloomily.

"Your great-uncle did not explain much of the practical side of the Mage Guardians, did he?" Gutrune asked.

"No, just the obligations. And some of the history," Ardhuin said.

Gutrune looked even more amused. "You need not concern yourself with the financial details, for—"

A knock interrupted her, followed by the entrance of a palace servant with a crease of worry between his brows. He spoke rapidly to Gutrune in Preusan, but Ardhuin heard enough to understand. Even if she hadn't, the stunned look on Dominic's face would have told her. Visitors asking for her, by name.

"How long ago did you leave this friend of yours?" Markus wanted to know.

"Less than an hour! It can't be her—can it?" Dominic protested.

Markus rubbed his forehead. "If it is, we should put her in charge of our military mobilization plans. Or the trains. We need to stall for time."

"Tell them that Fraülein Andrews and I are…away, visiting my family's estate. We are expected to return in a few days," Gutrune told the servant, who bowed and withdrew.

"It won't work," Ardhuin said gloomily. "She'll come back. Often. And when she doesn't get what she wants, she'll find out where your family's estate is and go there." The longer it took, the longer the lecture would be, too. There was no way out of it.

Gutrune looked thoughtful. "Undesirable, since it would not be difficult for her to find out we were never there. How long, in your opinion, before she proceeds to this extreme?"

"A day, at most. I can't be sure." Ardhuin closed her eyes, unable to think of a way to stave off disaster. "The university wants me for a ceremony tomorrow, though, and I don't know how long it will last."

"Then a distraction is clearly called for," Markus said, sounding entirely too cheerful. "I have a great desire to meet such a formidable lady, and Herr Kermarec needs to ask all the proper permissions. Can your friend be relied on to assist? It would seem he told her the whole the instant he saw her again."

"I am sure he told her what he did purely in self-defense," Dominic protested. "And he didn't tell her everything, or she would have been asking for me as well."

"Yes, very true. So, our duty is clear. We must act as the sacrificial diversion, while the ladies complete their university business in complete secrecy. By the time they are finished we should be able to report our conclusions from the scouting expedition and decide what to do next."

It sounded like he was planning a war. Ardhuin had to admit that was probably the best way to approach it.

❧

I can do this. I burned manacles off my own wrists. Dominic stared at the completely innocuous hotel that Madame Andrews honored with her presence, squared his shoulders, and went up the steps to the entrance.

Debate had raged long after Ardhuin had gone up to sleep and the conspirators could talk more freely about what was, to his mind, the largest obstacle. They had decided it would be best for Dominic to appear first, and alone. After a reasonable interval, Phillipe and Markus would make their appearance—either to continue to distract Madame Andrews, or to rescue Dominic from disaster.

Now, however, he began to wish they were with him. Too much depended on making exactly the right kind of impression. Such was his nervousness he had some difficulty making his request at the front desk understood. When the hotel servant returned and asked Dominic to follow him, he could only nod in response. Was Madame Andrews really going to meet with him, alone? The hotel staff didn't seem to think anything of it, which was strange, too.

The servant knocked on the proper door, and when it opened Dominic understood why he had been asked to come up instead of more properly waiting below. A tall, bearded, older man with a strong resemblance to Ardhuin stood there, peering at him in a slightly near-sighted way.

"Monsieur Andrews?" Dominic gasped. Nobody had mentioned that her father was in Baerlen as well. "I am—that is, permit me to introduce myself. I am Dominic Kermarec, and I—"

"Oh, *there* you are!" A petite, golden-haired whirlwind suddenly appeared at M. Andrews' elbow. "What *excellent* timing you have, for if you had been but half an hour later, we should have missed you, having left for the palace to seek you out!" Ardhuin's mother gave him a brilliant smile, then looked up at her husband, still studying Dominic in silence. She tsked at him in exasperation. "Thomas! Your manners! He's not a specimen in a glass case, you know. Do sit down. There is so much I mean to ask you—oh Thomas, would you be a dear and ring for tea?"

Stunned, Dominic followed the pressure of Madame Andrews' imperious little hand and sat, only realizing when he made contact with the seat that he had forgotten to check that there was something to sit on. While she chattered happily about her trip and the amazing coincidence of meeting up with Phillipe in Baranton, Dominic struggled to regain his mental balance. At first he thought Ardhuin and her mother had nothing in common. Madame Andrews was delicate, tiny, exquisitely dressed, and never silent. Not a single golden hair was out of place. He had a sudden flash of memory, a vision of Ardhuin levitating out of the smoke and dust in Denais' house, and had to choke back an entirely inappropriate laugh, thinking of her probable reaction.

Then he saw her quick, flashing smile, and the resemblance was there. Ardhuin just didn't smile that much. He should change that.

"But how did you come to visit Peran?" Madame Andrews asked suddenly, and he gulped. Time to pay attention. He had to remember to keep his story straight—after all the hours they had spent coming up with it, it would be a shame to forget it now.

"I had the honor to pursue some research with Monsieur Morlais during my university years. He was kind enough to remember me in his passing, and it was my pleasure to assist in the disposition of his estate. It was then that I met your daughter," Dominic said, hoping the mention was sufficiently casual.

"Do you know when she will return?" demanded Madame Andrews. "I can't imagine how so many of her letters went astray like that. We had no idea where she was! Next time we go on one of your little trips to the ends of the earth, Thomas, we take her with us so I can keep an eye on her," she said, shaking her finger at M. Andrews and scowling. Dominic's heart dropped into his stomach. "Not that she would find it very amusing, poor girl. We did not encounter much civilization in our travels, did we dear?" M. Andrews shook his head. "But I am so *delighted* to hear Ardhuin is staying at the Imperial Palace. She used to be so reluctant to go out in society, and here she is, mixing with the most prominent people of Baerlen practically every day!" She gave a beatific smile.

When she isn't embedding them in walls or uncovering their plots to overthrow the government, thought Dominic, trying to smile back. Fortunately, the tea arrived and allowed him a few moments to collect his thoughts.

"I knew she would enjoy herself if she would just make a little effort. I suppose there were a great many splendid parties?" asked Madame Andrews, handing him his teacup.

"Er, I was—that is, I believe so. I was unfortunately unable to attend. My business took up much of my time," Dominic stammered, resolving to warn Ardhuin and Gutrune to make up some dazzling parties to describe. He could tell Madame Andrews would not be satisfied with anything less.

"Your business?" she asked, one delicate eyebrow raised.

"Monsieur Morlais had some…affairs of delicacy with the government here. I was asked to, er, complete them."

"Oh, so *that's* why you were staying at the palace too. How nice for Ardhuin to have someone she already knew…but I forget, you said you were not able to attend the parties. How sad!" She sipped her tea. "Uncle Yves had business with the government? But—" she stared at him, astonished. "Are you a *magician?*"

Oh dear. This was a complication their planning had not foreseen. "No, not at all, Madame. I am a writer, only. Er, a writer of works on magic, that is. Of course. Naturally. Otherwise how would we have met?"

"If they are delicate government matters, he will not be permitted to discuss them," M. Andrews stated in a deep voice. Dominic was startled to hear him talk at last, but grateful that he had been rescued from his floundering.

Madame Andrews gave Dominic a look that was half apology, half mischief. "I will say nothing, I promise!"

A knock sounded at the door, which M. Andrews answered. Dominic knew who it must be before he returned.

"More guests, my dear," he said with a humorous look. "They should be up directly." He glanced at the tea table. "Will this be enough?"

Markus and Phillipe, already? How long had they been talking? Propelled by sheer terror, Dominic managed to stumble out an incoherent explanation of the real reason for his visit. "And I love her very much," he mumbled at the end, trailing off in despair. He'd ruined it. Why would anyone want such an idiotic son-in-law? What had he said? He couldn't even remember.

Then he was engulfed in a flurry of exclamations and soft kisses on both cheeks. Somehow, he managed the presence of mind not to drop his teacup.

"But this is *delightful!* I will confess, I had wondered…oh, how *annoying* that Ardhuin isn't here! We have so much *shopping* to do."

Dominic suppressed a shudder, imagining Ardhuin's likely response. Noticing M. Andrews had not said anything and was looking thoughtful, he asked, "Sir? Do you have any objection?"

M. Andrews blinked at him. "Ardhuin has a good head on her shoulders. If she really wants to marry you, I don't mind."

As soon as Phillipe came into the room, Madame Andrews pounced upon him and told him the news. Markus stood there, looking dashing in his uniform, only the slightest quivering at the corners of his mouth betraying him.

"I beg your pardon for the intrusion, Madame," he said, bowing gracefully. "I was looking for Herr Kermarec, and was informed he might be here." He gave Dominic a significant look.

"Permit me to introduce *Schutzmagus* Asgaya," Dominic said hastily. "Er, is it anything urgent?"

"No, it is merely that your presence is requested at the palace this evening, if convenient," Markus said with a grin. "The project is expected to be complete this afternoon."

He must mean Ardhuin's ceremony, Dominic decided. In the general chatter, he motioned Phillipe aside.

"What the devil did you tell them?" Dominic asked in a frantic whisper.

"Why? Didn't it work out?" Phillipe asked, looking surprised. "Don't tell me you've changed your mind. I *did* warn you."

"No, I haven't changed my mind! But they didn't ask me anything. She's delighted! The woman lives for fashion and society, neither of which I have any connection to."

Phillipe bit his lip. "Yes, but I do, and you are my friend. Perhaps I encouraged her to think we came from the same circles—all you have to do is not correct her misapprehensions, so it isn't precisely *lying*."

"Well, if she tries to hold the wedding in the Rennes Cathedral she'll figure it out fairly quickly," Dominic snapped.

"Don't worry, I dropped a few hints that you didn't care for the social whirl," Phillipe said in a soothing, quiet tone. "So, when is the happy day?" he asked, more loudly.

"Oh, there is so much to do!" exclaimed Madame Andrews. "I will need to sit down with Ardhuin and come up with a guest list, and decide where it should be—Baerlen is rather remote for most of her family—it will take at *least* a month. Why, we must still arrange for her trousseau!"

Markus shot a quick glance at Dominic and must have seen the horrified expression on his face.

"Madame, I must regretfully inform you that there are certain reasons —" he broke off and stared at Phillipe.

"Ah, you may speak freely in front of him," Dominic said, solemnly.

Markus nodded and continued, "Matters of state, in fact, which would make the King and the government of Preusa greatly prefer a small, private ceremony, if at all possible."

Madame Andrews' face fell. "Oh, but…she will be so *disappointed!*"

"If she objects, then naturally I will respect her wishes," Dominic said promptly, having no doubt at all what Ardhuin would decide. Markus gave him a wink.

"If Madame wishes, I would be happy to escort you to view the palace chapel," Markus said, giving her another courtly bow. "I believe Madame will find it acceptable."

"Oh, well, the *palace*," Madame Andrews said hesitantly, looking more interested.

"You would not want to throw any difficulties in their way, my dear," M. Andrews added. "There must be a very good reason for this request or they would not ask it."

Madame Andrews threw up her hands. "I will talk to Ardhuin," she said with finality. "You can't simply deny her the most important day of her life on a *whim*."

The granting of her *ars magica* degree at the university was quietly done to preserve her secret, but it was still impressive—the magical faculty in their rich robes gathered in the old paneled praesidium, taking their places in the steeply banked seats. Ardhuin kept the happy glow of knowing she was loved like a cloak about her through all the ceremony and attention that would earlier have put her in an agony of discomfort. She had worn a simple grey silk dress, thinking it the closest thing she had to an academic outfit, and then was dismayed at the rich colors and gold embroidery.

"Your robes are waiting for you," her sponsor, von Westerhof, told her with a gently mischievous smile. He led her to a small room connected to the praesidium, where the Adaran *sofon* waited. The old man carried in his arms a robe of deep green silk brocade, cleverly woven in a pattern of leaves. Some of the leaves were picked out in delicate lines of gold embroidery, and down the front edging was the symbol she had seen in the Adaran tree: two birds flying over a mountain.

"The people wished to thank you for your defense of the Closure," he said, and without any further words placed it around her shoulders. It was heavy, and rich, and the most beautiful thing she had ever owned. She told him so.

"Go, and speak the words," he said simply, and smiled. He placed two fingertips briefly on her forehead. It felt like a blessing.

Armed with her new robes, she walked into the deep well of the praesidium and stood tall before the *ars magica* faculty of the University of Baerlen, the most famous in the world. The rustling of robes stilled and she felt every eye upon her, but instead of the fear that had been present in every other public appearance, she felt strength.

Ardhuin summoned power, gathered it, invoked the golden light of the *gloire,* and said the words. *"Ecco, maga est!"* Behold, I am a mage. The words of becoming. A statement, and a challenge.

And the faculty replied with one voice, *"Veritas!"*

Dominic extended his hand to help Ardhuin down from the train platform. "Are you certain he understood the telegram? I don't see him here."

She smiled. "He understood when I sent them before. Michel doesn't like the trains. He's probably waiting outside with the cart."

Indeed, Michel, the sleepy old horse, and the battered cart were all waiting together outside. Seeing them, Dominic felt that he had come home at last. Michel followed in his customary silence to load the baggage.

Madame Daheron waved to him excitedly from the ticket window. "Are you back from your wedding trip at last, then?"

Dominic stared at her. "I beg your pardon? How did you know I was married?"

"Ah, it's your servants that told me! They'll be that glad to know you and your lady are back at last. They're staying at the *Chat Gris,*" Madame Daheron added, looking severe. "You should have arranged to leave them a key, so they could prepare the house against your arrival. But no doubt you had other matters to attend to," she said, giving him a motherly smile.

"Er, yes. Precisely. The *Chat Gris,* you said?"

He found Ardhuin, who took one look at his face and promptly asked what had happened.

"Do we have servants?" he asked, feeling bemused.

"No. Why do you ask?"

"Well, somebody told Madame Daheron that's what they were. Oh, and they knew we were married, too."

"The King was very generous," Ardhuin said, looking anxious. "He provided our entire wedding, but I doubt his generosity would extend to hiring servants for us. How strange."

"Yes, I rather felt he was enjoying himself," agreed Dominic. "Your mother was not expecting royalty. It was a near thing at times, but that did the trick."

"Not to mention Markus looking romantic with his arm in a sling and flirting with her shamelessly," Ardhuin said, grinning. "I wonder my father did not object."

Dominic gave her a lofty look. "Your estimable father knew exactly what was going on, and was greatly amused. It was a pity they had to leave so soon afterward; I would have liked to spend more time with them both."

"Really?" Ardhuin jumped up to the cart seat before either he or

Michel could assist her. "Maman was talking you silly. She still thinks you are one of Phillipe's well-connected friends, you know."

Dominic stood looking up at her. "I liked discovering traces of you in each of them."

Ardhuin stared at him. "I am nothing like Maman!"

"You are more subtle, of course. I suspect the moderating influence of your father," Dominic said, smiling at her expression of shock and climbing up to sit beside her. "Even Phillipe commented on the resemblance. He was quite cast down to hear you had no sisters."

She laughed. "You are making that up. I remember you telling me he has a great weakness for a pretty face."

Dominic raised an eyebrow. "Very true. Now, however, he tells me I am responsible for raising his standards to an impossible height, having introduced you to him. I don't suppose you have any female cousins instead?"

"He was just being polite," she said, and sighed.

"It is not particularly polite to refer to your best friend's bride as a 'stunner,' " Dominic retorted, "but you *did* smile at him. Perhaps you did not notice he didn't speak for nearly ten minutes afterward? Ever-talkative Phillipe?"

Ardhuin opened her mouth to reply, then closed it, looking puzzled.

Dominic had Michel stop at the *Chat Gris*. He was not entirely surprised to see Henri and his wife come out to greet them. Henri moved a little stiffly still, but both were much improved in health since the last time he had seen them a few weeks ago.

"Estelle and I agreed it was only right, after what you did for us," Henri said. His wife, a calm, pleasant woman, nodded.

"Are you quite certain you wish to be in another…a magical establishment?" Ardhuin asked carefully.

"Oh yes, madame. We are both accustomed," Henri assured her.

Dominic exchanged a questioning look with Ardhuin. She shrugged. "I'll, ah, send Michel back for you," Dominic said. He got back in the cart and they started off again. He felt stunned.

"Dominic! How on earth are we going to pay them?" Ardhuin whispered urgently.

He shook his head. "How could I tell them no, after all they've been through? And you know, their experience will be advantageous. It isn't as if you could find such servants anywhere you looked."

"It will be nice, I suppose—oh look, there's Peran!"

Her house—and his house too, now—was still intact, if a little weather-worn.

"The yard looks dreadful. I have a lot of work to do."

"You need to work on your book!" Ardhuin said, shocked. "I suppose we'll have to hire a real gardener next."

The wards were still intact, but weak, and Ardhuin claimed none of her traps had been triggered. They both busied themselves with moving trunks and unpacking until the bell rang at the door, announcing Michel's return.

"I'm going to have to come up with some way of adjusting the wards for them," Ardhuin said, running down the stairs. "I don't suppose they would welcome being shut out by mistake."

In addition to Henri, his wife, and their minimal baggage, Michel deposited a large wicker hamper on the step before returning to his cart. Henri opened it, and a familiar orange-and-white cat jumped gracefully out and immediately began grooming himself.

"That's not the same…I thought he was killed when the mansion collapsed!" Dominic exclaimed.

"Oh no, sir, he's a very resourceful cat. Intelligent, if I may say so," Henri said indulgently. "Everyone seemed to think he should come with us."

"I agree completely. That cat saved my life," Dominic said. "I will personally give him a saucer of cream at the earliest opportunity."

"Speaking of which, I suppose the larder will be quite bare with you being away so long," Estelle said thoughtfully. "What would you wish me to prepare for you, madame?"

Ardhuin went off with Estelle to explain the state of the kitchen as best she could, and Dominic tried to soothe Henri's feelings, greatly ruffled by the thought of Ardhuin in the habit of traveling in Michel's cart.

"There is a carriage," Dominic said. "It hasn't been used in some time. I suppose we could get Michel to drive it when—"

The bell rang again. Dominic looked at Henri, surprised. "Were there any other prospective servants with you?"

The old man shook his head, and with grave dignity went to the door as if that had been his task for years.

"Yes, sir?"

Dominic could see a man in the uniform of the Queen's Hussars standing on the step. He bowed and stated he had a message for Madame Kermarec.

"I shall see if she is at home to visitors," Henri said, and made his way towards the kitchen. Dominic preceded him at a much more rapid pace.

"Who?" Ardhuin blinked at him, as he blurted out what he had seen. "Does the whole world know about us? I thought we went to a lot of effort to keep it private."

"We did! I want to know why a Queen's Hussar is standing on our doorstep," Dominic said, in some agitation. "Those are the private guard of Queen Anne, and are not used to deliver mail. What does he want?"

"I suppose we should find out," Ardhuin said, and handed off a very long list of what appeared to be shopping to Estelle.

The man bowed profoundly to Ardhuin when she appeared, offered a large, ornate envelope with both hands, and then turned and left.

"It has a magical seal," Dominic observed. Ardhuin let power flow over her hand and opened it.

"So, her Majesty seems to know about me. I think we know who to thank for that. Oh. Oh my." She stared at the letter, motionless. Dominic finally could no longer contain himself.

"What is it? Is anything wrong?"

"It's from *her*, Dominic. The Queen herself! Our gratitude for assuming the burden of Mage Guardian of Bretagne, so on, so forth, the right of requesting a personal audience…more verbiage…kindly inform the Minister of the Treasury of the desired deposition of the yearly stipend…stipend? What stipend?" She held out the letter to him.

"It would appear they do not expect you to provide the magical defense of Aerope out of your own pocket," Dominic said, glancing at it. "And a good thing, too. We can afford that gardener now, I think. I wonder if Michel would be willing to be our regular coachman, since he already performs that function at need. Is the stipend…usual?" He glanced carefully at Henri, standing some distance away.

"I have no idea. My great-uncle never mentioned it, but…but he did seem to think I would be able to support myself and the staff to maintain this house on my own. Now I know what he meant."

"Did you read the last part of the letter?" Dominic asked. "Is she serious? How does she expect you to find other…others like yourself?"

"Someone has to do it," Ardhuin said reasonably. "I certainly don't want to be the only one. I don't even know where to begin, though."

"Does Madame speak of the Mage Guardians?" Henri asked. They both stared at him, shocked, and he smiled slightly. "My former master spoke of them often, and intemperately. Since Madame was able to defeat him, I assumed you were one of their number. He feared very little, but the Mage Guardians gave him pause."

Ardhuin took a deep breath. "Quite. I trust your discretion, Henri."

He bowed. "Madame, my life is at your service."

Dominic took her hand. "Come, let us consider the matter in the library. Who do we need to replace? Preusa, definitely. I don't want to go back there anytime soon, at least not until it thaws. What sort of requirements do we have?"

Ardhuin started up the stairs beside him, her upper lip caught between her teeth in the way that never failed to make his heart race, and he wondered how long she would want to work on this—or if he could persuade her to postpone it until tomorrow.

"Shall I bring tea to the library, Madame?" Henri asked.

"No! No tea. We need to think," said Dominic firmly. "Alone."

The End

ABOUT THE AUTHOR

Sabrina Chase was originally trained as a Mad Scientist, but due to a tragic lack of available lairs at the time of graduation fell into low company and started working in the software industry. She lives in the Pacific Northwest and is owned by two cats.

Further sordid details may or may not be available at her website, chaseadventures.com